The
Atlantic Affair

A CHARLES LANGHAM NOVEL

The
Atlantic Affair

By Gary Paul Stephenson

LANG
BOOK PUBLISHING

BOOK PUBLISHING

langbookpublishing.com

Cover design by Blair McLean

National Library of New Zealand Cataloguing-in-Publication Data
Lang Book Publishing 2017

ISBN 978-0-9941446-8-3 – Paperback
ISBN 978-0-9941446-7-6 – Hard Cover
eISBN 978-0-9941446-6-9 – eBook

Published in New Zealand
A catalogue record for this book is available from the National Library of New Zealand.
Kei te pātengi raraunga o Te Puna Mātauranga o Aotearoa te whakarārangi
o tēnei pukapuka.

This book is dedicated to my wife, Davina, for her love and patience while I penned this work.

Table of Contents

Chapter One

The London Apocalypse

The noise of the letter box closing with a loud metallic clang aroused him from his heavy sleep. He pulled the old tattered blanket back and swung his legs out of bed and placed his feet on the cold wooden floor, scratched his fingers through his hair, and then pulled on an old blue towelling bathrobe that lay over the end of the bed. He padded bare foot from the dark single bedroom across the hall with its peeling paint and cold red tiled floor to the front door. He picked up the post from the grubby door mat and leafed through the envelopes.

Amongst the usual final reminders and colourful marketing flyers was a large white padded envelope bearing an airmail sticker and customs declaration form. He threw the others into the overflowing bin by the side of the hall table and ripped opened the white envelope, removing a thick wad of papers. He walked into the small dimly lit lounge and picked up his half rim glasses from the coffee table. He lit a cigarette, dropped into the worn armchair, and laid the contents of the envelope on the coffee table. He divided the contents into three piles. Cash, official looking documents, and the single sheet neatly typewritten on both sides. He had not expected to hear from the organisation after he signed up at one of their clandestine meetings many years ago. But, on a regular basis, they had asked him to do small jobs. Picking up a parcel here and delivering it there, taking a car from one town to another, placing an advert in a paper or corner shop window that made no sense to him. Always small jobs, for which he could see no real purpose, but he did them anyway, and they paid well.

Drunk and morose in a pub he had started talking to a group who, it turned out, were members of some extremist evolutionary group. He tried to recall exactly who they were. They were not white supremacists or Anti-Semitic or anything like that; they were concerned about the purity of the gene pool, the survival of the true human race or something or other. He rubbed his jaw. *What was it they were linked to?* Ah, yes, that is it. The Schutzstaffel. Yes, that was it, the Schutzstaffel.

The group was German in its origin but what the word meant he could no longer remember. Mind you, he couldn't remember much except that a week later he went to another of their meetings in a small hall where he had signed up for the monthly retainer that they promised to pay. The retainer kept him in cigarettes and whisky and paid for his small rundown grubby flat in London. He grabbed the whisky bottle from the coffee table, poured some into a large glass, and drank it down, feeling the warm glow radiate through his body. He read the letter, shrugged, read it once more and then glanced at his watch. All they wanted him to do was to collect a car from a freight importers depot at Southampton docks and drive it to London. The envelope contained all the documents he needed along with detailed instructions on the answers to specific security questions he would be asked on collection of the vehicle. It told him the day he was to collect the car, what to take with him, plus a map showing him where to park the car in London—and at what time he was to turn the engine off. (they were very specific about that.) He checked the date and realised that he was to collect the car that day and park it at the designated spot late that afternoon. He rubbed his chin, feeling the three days of stubble and decided to have a shave and tidy himself up before leaving.

He looked in the bathroom mirror at the gaunt face that stared back at him. The sunken cheeks, black bags beneath the eyes, the hairline was receding and the grey increasing. The years following the crash that had led to the death of his wife and only child had ruined him both physically and mentally. The crash was caused by a drunken truck driver on drugs. He had been driving, but the crash had not been his fault; yet the guilt of being the only survivor was overwhelming. Why had he survived when his wife and child were taken? He would have done anything to change places. Psychotherapy and anti-depressants had little effect. Nightmares were a regular occurrence as were the night sweats. He was unable to hold down his job, even with his boss's empathy. Once a highly respected senior manager for an international conglomerate, he had everything a man in his forties could want: a house in the country, company car, pension, health plan, smart and attractive wife, lovely child and holiday's abroad twice each year and the future looked good. Then on the way back from a trip to the zoo his life was changed; no, his life was destroyed. Shunned by family and friends whom he had ignored, although he knew deep down their intentions were good, he sought solace in drink, solitude and self-pity. He shook his head to clear his thoughts and continued to shave. Those thoughts won't bring them back, which is all he craved, to be with them again for eternity.

Feeling his newly shaven face with his hands, he cleaned his teeth and combed his hair. Wearing fresh clothes, he collected his wallet and raincoat from the bedroom, stuffed the documents and letter into the deep pockets, picked up his keys and left the flat. He turned up the collar of the raincoat, put his hands in the pockets and descended the three stone steps to the pavement and walked through the grey morning rain to the nearest underground station. London in autumn was not his favourite season with its grey skies, bone chilling wind, and rain, which made London dreary and its citizen's bad tempered and unwelcoming. His tummy grumbled from lack of food but that could wait till the train journey or the car drive back. The tube train was packed with people going about their daily business, and after a few stops he arrived at Waterloo station, where he purchased a ticket to Southampton.

The train was leaving soon and he had just enough time to buy the daily newspaper before he boarded and found his seat. As the train worked its way through the suburbs of south London, he wandered through the train to the buffet car and purchased two hot pies, coffee and some crisps. Back in his seat he swiftly consumed the pies and drank the warm liquid that tasted slightly of coffee and felt more relaxed with the food in his stomach, the first food he had had for at least two days. He crossed his legs and slowly crunched on the crisps while scanning the newspaper for anything slightly interesting, before closing his eyes and taking a nap. He woke as the train entered the station. It was still raining when he stepped off the train and walked through the station towards the taxi rank. He waited in line beneath the canopy with his hands in the pockets of his raincoat to keep warm. He did not have to wait long until it was his turn and he sat in the back of the warm car and gave the driver the address.

The import agent's offices were located at the front of a huge bland warehouse surrounded by many other identical buildings. Inside sat a young receptionist typing away on a computer keyboard entering data on a screen that was hidden behind a long low black and chrome counter that looked very expensive. She looked up and beamed the smile that only slightly resembled sincerity.

"Good afternoon, sir. Can I be of assistance to you?" she asked.

"Eh, yes, I am here to collect a car on behalf of a client of mine."

He pulled the documents from his pocket, unfolded them and handed them to the receptionist. The receptionist swept her long black hair from her eyes and looked through the documents and pulled one sheet out, typed on the keyboard then picked up the telephone.

"Jerome, I have a man here to collect a car, our reference numbers on the paperwork are JW187AH435." She put her hand over the mouthpiece.

"Won't keep you long, sir." she smiled before returning her attention to the phone. "Thanks, Jerome," she said into the mouthpiece and put the handset down. "Jerome has the authorisation paperwork and will be with you shortly. Please take a seat and help yourself to a coffee while you wait."

He looked at the coffee machine and decided to just sit down and make himself comfortable. It was not long before a tall man in a navy blue business suit with a crisp white shirt and yellow tie entered the reception area holding a manila folder. He took the documents from the receptionist and sat beside him.

"Good afternoon, sir, my name is Jerome." He smiled as he introduced himself and shook hands. "So, the first thing I need to do is run through the precise protocols that we have on file from the shipper to confirm that you are the person authorised to collect the vehicle. Firstly, your passport please." He handed over his passport, which Jerome checked against a scanned colour copy from the manila folder. "That's okay." He handed it back. "Now, you should have for me a nine digit code plus the name of a woman and the name of a planet, all recited from memory, which should match what's in this sealed envelope." Jerome took a white sealed envelope from the folder, opened it and remove a sheet of paper.

"Yes, the code is 748241368, the woman's name is Angelina and the planet is *Jupiter*."

"That's correct. I must say that this is all most unusual. We never have these sorts of protocols to go through. It's certainly a first for me, a bit cloak and dagger, like a scene from a James Bond movie." he chuckled. "The vehicle has cleared customs and all import duties have been paid up front. Also, as instructed and paid for by the shipper, the car has been fully fuelled and has been charging since arrival. Please come this way and I will show you to the vehicle."

He stood up and led the way through the door into a packed and noisy office. He stopped to pick up some keys that lay in a tray on a desk and walked through another door that opened onto a huge brightly lit immaculately clean warehouse packed from floor to ceiling with racks of palletised cartons. Forklift trucks beeped as they reversed amongst the ceiling high racks, their amber lights flashing constantly. Cordoned off with orange cones, near some wide open roller shutter doors, sat a white Toyota Prius. He handed the keys over.

"Just sign here and then you can drive out through that door there." He pointed to the large open roller shutter door just to the left of the car. "Turn right to the main road."

"Thank you for all your help," he said signing the document while Jerome removed the cones and unplugged the car. Jerome took the signed document and tore off a copy.

"That's your copy and here's the cars power cable. Have a good day, sir." Jerome smiled and made his way back to the office.

He opened the door and threw the charging cord onto the rear seat with the signed piece of paper. He sat in the car and adjusted the seats position and back rest angle before closing the door and starting the ignition. He looked at the controls and found the windscreen wiper control and light switch. He exited the building and followed Jerome's instruction to the main road and headed back towards London in the rain. After an hour he pulled into a service area and purchased a burger, fries and large coffee. Back in the car, he ate the burger while he typed the name of the London address into the car's built-in navigation system. He folded the fast food wrappers, wiped his mouth with the napkin, placing the rubbish in the door bin and started the engine. He drove off, carefully following both the on screen instructions and voice directions.

On arrival in London, using the navigation system he easily found his way through the maze of busy streets and one way systems. He slowly cruised along the designated street until he came across a space large enough to park the car. He neatly parallel parked into the space and turned the engine off.

"Right, what were the other instructions?" he said to himself and pulled out the letter and started to read out loud. "Okay, let's see, after switching off the ignition and removing the key, engage the immobilisation system. The immobilisation system is engaged by pulling down the red cover and pressing and holding the white button for five seconds. The white button is located beneath the red cover on the right hand side of the steering column beneath the dash."

He put the letter down on the passenger seat and looked under the dash. There, near the back behind the steering wheel on the right hand side was the red cover, which he pulled down to reveal the white button. He sat up and looked around. From Great Peter Street he could see the Thames between the trees across Millbank. The cars navigation system showed him the Palace of Westminster and Downing Street were to his left; Buckingham Palace was behind him. River cruises left from Westminster Pier and, if his memory served him well, you could hire boats from there.

Why they wanted the car parked here, he could not fathom, but it was not up to him to question their reasons. They could be smuggling gold, drugs or crystal meth; he did not care as it was none of his business. He looked at his watch. He had just ten minutes to wait until the time they wanted him to turn the ignition off. While he waited he thought he might as well find out where they wanted the keys sent or placed. He picked up the letter and read it again. He frowned, puzzled as to why they did not mention that. They must be sending another letter, he shrugged. Ten minutes, well, eight now. He turned the ignition off, removed the ignition key, leaned down and pressed the white button.

He saw an intense bright flash, felt immense heat and heard a gargantuan noise in the millionth of a nanosecond that his brain still functioned before it and his entire body were vaporised into billions of molecules mixing with the infinitesimally small particles that used to make up the Toyota Prius as the six kiloton nuclear bomb carefully and meticulously built within the cars battery compartment ignited. There was no time for his life to flash before his eyes, no time for sorrow or recrimination. No time at all.

The blast threw thousands of tons of earth skyward, creating a huge crater three hundred metres wide and forty four metres deep at its centre. The shockwave thrust outwards like ripples in a pond at the speed of sound, shattering everything in its path, trees, cars, buses, buildings, road signs, bridges and people. At the further most point of the shock wave, windows of buildings were blown inwards killing the occupants with shards of glass before the heat flash that followed seconds later incinerated them and everything and everybody in its path. Iconic London tourist landmarks were destroyed in the first few seconds: London Bridge, the London Eye, the Parliament buildings, Elizabeth tower that housed Big Ben, St. Paul's, even Buckingham Palace. Main business and political centres of the United Kingdom were flattened in the seconds before the fire storm burnt the remains. The blast and fire storm destroyed everything in a six kilometre radius. The River Thames rushed in to replace the waters that had boiled and vaporized in the initial blast, causing tidal waves upstream and downstream, sinking the burnt out remains of boats tied to their moorings. The mushroom blast cloud rose kilometres into the sky, containing trillions of radioactive particles that would kill tens of thousands in the coming weeks, months even years. Men, women, children, all races, religions and creeds, it cared not.

Those who survived the initial blast stood in shocked awe as the blast cloud rose high into the sky forming the symbolic mushroom shape. They tried to fathom what had occurred and why, until they too were burned alive, stripped of their flesh down to the bone by the firestorm that followed the shockwave. Pedestrians further away who looked at the blast flash were temporarily blinded. Cars crashed as drivers looked in horror towards the source of the colossal noise before, they too, were burnt alive, only inside their burning cars. An Airbus A380 carrying three hundred and sixty passengers and crew on final approach to runway 27R at London's Heathrow Airport was caught in the blast and tossed around like a toy. Passengers screamed, the cockpit awash with the sounds from multiple alarms. The pilots helpless to control the massive jet as it skewed and twisted with one wing tip pointing skywards, plunging to the ground in a residential area near Hounslow, killing all on board and countless souls on the ground. Two Boeing 737's, both climbing under full power after take-off 40 seconds apart, one on route to Munich, the other Shannon, were tossed around, the pilots calmly trying to gain control before they too were swatted to the ground.

An estimated two and a half million souls died on that Wednesday afternoon as a direct result of the initial blast, many more would die later from the effects of radiation.

Thousands of miles away Gustav Axmann calmly looked at his watch, knowing that, if his plan had been carried out, then the devastation of the British government and its monetary centre would be complete. The British would be impotent, their role on the world stage totally undermined. He would wait for news of his latest and most audacious endeavour whilst meticulously planning his next.

Chapter Two

Chequers. The Prime Ministers Country Residence

The Prime Minister had spent the morning, including a late lunch, in meetings with his senior cabinet ministers in the Hawtrey room of his country residence, Chequers, fifty kilometres northwest of London, in the county of Buckinghamshire. Chalmers liked Chequers and its one thousand five hundred acres, where he could, if it were not drizzling, walk and free his mind from the pressures and decisions that being Prime Minister constantly demanded. He often thought back to David Lloyd George, who, in 1921, became the first Prime Minister to have use of the house. What would he have made of life today with the rise of terrorism, wars across the world, the global finance crisis, the intrusion of social media and the immediacy of any news, not to mention climate change and the infernal politics and infighting that came with being part of the European Union, which demanded more and more money and,, ultimately, in his mind achieved very little except for increasing the number of bureaucrats in Brussels.

His next scheduled meeting, at four in the afternoon, was to discuss the options regarding the United Kingdom's withdrawal from the European Union. After that it was back to a major Cabinet meeting to evaluate issues facing his party at the next election. Out of habit he looked at his watch and noted he had fifteen minutes to complete his final review of the papers. The citizens had shown very clearly that they had had enough of paying billons into the European Union without getting anything tangible in return except for more red tape and interference with United Kingdom laws. Scotland had voted to stay in the United Kingdom but wanted out of Europe. Ireland had initially done well under Europe but was now suffering very badly and wanted to cut all ties. The United States President had sent his ambassador to personally deliver his strong opinion that it was not in the United Kingdom's best interest to withdraw; the European Union President, the German Chancellor and French Premiere had also sent ambassadors, each warning that withdrawal would damage the United Kingdom's economy and standing on the world stage, something that bothered Chalmers greatly. How did they know of a meeting that only he and his two closest ministers knew about?

Europe would greatly miss the monies it received from The United Kingdom, he knew that. But what would America lose? He looked through the briefing papers and found exactly what he needed to answer that question, two papers. The first one from the Foreign Office and another from the Ministry of Trade and Industry. He had just enough time to scan through them.

He was sitting at the antique desk at one end of the Hawtrey room with its quaint charm reviewing papers in preparation for that meeting. He felt much older than his fifty years, but this job did that to you. The constant pressures, stress and worries aged you prematurely, no matter how well you exercised or how carefully your diet was controlled. He had placed his navy blue suit jacket over the back of the modern comfortable chair, pulled down his gold and blue striped tie, and undone the collar button on his crisp white shirt. A decent cup of coffee and his favourite cognac were both making the task a bit easier. After tonight's meeting, which would be followed by the usual seven course formal dinner with a variety of wines, most of the ministers would leave for their constituencies or their London homes or residencies if they had parliamentary business in the morning. There was only one meeting scheduled tomorrow, and that with the Chinese ambassador and the China trade delegation. Chalmers would be staying at Chequers tonight along with his Foreign Minister and Trade Minister. His wife and two children were at their home in Bedfordshire.

His reverie was broken when a senior aide knocked on the door and entered walking quickly and quietly over to the Prime Minister. The aide, looking white as a sheet stopped in front of the desk, looked directly at Andrew Chalmers, who looked up and frowned. The aide spoke quietly and with deliberate slowness.

"Prime Minister!" The aide cleared his throat before uncharacteristically rubbing his hands and continuing hesitantly. "We have just received grave news that a huge explosion has hit central London. Information is still very sketchy to say the least, but at this stage we know for sure that the devastation is widespread and the epicentre was in central London." He took a breath before continuing. "We have unconfirmed reports describing a mushroom shaped cloud that's usually associated with nuclear type explosions." The aide continued to look directly at Chalmers, shaking slightly.

Chalmers who had sat in silence and disbelief, his mouth agape as his aide had spoken, stood up in shock.

"Jesus Christ, are you sure?" He walked a little uneasily around the desk, the fingers of his left hand running along the wooden edge of the desk by way of support.

"Both the Chief of Defence Staff and the Chief of The General Staff are flying in by helicopter from the Twenty First Signal Regiment in Bristol," the aide said. "They will do a reconnaissance pass over London, if it's safe to do so, before arriving here."

"Oh, my word. This is just unbelievable." Chalmers said quietly looking down at the floor. "Thank you. Nicholas, pour me a cognac please. And you'd better have one yourself."

"Yes, sir, thank you."

The aide replied and walked across the room to a large antique bar and took out two cut crystal glasses and a dark bottle of cognac.

Chalmers tried to think clearly, his mind was racing over the many issues and problems that would need to be resolved, the many dead, his friends and colleagues who were in London, the injured, the state of hospitals and doctors, law and order, who and why? He quelled his racing mind and breathed slowly. He sat on the edge of the desk while the aide poured his drink. He picked up the telephone and dialled an internal number, his hand shaking. When the Secretary of State for Defence answered he spoke, his voice strong.

"You've heard the news, I take it. Well, you had better get all your military chiefs together, Fleet, Army and Air Force and find out exactly what the hell has happened. They can talk to their people while they are on the way here. I need to know what it was and who were responsible?" He looked up at the ceiling his eyes tightly closed. "If that's the case, then the highest ranking person will have to take their place." He replaced the receiver and took the cognac from his aide. "Get the Chequers Cobra room operational and I want all agency chiefs here within the hour, or their deputies depending on who was where and survived."

"Yes, sir, " the aide replied, downing his cognac as he made his way to the door and nearly colliding with the Home Secretary, Lucinda Grey who had her head down keying buttons on her phone. Grey was tall and her slim figure accentuated by the beige knee length skirt and matching jacket and her wavy blonde hair. At thirty eight years old she was the youngest member of cabinet and enthused energy and action. The fact that she was not married nor divorced raised some eyebrows and rumours abounded about her sexuality, which she ignored. Was it her fault that she had yet to meet the man who could stand up to her very exacting requirements?

"This is terrible. I have made contact with the Chief of Police and the Director General of MI5, and they are on their way here." She put the phone to her ear. "Still no answer from the Chief of SIS, I'm afraid." She sat down in one of the two couches either side of a long low table.

"I think he is in Iraq at the present time," Chalmers replied, sitting on the opposite couch. "I cannot believe this has happened. Who in their right mind would undertake such a senseless act?"

"Any number of terrorist groups," barked Malcolm Brooke, the Secretary of State for Defence as he strode into the room.

His tall frame, clothed in a loose fitting suit that looked like it had been slept in, was capped with a mop of long grey unkempt hair that only enhanced his dishevelled presence, which belied his razor sharp mind. "We have troops all over the world fighting many terrorist groups alongside our allies. This is their coup de grace. Their ultimate act of terror. All world leaders will now be wondering if their capital city is next."

He sat next to the Home Secretary, his voice controlled and calm. He knew that the time for grieving what had happened and what was lost could come later, but now the country needed him at his best.

"Could be the IRA, ISIS, Al-Qaeda, but I don't think so. All our sources have been quiet. Just the usual banal chatter." He shifted in the seat. "The Chief of Defence Staff has confirmed it, by the way. A nuclear blast not far from Parliament, or what was Parliament I should say. London lived through the blitz but this is on another scale altogether. This was obviously targeted to destroy the very beating heart of our country and all the things we British hold close to our hearts. The Royal family, Government, the civil service and commerce."

"The Cobra room is ready and all available listed personnel are gathering there now sir," said the Aide, popping his head around the door.

Chalmers stood up and went to his desk to retrieve his suit jacket from the back of the chair, put it on and, straightening his tie, re-joined Grey and Brooke.

"Thank you. Come on you two, let's go. All operations will be run from there and that's where everyone will be directed as and when they arrive. What more do we know?" He looked across at

Brooke as they left the Hawtrey room and followed the aide. His face grim at the reality of what had taken place.

"Buckingham Palace was destroyed. Luckily the Queen was in Balmoral with her immediate family. Parliament is erased and the Bank of England is no more. What the state of the gold in her vaults is, we may not know for a very long while and the stock exchange, well, that's destroyed."

As they descended the stairs to the Cobra room, he looked at Chalmers and knew what question would come next and answered before Chalmers could speak.

"How many people are dead? Well, Westminster and the City are totally destroyed so, there is at least nine hundred and eighty thousand people a day in Westminster on average and another four hundred thousand people in the city. So we are looking at well over a million dead, and I wouldn't hesitate to guess at another million or so injured. The main central London hospitals are out of action. They would have been either destroyed or severely damaged. And, even if they were not, they would have no power nor the staff, who would be either dead or severely injured."

They entered the austere, brightly lit clinical Cobra room, housed deep underground with its banks of screens showing data and live feeds at one end of the long table with more screens in the walls on either side showing different data and live feeds. Five people who were already seated and deep in conversation went silent and stood as Chalmers entered and took his seat at the head of the table.

"Gentlemen, Ladies," he said acknowledging their presence. Brooke and Grey took their allocated places. "I believe that we have a disaster emergency response plan for this eventuality already worked out?" Chalmers queried, trying very hard to put emotions aside and appear in control which everyone in the country would expect as their leader.

"Yes, sir," Grey confirmed, pushing her chair back and walking to a drawer system built low into the wall. She pulled out the second drawer down and retrieved a green box that she laid on the table while using the heel of her left foot to close the drawer. She looked up as a phone rang and continued to open the green box and retrieved numerous folders that she started to set at each place around the table.

"This, Prime Minister, this is the DER plan for this scenario. It contains estimated casualty figures, evacuation centres, nearest usable hospitals, temporary military hospital locations, water and food stations, troop requirements, northern resources that will be required to relocate to provide aid. It also advises on monetary, monarchy, trade issues and foreign diplomacy."

She sat down.

Chalmers opened the thick folder and leafed through the pages of detailed text, maps, Gantt charts, graphs, tables filled with numbers, before returning to the first page.

"How quickly can we have the affected area cordoned off and people evacuated?" Chalmers asked looking around the table.

Brooke, who had been animatedly talking on his phone put it down, looked up at those around the table and spoke, his voice controlled.

"That was The Chief of Defence Staff. They have just flown over the area. It's really bad." He shook his head. "He has a copy of the DER with him. He has mobilized troops from Bristol, Aldershot, Windsor, Romford and Croydon. They are equipped with Geiger counters and will start on two fronts simultaneously, cordoning the area off starting at the furthest predicted outer perimeter of the estimated fall out range and evacuation of the area downwind of the explosion. Regiments from East Anglia and the Midlands are readying for deployment to set up Evac centres. Two aircraft have crashed at Heathrow with full fuel loads, putting the runways out of action."

"Thank you, Malcolm. Well, Home Secretary, it appears from this that you are the DER co-ordinator." Chalmers said solemnly looking at Grey. "Quite a responsibility, I would say for one so young. But I am sure you will do your utmost and obviously seek help and rely heavily of the heads of all agencies. Any issues, just remind them that you speak with my full authority and that of her Majesty the Queen as mentioned here in the first paragraph on page two. I am aware that we do not have the full complement here as of yet, but let's make a start." He looked up as people walked in and took their places at the table.

Grey cleared her throat, remained seated and acknowledged the Prime Minister with a nod of her head.

"Thank you, Prime Minister. I may remind you and everyone here that, although I sorry... we, have trained for this, this is real life and not an emotionless training simulation. We have millions of souls depending upon us for help and the decisions we make today, each and everyone one, are a matter of life and death. If I may start with the checklist on page three and go through each item line by line so that everyone here knows their full duties and responsibilities. You can advise on any status updates as we go. As people arrive, and I note that most now have, we will revert back to their area, then continue on from there." She looked at the screens. "We have agents in the field at various strategic locations as detailed in the DER. They will have activated automatically and should start reporting in on the data screens. If any of those locations were compromised, they will report from their nearest alternate location. Should an agent be incapacitated, they will be replaced as soon as we are aware of the fact. It sounds cold hearted, I know, but we need to think of those who are injured awaiting aid rather than those who have died." Grey poured some water into her glass from a crystal jug and took a long drink before continuing. "So, let's get on with the check list starting with item one, page three."

Chapter Three

Calm at Sea

The sky was a dark blue with stars just starting to become visible amongst the thin veil of cloud. The low recessed external downward facing lights lit the teak deck and furnishings in a warm blue glow and, as designed, did not impinge on the night sky keeping the view of the stars vivid. A light breeze flowed across the deck as Charles turned on the main external screen and left the communications channel open. The screen automatically showed the view from the forward facing camera mounted high above on the star deck. Ex-Senator and Presidential aide Duke Warren, who was now more of a permanent resident on board the superyacht, arrived, making his way across the gently moving deck. He was wearing a white polo shirt and grey slacks. Warren was tall and kept his hair very close cut, near bald some would say. He was swiftly followed by Charles' right hand man Max in his obligatory black polo shirt and black slacks, which suited his medium height and short cropped black hair.

"So a nice cold Tiger beer for me, I think," Max said on his way over to the outside galley and bar area, where a steward was in attendance. "What does everyone else want?" he asked resting one buttock on a bar stool while leaning his right arm on the bar.

"I'll have one of those," Duke replied, taking a seat next to Anne Langham, who, in a white blouse and blue skirt that accentuated her fair skin and dark hair, decided on a nice cool Pinot Gris. Anne rarely wore make up, letting her natural complexion shine through. Charles, wearing a dark orange tea shirt and tan shorts that complimented his healthy tan and greying fair hair, joined the men in a Tiger beer.

As they sat around the large teak table laid out with porcelain plates and silverware with fresh orchids as the centre piece, two stewards started to serve the first course of the barbecue, a refreshing Caesar salad. They were on Charles and Anne's luxurious superyacht *Sundancer*, cruising from San Francisco to their secret underwater Kermadec headquarters in the Pacific Ocean, eight hundred kilometres north of New Zealand. *Sundancer* was Charles and Anne Langham's permanent home and office from which they ran their conservation and environmental operations. On arrival at the Kermadec Islands, they would refuel, pick up supplies, a specialist research team and their son and daughter before heading to Indonesia and their two new projects.

The one hundred and eighty five metre *Sundancer* was powered by seventy five thousand horse power from her four Rolls Royce engines coupled to shallow water jet propulsion units capable of driving the huge yacht at forty two knots through the water. For now she cruised at twenty one knots on just the two outer engines, her automatic gyro stabilisers keeping the pitch and roll to a minimum. Unseen, some thirty two crew members quietly carried out their duties across the eight decks to ensure the smooth running and safety of the yacht. Three specialists manned the surveillance room that housed the very latest in communication, surveillance and sonar technology. The same team manned the concealed armaments that would keep the passengers safe in case of pirate attack. Below the surface of the sea and out of sight were the two submarines belonging to World Earth PLC, the organisation that Charles and Anne had started after selling his worldwide business interests so that he could, instead, concentrate on conservation. The submarines, *Mercury* and *Jupiter*, had flanked *Sundancer* and kept pace with her from the United States of America. Amongst the bright stars was a wonderful full moon, slightly obscured by a thin layer of wispy cloud, as if by a veil of lace, which lit the wake created by *Sundancer's* bow and the water ejected by the two water jet propulsion units leaving a trail of sparkling phosphorescence.

The only sound, save for the four diners, two stewards serving the food and the chef busy at the outdoor barbecue, was from the waves as they broke into white foam with that soothing whooshing sound that only the ocean can make. The deep hum from the engines could only just be felt through the decks, felt more that it could be heard thanks to the intensive sound insulation and specially designed engine mounts.

Charles thought back to the meeting with the United States President, which had left him relaxed in the knowledge that this new administration would now do more to protect the flora and fauna of planet Earth. Months earlier, Charles had had the privilege of presenting his views, backed up with scientific evidence, to the United Nations, on the state of the planet, which included an in-depth study on what was required to be done to protect all that was left and how to recover the many species on the brink of extinction. The presentation was greeted with the usual political excuses and inactivity, and in Charles view, ineptitude. With the new United States President taking action, other world leaders would undoubtedly follow his lead.

On becoming President, Christopher Johnson, asked Charles to run through the entire presentation at their private meeting in the Oval office in the West Wing of the White House. The Oval office, decorated to suit the style of each President, featured the well-known three south facing windows behind the President desk. The northern wall housed a grand fireplace in front of which sat two ornate chairs. In the centre of the Oval office were two settees resting either side of the Oval rug. More than most rooms, the Oval office has four doors. The east door opened onto the rose garden, the west door led to a private study and dining room, the northwest door led to the main corridor of the west wing and the northeast doors opened to the office of the Presidents Secretary. Like all visitors, Charles and Anne had not entered via the front door of the White House, but by one of the side doors, which were guarded by three armed security guards. Though surprised by the Presidential request, Charles had happily obliged and ran through the entire presentation. He was also surprised at how intently President Johnson had concentrated on each slide. The President had asked many sensible and thought provoking questions and had shown his shock at the overall rate of species extinction and rain forest destruction. As Charles had expanded on the data displayed on the last slide, the President had asked for a copy of the presentation to be left with him.

At the back of Charles's mind though was the nagging worry

that Gustav Axmann and his cohorts were still on the run and no one knew where they were or what they were up to. He pushed the thoughts away and looked at the delicious rump steak that had been served from the barbecue. It would be great to get back to the true calling that he had developed over the years, the true love of both himself and his wife Anne—conservation. They had committed huge resources and monies to reversing the damage done by rain forest destruction and—by actively buying thousands and thousands of acres of rain forests and managing the resulting restored habitats with the local tribes—reducing the high extinction rate. His presentation to the United Nations, which detailed the current extinction rate, the reasons why it was so high and what needed to be done to reverse the current levels, had been met with reservation by many of the attendees. But now, with the United States on board, together with the English, New Zealand and Australian governments backing his views, things could change. The Axmann incident in the Pacific had derailed their progress, so now was the time to get back on track. But where was Axmann?

"You're thinking about Axmann again, boss?" Max asked, noting Charles's quiet demeanour and tell-tale creasing of his forehead. A steward topped up Anne's wine glass with New Zealand Pinot Gris and placed new bottles of Tiger beer in front of the men. Charles placed his empty Tiger beer bottle down and fingered the damp sides of the new ice cold bottle before cutting into his steak.

"Yes, I am. I do not think for one moment that he is not going to try and find another way of fulfilling his plan. His kind, the SS and Nazi's were results orientated, no matter what the cost, and human life to them was cheap. They would willingly, and in many instances did, sacrifice their own for the common good and the cause."

"Darling, there is nothing we can do." Anne looked across the table deep into her husbands troubled brown eyes. "Besides, with the security measures now in place at United States ports, there is no way he could leave American soil. As long as Gustav is still in the United States, he's harmless."

"True, but let us not forget that he and his cohorts infiltrated two of the most secure weapons facilities in the world, and it would be very foolish to think that they did not data mine the computer systems while they had the chance. They could very well have given themselves new identities and security clearances for who knows what. And we still do not know exactly what they stole!"

"Look, Charles," Anne said sternly, placing her knife and fork on her plate and resting her chin on her hands. "We have a lot of work to do in Borneo and Sumatra on both the Orangutan and Sumatran tiger projects, which will keep us busy for some time to come. It's extremely important that we get there as planned, to see for ourselves what progress has been made in the past year and what further resources are required. We must ensure that Cathy and Chris will be safe." She wiped her mouth with the napkin. "The United States can sort Gustav out. I am sure that President Johnson will call on us if he needs our help."

"Anne is right, Charles," Duke butted in. "Besides, I would like to see what you guys are doing in Indonesia. I might be able to help with any dealings with the local authorities. Some of the current government guys are old friends."

Charles smiled. "Okay, Anne. You are right as always. Irdonesia must and will come first." He put his knife and fork down and leant back in his chair and stretched his arms above his head. "Now it's time for some coffee and liqueurs." Before Charles could stand up the display chimed. Charles flipped a hidden cover up revealing a keyboard inlaid into the table and tapped a few keys. Marge appeared on the display, her face was grim.

"Charles, we may have a big problem. I need to come aboard and talk to you about it now, if that's okay?"

"Sounds ominous." Charles recognised the sincerity in her voice. "Okay, tie in with Captain Whitcome and make the arrangements to come aboard." Charles disconnected the call. The display chimed again. "What now?" said Charles with an edge to his voice as he answered the call and a face appeared who Charles recognised as Grant, the head of *Sundancer's* surveillance team. Grant was not your usual computer geek, although he was a computer geek. He was tall and lanky with black short hair neatly parted on the left. His blue eyes shone brightly. He had a laid back manner and was always calm even in a crisis with a mind as fast and as sharp as any computer.

"Charles, reports are coming in thick and fast about a probable nuclear explosion in London. It's on the BBC world news right now," Grant said, his voice calm as always. "Do you want me to relay it to you?"

"Thank you, relay it to this screen," Charles said.

"Coming up now," Grant said, as his face disappeared from the screen to be replaced with the BBC World News. Everyone altered their chairs to get a clear view of the large sixty-five inch screen. They watched, listening in silence, riveted to their seats as the horror of the devastation and loss of life unfolded. No one spoke during the broadcast, just gasps of disbelief broke through the tense atmosphere.

At the end of the report Charles turned the screen back to a view of a waiting Grant.

"Grant, keep us advised of any further developments," he said before turning the display off leaving the communications channel open. "Coffee and liqueurs all round please," Charles said quietly to a steward, running his hand over his brow. "Almighty heaven, I think we could do with it after that news. What a terrible thing to happen. No one stood a chance, and those that survived will be horrifically injured."

"Axmann?" questioned Duke.

"Could well be. The United States should be able to analyse the isotope and see if it matches the Nevada materials that are missing. But, Christ, there must be hundreds of thousands dead. It's inconceivable that anyone in their right mind would do something with such destructive force. It must be an accident."

"We're slowing down," Max said, standing up and walking over to the side rail. He peered over the side to the surface of the ocean four decks below.

"Find out if both submarines are surfacing, will you?" Charles asked the steward as he was served his coffee and cognac.

The steward went to the bar, put the tray down and picked up a phone and called the bridge. After talking and listening for a while he picked up the tray and returned smartly to Charles, leaning down and speaking softly into his right ear.

"The Captain advises that the submarines *Jupiter* and *Mercury* are both surfacing and only *Jupiter* will be coming alongside. Marge is preparing to board *Sundancer*. *Mercury* will run on the surface just off our port bow to let the crew get some air," the steward said quietly and went back to his duties of serving coffee and cognac to the others.

"Marge must have got more information from somewhere," Max commented returning to the table.

Anne looked at her husband. "Well, we will find out soon enough, but in the meantime, finish taking your medications and drink your coffee and cognac."

Max, restless as always when things were happening, picked up his coffee and went back over to the railing and looked over the side as one of the submarines came alongside and docked at the lowered hatch. He would never cease to enjoy watching a submarine as it broke surface. He watched as Marge emerged from the submarine in a tight fitting trouser suit, her curly auburn hair blowing in the breeze as she crossed confidently over the gangway to the lowered hatch. The gangway was retracted and the hatch was closed. The submarine moved slowly away as the conning tower of another submarine broke the surface in the distance.

"Both *Mercury* and *Jupiter* are on the surface port side and Marge is on her way up," Max said as he sat down.

Charles could feel *Sundancer* increase power to a steady but slower than normal speed to match that of the submarine so that they could keep pace while surfaced.

Marge emerged from the lift walked through the sumptuous luxury of the informal dining room and long aft lounge and out onto the expansive rear deck. "Hi, all," she said as she walked over to the table. "Mind if I join you?"

"Of course you can, Marge," Anne replied. "Steward, another coffee please."

The Chef walked over to Marge and said, "I have a steak that I can cook if you are hungry?"

"Eh, yes, might as well, rare to medium, please," Marge replied as she sat down. The others took their places at the table again. "Can't get barbecue steak on a submarine," she said. "Looking at all your faces, I can obviously see that you have all seen the news, so you know that this is not exactly a social call. You have watched the BBC World News I assume?" As Charles nodded she continued. "Keith has brought me up to date with the conversations that he's been having with the President, his security advisor and the CIA, and we need to discuss them. The President has had a call from Gustav Axmann."

"I see, not totally unexpected," Charles replied, his voice hesitant showing his tiredness. He held up his hand as a signal to Marge to slow down. Trying to think of too many things at once caused cognitive fatigue bought on by his Multiple Sclerosis. "I think we have staff on board *Sundancer* and the submarines, actually everywhere, who have UK relatives. We will need to see if anyone is directly affected," he said, his mind going off on a tangent. "Then we will start with your news and work our way forward slowly, shall we?"

Max stood up, went to the railing, looked over the side and then returned to the table. "Both subs are running on the surface, letting the crew get some fresh air. I'll go and see the Captain about the crew member's boss, and I'll get onto Keith," Max said and left to make his way to the bridge.

"Charles, we have a problem and I truly believe that it is all related back to the Pacific incident," Marge said before starting to explain in a slow precise manner. "Our sensors in the Atlantic, which as you know have an expanded diamond formation of greater size than those in the Pacific, together with those of the Scripps Institute in the Gulf of Mexico, have been picking up variations in temperature and acidity across a range of depths. But that's not all. We have increases in mineral absorption, which in itself is not unusual and usually of no concern, if it were not for the fact that the minerals in question are radioactive!"

Charles immediately looked up and over at Marge. "And how can that be? What would the possible causes be?"

"Someone is dumping radioactive waste. It's the wrong ocean to be linked to the Fukushima incident. Nuclear power plants in northern Europe are the biggest sources, but those levels are monitored and the readings we have far exceed those. Then we have mining and refining of thorium and uranium and such, but again the levels far exceed the nominal range. The only credible explanations are that either a warhead has been lost overboard or dropped from a plane, its casing damaged in the process, or someone has purposely dumped illegal nuclear waste."

"Won't be the United States," Duke said. "They have way too many safeguards. And the administration would never let that happen again."

"Does this have anything to do with the call from the President, Marge?" Charles asked before taking a drink of his cognac.

"Yes," replied Marge, she paused as she searched for the right words. "When they entered the two Nevada facilities being used by William Paige and Glenn Haines to build their dubious nuclear arsenal for the previous President or as we now know, unwittingly for Gustav Axmann, all records and everything initially seemed to be in order. However, when the CIA and

NSA concluded their full audit, at least two complete weapons were missing and one and a half kilos of fissionable weapons grade material along with some of the hardware required to make another weapon were unaccounted for. Someone had gone to a lot of trouble to cover the paper trail, but they could not cover up an item by item intensive physical audit, computer audit and paper trail."

Max who had returned and sat down, let out a slow whistle. "Grief, we have two weapons, or one if the London bomb was one of them, fissionable material, one freighter, a submarine and the ex-Nazi Axmann on the loose. Without seeming to be an alarmist, I think the United States has a big problem on its hands, or should I say we have a big problem on our hands."

"Marge, I assume that our ocean monitoring technology can trace the origins of the irradiated water?" asked Charles.

Marge thought for a few second before answering.

"Within certain parameters, yes, but so far we have many multiple trace sources and will need to map and refine those to calculate the source trace. But it can be done, I can get Keith to run a program on the computer at Kermadec."

"Okay, one step at a time. Firstly, I think we need to head for Hawaii and take a closer look at the office that we believe was used by members of the Axmann team. That's your area Max so I'll leave it to you to see what you can find. We will anchor just offshore and go in on the Bell. I am sure Anne will take the opportunity to do some shopping, so we will go with you. Security detail, I want Miles to accompany us, and so you can take Ralph. Tell the Captain of the new destination and get him to contact *Jupiter*, I want them to stay with us."

"Sure thing, boss." Max stood up and taking his cognac with him went to see the Captain.

"Yes, but after Hawaii we head for Indonesia," Anne said frowning. "You are not going to get fully immersed in this Axmann thing again. Think of the Orang-utans and your health!"

"I agree, Darling, but if we can help a little on the side especially with the technology that we have at our disposal, then we should. *Mercury* and *Jupiter* together with the teams back at Kermadec stand a better chance of locating the source of the radioactivity than the United States can do on their own." Charles looked into Anne's eyes and placed a hand on her arm. "But you are, of course, right. I would not let this stand in the way of the Indonesia project, but at the back of my mind is the worry of another London. If we can help stop millions from dying then we must do what we can and that's what I am trying to balance here." He looked over at Marge. "Marge, see if you can isolate the radioactive mineral traces, track the currents, where there coming from. Send *Mercury* to the area of the highest readings and see what they can trace. Can you triangulate using the sensor readings?"

Marge rubbed her neck. "We have not managed to yet. As I said we are picking up readings from various sensors, and there is no logical triangular pattern we can track. James is looking at satellite imagery and oceanic currents. Keith reckons it's probably from a freighter that is purposely taking an erratic course to its destination. He seems to think he recognises the pattern from his naval days and is racking his brain to recall it. Anyway, we are trying, but if it's a freighter, then it has its beacon turned off, which indicates that it does not want to be found. I need to brief Keith on the program to run on his computer."

"And the call from Axmann to the President?" asked Charles.

"Oh yes. He simply said London was number one. Which American city will be number two?" She shrugged her shoulders. "Nothing else. He said those words then ended the call."

"Okay, after Hawaii, we will head down to Kermadec, then onto Indonesia as planned, but *Jupiter* will join *Mercury* in the Atlantic and I want you on-board leading the group."

"Great idea, if nothing else comes up we can pick up changes in reading strengths as we go and, hopefully with both subs we can close in and isolate the source."

"It's a long shot and means we can't stay in Hawaii very long as we have the Indonesia team waiting at Headquarters," Charles stated, feeling *Sundancer* alter course as Max returned to the table.

"All done, boss. Captain says we should arrive at around five in the morning, so in about seven hours," he said as he sat down to finish the last course of his meal, fresh strawberry sorbet. "What have I missed?"

"You'll have one day in Hawaii, and then *Jupiter* will head for the Atlantic whilst we head to Kermadec and Indonesia as planned. Get Keith on the screen from Kermadec and get Grant to patch in Ryan O'Hare if you can," said Charles. His mind focused on the singular possibility that Gustav Axmann was up to no good on the freighter and he felt sure that the weapons and material were on-board. But where was he headed and where was the submarine that he had at his disposal? He watched Max call up Keith and waited while Grant patched in Ryan O'Hare in the White House. He smiled when he saw Ryan O'Hare's face appear on the screen and acknowledge everyone in view.

"Ryan, good to see you. Look, we think it would be a good idea if we were to search the Hawaiian office used by the Axmann team, if that's okay with you? Can you advise the coastguard, immigration and the local police to provide us with assistance? We will anchor offshore and fly in on the helicopter and land in the park next to the office building," Charles said.

"Sure, Charles, that's fine. I will let the naval commander know. They can give you some security back up. I'm flying down myself at six o'clock, so let's meet up. I'll call you as soon as I arrive."

"Great, Anne will be doing some shopping and, knowing our chef, he'll jump ashore as well to get fresh ingredients. We will be on the ground for one day only. I want our submarines to help to track the radiation anomaly that Marge has picked up in the Atlantic, if you could use the help?"

"All help greatly appreciated, Charles. The President is very concerned about that especially after the London incident and the call from Axmann. He has raised our DEFCON status to two. We had a meeting in the Oval Office earlier today with Homeland Security, the FBI, NSA and the CIA. You'll be pleased to know that he insisted Thomas attend. It caused quite a stir when the leader of the President's private army entered the Oval office fully armed. We have the biggest man hunt operation on since Bin Laden," O'Hare said.

"What action has he instigated in tracing the radiation?" Duke asked.

"We have satellites over the Atlantic with scientists pouring over the images, and four of our Virginia class submarines heading into the Atlantic to work alongside two aircraft carriers which are already there."

"Ryan, one of our submarines is on its way to the Atlantic now, the other will follow when we leave Hawaii. They have the latest sensor technology and water analysis equipment aboard and are plugged into our senor array which will be very useful. Keith, get *Launch One* on its way from Tonga and head at full speed for the Atlantic," Charles said.

"Consider it done," Keith replied, turning away from the screen.

"What's *Launch one?*" queried O'Hare.

"She carries our submersible called *Deep Sea*. She's a very fast vessel and packed with the latest technology. *Deep Sea* is packed with sensors and capable of extreme depths."

"That's a good idea. Oh, just a thought. Can I base myself on *Sundancer* for a while?"

"Sure you can. See your tomorrow."

"Goodnight all," O'Hare said finishing the call.

After Ryan left the call, Charles looked at Keith on the screen. "Keith, get James to hack into those satellite feeds and put them through the computer. Marge will tell him what to look for." Charles leant back in his chair. "That's all, I'm calling it a day."

"Goodnight all," Keith said.

After the screen went blank, Charles stood up and took a long deep breath and looked up at the stars. It was a balmy night with the breeze caused by *Sundancer's* speed a welcome relief.

"One last coffee and cognac and then to bed I think," he said aloud. "Steward another coffee and cognac all round please." Charles called. Anne passed him his Neurontin capsules and a glass of water, which Charles downed. A steward with a large silver tray started clearing the table, taking the loaded tray behind the outside galley and placing it into a dumb waiter. He picked up a clean tray and continued clearing the table. Another steward quietly served coffee and cognac. The chef with the help of two other stewards from the main galley starting clearing away all the utensils from the large outdoor galley, closing all the doors and covers, wiping them to a shine and leaving for the main galley below decks. Charles enjoyed the peace and quiet as everyone sat around the table in silence and enjoying the freshly brewed coffee. "Marge, as you are staying on-board tonight, you can use your usual executive guest suite."

"Thanks, I think I have a change of clothes and spare toiletries in there," Marge said.

Charles looked at the stars and moon overhead and then looked round till he saw Max.

"Max, did the London bombing affect any of our crew?"

"No, none had any family in London, but all the British crew members are suffering from shock and disbelief. I sent the worst affected to see the Doctor. Keith and Captain Simpson have both done the same."

"Good idea. On the ball, as always."

"Do you think Axmann will target an American city next?" Max asked.

Charles drained his cognac and stood up, his hands gripping the back of his chair.

"Yes, it would fit his aspirations to hit the seat of government of his enemies. He's hit London, so that means by all accounts Washington is next. On that cheerful note, good night, and more fun tomorrow in lovely Hawaii."

Anne rose from her chair and clasped his left hand and they made their way into the main saloon and through to the lift. After the short ride down to deck two, they walked quietly hand in hand along the luxurious corridor, subtly lit and lined with original oil paintings. They arrived at the cherry wood door to the owner's stateroom, which, although expansive, was warm and inviting. The suite stretched the full width of the vessel with huge picture windows on one side and on the other side a large section of the wall which could be lowered to form a large private balcony and swim platform. The floor was covered with a deep pile white wool carpet. Two archways were on the wall opposite the king sized bed with its built in cherry wood bedside cabinets. The bedside tables housed reading lamps, phones, controls for the lights, stereo, TV, and balcony controls. One of the archways led to a cherry wood door that opened onto the stern bathing platform. The other archway led to the large bathroom suite with spa bath, shower, vanity unit with twin basins, toilet and off to one side, walk in wardrobes. Oil paintings and bookshelves completed the furniture. Charles had a shower and then reclined in bed reading a book by Clive Cussler. At the foot of the bed was a large cherry wood unit from which a large display unit rose. Charles chose some quiet music. Anne left the bathroom and climbed into bed naked beside him. He turned off the main lights and switched on the bedside lights so they could both read. Charles quickly fell asleep and Anne closed his book and placed it on his bedside table. From her bedside table she turned off his reading light, shut off the music and retracted the display unit. Deciding it was late enough, Anne put her own book down, turned off her reading night, leant over and kissed Charles goodnight and lay in the dark, feeling the motion of the superyacht as it headed towards Hawaii.

Chapter Four

Gustav Axmann

Gustav sat at the grey metal desk in the dark smoky cabin of the freighter and stubbed his cigarette out in the already overflowing grey metal ashtray. A tall man, he sat hunched over the desk looking through thick glasses at the laptop screen. His receding hairline of fair hair was far more grey than fair, and thick eyebrows emphasised gaunt brown eyes. Papers and maps littered the desk alongside a bottle of schnapps and a half filled glass that he held in one hand to stop it sliding on the desk against the roll of the freighter. On the wall in front of the desk, hanging from a screw head, was an old heavy picture frame which held a fading photograph of his hero, Adolph Hitler. On the wall to his left hung the flag of Hitler's Germany, the swastika. Once a member of the Hitler elite, he had held the rank of Oberst-Gruppenfuhrer in the Schutzstaffel and reported to Heinrich Himmler himself. He fled Germany using the Odessa route, in 1945, on hearing of Hitler's demise. He took with him his most trusted comrades and as much gold and antiquities as they could carry. Those who could not travel with him, he ensured, would get word on how to follow him. On arrival in Argentina, they settled for a while until Gustav decided that too many of his kind were arriving in Argentina and that they would eventually be sought out by the allies there because the larger numbers posed a greater danger. They were bound to be found at some stage.

He developed a plan to head to Brazil and put it to the group, who elected to leave the relative safety of Argentina and head with Gustav to Brazil, where they could survive in anonymity. He kept the old customs and ideals alive and, as the families and new generations grew up, he inducted them into Schutzstaffel thinking. Even with their numbers growing, their true identity and background remained unknown to those they interacted with; they remained a very close knit group with Gustav Axmann as their leader. All the children were privately educated and, with the help of money and the influence of the group, many held senior positions in government agencies or were promoted up through the ranks of the companies the group owned. Their foray into the world of drugs had proved extremely lucrative. Their tyrannical hold over the local heroin and cocaine cartels was founded on their distribution capabilities and ruthlessness over any who refused to come to heel and agree to supply solely to Axmann.

Now, thanks to the devastating raids on the drug cartels by the Brazilian government, they had lost not only the entire income from their drug empire but also the substantial investment of time and money, a horrendous loss but not a fatal blow. Their legitimate businesses, which covered a range of industries including car dealerships, supermarkets and distribution, all remained. Contacts in government, either their own people who had risen through the ranks over many years or persons on their payroll, had proved useless when the raids had occurred. The had provided no prior warning of any pending raids, which had infuriated Gustav and many had paid for that failure with their lives, not just those who died in the attacks, but many at that hands of Gustav's own assassins. With deep regret, he had accepted the loss of his United States contacts and the access to the majority of the nuclear weapons. He had not come away empty handed though; he was far too clever for that.

When the former deputy head of the CIA, Glenn Haines, had failed to meet the head physicist at the airport as arranged, backup plans developed by Gustav came into immediate play, which involved five senior technicians from the assembly plant departing with one complete weapon, another nearly complete weapon and parts for one more. Two technicians from the processing facility left with enough weapons grade material for a further weapon. Each group was led by a member of his extended family who had infiltrated the plants as security guards without the knowledge of Haines or the former military advisor to the President of the United States, William Paige. This he had calculated and planned for over a long time, with every move and timing to the second worked out to perfection.

A private plane had flown the group and their freight to the east coast, where they owned a small distribution warehouse. Two technicians built one of the bombs into the large compartment that held the batteries in the floor of a Toyota Prius. They removed only some of the central batteries, enabling the weapon to remain concealed. Gustav used a contact he knew at a sea freight export company to ship the car in a twenty foot container to Southampton. A sleeper agent in the United Kingdom would pick the car up and drive it to a specific location. The group, with the other partially completed bomb and fissionable material, then boarded a large launch which took them to the freighter lying offshore. Even now, they were down below working on the assembly of the second weapon.

The arthritis in his knees and shoulders was giving him a lot of pain. He reached over for the bottle of schnapps and took a large gulp. He had never heard of this guy Langham, who had thwarted his attempt to destroy the United States, and that bothered him. He had a feeling deep in his gut that this Langham had been involved in the drug raids; he had no proof, but the secrecy and surgical way it had been carried out pointed in that man's direction. The new President and his aides were unknown entities. He thought he knew who his enemy was but he would not let an impudent Langham derail his plans; and, too, the arrogance of the new President had got under his skin. His mind was set. The United States and the United Kingdom had once before thwarted the Fuhrer's plans, and he had vowed to continue the fight to the end. With his wife's death from cancer shortly after their arrival in Brazil, he had put his heart and soul into destroying both countries, and would not allow the recent events to divert him from his plans. He had sacrificed far too much of his life for that to occur. But Langham would pay, he would make sure of that.

The ship heaved as the weather worsened, and Gustav closed his laptop and note book, took another gulp of schnapps, and with both hands on the desk heaved his body upright. He turned towards the door at the sound of someone knocking.

"What is it?" he said grumpily, carefully making his way to the door, stumbling against the motion of the ship. He opened the door and faced the head physicist member of his team.

"Well?" he asked.

"We have had to stop work now. It is far too dangerous with the motion of ship. We cannot work safely. I have told the teams to secure all the equipment," he said looking slightly green. "And I have three of the team laid up with motion sickness."

"Very well, very well," Gustav said with a wave of his hand. "Find out from the Captain how long before we reach Matagorda Bay. You can finish the assembly there when we get to the cottage. That was always the plan anyhow."

"Yes, sir. I will ask him now," the head physicist said and closed the door and hurried along the gangway, holding on tight to the handrail as the ship rose and fell in the increasingly rough seas. He opened the heavy bridge door; the motion of the ship and high winds slammed it shut behind him. The Captain was sitting in his chair, smoking a pipe, while the helmsman stood in front of his chair resting his backside against the seat cushion, his feet firmly planted on the deck. Except for the glow of the instruments and electronics the bridge was dark, the ceiling lights turned off.

The Captain drew on his pipe and let the smoke swirl from his lips as looked at the head physicist.

"Ah, professor, how are you?" More smoke swirled from his mouth.

"Okay, I'm okay, but we have had to cease work due to the pitching of the boat."

"Ship, professor, this is a ship," said the Captain, pointing his pipe at the head physicist.

"Whatever! Axmann wants to know how long before we reach Matagorda Bay?"

"Eight hours to nine hours with the weather that's closing in," replied the Captain as the ship heaved, crested and then fell down a large wave with a cascade of water washing over the bow and leaving water running down the bridge windows. "I hope you have everything secured down below."

The head physicist stood, legs apart against the roll of the ship, bracing himself further by holding onto the chart table with both hands. "Everything is secure. You mean this weather is going to get worse?"

"Yes, it is getting worse. As we get further south and into the Gulf it will improve. Tell Axmann the submarine is just outside the bay now and is resting on the sea floor. It cannot enter the bay. It is too shallow for them to hide on the bottom. As we get closer, we will get the shrimp nets and crab pots out on deck and display our fleet number and head for the dock and get moored up under the cover of darkness."

The head physicist left the bridge, the door slamming behind him and returned to Gustav Axmann, in his cabin, and gave him the news.

"When the weather improves get everything ready for transfer to the cottage. I want everything transferred as soon as we dock before everywhere gets busy. We can complete the weapons in the large workshop next to the cottage," Gustav said and dismissed the head physicist and stretched on his bunk and closed his eyes. "Soon, very soon, I will complete my life's work," he said to himself as he fell into a restless sleep.

Matagorda Bay is a large estuary separated from the Gulf of Mexico by the Matagorda Peninsula and fed by the Lavaca and Colorado rivers. The bay, covering four hundred square miles and sparsely populated, gave ample space for the sight of a newcomer to go relatively unnoticed. The submarine would have to navigate very carefully to ensure it stayed in the deepest, dredged channels of the bay. The submarine commander wanted to stay no longer than absolutely necessary. According to Axmann, he had about two weeks before he would be required to enter the bay and receive the weapon. He peered through the periscope and, with nothing in their vicinity and with nothing on sonar, he surfaced the submarine to recharge the batteries and give the crew some air time.

The freighter, now disguised as a fishing trawler, headed in the darkness to the main quay. The town was an old town established in 1827, with a population in the low two thousands, although the county itself was nearer to thirty six thousand. The sparseness of the population was one of the main reasons that Axmann had chosen the town. The ease by which the vessel could be moored up without much attention and the relative privacy of the large rented cottage with huge garage cum workshop miles from any neighbours suited his purpose. He sent one of the younger scientists to collect the Ford F-150 truck that he had hired from the local Avis depot, which would be parked near the quay with the keys in a magnetic holder under the front driver side wheel arch. He instructed everyone else to gather their equipment on deck and be ready to load up. With the truck's ability to carry no more than four passengers, plus the driver, two trips would be needed to get everyone and the gear to the cottage. He looked at his watch over and over; they had more than enough time to complete the exercise before the townsfolk woke up. Once unloaded, the freighter cast off its lines and headed back out into the gulf to start its journey back to its home port in Hawaii. Gustav watched it go before getting into the passenger seat of the F-150, with the last of the equipment and the final three technicians. The main road to the cottage was sealed and they passed only one other vehicle on the journey, which pleased Gustav. They had seen no pedestrians; he smiled a rare smile when Michael, the youngest scientist and allocated driver, confirmed that he had not seen anyone during the first trip, either.

The long gravel side road that lead to the cottage wound its way through dense shrub, trees and marshland. The cottage and workshop stood alone, surrounded by trees and shrubs with two large lawn areas and set well back from the Colorado River. The cottage was a single storey five bedroom wooden building with a red metal roof. Off to one side and set slightly back was the large, old wooden workshop with two wide and tall wooden sliding doors. An eight metre fibreglass boat with a pair of large four stroke outboard motors was moored at the private jetty, reached from the back of the cottage by an old cracked concrete path through the expansive grounds. Gustav had paid the real estate agent six months rental in advance, and he purchased the boat from a local dealer via the internet and had it fully fuelled and delivered as part of the deal. Gustav wandered around the expansive shrub filled grounds, happy that they could not be overlooked from the road, river or nosy neighbour. He returned to the house, checking that everything was in place and working. In the kitchen he checked the cupboards and found them, as expected, fully stocked with tins of food, soup, tea, coffee and sugar. Cheese, butter, eggs and long life milk were in the fridge; the freezer was fully stocked with meat, pies, burgers, and sausages.

He smiled to himself at his choice. It would be okay for the short time they would spend here. He put the kettle on; might as well have a coffee while everyone else unloaded and set up the equipment. He sat at the large rectangular wooden kitchen table and was about to take a drink of his coffee when Julian Beech, the head physicist, came in looking decidedly worried. "We have some serious issue," he said. "There has been a leak from one of the containment units. We have it sealed now and the cooling system containment is restored, but it does mean that the freighter has radioactive liquid on board, some of which would have now drained into the bilge and into the gulf and the Atlantic. We should tell the Captain to hose the floor of deck two storage area and to flush the bilge as a matter of some urgency."

"Okay, okay, no need to panic. Contact the Captain and tell him to do so but only once he is clear of the gulf. Has anyone here received a dose of radiation that I need to be worried about?" Gustav asked, holding his hot coffee mug in both hands.

"No, we were below two hundred mrems per hour," Beech advised.

"Okay, that's good. So explain to me what caused the leak?"

"A small crack and a broken seal, most probably caused when the boat crashed off one of those darn waves. We lost about twelve litres of liquid coolant. We had some spare and have used half of it due to this."

"Okay, now, more important matters." Gustav looked at Beech closely. "How many days to finalise the last two weapons?"

"It will take about a week and we may need to obtain more parts, which will delay one, possibly both of the units. I had a look at what was taken from the facility and I would say that in the panic one or two boxes of parts were not loaded. I will do a full inventory once we have unpacked and then I will know for sure." Beech said, anxious to leave and call the freighter Captain.

"This is not good," said Gustav standing up, his eyes blazing. "Everyone had their job to do. I am not happy. Why did we not know this when we built the Prius weapon?" he screamed. "Never mind, never mind. Tell me as soon as you can. I have a strict timetable that I cannot and I will not waiver from. Now, leave me!" he shouted and turned his back on Beech.

"Yes, sir," Beech said, and left the kitchen and went along the corridor, passed the living room to the front door. The décor was old and very plain to say the least; only the bare essentials for day to day living were provided, which was in line with how Gustav was running the operation, thought Beech. He walked across the lawn and down the path beside the cottage to the workshop. It was very hot and humid with heavy dark low cloud, headache inducing weather and, as soon his shirt was sticking to his back, he looked at his watch, still not midday. The floor of the workshop had been swept clean, and now the rear half was covered with polythene sheeting. A tubular frame work had been assembled at the rear of the workshop, and was enclosed by thick clear plastic panels with a double door at one end acting as an air lock. Two ventilation tubes were connected to the enclosure; one of them connected to a filter system before leading outside through a small side window, the other connected to a pump. Inside the enclosure, which now had positive air pressure, was a large oblong cylinder that hung by thin metal guide wires from a metal frame work. Along the rear wall of the enclosure was a long metal bench on which sat a fat short stainless steel cylinder. On the floor of the workshop were open boxes. A group of three technicians were busy working on a large worktop that was littered with machined parts and tools, while another technician was putting on a white suit and helmet with its own air supply cylinder.

"Okay everyone, gather round," Beech called as he walked to the centre of the workshop. "I have just seen the Reichsleiter, who as you can guess is very unhappy. He has stated that we must do an inventory and quickly ascertain what is missing. Right, let's get started," he said, clapping his hands.

One of the technicians came over with a clipboard. A tall man with very fair hair that matched his fair skin and deep blue piercing eyes. "I have the list of what we should have here and what I think we have missing," he said with a distinct Germanic accent. "If what I think is missing is actually missing, then we will require very accurate machine shop capabilities, which I doubt will exist locally. Plus we will need to get the parts made in separate facilities to avoid questions. So, I will look for these parts only while you do the inventory. It may save some time and be better for my father's nerves."

"Seems like a good idea," Beech said, not wanting to upset Gustav's eldest son. He watched as Albrecht walked over to the bench with clipboard in hand and started searching. Beech joined the others and started the full inventory.

After two hours Albrecht and Beech found Gustav in the living room, which, with the curtains closed, had a musty air. "Well, what have you found, what good news do you bring me?" Gustav said staying seated at the end of the settee, cigarette in hand.

"It is not good news, father," Albrecht said. Beech was happy to stand aside and let Gustav's son break the bad news. "We have two boxes that are missing which contained some parts of the main ignition cylinder assembly required for both units. I have checked and I have the technical drawings of those items, but we will need to have them made and they are, as you know, high precision machined items unique in their design. We must find three unrelated companies in separate towns that have the capabilities we require."

Gustav drew deeply on his cigarette. "Can we do this via the internet rather than travelling around this country?"

Albrecht simply nodded.

"I cannot see why not. The parts can be delivered by different courier companies to avoid raising any undue suspicion," Beech offered, wanting to be the bearer of good news. "By having the eight pieces made at various facilities we will avoid anyone piecing together their real purpose."

"Do it. Money is no object. Pay for very fast service and remember they must return all the engineering drawings and any cutting programs, disks or whatever else it is they use." He waved them away with a flick of his hand but then continued speaking after something else came to mind. "When the parts arrive, erase all electronic evidence of the emails and drawings. We have a software virus we can send to the companies to wipe all the data?"

Beech was always ready and happy to reply to Gustav when he had good things to report. "Yes, I have a software virus that can be embedded in the first email and activated on a given date when it will wipe all the drawings and the email path."

"Okay, don't just stand there, leave, get on with it, out!" Gustav snapped.

They left the room and walked to the study where Beech had set up the two laptops.

"Do you have those drawings in electronic format?" Beech asked.

Albrecht pulled a USB drive from his pocket and held it up in front of him.

"Of course I do. I have all the drawings on here."

"I'll write the email and save them as drafts with the virus loaded and ready to activate in four weeks while you search for the companies. You know what is needed but I can write English American better than you," Beech proposed with a smile.

"Systematic as always, Julian!" Albrecht gave him a friendly punch on the arm. "I'll rename the parts and remove any reference to what they are. I'll give them new part numbers, new names and add one of father's company logos as well and update the USB drive."

They sat down at the laptops and started to work. After two hours they added the files and email address of the three selected companies and sent the emails to them under the guise of an experimental deep ocean pump mechanism. All they could then do was to wait for the replies to arrive. In the meantime Albrecht returned to the workshop and carried on with finishing the most deadly of the weapons as far as it could be finished while they waited for the parts.

Beech walked outside with the satellite phone and called the freighter Captain, to give him the news.

On board the freighter, after guiding the ship through the gulf and heading north east, the Captain was relaxing in his cabin when the news came through from Beech to flush the decks. He instructed his crew to connect hoses to the sea water pumps and wash down all the decks and switch the bilge pumps from automatic to manual and turn them on. He did not tell them the reason why, for fear of alarming them. He was relieved the storm had passed and they were sailing in very calm seas on route back to Hawaii. After two hours of hosing down decks and bulkheads, he was satisfied that they had done all they could, but without the use of a Geiger counter, he could never be sure. As an extra precaution he told the First Mate to lock the deck two storage area.

Chapter Five

Hawaii

When Charles awoke, he reached for the control console on his bedside table and opened the balcony of the owner's stateroom. As the large side panel folded down and the swim ladder extended, sunlight filled the stateroom. He sat up and looked out at the clear blue sky and across the blue green ocean to the western coastline of Oahu, the third island in the Hawaiian Islands, sometimes called The Gathering Place, home to the vast majority of the one and a half million Hawaiian population and the state capital Honolulu. He stretched and breathed in the warm but fresh salty air that was filling the stateroom's air conditioned ambience. He switched on the display, which rose from the cabinet at the end of the bed and saw their location on the GPS display he selected. He switched to the superyachts status screen and noted that they were at anchor. He swung out of bed, stepped into the dressing room, and pulled on some swimming shorts. He walked over to the platform and dived into the warm sea and swam away from the superyacht for a short distance before turning back and heading for the balcony, where he saw Anne in her bathrobe looking at him.

"Come in, it's lovely," he called, holding onto the balcony's boarding ladder.

"Later, we have a helicopter to catch and you need your breakfast and your medication before we take off," she said and held his hand as he climbed up the boarding ladder onto the balcony. He took the towel and started to dry his tall slim frame and thick fair greying hair.

"Okay, you win, but I needed that. It was refreshing and reviving." He padded over to the bathroom and took a shower before dressing suitably (in grey slacks and white tea shirt and moccasins) for the trip to Honolulu. He sat on the bed and Anne handed him a pre-filled syringe that contained a disease modifying drug as part of his fight against Multiple Sclerosis. He injected it into his leg, then snipped the needle end with a needle cutter, and placed the used syringe in a sharps container.

"Okay?" asked Anne.

"Yep, let's get going."

They took the private aft lift to deck one and then walked up the circular staircase, which led to the rear of the main deck. The breeze was warm and they could smell the salty ocean as they walked the length of the vast deck to the large teak table, where Max and Duke were already seated, eating a full English breakfast. Abbey, who had been sitting beside Max feasting on the occasional piece of sausage, barked and went charging along the deck to greet them. She walked eagerly alongside, snuffling their hands and, when they sat down, she sat beside Anne, anticipating some food falling her way.

"Good morning, everyone ready for a busy day?" asked Charles as he sat down and placed the napkin in his lap.

"Sure thing. Boss. I've had the guys clean the Bell, my kits on board and I've roped in Grant, as head of surveillance team, I thought he might be very useful if I find any computer gear. I've stood Ralph down."

"Sounds like a good idea. Duke, what are you going to do today?" Anne asked.

"I'm meeting up with Ryan at the airport, and then we are heading for police headquarters to investigate the company from there. We might be able to uncover some more information on the company and its people, their movements, you know, that sort of thing." He picked up his coffee. "Unless you had anything else in mind, Charles?" said Duke.

"No, that's good. I am under strict instructions from Anne to take it easy today. So it's a day of shopping, rest and relaxation."

Anne looked across the table at Charles. "Shopping with the chef for starters, so firstly Tamashiro fish market. Then the farmers' market, after which chef leaves to do his own thing and you have me all to yourself," Anne said as the steward put a full plate in front of her and one in front of Charles.

"Earl Grey tea, Mrs Langham?" asked the steward.

"Yes, please dear. And for Charles, as well," Anne replied as she filled two glasses with freshly squeezed orange juice and gave one to Charles. Charles took a prepared set of tablets and swallowed them with s orange juice before tucking into his breakfast of two sausages, bacon, baked beans, grilled tomato, one poached egg and freshly toasted brown bread.

"Shopping with a woman would hardly constitute taking it easy and having a rest in my book," joked Max.

"You are on dangerous ground, Max," laughed Anne.

"Anyone heard any more about London?" Charles asked, switching on the large display and choosing the BBC World News service.

"Yes, looks dire. The Americans have studied some satellite imagery and put the epicentre near the Thames, between Buckingham Palace and the Parliament buildings. They reckon on the weapon being around the six kilotons range and estimates are at one and a half million dead and half a million injured. The British Prime Minister has ordered a state of emergency and instigated military law. Emergency services and the Armed Forces are setting up mobile hospitals but they are stretched well beyond capacity," Duke replied and drained his coffee before continuing. "Buckingham Palace was wiped out along with central London, the business district and the Bank of England. It will take years for the economy to recover, the pound has already fallen against most world currencies and the UK stock market has fallen five thousand points overnight, wiping billions off company values. Most other stock markets are in freefall."

"Trust you to think of the monetary side, Duke," Anne cut in sharply. "Innocent children, babies, husband and wives have been killed or horribly injured. That's more important surely."

"Anne, I agree, but the world we live in always converts disasters into monetary terms. I bet this news broadcast states the amount of damage done in monetary terms before the casualty numbers," Duke said softly.

"Their European partners are sending supplies and medics," Max put in. "The Channel tunnel is closed for security reasons, which is slowing everything down. Everything has to go by ferry and all British ports are now under military control and the security measures in place are slowing the release of supplies."

"Not surprising, really. They won't take a chance on another bomb entering the country," Charles said.

After breakfast they made their way up the exterior staircase, to deck eight and the helipad, where they found the chef and Grant waiting and admiring the view. Two deck crew were on hand to provide any assistance that may be required. Once everyone was on board the Bell 525 Relentless and seated, Max went round closing and securing the doors before climbing aboard. He put his flight helmet on and spoke into the microphone.

"Seat belts on please," his voice came over the speakers in the cabin area as he started up the electronics and the two GE CT7 power plants which started to turn the rotor blades. The flight was short and uneventful. Charles always enjoyed the flight around *Sundancer,* especially when she was sitting in such beautiful surroundings. He could see the garage on the port side being opened and both the eight metre rib and fourteen metre launch sitting on their retractable launching cradles. The launch would ferry the chef and his purchases back to *Sundancer.* The Captain, Charles knew, would have three crew in the rigid inflatable boat checking and cleaning *Sundancer* along her waterline.

Max found the large park area close to the office building and noticed that it was cordoned off by red and white police tape and that police cars were parked at each entrance with their blue and red lights flashing. He slowed the Bell 525, extended the landing gear hovered over the park, looking around at the clearance between the rotors and trees before bringing her to a gentle landing near the centre of the park. The rotors slowed and by the time everyone had their seat belts undone, they had nearly stopped.

"Everyone back here at five o'clock," Charles said before looking around at the chef. "Except you. I understand that you have one of the launches organised to take you and the food back."

"That's correct, Mr Langham. I thought it would easier, sir," the chef said and opened the door and climbed out, turning to help Mrs Langham.

"I reckon Ryan's here already and organised all this. Saves me a trip to the airport!" Duke said, motioning to the police vehicles that were stationed at each entrance to the park. "I thought so." He laughed pointing as he saw Ryan O'Hare's tall and broad frame resplendent in black suit, white shirt, striped tie and black sun glasses, walking towards them. Ryan smiled and shook hands with each in turn.

"I have heard a lot about your dishes from Duke, and I am looking forward to tasting them," he said when introduced to the chef. "Okay, let's get going, for we have a lot to do."

"See you later," Charles said as they made their way towards the markets, leaving Max and the surveillance operative heading into the office building, and Duke and Ryan for a police car.

At the office building, Max entered the marbled lobby of the five storey glass and steel office building and ran his finger down the list of tenants.

"Ah, second floor," he said his finger running along the name of the company.

Ignoring the lift, they took to the stairs and in a few steps they were at the door to the office. Max pulled out a small leather wallet and looked at the lock pick set, chose two pieces and in a few minutes heard the lock click. "They make it look so easy in the movies but it takes a lot of practice," he said as he handed Grant a pair of latex gloves and put a pair on himself before opening the door and entering the office. Grant carefully closed the door behind him and turned the lock. Inside it was dimly lit with Venetian style blinds almost closed shut at the windows, but providing some shade from the bright sunlight of the outside. The office consisted of just three rooms. A small kitchenette with sink, refrigerator and cupboards, a bathroom with shower and the main office with two large modern metal and glass desks. Luxurious leather high back executive desk chairs behind the desks and two smaller chrome visitor chairs in front of each desk. One large five drawer filing cabinet sat in the corner next to a large world wall map. Tower style computers sat on the floor beneath each desk; the desks were bare except for computer screens, keyboards and mice which sat in the centre of each desk.

"Looking at the carpet, I would say this office is very rarely used. You take that computer, I'll take this one," Max said and sat in one of the leather chairs, leaning down and turning on the computer. He pulled the keyboard and mouse closer to him and switched on the computer screen and waited while the computer booted up.

Grant put his hand inside his jacket pocket and pulled out two larger than normal USB drives.

"Plug this into the USB port. It will install a little program of ours which will help bypass any passwords," Grant, the head of surveillance, said.

"Sneaky, but I approve," Max said, taking the USB drive and leaning down to plug it into the computer. He sat back and watched the screen as the computer booted up. "Ah, here we go," he said as the password screen appeared. He leaned forward and rested his arms on the desk top while he watched as the username and password fields were automatically completed and accepted. "Well I never! How did it do that?" he asked looking over at Grant with a slightly astonished look on his face.

Grant had inserted another USB drive into the other computer and sat watching the screen while the program on the USB drive did its work.

"The program stalls the computers start-up program and data mines the code to find all the usernames and passwords and their relevant program entry codes," explained Grant. "Given that we have no idea how safe we are or how long we can stay here, I thought it might help. Now can you see the copy menu yet?"

"Yes."

"Choose 'yes' and it will copy the hard drive through the USB's wireless connection via this little wireless booster to our systems back on *Sundancer*." He pulled out a black slim case from his inner jacket pocket. "I'm doing the same. We can concentrate on searching the office and by the time we've done that all the data should be copied and we can get the hell out of here."

"I am very glad I thought to bring you along," Max said, a big smile on his face. He stood up and went over to the filing cabinet. "Mind you, I am not sure what Charles will make of your activities," he said opening the top drawer of the cabinet.

"Don't worry, he knows. Keith, James and I developed the software and wireless booster some time ago for a covert operation Charles required. James has continued to develop it over the years," replied Grant.

"I don't suppose you have one of those mini cameras on you?" asked Max as he leafed through the files.

"Nope, but I know you do."

"True. What have we here?" Max said pulling a file from the draw. "Plans of the city of London and Washington DC, with different blast radii and casualty figures annotated on them." He pulled a mini camera from his pocket and started to photograph the documents. He put the folder back and carried on looking through the rest of the drawers, pulling folders out, examining them, taking pictures of some further documents.

"Okay, now this is interesting. It's like an old medieval world map of the United States eastern coastline and Gulf of Mexico." He took a few pictures and replaced it. "Nothing more here," he said closing the bottom drawer as Grant pulled the two USB sticks from the computers before shutting them down.

"All set," Grant said.

They left the office, Max carefully locking the door behind him.

"Remove your latex gloves, looks silly otherwise," he said as he removed his and put them in his jacket pocket. Grant removed his gloves and dialled a number on his mobile as they descended the stairs. Back on the street, Max put two fingers in his mouth whistled up a taxi.

"All the data has been received and is on one of our separate secure drives being thoroughly virus checked," Grant advised Max as the taxi weaved its way through the midday traffic to police headquarters. He looked at his watch. "We were there for just under two hours, only it seemed like a lot longer."

"You're right, and it would have been a whole lot longer without those USB gadgets," agreed Max, checking his watch.

"Let's hope the data is useful, but for now I need a strong coffee."

The taxi pulled up outside police headquarters, and Max got out and Grant paid the driver. They entered the police headquarters and Max leant on the reception desk and spoke politely to the officer on duty.

"Can you tell Ryan O'Hare that Max has arrived?" He gestured to a large white unit on the far wall beneath which was a leather settee. "I will be over there near the air conditioner."

Before Max could move the officer said, "We were told to expect you, sir." He motioned to another officer to come over. "Please take these gentlemen to Mr O'Hare, who is with Deputy Chief Makino."

"This way gentlemen, if you please," said the officer, and they followed him to the lift and rose up three floors. When the lift doors opened they stepped out into a large open plan office with glass walled offices down the left hand side. In one they could see O'Hare, Duke and another person whom they assumed to be Deputy Chief Makino.

"We can take if from here, officer," said Max as he strode casually over to the office with Grant. "Hi, all. How are things going here?" he asked as he opened the glass door and entered the coolness of the office.

"It seems that there is no one on any police record connected with the company. The office address is clean," O'Hare said. "So we have drawn a blank. We checked the name Gustav Axmann and came up blank there as well." He sighed. "Rather frustrating to say the least. How about you guys?"

"Found two computers and have sent the contents to the *Sundancer* system for full analysis and there was a single filing cabinet, mostly rubbish except for one file which contained amongst other things maps of London and Washington with nuclear blast radii and fatality information. I have a copy of the file," Max said patting his pocket.

"Interestingly, there were no telephones or telephone lines, which means all communication and computer Wi-Fi connections must have been made via secure mobiles or satellite phones," Grant advised. "They obviously had trust and security issues."

"And things to hide," said Duke. "How long will it take to analysis the data you found?"

"Guess we'll have to run some algorithms to reduce time by using key words or phrases and run a program to search for known names, places, things we know. So say twenty four to forty eight hours," Grant advised rubbing his right ear. "Really depends on how much data there is."

"If we can find names, we can run those through your data base, Deputy Chief."

"And I can run them through immigration control and tell you when they arrived and when they left," Makino said.

"And where they arrived from and departed to?" asked Duke.

"Yes, no reason why not," answered Makino

Duke checked his watch. "Right, back to *Sundancer*. The sooner we mine that data the better. Thank you for your time Deputy Chief," Duke said shaking Makino's hand.

"My pleasure. I'll see you out and get a vehicle to return you to your helicopter. Always good to see you Ryan," he said, putting a hand on Ryan's shoulder and guiding them to the lift. "Don't leave it so long next time. Grace will be annoyed enough that you have been here and not seen her."

Max sat in the Bell 525 and called Charles and Anne on his mobile to let them know they were ready for departure. Charles advised that they would be there in ten minutes. As good as his word, Anne and Charles arrived by taxi with a few bags and boxes, which were quickly stowed before Max increased power and lifted the helicopter clear of the trees, retracted the landing gear and accelerated towards *Sundancer*, the helicopters nose dipping as it accelerated.

"Did you guys find anything useful?" Charles asked Grant and Duke.

"Well, we came up blank, but from what I hear Max and Grant may have hit the jackpot," Duke advised smiling at Grant.

"Maybe, we will know for sure one way or another when we analyse the data we downloaded from the computers." Grant said.

"Tell me more?" Charles asked a wry smile on his face.

"We used the USB downloaders and the wireless booster on two computers at the office to dump their contents onto the secure server on *Sundancer's* main system."

"Good thinking," Charles said. "Let's hope there is some useful data there that we can use." Charles closed his eyes and leant his head into the headrest.

Ten minutes later, they circled *Sundancer* before Max levelled off and flew down the port side of the superyacht until he was level with the helipad on the sea view deck, extended the landing gear and slid the Bell over the helipad and gently touched down. Ryan, Max and Grant headed straight for the surveillance room to start work on the data from the two computers while Charles and Anne walked through the library and formal dining room to the bridge to see the Captain. Duke headed for the lower decks to wait for the chef.

On the bridge the Captain, John Whitcome, was busy plotting the course to the Kermadec headquarters on the large touch screen chart plotter. Martin Deeks, the Technical Officer, was talking to the engine room and checking display screens as he started the four Rolls Royce engines. First Officer, Franklin, was busy on the VHF radio talking to the launch that was approaching at high speed loaded with the chef and the bags and boxes of the produce he had purchased.

"Launch will be recovered and stowed in ten minutes Captain," Franklin said.

"Thank you, Franklin. When will you be ready, Martin?"

"When the launch is recovered and the external doors are closed, we will be ready to power up," advised Martin, without looking up from the screens that displayed all the engine parameters.

"Give me the all clear as soon as you have it gentlemen. In the meantime, Franklin weigh anchors, Martin, thrusters to station keeping if you please," John said and turned when he saw Charles and Anne. "Good afternoon, Sir, Ma'am. How was the trip?" he asked.

"Very nice, thank you. Chef has quite a variety of fresh sea foods, fruit and vegetables, so everyone should be happy," Anne replied.

"How about the investigation?" he asked looking at Charles

"Not quite so good. Max and Grant downloaded a load of data from two computers in the offices. They are down in the surveillance room now starting to trawl through it all. Police headquarters was a bust unless we can give them more names or facial images," Charles explained.

"Marge is back on board *Jupiter* and is heading for the Panama Canal chasing to catch up with *Mercury*. She did not want to hang around. She's eager to start tracing the radioactivity," Whitcome said.

"All clear, Captain," Franklin called out, looking over his shoulder at the Captain.

"Ready when you are, Captain," Martin confirmed.

The Captain looked at Charles. "Kermadec?" he asked, raising his eyebrows.

"Yes, we head for the Kermadec headquarters," said Charles.

"Franklin, thrusters off, extend stabilisers, make twenty six knots, steady power increase across all engine, make course Kermadec," John Whitcome ordered.

"Yes, sir," replied Franklin, tapping commands on the display screens in front of his position that shut down the thrusters and deployed the stabilisers, he then placed his hand across the four throttle levers, slowly and steadily easing the throttles forward, watching the speed increase on the navigation display in front of his position. When he saw twenty six knots, he carefully adjusted each throttle to balance the engine revolutions. All over the superyacht the raw power could be felt as a gentle and subtle vibration and faintly heard as she quickly gained speed and the quiet deep roar of her four huge engines, totalling seventy five thousand horsepower, increased sending a cascade of white frothing water out of her four water jets as the bow eased gently upwards and the stern settled slightly deeper.

"Nothing to do now but enjoy the cruise until we reach Kermadec," the Captain said thoughtfully. "Weather is excellent all the way so we can maintain a steady twenty six knots for a fast and comfortable ride."

"Thank you, Captain," Charles said. "Join us at seven pm for dinner on the main deck. Chef has a surf and turf barbecue planned."

"Very well, thank you," the Captain replied returning his attention back to piloting the superyacht.

Charles and Anne left the bridge and crossed the full width corridor which featured two spiral staircases at each end and heavy doors that gave access to the outside gangways and entered the Sea View dining room. The dining room was dominated by a large polished cherry wood table and twelve chairs, which sat centred on a Persian rug surrounded by parquet flooring. The table, when the dining room was to be used, was normally laid with silver cutlery and cruets, cut crystal glasses, and fresh flowers in a cut crystal vase as the centre piece. These were carefully stowed in the matching polished cherry wood cabinets built into the port wall between the windows. The walls were cream with large floor-to-ceiling windows. Lights, recessed in the ceiling and at floor level, could be controlled to give just the right amount of light and colour. A large display screen was recessed into the wall at one end. Charles and Anne walked to the rear of the room, past the glass passenger lift and through the double doors that led to the library. The library had expansive windows and shelves lined with books. Suede lined ceiling with recessed led lighting and a deep pile rose wool carpet gave the room a warm cosy feel. Two cherry wood desks, two high back three piece settees with two armchairs to one side facing the display screen with a low cherry wood table in the centre. A keypad and mouse were recessed into each desk and table top next to pop up display screens. At the far end was a tinted glass wall beyond which sat the Bell 525. Charles stopped at the base of a circular staircase, which was built into the wall on the starboard side of the library, next to the lift. He pressed a button that opened the sealed hatch at the top of the staircase with a hiss. He stepped aside and let Anne climb the stairs to the uppermost outside deck called the Star deck.

He moved aside as Abbey, Cathy's Border Collie nudged past and charged up the stairs. The Star deck was the highest deck on board the superyacht and at its centre was the main electronics mast. The circular space was covered by a matching circular tinted glass roof that curved downwards at the edges with very narrow supports from the central electronics mast. The rear area was fitted out for the ultimate in relaxation with sumptuous lounger chairs, tables, bar, concealed galley, a large display screen and spa pool. Lights twinkled from the glass roof supports. Anne went to the bar and poured two gin and tonics and handed one to Charles as he sat down. The breeze caused by *Sundancer's* speed of twenty six knots was mostly dissipated by the tinted glass windbreak, but the breeze that did find its way through was welcoming and cooling. Charles took a drink from his glass and enjoyed the cool freshness of the gin and tonic.

His mind was full of a jumble of thoughts that he needed to break down and work through one by one. The first question was the easy one because it had no answer yet and that was, "Where was the radiation trail emanating from?" They would ultimately answer that question only once they picked up the originating radiation trail and followed it to its source. The next question again, an easy one to ask but one that again had no answer as of yet, "Was Axmann involved?" He turned to Anne, who was lying on one of the reclining chairs, with the back rest almost straight.

"Should we really be getting as deeply involved in this as

we are?" he asked. "It's not really our role to be the police or Secret Service. I don't mind helping to track the source of the radioactivity which could be, though not very likely, but could be, from a natural source. But chasing down Axmann and those missing weapons is not really in our remit and it is putting us and everyone in our company in grave danger."

"I know and understand your concerns, darling. But we have gone beyond the point where we can just walk away and, if we did, those weapons will do us and many others greater harm than if we continue on our course of action and stop them being used." Anne looked into his eyes. "It's safer for all concerned if we can help find those weapons and this madman while, I must add, we continue on our course to Indonesia."

"Have you read the report on Gustav Axmann that Keith sent through?" asked Charles, lying back on the lounger and looking at the stars that were beginning to show in the darkening sky.

"No, I haven't read it yet."

"It makes interesting reading but also indicates that we are dealing with a very smart, ably capable and extremely dangerous individual who wants to see the Reich rise from the ashes. He has a large dedicated group of followers, said to be in the thousands, and has re-established the Nazi Party, albeit outside his homeland with those that fled Germany with him. On the thirtieth of April, 1945, just a few hours before committing suicide, Hitler signed the order to allow a breakout and passed it to Axmann, who then left the Fuhrerbunker with an SS doctor. Can't recall his name but it's in the report, and with Martin Bormann. When they started to follow the railway lines to Stettiner station, Axmann decided to go his own way and headed in the opposite direction and escaped capture by doing so. He gathered his group and fled Germany and took with him the greater part of the Nazi treasure, which he has used to good effect funding the re-emergence of the Nazi party." Charles took a sip of his gin and tonic and carried on. "During the war he was Oberst-Gruppenfuhrer in the Schutzstaffel and reported directly to Heinrich Himmler himself, who as we all know was the most powerful man in Nazi Germany and one of those most directly responsible for the Holocaust. And it is clear that Axmann was very personally and heavily involved in the orchestration of the deaths of millions of people. Anyway, after the war, he originally positioned himself as the new dictator of the Fourth Reich, but it is thought that he chose to take the position of Reichsleiter instead and leave the position of Der Fuhrer to his eldest son. Basically, darling, he is trying to finish what Hitler started and we have now positioned ourselves directly in his firing line."

Anne smiled at Charles and began speaking: "We have some of the smartest minds in the world working for us and formidable technology that world leaders would love to get their hands on, and so I am sure that we are capable of beating this Axmann character. Besides I am pretty sure our team would tell us to leave well alone and pull us back to the undersea headquarters if we were not safe."

"I know, but I think we need to beef up security and the alertness on board. I think I'll go to the bridge and talk to the Captain, Max and Keith." Charles stood up and went to the staircase. "Back in a tick," he said as he dropped down the stairs. He left the library and made his way across the vast corridor to the bridge.

"Good evening, sir," said John Whitcome the Captain, turning in his deeply upholstered Captain's chair. The bridge was quiet and lit only by the displays that showed and monitored all the systems on board the superyacht.

"Good evening," replied Charles. "Get Max up here and link in with Keith, please." Charles went over the large monitor table that consisted of a very large flat sixty inch display laid into the cherry wood and leather table top. The system could show anything from engine instruments, images from the multitude of cameras around the superyacht to navigation maps which could be overlaid with radar and sonar. "Show me where we are, please," he asked Franklin, the First Officer.

"We are here, sir," Franklin said pointing out an icon on the map. "Sixteen hours from Kermadec."

"And where are our submarines and *Launch One*?"

"Max is on his way and Keith is just here," the Captain said, tapping the menu on the large display, causing a quarter section of the screen to change and show Keith linked via camera. "*Jupiter* is just here, eight hours from the Panama Canal. *Mercury* is here, and *Launch one* is right here, seven hours south east of Tonga."

The bridge door opened and Max entered and joined the three around the display table. "You've read the report and want to beef up security, I assume?" he said to Charles. Max had a way of knowing in advance what was going through the mind of his boss, born through years of close service.

"Yes, it's obvious that this Axmann fellow is highly dangerous and will without any shadow of a doubt, inflict death on anyone who gets in his way and, as we have already done that, one can only assume that we are on his radar and in immediate danger.

With that in mind I want to have both submarines and *Launch One* on full lock down alert status. All crews are to be on the alert at all times and a drill run within the next twelve hours. I also want *Sundancer's* defensive systems tested and a crew arms drill to take place in half an hour. Afterwards all deck defence hatches are to be kept clear. Keith have *Launch One* follow suit and contact both submarines as directed and test all the defence systems at the Kermadec base and put all our operations worldwide on alert," Charles said while keeping his eyes focused on the map.

"Yes, sir. I will contact all our bases and get James to test all our systems here," Keith said. "I assume you want all the aircraft secure as well?" he asked.

"I do. Where are they now?" Charles asked Keith.

"The 747 and Lear are at Auckland International and the A380 is due to land there in, let me see . . . ." He cued up a small screen inlay and ran a finger down some figures. "In about three hours, she is scheduled for a refuel before loading and heading to Indonesia with supplies ready for your arrival."

"Okay, sounds good. Get the Lear to Indonesia for me in case Anne and I need to use her. The 747 should be loading for the Ethiopian famine work. Talk to the security team and put them on alert."

"Okay, I'll get that all sorted now," replied Keith.

"Another thing, Keith. Tap in to all communication systems that you can, legal or otherwise, and increase the surveillance levels, and liaise with Grant. Talk again soon," Charles said. "Now, Max, I want the *Sundancer's* surveillance team to heighten monitoring of communications, radar and sonar round the clock, so check their rosters. The Bell 525 is to be ready at all times for take-off with the electromagnetic pulse unit plus missile pods attached."

"Yes, boss," Max said and turned quickly and left the bridge.

"Captain, in twenty five minutes sound the alert and note the time it takes the crew to get each system ready to fire."

"No problem. May I also suggest that, as we near Indonesia, we secure all the external doors, there are a lot of pirates operating in that region and we cannot get a guarantee of protection from the local Navy," the Captain suggested, tapping an area on the display table's map.

"Yes, I'll tell Ryan, Duke and Anne that external access will be the Star deck only. Just give us a heads up before you lock down," Charles agreed and leant back over the display table.

The Captain returned to his Captain's chair and sat down. He called Martin Deeks over to him and briefed him on the conversation he had just had with Charles Langham. Martin listened carefully then returned to his position on the port side of the bridge and ran through some of the menus on the array of screens in front of him, happy that all the superyachts systems were functioning one hundred percent. The Captain checked their course and called up the latest weather report. All through this the atmosphere on the bridge remained that of professional calmness. Charles stayed at the large table display with Franklin and watched as the icons that represented the submarines changed position.

"The submarines are manoeuvring into their new positions," Franklin said pointing to the two icons so that Charles could see which icons they were. "And these figures show our distance, speed, course heading and time to destination, which is Curtis Island, Kermadec."

"Thank you, Franklin," Charles said and left the table and, on his way to the door stopped by the Captain. "Captain, after the drill don't forget to join us for dinner on the main deck for the surf and turf. You can brief me there on the drill performance," Charles said and left the bridge to return to the Star deck where he found Anne with Abbey lying at her feet having her ears ruffled. "She'll have you doing that all night," laughed Charles.

"She's such a loving dog. She's been following me everywhere I go. I think she believes I'm her surrogate Cathy."

The phone rang and Charles answered. "Hi, Marge. Wait a second while I'll put you on screen. So, what's up Marge?" Charles asked, looking from Anne to the screen.

"Well, from the data that James has sent me from the satellite information and when I overlay it with data we have on currents, I can quite clearly see that the radioactivity started off the east coast of America in the Philadelphia region, tracks south towards Gulf of Mexico then back out to sea, heading east where there is an increasingly large bloom lying just north east of the Bahamas, where the trace ends," explained Marge.

Charles rubbed his chin and looked deep into Anne's eyes while he took in what Marge had said.

"There's no way that this is a natural phenomenon then, and the effects on marine life could be devastating. So three questions. Question one is how can we clean this mess up? Secondly where is it from? And lastly what's in that area on the sea bed?"

"Well, I'll keep tracing the source, but at least we now have some areas to focus on, a start point and a finish. I'll get back to you on the other questions shortly. Bye, for now," Marge said smiling and waving her left hand at the screen.

Anne stood up as the screen went blank.

"Time for dinner Charles."

She ruffled Abbey's neck, come on Abbey." Abbey charged to the stairs and slowed as she carefully descended the circular staircase with Charles and Anne following, gin and tonics in hand. At the base Charles tapped the keypad and waited while the hatch lowered and sealed with a hiss of air. They took the lift from the library down to the expansive main deck lounge. Charles went to the electronics console and opened the full height glass dividers so the lounge opened directly on to the vast rear deck with its swimming pool, spa pool, outside galley, bar, barbecue, Pétanque court, and teak tables and chairs. He turned on the deck lights, pool lights, mast lights, and the underwater hull lights. Pressing more buttons, he turned some music on, and the lounge lights changed colours. He ordered coffee from the waiter and sat on one of the settees next to Anne. The lift chimed and Max and Ryan came over to them. Max walked as always in a controlled power walk and laid an A3 photocopy of an old yellowing map on the table.

"Guess what we found, a treasure map," he said, sitting down opposite them in one of the high back plush armchairs and signalled to the waiter for a coffee.

"Oh come on Max, a treasure map?" chuckled Anne. "X marks the spot!"

"Well, actually, it's an old Nazi map, which originates from the office of the Fuhrer. The Third Reich were on an extraordinary hunt for the power that they believed came from a master race of pure supreme beings. It is well documented that they searched Egypt for ancient maps and artefacts that could point them to the source of that power. They even searched for evidence of Atlantis. And this map shows clearly where they thought Atlantis lies. Off the United States eastern coastline. Look."

Max laid the map on the table and used the coffee cups to hold three of the corners and the crystal fruit bowl to hold the fourth corner. "See, just here is where they say that the ruins of Atlantis lie." He pointed to a mark on the map and then took a sheaf of paper from his left inside jacket pocket. "But this is the real kicker. One of the files we downloaded was a copy of a report from a group of Nazi scientists to Hitler himself. In the report they say that they have identified the location beneath Atlantis where the real power of the city and its people lies. They then go into great detail about how to harness that power to the benefit of the Third Reich." He placed the copy on the table. "Buried deep underground in a cave at the centre of the city. It reads almost as though they may have actually been there and investigated the place." He sat back and looked at Anne and Charles. "I have the guys pulling up satellite images of the area and all the oceanographic data they can find."

"I don't believe it," Anne said incredulously. "Are you seriously trying to tell us that Hitler believed in Atlantis and you are searching satellite imagery trying to find it?" Anne crossed her legs and gripped her hands around one knee. "Pull the other one."

"Incredible as its sounds, yes." Max sat back and smiled. "Hitler stated that in the depths of his subconscious every German has one foot in Atlantis, where he seeks a better Fatherland and a better patrimony. He also said in October 1941 that, according to a Greek legend, there is a civilization known as prelunar and we can see in the legend an allusion to the empire of the lands that sank into the ocean. On his orders, Reichsfuhrer SS Heinrich Himmler set up the Ahnenerbe Institut, the National Heritage Institute, to conduct research into possible ancestors and descendants of the Atlantean peoples. Himmler sent archaeologists all around the world searching for these connections and used his top scientists in the field to find similar genetic traits to prove a common ancestry. Josef Mengele and his hideous medical experiments were all to try and find the biological connection. Himmler and Hitler also followed Blavatsky, who in her book, *The Secret Doctrine,* published in 1888 proclaimed that the people of Atlantis were a fourth root race succeeded by the Aryan race." He looked at Anne who seemed puzzled.

"Fourth root race? What's that?" she asked.

"It's a form of racial evolution rather than primate evolution, so the Aryan race is the fifth evolutionary race and, thus by far the most superior. Blavatsky was Aryan."

Charles look at Anne and then across at Max. "This is all well and good Max, but I fail to see what it has got to do with our conservation objectives or Axmann?" he asked.

"Well, to try and cut a long story short. Himmler's other favourite, a man called Herman Wirth, who was placed in charge of the Ahnenerbe, in 1935. He estimated that after the North Atlantic Ocean floors continental shift, Atlantis stretched from Iceland to the Azores. Meaning that Cape Verde and the Canary Islands are the only parts to remain above water following submergence. Himmler allowed Hurth in 1937, after Herman Wirth left the Ahnenerbe, to undertake an expedition to the Canary Islands with a research team."

"So, I know I am a bit fatigued, but I still don't get the connection," Charles remarked.

"It's simple really. The map shows the boundaries of Atlantis with Cape Verde and the Canary Islands clearly marked. Atlantis was a huge island which the Egyptians believed was larger that Libya and Asia put together."

"I still don't get it." Anne looked more puzzled and shrugged her shoulders, Max took a printed sheet from his pocket and unfolded it.

"I just got this from Marge. It shows the radioactivity traces that Marge is tracking are in this area. If we take everything we know that Hitler and his cohorts believed and overlay this old map with this new one then the centre of Atlantis now lies here." He stabbed a finger at the printed sheet. "Is that a coincidence?"

"Okay," Charles laughed. "But I am not going to start sending our teams in to search for the ruins of Atlantis." A siren sounded in the lounge and on the after deck.

"Ah, the Captain has initiated the readiness drill."

On the bridge, Captain Whitcome looked over at the Technical Officer, Martin Deeks. "Martin, sound action station please."

Martin leaned forward in his chair and tapped on a small screen to the right of his main screen. Immediately sirens sounded throughout the ship. External doors and windows closed and sealed with a hiss. Below decks bulkhead doors closed. Deep in the bowels of the yacht, the main air conditioning system increased in power and drew in air through external filtered air vents. On the bridge, Franklin, the yacht's First Officer, gripped the four throttle and pushed them slowly forward to their stops then eased each back individually to balance the revolutions of each engine. He started a slow turn to port and readied for a slow turn to starboard as the superyacht accelerated through the waves

In the surveillance cabin, the two operators on duty concentrated on their individual tasks. One raised the four missile launchers from their below deck positions and scanned the area with radar and high definition cameras. The other scanned the area beneath the waves with sonar and high definition cameras and lights built into the hull below the water line.

"I think I'll leave the forward torpedo systems inactive. What do you think?" he asked his colleague, who was by rank his senior.

"Agreed," replied Grant. "I ran an auto systems check on them while we were in Hawaii and it was all clear."

Charles, Anne and Max watched as the yacht's crew made their way quickly to their pre-planned places. The full height bullet proof glass doors that opened the lounge to the vast afterdeck started to close. At the stern two concealed deck hatches opened, one on each side. From beneath the deck weapon systems were raised and started to scan and tilt. Each weapon system consisted of six long tubes from the front of which the pointed black nose of missiles could be seen. Charles knew the same was occurring near the bows. He had worked closely with the designer and builders to ensure *Sundancer* was not only self-sufficient but that she could weather any storm and be secure against the growing piracy that prevailed in many of the seas and oceans she needed to navigate. The Italian shipyard where she was built and all personnel involved in her design and construction were bound by far reaching confidentiality contracts. To keep matters simple, the same yard built all the eight metre rigid inflatable boats and fourteen metre launches that were stowed in the two garages on each side of the superyacht. All members of the crew had been carefully selected by Charles, Max and Captain Whitcome for their character and personality as much as their skills. They needed the ability to get along with each other over long periods at sea and to work as individuals together in a close knit team. Charles saw that the crew stood at their stations armed with assault weapons and wearing the latest Kevlar bullet proof vests.

The sirens quietened and the Captains voice came over the system.

"Record time everyone, well done. Return to normal duties, Captain out."

Charles watched as the glass doors re-opened and felt the breeze caused by the differential between the air conditioner running at full power and the outside air.

Duke appeared on deck, stumbling slightly as the superyacht turned quickly back on course and powered down rapidly from full throttle to the original cruising speed on twenty six knots. "Jeez, never thought I would see that on a private yacht." He took a seat next to Max. "Are those missile launchers for real?" He pointed to the port side launcher as it retracted back into its housing beneath the deck.

"Oh, yes, and controlled by the guys in the surveillance room. They light up the target. The missiles do the rest."

"Will nothing ever surprise me on board this vessel?" Ryan said casually. "Thomas told me all about *Sundancer* over dinner one night but I think he left quite a bit out!"

"Ah Captain, good drill. Now tell me, as a seafaring man, what are your thoughts on the legend of Atlantis?"

Charles turned towards Captain Whitcome, who was walking with military bearing in his Captains uniform through the lounge towards them.

"A wonderful legend, no more, no less." He sat down, easing the material of his trousers at his knees as he did so. "I am of course conversant with what Max has described. But suffice to say it is a very good myth about the gods. The Atlantic is named after Atlas of course, the son of Poseidon. All true mariners know the story."

Max looked hurt, saying, "Oh come on, neither Hitler nor Himmler would expend so much effort at a crucial and pivotal time in their political careers if it were just a legend."

"Max, I know, but we have Indonesia to get behind and that is our priority, after that it's back to Africa and the famine relief teams." Anne leaned forward. "More important than chasing down some legend."

"That's not what I am saying." Max looked intense. "I think Axmann may be following up on the Atlantis theory and the power source that is said to be down there at the centre of the city. Why else would he have these maps?"

"In that case, my dear Max, we will cross that bridge if and when we get to it. Now let us take our minds off the troubles." Anne smiled and stood up. "Anyone for a game of Pétanque before dinner?"

Charles was the first to stand up.

"Sounds like a wonderful idea, my love. Come on, everyone."

"Never played it." Ryan stated as he stood up.

"Neither have I, but I have seen Cathy and Chris play it many times and it seems easy enough." Duke raised his arms in defence.

"Where are they, by the way?" Ryan asked.

"At the Kermadec Headquarters. They are central to the orangutan and tiger projects and will be leading the efforts and staying on for six months after we leave," Anne replied, pressing a button on a white cabinet which, with a quiet electric hum, opened to reveal an assortment of outdoor play equipment.

"They are in separate countries, so will Chris work on one and Cathy the other?" Ryan questioned.

"No, they will have one of the company's helicopter and a pilot at their disposal," Charles explained as Anne concentrated on her first shot. "They will both be in Borneo to start with before Cathy transfers to Sumatra for the endangered Sumatran tiger project."

Chapter Six

Chequers: The Cobra room

The Prime Minister looked around the Cobra situation room, now full of its required complement of staff. The room had the antiseptic feel of a hospital operating theatre with its stark bright lighting and hive of activity with aides entering with folders bulging with sheets of paper, some whispering in their Minister's ear. He looked at his watch and then the various clocks on the wall showing the times of various cities across the world. It was five in the morning, some nine hours after the bomb had exploded. It seemed like a lifetime ago. He had not slept since the explosion and was tired and had the sort of headache you should have only on the morning after the night before.

He rubbed his temples and looked around. The first meeting had laid the groundwork and achieved a great deal setting in motion the DER operation, assigning ministers and officials to their roles and, on the more sobering side, filling the vacant positions left by those officials who were missing, presumed dead. He stood up and rapped his knuckles on the table.

"Right, let's get started. All non-Cobra members, please leave. Lucinda once everyone is out and the doors are closed, you may start."

He sat and gestured to his aide, who ushered people through the doors as they were closed behind him by two armed security personnel.

Home Secretary, Lucinda Grey, looked around the room acknowledging those who were senior to her as well as those who had only just arrived.

"Ladies and Gentlemen, we will forgo the normal formalities of introducing everyone, those of you who are new to this team will all get to know each other well enough over the coming hours and days. I will get right on with the current situation as we know it." She cleared her throat and took a sip of water. "Excuse me, it's been a long night and I have done too much talking. We now know it was a nuclear weapon in the five to six kiloton range centred on the banks of the Thames between the Houses of Parliament and Buckingham Palace."

She pointed to the large display on the wall at the end of the table, which displayed a map showing an area of central London with concentric circles radiating out. "This is a high altitude aerial shot care of our American friends. As you can see, the area affected is some five to six square kilometres, so central London has effectively been wiped off the map and, with It the civil service, the financial and business districts. The area that most people see as the seat of law and order if you like. Casualty numbers are still being corroborated but we are talking at least in the mid to high hundreds of thousands. We may never find all the bodies as many would have been instantaneously evaporated." She wiped her brow. "The armed forces have a cordon in place at seven kilometres from the epicentre and triage centres every five kilometres around that perimeter are under construction.

Major hospital tents with surgical wards are being erected and a call has gone out for surgeons, doctors and nurses nationwide. London Heathrow airport is closed and heaven knows when it will reopen. Gatwick and Stanstead are closed, having taken the load from Heathrow. Luton took some of the load but is now closed due to an emergency landing that didn't make it. Trained specialists are gearing up to enter the cordon to help survivors on the edge of the cordon, who cannot make it out on their own. Due to the nuclear fall-out, many are feared buried under radioactive debris and, if they are alive, there is nothing we can in reality do for them. Fires are raging throughout the blast zone and the wider London area. The offices of Her Majesty's Government and the Houses of Parliament have been officially transferred here. The BBC and ITV have moved their centres of operation to Cardiff and Birmingham, respectively, and are setting up outside broadcast units here ready for you to address the nation Prime Minister."

"Thank you, Home Secretary. Do we have the resources to help those who are injured, I mean those affected by the radiation?" Chalmers asked gravely.

"Well, Prime Minister, those from the blast zone affected by burns we can treat for pain, but their prognosis is death and, quite soon, I would say. Those who have suffered from a medium to high dose of radiation will die in a few weeks or months down the track. Those who have received a small dose may develop cancers later in life. We really are in the depths of the unknown," the thinning haired, slim Health Secretary stated slowly and quietly. Gerard Mackintosh was a well-liked Minister known for his quiet respectful but frank and honest manner. He removed his glasses and rubbed the bridge of his nose. "We can treat broken legs, arms, cuts, amputation, concussion and the like as normal but the damage by radiation, no. We will need to isolate those poor souls and treat separately and as humanely as we can." He looked at his notes. "And we will need as many crematoria as we can commandeer to receive the huge numbers of bodies to prevent disease. The number of dead will be beyond anything we have seen before and, to be frank, vast funeral pyres may be an option of last resort that we may have to consider."

"God, I hope not. There would be a public outcry. But it will mean vast teams just to identify the dead and where necessary, taking finger prints, dental records or DNA," Grey said grimly. "I have identity teams being readied now and the army has vehicles and body bags on route but from the looks of the numbers I think we will fall very short. Ten crematoria are gearing up with more staff and ready to work on a twenty four hour basis. We are looking further north for more."

"We will have to monitor the numbers very carefully, indeed. I do not like the idea of public funeral pyres, but, if the need arises, we will have to make those decisions. If we cannot identify all the dead, then so be it. This is a very unusual situation. We must do the very best we can. Lucinda, get hourly reports on numbers and how we are coping. Report here hourly on whether we are behind the ball or in front," Chalmers said clearly.

Malcolm Brooke, the Secretary of State for Defence, removed his glasses. "Prime Minister, one thing we have to take into account is that we do not know whether this attack was a one off, or whether there is another bomb in Manchester, Birmingham, Edinburgh or who knows?"

"What do you suggest we do, with our resources already stretched to the limit?"

"Sir, I suggest that whilst we have military rule in place, we also put in place a curfew and close all ports and call in the Americans for help. They have two aircraft carriers in the North Atlantic that would be of vast help with personnel and equipment."

"Good ideas, which would help the situation enormously." He glanced at the Police Commissioner. "Instigate a curfew now. Liaise as necessary. Let us say a forty eight hour lock down initially while we work on a rota system for people to access food and water. I know it will stretch your resources to the limit but looters and riots will make things worse and be a bigger draw on your resources. The Territorial Army will be at your full disposal."

The Police Commissioner said nothing, just nodded and quietly sighed knowing his forces would be stretched thinner than ever before even with the Territorials, and that there was nothing he or anyone in the room could do about it, so why burden everyone with the question of resource?

"Lucinda, close the Channel Tunnel, all sea and airports until further notice," Chalmers said. "I'll talk to the President. Foreign Secretary, talk to your European colleagues, see what help and advice they can offer and explain the port closures. Meeting adjourned. Let's get to it, because a lot of people need our help." He stood up. "Everyone back here in an hour."

Chalmers sat while everyone filed out with their papers under their arms, phones to their ears, busy in their own worlds gathering information, giving orders and arranging meetings. When everyone left, his aide walked in and sat beside him, placing a cup of coffee in front of him.

"Get me President Johnson," he said and lifted the coffee cup to his lips while the aide picked up the phone and made the call.

Chapter Seven

Matagorda Bay

Axmann watched on his laptop in the dusky lounge of the cottage the news reports from London. He shifted on the settee trying to get comfortable. He was immensely pleased with the outcome of the car bomb. At first he was not convinced by his technician's confidence that they could install the nuclear weapon in the battery compartment of the Toyota Prius and get it through the United Kingdom border inspection, but they had exceeded his wildest expectations. The BBC reporter was solemnly describing the aerial photographs of the scene, which was being described as the result of a six kiloton nuclear weapon. The devastation was absolute: nothing left of central London, and millions feared dead or injured. The Prime Minister was due to address the nation shortly. Axmann grunted and closed the lid of the laptop.

He stood up, grabbed his carved wooden walking stick and went into the kitchen, where he took two pain killers before he made his way from the cottage to the workshop. He found his son Albrecht and Julian Beech in discussion looking over some detailed assembly drawings.

"We did well, my friends. London is in ruins and the Americans are bound to panic, as will France and the Netherlands. They will be so focused on helping the English and watching their backs that we will have an open route to success." He shook each by hand smiling. "Now, tell me how are we progressing with the two bombs?"

"Father, one is nearing its completion. I would say thirty six hours. What do you think, Julian?" Albrecht looked at Beech more for agreement than confirmation.

"Yes, we are concentrating on the first weapon while we wait for the rest of the new parts to arrive," Julian confirmed, his hands fiddling in the pockets of his white coat. He never liked to be put on the spot before Axmann, who was known for his short temper, and even with his frail frame still towered over him in stature. He was also highly concerned when he heard about the two aides that Axmann had shot dead for failing him recently.

"Good, the weapon is eight kiloton, that is right?"

"Yes, father," Albrecht nodded.

"The last one is the big one. Yes? Ten kiloton, am I right?"

"Yes, you are right, of course, father. And the casing is being made for a depth pressure of five thousand feet, as you specified."

"Five thousand feet? First I have heard about that," Julian exclaimed before catching himself and calming his voice. "We will not be able to pressure test its containment vessel. We do not have the right equipment here to do that. I can acquire some equipment and do a relative test on the seals, which will take more time and lead to more exposure for us, I would think."

"Ach, there was no need for you to know. Albrecht does the case design not you. Anyhow five thousand feet is not required. It is just my precautionary measure. Now from my latest information,

I do not believe we will need to go that depth," Gustav said with a wave of his hand. "How long for the last weapon?"

"We will work through that now, father," Albrecht said, and bowed his head slightly. "We are waiting delivery dates from the suppliers of the final parts that are due very soon."

Gustav raised his walking stick and waved it at the two men.

"Well, stop standing around here and get me the date," Gustav yelled and hobbled away, the arthritis in his knees and shoulders giving him a lot of pain. The other workers stopped what they were doing and watched in silence as Axmann left the workshop.

Back in the quiet of the lounge, he sat down stiffly in the settee, opened his laptop and quickly found the document he was looking for, scanning the page for the detail he needed. He made a few notes on a pad, and then opened up a large scale oceanographer's map and cross referenced the data on the pad against the map. He scratched his head, got up with the aid of his stick, and went into the kitchen and poured a coffee, took some more pain medication before returning to the settee. He folded the map and closed his eyes deep in thought, a frown creasing his brow. The pain medication started to ease the deep aches so he could concentrate his mind on his thoughts. His Fuhrer would be pleased with what he had achieved so far and overjoyed at his future plans. He only wished that Adolf Hitler was alive today to see what he was about to achieve in his name, the name of his hero. If only he could calculate the exact location, then he would know for sure how deep the weapon would need to go. He decided to rest his mind and return to the problem later. He had time; the weapon was not yet finished. He smiled to himself and fell asleep, the result a mix of alcohol, medications and age.

Chapter Eight

The White House

President Johnson sat in the Oval office, waiting for his Chiefs of Staff to arrive. He quietly reviewed the telephone conversation he had just had with the British Prime Minister, who had called to ask for aid following a devastating nuclear attack on London. He could really do with his Chief of Staff, Ryan O'Hare, right now, but he was on *Sundancer* with Charles Langham and he had not heard from him since he left Washington for Hawaii a few days ago. He was aware that Ryan was following up an important and significant lead on Gustav Axmann, but had hoped to hear from him by now. After this meeting he would put a call through to Charles Langham's superyacht *Sundancer.*

Clive Harris, the Defence Chief, entered the Oval Office followed by Legal Counsel Jeannette Rouse, FBI Chief Jerry Wozniak and newly installed Presidential Military Advisor Stephen Anderson.

"Good Morning," the President said, smiled and waved them to sit down. "I have just come off the phone with the British Prime Minister." He walked around to the front of his desk and sat in the armchair between the two settees. "He has requested our aid following the nuclear attack on London. He has asked that we send two carriers immediately, both to Bristol."

"I have heard about the attack," Jerry Wozniak shifted slightly and unbuttoned his jacket that was threatening to burst against his bulk. "Darn awful to say the least. Our scientists picked up a large blip on their earthquake monitoring equipment and centred it in southern England. We also had a report from the International Space Station about a bright flash."

"Okay, okay, that's fine. But for now we need to concentrate on what help we can give. Do we have two carriers available to send?"

"Yes, Mr, President. Three in the Northern Atlantic. The *USS Eisenhower* is still in dock undergoing intensive repairs to her electronics, thanks to Charles Langham. The *USS Nimitz* and *USS Carl Vinson* are engaged in the search for the origins of the radioactive trace. We can disengage both and send to England immediately. The admirals can be fully briefed on route with the operational requirement of the British." Anderson tapped on his tablet. "We can have *USNS Comfort* operational in five days. She's a hospital ship which may be of great use."

"Do that, both carriers, fastest speed and see if we can deploy the *USNS Comfort* in less time, every day counts. The situation in London is critical and we owe our English friends the fullest support."

"We can fly in support, Mr. President. A few C-17 Globemaster aircraft could carry and deploy field hospitals and personnel a lot faster," Harris advised.

"Out of the question. All airports capable of landing an aircraft of that size near London are out of service. Aircraft carriers with long range helicopters are the best option. Charles

Langham has two submarines heading into the Atlantic to assist with tracking the radioactivity and they are better equipped for the task than are our carriers. I understand that their deep sea submersible carrier is also on route to assist, so we can afford to redeploy the carriers to assist our friends. Now, any idea on who might be behind this atrocity?"

"We have many reasons to believe it to be Axmann," Wozniak said as he looked directly at the President. "We are fully committed to the fact that he was behind the theft from Nevada. Plus, we know he was up to his neck in it with my predecessor Haines and Anderson's predecessor William Paige. He even threatened you, Mr. President."

"Have we any leads at all on his whereabouts?"

"None at this time, sir. He has gone to ground and off the grid, and he has covered his tracks very well. But we have all the agencies on the case, CIA, NSA, FBI looking for anything at all out of the ordinary. We also know that whoever stole the material left some critical parts behind that they will need if they are considering building another weapon. We are looking for anyone who may be contacted to machine those parts."

"Okay, get those vessels on the way and put pressure on the teams to find this man and his cohorts."

Johnson stood up and made his way back to his desk and sat down while the others left the office and closed the door. He picked up the phone and called his secretary and asked her to connect him via video link with Charles Langham's superyacht *Sundancer*.

Charles and Ryan appeared on the screen. "Hello, Chris, how are you?" Charles said smiling. "I have Ryan here next to me."

"Hi, Mr. President. How are you sir?" Ryan said a little more formally.

"I'm very well gentleman, thank you. Now Ryan, how did your investigation go?"

"We downloaded a lot of material that is being analysed by the computers on board *Sundancer*. So far we have nothing concrete to go on sir." Ryan rubbed his eyes. "I've decided to stay on board while we trawl through the data. Max picked up a Nazi map which harks back to their Fourth Root cum Atlantis theories and is certain that Axmann believes that the power at the centre of Atlantis is true."

"Sounds like Max." The President chuckled. "Keep me up to date. I assume you have heard about the London incident?"

"Yes, we have. We saw the BBC news. Absolutely terrible," Charles answered.

"We're sending two aircraft carriers to assist. The FBI and CIA both believe Axmann instigated the bomb."

"That's our belief, too. The isotope signature should tell us whether it's a match to the material that was stolen," Ryan said.

"Now, why has no one here told me about that?" the President said thoughtfully.

"It would implicate the United States in the bombing, that's why," Ryan said, his voice edged with sarcasm. "Typical arse covering by the CIA, I would say."

"Ryan, I will get Thomas to obtain a sample of the London weapon material for you to check. I will get the isotope signature from the Nevada material to you on board *Sundancer*. Charles, you have the equipment on board *Sundancer* to compare the signatures I've heard. Is that correct?"

"Yes, Mr, President, we do. If there is anything else we can do, let me know."

"Thank you, Charles. I appreciate the offer. By the way, Thomas and his activities and objectives are between us. Good day gentlemen, and thank you, again."

The President clicked off the call and sat back in his chair and ran his fingers through his hair. His brow creased in deep thought. Nuclear blast on London using a weapon of American origin. How worse could things get? How was it shipped from American soil to London? Many questions that needed an answer and promptly. He picked up the phone. "Get Jerry Wozniak back here and get me another coffee." He read through the notes on his tablet while he waited, only looking up to say thank you when his secretary placed a fresh cup of coffee on his desk.

"You wanted to see me, Mr. President," Wozniak said, standing in front of the desk. President Johnson had not seen or heard him enter and looked up slightly startled.

"Yes, yes, take a seat. I have just spoken to Charles Langham and Ryan O'Hare and they raised an issue that could cause grave embarrassment, not only to this administration but the country as a whole and on the world stage."

"And what would that be, sir?" Wozniak looked perplexed.

"If the weapon or material used on London came from the Nevada facility, then this country could, by association, be implicated in the bombing."

"I see. Your primary concern is that the isotope signature could be traced back to the material in Nevada? But that concern arises only if the isotopes match."

"And in all probability you and I know they will match. The coincidence factor is far too high for them not to match. Would you not agree?"

"Mr. President, while I agree with your statement, that coincidence is only of concern if the isotopes signatures do match. We can circumvent that by supplying material via the Nevada facility but originating from, say, Los Alamos."

"No, we will not undertake that kind of subterfuge. We must trace the route of the material once it left Nevada. How did it leave American soil? How did it travel to London? How does it tie back to Axmann? We must find the link to Axmann and track this man down. I want people on the ground in the UK tracing the arrival of the material."

"We are running back through satellite imagery just before the bomb exploded, which should help pinpoint the location of the device and how it was contained. We know what the minimum size of the containment vessel would be. We think it must have been in the back of a truck or van." He interlaced his fingers. "If it's a vehicle, we may be able to track back to its origin point. But, we have no one on the ground that we can contact. The Embassy was destroyed in the blast."

"Oh, God."

"I have a team trying to contact everyone on their satellite phones, home numbers, each and every number we have, just in case anyone was away from the Embassy." He raised his hands "So far no one is answering, so at this stage I am getting an undercover team ready to leave to join *USS Nimitz*."

"Take Thomas and his team. I know they are my private armed forces team but they are of more use to you now. Tell me as soon as you know anything and liaise closely with the British. Thomas will brief me directly. The British traffic camera system may come into its own on this."

"Very good, Mr. President." Wozniak stood to leave.

"And don't forget." The President stood up. "We play it clean with the isotope and concentrate on finding Axmann, and clearing up this mess."

"Yes, sir. That is understood." Wozniak turned and left the Oval office.

After Wozniak left, the President took his secure cellular phone from the left hand top drawer of the desk and pressed two buttons, a quick dial to Thomas.

"Thomas, where are you? Good, come on over we need to talk in private." The President placed the handset on his desk and started to browse through the days briefing. Thomas arrived within five minutes. Thomas was a bull of a man, having dark but clean features, shortly cut black hair swept back neatly, and muscles bulging beneath a tailored black suit. The previous President, Mike Read, had enlisted Thomas and his team to take out Charles Langham. When a meeting of the G8 demanded the cessation of threat activity, President Read had ordered the Navy to destroy the boats that Thomas and his team were on. Only Thomas and one of his team, Connor, had survived the attack and been rescued by *Sundancer* which they had been chasing. From that day, Thomas had become a trusted friend of Charles Langham and enlisted into the service of the new President, Christopher Johnson, whom he now stood before.

"Thomas, I want you and your team to go to the United Kingdom with Jerry Wozniak and his FBI team. You will take your orders from him but work under my direct command. You will follow his orders only if they do not contradict or conflict with mine. Under no circumstances is there to be any tampering with evidence relating to the isotope signature of either the London or Nevada material. The material is to be analysed aboard *Sundancer* and delivered untouched and uncontaminated. When you have a sample of the material, get it back to the carrier and loaded on a suitable aircraft for an air drop to *Sundancer*, which I understand will be near Sumatra or Borneo. The aircraft will probably need to refuel in flight. You will need to arrange all that with the Fleet Commander behind Wozniak's back. I want you to use everything you have at your disposal. Charles and his team have offered their fullest assistance to trace the origins of the weapon and hence locate the whereabouts of Gustav Axmann and his next target." He looked into Thomas's eyes. "Most of that coincides with the orders given to Wozniak. But I do not fully trust the FBI. They tend to work to their own agenda and their own interpretation of what this administration, or rather, what I want."

"I understand fully, sir. My team will carry out your instructions to the letter. I will make contact with Miles Channing. He is the Security Chief for Mr Langham, if that's okay, and bring him up to speed," Thomas said, still standing erect.

"Yes, do that and keep me advised on my secure cellular. Ryan O'Hare is on *Sundancer*, He can be trusted if you cannot contact me for whatever reason. I will have a Presidential warrant drawn up and given to you before you leave. It will provide you with my full authority, so use it as you see fit. Good luck, and bring my team, your team, home safely."

Thomas nodded, turned and left the Oval office. President Johnson felt more at ease in the knowledge that he had Thomas covering his flank and rear. He turned his attention to drafting the warrant and passing it to his secretary before getting back onto the affairs of state and returned to the pile of briefings on his desk.

Thomas left the Oval office and made his way to his team's headquarters, calling each member in turn and telling them to meet him at their headquarters immediately. When he arrived, all seven members were waiting around the conference room table, steaming mugs of coffee in their hands. All were dressed in a similar way to Thomas: black shirts, trousers and jackets, which with their short hair and wide shoulders evoked a menacing atmosphere. None rose when Thomas entered and took his seat at the far end of the glass and aluminium table and he did not expect them to.

"Gentlemen, we have a new mission to perform for our leader. We are to head for the *USS Nimitz* and join the FBI team led by Jerry Wozniak heading to the United Kingdom. On the surface we will follow his orders but only when they do not contradict those I have just received from our President. We will have a Presidential warrant that endows us with the authority of the President. We are to collect material from the London blast zone and ensure that there is no contamination of evidence by our friends at the FBI, and we are to seek and find Gustav Axmann. On the way here I spoke to Miles Channing, who most of you have met, and he is ready to assist as and when we need it." He looked around the table. "Any questions?"

"When do we leave?" Connor, the second in command, asked.

"As soon as I have the warrant in my hand, and you guys have all the equipment in the truck and ready to roll to Nellis Air Force base."

"Any specific equipment?" Connor asked.

"Weapons of personal choice as usual, secure satellite communications, hacking kit, two drones, radiation suits, medical packs. You know the drill. Okay, drink your coffee, get your kit. Time is not on our side."

Chapter Nine

Matagorda Bay Incident

Albrecht put the micrometer down and wiped the sweat from his forehead.

"This humidity is impossible. My hands are covered in a film of sweat. How can we accurately measure these parts?" He rolled the part in his hand. "I know it does not matter if we damage the test parts but it is essential we measure accurately."

Albrecht and Julian had decided to order a spare of each item they needed specifically to use for sacrificial measuring and testing to ensure that the parts met the exact requirements of the specifications and dimensional drawings. They had all but one of the parts and had set up a bench to start the laborious task of checking each and every dimension and hardness testing. With laptops open, measuring equipment before them, they sat on hard stools facing the wall near the front of the workshop.

"There must be more portable air conditioners in town?" Julian replied after downing another 500ml bottle of iced water. "We can send one of the team into town with cash to pick another unit identical to the one we are using in the positive air assembly chamber. If we go to the same store we should avert any suspicion."

"Father will not be happy, but we cannot do this work in the chamber, because we would risk contaminating the weapon and we cannot remove the air conditioner from the chamber either. We have no choice. I will go talk to father."

"You know he is going to ask when the last part is due to arrive and all we know is that it is on its way by courier but we have no track or trace. He won't be happy about that, either" Julian said quietly.

"Yes, yes, I think I'll be in for a rough ride. His arthritis is made worse by the climate here and he is drinking and smoking more. He is taking far too many painkillers. He was so strong, even after the drug raids and the Davison seamount destruction, as long as he had his stick he could still walk true and strong. He's changed a lot since we arrived here. I had better go, and the sooner we can get the air conditioner the better." Albrecht looked grim.

"Check on the progress of the eight kiloton bomb. Some good news may help," Julian called to Albrecht as an afterthought.

Albrecht waved a hand in thanks and detoured passed the three technicians who were busy assembling the case for the ten kiloton bomb to the positive air pressure chamber, where two fully suited technicians were putting the finishing touches to the eight kiloton bomb. One looked up through his hood, picked up a clipboard and wrote the words "Ready tomorrow" on a sheet of white paper clipped to the board. Albrecht made an okay sign with his fingers and smiled to himself. At least he had really good news to give, but he doubted it would placate his father enough to stop him having another temper tantrum, which was becoming a daily occurrence. He was worried about his father's health and the sooner they could get to a more suitable climate, away from this humidity, the better. He knew his father would not leave until all the work here was done and both bombs on route to their ultimate destinations, which no one in the group, not even he, was privy to. The cottage and workshop would be cleaned and all evidence destroyed. The F150 would take four people across country to a local airport, where they would fly to Argentina to return to their families. The boat sunk in deep water after the weapons, Julian, Albrecht, Gustav and the remaining technician had transferred to the submarine.

Albrecht found his father sitting on the settee in the lounge, which was dark with all the curtains closed and no lights on, even though it was just past eleven in the morning. Gustav, seemingly startled by the sound of someone entering the room, opened his eyes and sat upright, grabbing his cane which was resting against the settee near his right hand. Albrecht walked round to face his father, who he noted was surrounded by maps and looked as though he had just woken up.

"Father, I apologise for disturbing you. I have some news and a request."

"Well, go on, what is it?" Gustav felt rotten. He ached from every joint from his ankles through to his shoulders. He knew he had taken more pain killers than he should and taking them with schnapps was probably not a good idea, but it gave him some respite from the pain and just left him with an unbearable ache. He shifted trying to get some comfort and relief.

"The eight kiloton will be ready tomorrow father," Albrecht advised. "When we can load it up and transfer it to the submarine."

"No, no, no, that one does not go on the submarine until the ten kiloton is ready!" Gustav snapped. "The ten and the eight will come with us when we leave. Now what is it that you want?"

"I understood that only the eight kiloton weapon was going on the submarine." Albrecht wondered if his father was getting mixed up. With the amount of drugs and drink he was consuming he would not be surprised.

"Well, I have changed my mind on the deployment of the eight kiloton weapon. I have come across a target that is too tempting to miss. So, I ask you again, what it is that you want?" He banged his cane on the table. "I will not ask again."

"I need to get another air conditioning unit to enable us to do the test and measurements of the new parts. The humidity is making it too difficult to hold and measure as accurately as we need too."

"Well, get on with it then." Gustav had a sudden idea on how to make himself more comfortable. "And get two. One for in here. It may help my arthritis. Now get going. You have enough cash."

"Yes father. Can I get you anything else?" Albrecht got up and waited for his father to reply.

"No, I will be alright. I have a pot of coffee and painkillers. I just need to rest for a while."

Albrecht watched as his father leaned back and closed his eyes.

"Well, don't just stand there, get to work," he mumbled.

Albrecht left the cottage and walked back into the workshop and called the younger technician over. He had already been into town a few times and so was a known entity to the townsfolk and less likely to attract too much attention.

"Take the truck and go into town. We need another two portable air conditioners, same size as that one." He pointed to the unit in the positive air pressure chamber. "Go to the same place as last time. If anyone asks just say it is to set up one in each room the old man uses to keep him cool as he moves from room to room." He took some cash from his back pocket. "Here is enough money and make sure you fill the truck up with gas on the way back." Albrecht watched as the young technician removed his white coat, put a baseball cap on his head, picked up and put on sunglasses and headed out the door. He waited until he heard the truck start and crunch its way down the drive before walking over to Julian, sitting on his stool, and bringing him up to date. Julian was happy with the news and clicked on a drawing on his laptop and zoomed in on a dimension he wanted to check.

"That was quick," Julian said as he heard a vehicle coming up the drive, its tires crunching on the gravel until it made that unmistakable sound when the tires slid on gravel after the brakes have been applied.

"Can't be. He would not have returned so fast unless he forgot something," Albrecht said, carefully placing the tiny part he was measuring in its holder. He carefully placed the micrometer back in its case. He stood up and started to walk to the large front doors, Julian not far behind when one was slid open and a courier driver entered the workshop.

"Hi, there. I have a parcel for GA Holdings," the courier said looking around for someone to respond.

Julian and Albrecht looked at each other, noting the courier's eyes as he scanned the workshop.

"We have a problem here," Julian whispered from the corner of his mouth towards Albrecht.

"Hey, what you guys making? Mighty elaborate, whatever it is?"

"Well, you see, we're oceanographers and we are developing

a highly technical marine measuring device," Julian started to explain, walking closer to the courier while Albrecht circled behind. "It measures deep ocean currents, temperatures and salinity." He took the package and placed it on the floor.

"Where do I sign?" he asked.

"Just here." The driver held up his hand held device and passed it to Julian with the attached pen in his other hand. "If I didn't know better I would say it looks more like a bomb," he said and laughed.

Before Julian could sign for the package or reply to the couriers remark Albrecht grabbed the courier's neck in one hand, head in the other and quickly and expertly twisted. The courier's neck snapped, killing him instantly. The lifeless body slumped to the concrete floor in a heap. The atmosphere in the workshop changed as everyone stopped what they were doing and stared at the body on the floor. Julian staggered back in shock.

"What the hell did you do that for? You didn't need to kill him," Beech yelled flapping his arms in rage. "Oh my, oh my, all you have done is create a bigger mess, a bigger problem."

"He saw too much!" Albrecht yelled back. "I had to make a split second decision and I did. Get his van in here and check it for a tracking device. Most courier vans have them." Resuming his business-like manner, Beech slapped his hands to his side and marched to the doors and slid them open. The engine of the van was still running so he put it in gear and drove it into the workshop.

"Keep the engine running until we locate where the tracking device is," Albrecht called to Julian while he slid the doors closed behind the van. Julian checked beneath the dash and finding nothing popped the hood and jumped down. Albrecht joined him looking into the engine bay. "Ah, what's this?" He pointed to a black aluminium box with wires heading to the fuse panel.

"It's not connected to the engine, just to power, so that must be it. If we can provide power and isolate it from the van we can send it anywhere we like." Julian said thinking out loud.

"No, it's been tracked to this location on their system. Your right, I have caused a right mess but it seemed like the only option at the time. Look, we need to deliver at least the next parcel, maybe two parcels, kill the tracker at the last drop them dump the van. That way we can divert attention away from here."

"What about him?" Julian turned, looking at the body.

"We need his uniform jacket and hat for the drops. The body we take out in the boat. There are plenty of sharks out there. Now get his jacket and hat on while I see where the next deliveries are."

Julian looked at him his face shocked. "Sharks?"

"Have you a better idea. No body to trace and no better way to go," Albrecht said, and grinned grimly.

Julian lifted the body slightly and pulled the arms out of the jacket sleeves. "That's just sick," he said to Albrecht before he noted that everyone else stayed back, but were intently watching what their two superiors were doing. He stood and put the jacket on; it was about the right size.

Albrecht gave him the cap and handheld delivery device. "You had better sign this," he said. Julian grabbed the electronic device and signed it with the attached pen. "The next two deliveries are both on the small industrial estate on the edge of town. I'll call Michael and have him meet you there. After the deliveries, cut the power wires to the tracker and dump the van say twenty five miles north of town. Michael will follow at a safe distance and bring you back here."

Julian jumped into the cab and ran through the GPS. "This would be a good place. The 616 just off the 135. Lots of scrub bush to leave the van in. Can make it look like he pulled over and just left the van."

"Okay, you get going. I will call Michael and get him to meet you there. Take your phone so he can call you and a pair of wire cutters. Oh, and take some alcohol and a rag to clean surfaces for fingerprints." He looked at the body. "I'll sort this out and talk to everyone."

Julian retrieved his phone and grabbing a pair of wire cutters, alcohol and wipes jumped into the van and waited till Albrecht had opened the doors before selecting reverse with a crunch of gears and a grimace. As soon as the van was clear, Albrecht closed the workshop doors, grabbed a trolley and loaded the body on to it, covering it with a white cloth. He pushed the trolley over to the side door, and then walked over to the technicians.

"Gather round," he said hands on his hips, head high giving him an air of authority. "We have to protect us, the project and our families back home in Brazil," he said letting his Germanic accent come through. He was pleased at the nods of approval. "This poor guy saw too much and although he may not have understood what he saw, his talk could have alerted the authorities, a chance I could not take. Many thousands died in our London project, so he is just one more for our cause." More nodding of approval. "So, back to work. Not a word to my father."

He went back to the trolley and pushed it through the side door as the technicians returned to work. It was hard graft getting the trolley down the long undulating path to the eight metre powerboat, and he was covered in sweat and puffing hard by the time he reached the boat. He rested for a short time before bundling the body unceremoniously over the gunwale, followed by the cloth, leaving the trolley on the jetty.

He boarded the boat and covered the body with the cloth. He opened a rear locker and turned both battery isolators on and primed the fuel bulbs. He made his way to the hard top doors and went into the salon, found the keys, inserted and turned them. Both engines instantly came to life. "Brilliant," he said to himself in relief as both engines ticked over. He jumped back onto the jetty and let go the bow line and held it while he walked to release the stern line, which he held until he boarded the boat and tied it off on the side rail. He casually flipped the bow line over the bow rail and tied it off. He eased the throttles forward and moved into the centre of the river heading for the bay, conscious of obeying the speed restriction until he reached open water. He switched the bilge pump to automatic. He turned on the VHF radio and the large screen GPS fish finder, paged through the menu screens till he found the radar menu and powered it on, went back through the menu screens and overlaid the radar onto the GPS screen. He spilt the screen so he had the GPS with radar on the left and the fish finder on the right. He was pleased that his father had followed his suggestion of a large twelve inch screen model, which was very easy to read. He turned on the course tracker and saw the red line appear tracking his journey outbound, which he would follow on his return to get back to the jetty.

He reached open water and pushed the throttles to the limit bringing both outboards up to full power. The bow rose as the propellers gripped the water digging the stern deeper and leaving a trough surrounded by white tormented water. On the radar he could see the position of other boats and headed straight out to an area where there were no boats showing. He smiled, enjoying the sensation of the boat powering through the waves. He could have stayed out longer but after just over an hour he decided he was far enough off the coast. The sea state was smooth when he backed off the throttles to neutral and let the boat drift. He left the wheelhouse and went back to the open stern, steadying himself against the gentle movement of the deck. He opened a side locker and pulled out a large lidded bucket marked bait. He removed the lid and sank back from the smell. "This should attract the sharks," he said to himself and emptied the bucket over the side. All he could do now was wait. He sat on the gunwale and looked around until he saw the first fin slicing through the water. "Where there's one, there will be another," he muttered to himself. "I'm going to have to stop talking to myself." He saw another fin, then another.

He walked over to the body and lifted it onto the gunwale so half the body was outside the boat with the head just above the gently lapping waves. He took a knife and cut deeply around the neck ensuring both jugular veins were cut. Blood dripped into the water and spread out, bringing the sharks closer. He lifted both arms, slicing the wrists before letting them dangle in the water. He watched as more sharks moved in. He rinsed his hands and knife in the ocean, being extra careful to ensure no blood touched the boat. He heaved the body further over the side till he was holding just one leg with this left arm. He leant over the side and cut deeply into the other leg before letting the body and knife go. He quickly but thoroughly washed his hands and arms with the sea water keeping a close eye out for sharks. He looked away as the first shark moved in and made his way in to the salon to the sound of thrashing water behind him. He wiped his brow, checked the radar which was still clear, and spun the wheel, turning the boat slowly around towards the coastline and away from the feeding frenzy before powering up and following the course he tracked on the journey out to take him back to the jetty. He glanced back once and out of blind curiosity spun the boat back towards the sharks bouncing heavily as he cut through his own wake. He cut power and let the boat drift. He took the binoculars from the side pocket and searched the surface where the sharks were, the feeding frenzy ebbing. He could see no sign of a body. Satisfied that the evidence was erased, he threw the cloth over the side, powered the outboards up and headed to the jetty.

Julian was pleasantly surprised at how easy the two deliveries were. No one asked where the other driver was; in fact most ignored him and concentrated on the parcel and signing the electronic pad. After the second delivery he pulled up just round the corner and popped the hood, took the wire cutters and cut both wires to the tracking device simultaneously. Back in the van, he checked his position on the GPS and headed off towards the I35. The drive took longer than he estimated even though the traffic was very light. He kept the hat down over his face and his speed to exactly what the signs indicated. He turned left onto the straight road that was the 616 and saw the F150 parked on the right hand side and drove on by.

His phone rang. He picked it up and answered, speaking straight away.

"Michael, follow me till I turn off, then stop by the road. I'll drive the van deeper into the scrub, wipe it down then head back to the road trailing some brush to break up my footprints and the tire tracks."

He put the phone down and concentrated on the density and height of the scrubland and bushes. He slowed near a break in the scrub and, with no other vehicles in sight, drove off the road and into the scrub, the branches of the low scrub bushes scraping the van sides. He carried on for about two hundred and fifty metres before turning parallel to the road and stopping. He could not see the road and figured that the van could not been seen from the road, either. He removed the jacket and hat and placed them in a plastic bag with the ignition key. He stuffed his phone in his pocket. And started to wipe every surface he had touched or may have touched inside, and then outside the vehicle with the alcohol soaked rag. As a last thought he popped the hood, cleaning the leaver as he did so, lifted the hood and wiped the tracker unit and surfaces where their fingers may have touched during their search. Satisfied, he placed the alcohol and wipes in the plastic bag and breaking off a large branch trailed it on his route back to the road. He stayed back out of sight and called Michael.

"Can you see the van and is it clear for me to cross?" he questioned.

"I cannot see the van and, yes, nothing has come past since I started to follow you. It is still clear both ways," replied Michael.

Julian dropped the branch and walked to the F150, throwing the plastic bag in the rear before climbing into the passenger seat.

"Let's head back," he said looking over at Michael, "And face the music. I doubt whether Gustav will not know something has happened. He has a sixth sense for these things."

"He'll know, for sure. Like he knew to go the other way at Stettiner station?"

"Precisely, he is always one step ahead, for he's a wise old fox. He will strip Albrecht down a peg or two to show he is still the boss, but Albrecht is and always will be his successor, our Fuhrer."

Chapter Ten

Kermadec and the Navy

Sundancer started to slow down as she neared the Kermadec Islands HQ in the early hours of the morning. A slight one metre swell was running and a bright moon reflected on the oily surface of the sea. The night watch had been relieved by the full bridge compliment of Martin Deeks the Technical Officer, Franklin the First Officer and Captain John Whitcome.

"Approaching refuel pod co-ordinates," Franklin said, easing the four throttles back towards neutral before releasing his grip on them and tapping the small joystick lightly to the right. "On station now Captain."

"Then station keeping, if you please, Mr Deeks."

Martin swivelled in his chair and tapped on a display screen. "Captain, thrusters are at station keeping, retracting stabilisers."

"Thank you, Mr Deeks," the Captain said and pressed a button in his armrest. "*Sundancer* to HQ, in position, release refuelling pod, if you please."

The voice of Keith Pritchard, Operations Manager of Langham's organisation, who was permanently based in the underwater headquarters, came over the bridge speakers.

"Welcome home, *Sundancer*. Refuelling pod released on controlled ascent. Two submersibles will start loading passengers and equipment in 45 minutes."

"Thank you, Keith. We can see the pod on sonar," Martin said. "Good positioning, Franklin. Lowering port refuelling hatch."

"Franklin, keep your eye on the fuel pod and adjust our position as required," said Whitcome.

Below decks the level of activity grew as the crew closed bulkhead doors leading from the engine bay and fuel pump room, isolating them from the rest of the vessel and fed the four large diameter reinforced fuel hoses towards the lowered hatch. Crew who doubled as firemen donned their protective gear and took up their designated positions. The passengers, at four thirty in the morning, were oblivious to all this activity and slept on peacefully. The refuelling pod quietly broke the surface close to *Sundancer's* lowered hatch. Martin Deeks unlocked his chair from the floor clasp, spun round and rolled it to a control console at the extremity of the bridge. He now had the pod and the hatch in view and deftly used the thrusters to bring the superyacht closer to the pod until a crew member could step onto it with two mooring lines. The hoses were then carried onto the pod and attached to the fuel pumps. Martin saw the thumbs up from the technician on the pod and opened the fuel management menu of the display screen and tapped on four buttons.

"Pumping fuel at full rate. Estimate thirty eight minutes till complete, Captain."

"Thank you, Mr Deeks. Shut down engines one, two and four please," the Captain said.

Two hundred metres below sea level next to Curtis Island

in the Kermadec Islands sat the headquarters of World Earth. One hundred and forty people lived, worked, and played in the headquarters' building, which was made up of five pods linked to a large central pod. The pods were comfortably furnished with wool carpeting, lined walls and paintings to give the centre a feeling of warmth and homeliness for the occupants, who worked and lived for long durations of time at the headquarters. Access was limited to either deep-sea subs or through an elongated tunnel with a concealed entrance on to the remote island. Each pod was equipped with watertight doors that automatically opened and closed to allow access. Power was generated by tidal movement and thermal and solar energy. Except for some foods, the headquarters were self-sufficient. James Young sat at his console in the circular command centre on the uppermost floor of the deep-sea headquarters, overseeing the loading of the two submersibles that would carry the rest of the research team and their gear to the surface and then onto *Sundancer*.

James Young was the Operations Manager for the undersea base and took his role very seriously, remembering that Charles had seen something worthwhile in him during a visit to a rehabilitation programme and had offered him a low-key position. James soon proved more useful and talented and rose through the ranks quickly and was admired by his superiors and colleagues alike. James could not believe it when Charles offered him the Operation Manager position at the newly built Kermadec base; it was a dream come true and a heavy responsibility that he took extremely seriously. From his command position and multiple cameras around the headquarters, he could see the interior pod where the two submersibles docked with the undersea headquarters as well as inside each submersible. He watched as equipment cases were carefully lowered into one of the submersibles while people, including the Langham's children, Chris and Cathy, lowered themselves into the other. The interior layout of the submersibles left little room for comfort, with two seats in the cockpit which had one large circular thick glass window and four smaller circular windows, one to each side, one above and one below. Behind the cockpit were four rows of double seats, either side of a narrow aisle. The seats were canvas and easily removable to house experiments or cargo. James watched as the hatch on the submersible carrying the equipment was closed and secured before the loadmaster closed the pod hatch isolating the submersible from the pods atmosphere.

"Submersible two hold release until submersible one hatch closure," he said into his throat microphone.

"Holding, James. Will await your go for release," the pilot of submersible two said, giving a thumbs up to the camera.

James kept an eye on submersible one as the pilot closed the submersibles hatch and the loadmaster close the pod hatch. He watched the lights on his console turn green while the main pod access hatch light stayed red. The loadmaster exited the pod through the gangway hatch, checked his console and closed the large watertight hatch behind him, spinning the wheel and closing the levers isolating the room from the docking pod. The console lights went from red to green, showing that everything was ready for the submersibles to launch. James gave the word.

"Sub one clear for launch, sub two check your sonar, as soon as sub one is clear you can launch." Without waiting for replies he switched to *Sundancer's* frequency. "Captain, both submersibles are surface bound. How is the refuelling progressing?"

"James, we have stopped pumping and detaching the refuelling hoses as I speak. Thank you for the fuel. We now have full tanks," the voice of Captain Whitcome came clearly through the speaker on the overhead command panel above James.

"Hoses are clear, you can return the refuelling platform to its dock," the voice of Martin Deeks voice announced clearly over the same speaker.

"Thank you, gentlemen. Fuel platform submerging now. Submersible commanders, the fuel platform is descending two hundred metres off your port side. Submersible one dock with *Sundancer* on her port side rear platform, Submersible two forward port access hatch. Once unloaded return to docking pod immediately, time on surface is to be kept to a minimum. Out," James said clearly and watched the position of the fuel platform and submersibles on his sonar screen.

Submersible two moored next to a large platform that was forward of the now closing refuelling platform and commenced unloading the supplies. Submersible one moored next to a smaller personnel access hatch.

Cathy was the first to climb out, tall and tanned with flowing blonde hair blowing in the breeze, crossing from the submersible with confident ease. Chris was next, short blonde hair, tanned, tall and muscular. Four other researchers exited the submersible, one by one, taking deep breaths of the fresh sea air. Chris and Cathy helped the researchers cross from the submersible to the access hatch. Once everyone was clear, the submersible co-pilot released the mooring lines and closed the hatch. Cathy and Chris stood and watched the submersible slowly sink beneath the waves. They looked towards the stern and could see the other submersible still being unloaded when a klaxon sounded followed by the voice of Captain Whitcome.

"New Zealand naval vessel approaching, ten miles away on our starboard quarter. Get that submersible unloaded. We are getting under way in five minutes, Captain out."

Cathy and Chris closed the bulkhead door and made their way aft to see if they could help with the unloading.

"Mr Deeks, restart engines one, two and four please," the Captain ordered.

"Engines one, two and four started and all green. Submersible hatch is now closed, under power and moving away," Martin stated. "Loading bay hatch closed. Submersible clear and submerging."

"Very well, shut down station keeping thrusters. Mr Franklin, bring *Sundancer* up to twenty knots. Resume auto pilot course to Tonga," Captain Whitcome sat in his plush leather Captains chair. "Mr Deeks, extend stabilisers and check desalination plant please."

"Stabiliser fins extended and on fully automatic. Gyro stabiliser fully operational and desalination plant green. We have full water and fuel tanks" Martin said. "Five thirty, time for fresh coffee all round." He picked up the intercom and called down to the galley for fresh coffee.

The darkened bridge, with light only coming from the displays, resumed its air of quiet efficiency until Franklin noticed the radar blip.

"That New Zealand naval vessel has increased speed and altered course to match our heading. I would say she's on an interception course, Captain."

The VHF radio speaker came to life. "Vessel off our starboard bow, this is the New Zealand Navy, heave to. We intend to board you."

Captain Whitcome picked up the microphone and spoke with authority. "This is the superyacht *Sundancer*. Good Morning. We are heaving to." He nodded at both Martin and Franklin and continued speaking into the VHF microphone. "Please ensure your shoes are clean or you will be asked to wear shoe covers. Please board on our port side through the access hatch, which will be lowered with fenders deployed and well lit. You will be met by and escorted to the bridge by our security team. *Sundancer* out."

The Captain replaced the microphone as the smell of freshly brewed coffee wafted around the bridge. Martin stood and took the tray from the steward and placed it in the galley area at the rear of the bridge.

Franklin was busy taking the superyacht back from the autopilot and slowly reducing speed to bring the superyacht to a halt. Martin poured three mugs of coffee and passed them out on the way back to his console.

"Station keeping and retract stabilizers, please, Mr Deeks, at Franklin's readiness," Captain Whitcome said, blowing the steam from the mug of coffee before taking a sip.

"We are at a stop, Martin, so you can go to station keeping," Franklin called out.

Martin activated the station keeping programme and retracted the stabilizers while he called the security team and watched the naval vessel launch its rigid inflatable boat, which made its way quickly over to *Sundancer* and the waiting crew members who caught the thrown mooring lines. Two uniformed New Zealand

Navy officers climbed on board *Sundancer* and followed their escorts to the bridge, while two ratings stayed on board the Navy rigid inflatable boat, watched over by two *Sundancer* crew members.

"Well, may I ask why you have deemed it necessary to stop and board the superyacht *Sundancer* and who you both are?" Captain Whitcome asked indignantly of the two officers who entered the bridge escorted by two bulky guards led by Ralph Cohen, the security chief.

"We are interested in why you were hove to just off Curtis Island. I am Lieutenant Commander Mark Withers and this is Sub Lieutenant Nicholas Carter," Withers answered, standing rigidly in his starched uniform, trying to ignore the two burly men directly behind him. He looked around the bridge, his face showing he was astounded at what he saw.

"Well, Lieutenant Commander Withers, I am Captain John Whitcome, Captain of this superyacht *Sundancer*. The gentleman over there is Martin Deeks, our Technical Officer, and this is Franklin our First Officer. The two men behind you are fully trained bodyguards and that's Ralph Cohen, our security chief. The owners of this superb vessel are asleep in their stateroom and I would not like to be the one to disturb them. As to why we stationed ourselves just off Curtis Island is easy to answer. It is in the lee of the wind, which means we could use our thrusters to maintain our position more easily whilst we checked our desalination equipment. As you will know yourself, there is a three to four metre swell running, and where we were in the lee of the island it was a slight one metre. We had a diver in the water checking the hull inlets for any blockages, so it was much safer for him and his dive buddy that *Sundancer* was not moving about.

Also it meant that our owners stayed undisturbed." He calmly drank some of his coffee casually wiping some invisible dust from his trouser leg and continued. "We have just arrived from Hawaii and Mr Deeks noticed a drop in desalination output and the lee side of Curtis Island looked perfect."

"May we see your log please?" asked Withers.

"Why, of course, you may." Whitcome stood up carefully placing his steaming coffee mug in the holder on his arm rest and went to the large display table at the rear of the bridge and tapped the on screen menu and pulled up the latest log. "Here you are. This is our log, and this display here shows our course track and our schedule for our next destinations."

"Why did you move away as soon as you sighted us?" Withers asked looking up from the log.

"Lieutenant Commander Withers," Whitcome said, quietly resting his arms on the display table and sighed the sigh of someone dealing with a jobs worth. "We moved away as soon as the desalination equipment was corrected. You will note that in our log." Whitcome pointed to the log entry. "Tell me, Lieutenant Commander, what is your maximum speed?"

"Around twenty-seven knots, why?" Withers asked inquisitively.

"You see, we were accelerating towards twenty knots, as you can see in the log just there." Whitcome pointed to the autopilot read out on the screen. "We normally cruise at twenty six knots, not far off your maximum speed. If we were in a hurry to get away from you then we would have quickly accelerated to our maximum speed of forty two knots rather than heaving to as requested." Whitcome slowly straightened up and returned to his Captains chair and sipped his coffee. "Now, Mr Cohen here will escort you and your Sub Lieutenant back to your tender, and we will return to our course."

"We shall leave when you have answered all our questions." Withers stood his ground by the display table behind Whitcome. "I am not satisfied with your answer."

"If I may?" Deeks said looking at Whitcome, and deciding to try and defuse the issue. "Lieutenant Commander, if you look at the readout here you will see the output before and after our repairs plus the dive report from our divers who inspected the inlets." Deeks pointed to one of the screens on the bulkhead beside his chair. Withers walked across the bridge, taking a good long look at the displays and controls with widening eyes.

"Show me, please," he said as he stopped beside Deeks.

"This is the dive report showing, as you can see, start, duration, end time, maximum depth reached and the observation report with photographs which you see are time stamped." Deeks tapped on the screen. "This is the maintenance log from our engineer, which shows his testing before and after repair." Deeks smiled. "All automated you see."

"And this console which reads weapons control and armaments?" Withers said pointedly. "Not usual surely for a civilian vessel, and to my mind very disturbing, indeed." Withers whipped round to look at Whitcome and then at the bridge door which opened.

"Captain, what the hell is going on and why are we not under way?" Charles Langham asked, his voice strained but controlled as he entered the bridge in a thick towelling robe his hair untidy and the black shadow of an overnight growth of beard covering his face. The bridge went extremely quiet and the atmosphere intensified; it could be cut with a knife.

"We have guests, sir. The New Zealand Navy. They want to know why we were hove to off Curtis Island," Whitcome said standing up and to attention as he spoke. "I have advised them that we needed to carry out a repair to the desalination system. Mr Deeks has just shown the Lieutenant Commander here the maintenance and dive logs."

"Then you have seen all you need to see, Lieutenant Commander, and you may return to your ship," Charles Langham said. "You have delayed us long enough and disturbed not only me, but possibly my wife as well as my guests, which I do not appreciate. Ralph escort these gentlemen to their tender." Charles walked towards the Captain and stopped when the Lieutenant Commander halted his progress by grasping his right arm. Charles calmly looked at the hand that was restraining him. "You will remove you hand or I will have it removed and you in court for common assault," Charles said in a clipped voice.

"Not before someone explains why you have a control panel for weapons control and armaments," Withers said just before Ralph Cohen reached him and grabbed the Lieutenant Commander's arm with one hand and releasing the fingers gripping Charles's arm with his other, firmly pulling it behind the Lieutenant Commanders back in an arm lock. The two body guards moved quickly in front of Sub Lieutenant Nicholas Carter with their weapons drawn.

"No one touches, Mr Langham. You have just committed an assault," Ralph said maintaining his grip on the arm. "You two keep an eye on the Sub Lieutenant. If he moves, restrain him."

"Ralph, let the officer go, but keep a close eye on him, please."

Langham sat in the Captain's chair, which Whitcome had

vacated. He leant forward, resting his elbows on his knees, clearly exhausted. He spoke slowly and chose each word carefully. "Lieutenant Commander, this is a private yacht designed to my specifications and it is, in fact, my private home. We have on board the very latest state of the art equipment, which includes technology to protect us against piracy and also to ensure that no one gets too close to the hull whilst in port or at anchor. We can, for instance, detect divers and send either a high voltage charge or ultrasonic sound waves through the water around the hull. We have a host of technology on board that you will not understand so I do not intend to go into detail, albeit to say that we have been in New Zealand waters on many occasions and passed muster with your marine inspectorate." Charles looked closely at the Lieutenant Commander and put up his hand to stop him from interrupting. "I take the protection of my family, guests and crew very seriously and we are headed towards waters that are renowned for piracy." Charles unsteadily stood up. "Now, I have explained to you the weapons control panel and I can see from the way you are looking around this bridge, that you could have a host more questions, and, to be honest, I do not have either the time or inclination to answer them. I have given you more than enough of my time and you will now leave." Charles looked towards Ralph. "Escort these men from my home." Then to Whitcome. "Captain, resume control of the bridge and get us back on our course. We have a tight schedule and need to be in Indonesia on time, so you will make up for the time we have lost please." Charles walked towards the bridge door, slowing to turn to the Lieutenant Commander. "Unless you want trouble with your Navy Commander, Minister of Defence and Prime

Minister, not forgetting the United States President, I would leave *Sundancer* now. Good day sir."

Charles left the bridge and walked across to the corridor to the dining room and walked over to the lift and pressed the call button. He could feel the engines starting to hum beneath his feet and watched as the two Navy offices were escorted from the bridge to the lift. They stood quietly beside Charles with Ralph Cohen and the two body guards behind them. Charles entered the lift and stood to one side while the others entered. Ralph entered last and pressed two buttons.

"I assume your returning to your stateroom, sir?" he asked.

"Yes, thank you, Ralph. I don't think Mrs Langham has been wakened by this unwarranted intrusion into my home." The lift stopped and Charles got out and without turning around said. "Goodbye, gentlemen, and never try to stop or board *Sundancer* ever again or you will regret it for the rest of your careers." Charles walked away as the lift doors closed.

"I would listen to the man," Ralph said. "He holds a lot of sway with politicians and has enough money to not think twice about taking you to court for assault or illegally detaining *Sundancer*. Besides, you're a minnow compared to *Sundancer*. You are what one hundred and eighteen metres long, and we are one hundred and eighty five metres. You can reach twenty seven knots, we have a top speed of forty two knots and only need thirty two crew thanks to the automation," Ralph chuckled. "Besides I reckon we have more fire power than you." The lift stopped and Ralph led the way through the luxurious gangway down to the port side boarding platform. Ralph and the two body guards watched as the officers boarded the rigid inflatable and took their seats and the mooring lines were thrown on board by two *Sundancer* crew members. As the rigid inflatable moved away Ralph turned around. "Let's close up. The Captain will pick up speed very quickly."

The two body guards and one of the crew stepped back while the other crew member went to the hatch control panel and pressed the topmost button. The platform started to rise and hinge upwards until it closed flush with the hull. A hiss could be heard as the door sealed closed. "I'm returning to the bridge. You two can stand down after you have checked the latest information from the surveillance room."

Ralph made his way back to the bridge. He smiled quietly to himself, feeling the increase in speed and the slight tilt to port as the Captain increased speed and turned towards the navy vessel. He could feel the imperceptible lift of the bows and dip of the stern. He looked at this watch and saw it was still only five forty, a twenty-minute delay overall, that's all. Charles is just showing the strength of his organisation and the fact that he is pissed off at being woken up. Ralph knew Charles needed all the rest he could get. The fatigue caused by the Multiple Sclerosis that Charles had was getting worse. Everyone on board *Sundancer* was aware of that and hoped that the new disease modifying drug that Cathy had bought on-board and passed to the doctor would help. He would have a chat with *Sundancer's* doctor later in the day.

The bridge was buzzing when he arrived. "How fast, Captain?" Ralph asked.

"We did a nice long curve around them and hit thirty-eight knots till I decided that they had seen enough. We gave them a show with all the underwater and deck lights on. We are now gently slowing to twenty-six knots and coming round back on course. By eight o'clock we will be back on schedule," Whitcome said. "You were quick off the blocks when the Lieutenant Commander grabbed Mr Langham."

"He was out of line and I could see that Mr Langham was not feeling well and could have reacted very badly," Ralph said. "He was obviously fuming and highly concerned about why we had not picked up the navy vessel sooner. With our systems and those that James has at his disposal we should have had enough warning to get well clear. Plus, he was well fatigued. We need to quietly talk to the crew and bring them up to speed. He gets fatigued very quickly, and then he has a very short fuse."

"I agree with that. Let hope the new drug that Cathy gave the doctor helps. You talk to the lads in surveillance and James, find out what happened. Martin, talk to the section heads and pass the word and keep it low key, we do not want Mr Langham to find out. It would hurt him if he found out."

Lieutenant Commander Mark Withers and Sub Lieutenant Nicholas Carter returned to the bridge of the New Zealand Navy vessel.

"Well, that did not go very well at all," Withers said to Carter as he took his place in the Captain's chair.

"They did hove too when asked and were happy for us to board her," Carter said. "I would agree that they were not happy with the questioning, or should I say the questioning of their answers."

"They should have shown us more respect or should I say, the uniform more respect." He picked up the clipboard that lay on the table beside him. "Helm return to our patrol course." He started to write on the clipboard. "I really don't know who the hell they think they are, to talk to us like they did."

"Captain, the superyacht *Sundancer* is owned by a very wealthy conservationist who does a lot of work on famine relief, reversing environmental damage and he performs a large amount of conservation activity. I remember reading a transcript of a speech he gave to the United Nations. He has purchased land in the Amazon and Indonesia and works with local tribes on regeneration. In Africa he has teams working on famine relief sustainability programs and is now working in Sumatra and Borneo on tiger and ape recovery," the radio operator, Ham, explained. His nickname Ham, short for Radio Ham, had stuck with him since he started his tour of duty, simply because he did not like boiled ham.

"Thank you for that, Ham. Does not excuse bad manners," Withers replied.

"Did you meet Mr Langham?" Ham asked.

"Yes, he was very sharp and rude."

"His illness may have been playing up. I hear he has MS, so his fatigue may have made him appear rude especially if he just woke up," Ham replied. "If you excuse me for saying so, sir?"

"Enough said," Withers said with a gasp. "What the hell!" He watched as the sleek profile of *Sundancer's* white bow with water cascading from each side in a flattened V shape came curving towards them in an arc. Lights were ablaze all around the sleek vessel. The rising sun glinting off the menacing looking polished stainless steel anchor hull protection plates with a red glow. At close proximity to the New Zealand Navy vessel, she veered off, her long stylish hull roaring past on their starboard side, continuing its long curve leaving a churning froth of white water that glowed blue all around her.

"How can a vessel that big perform like that?"

"She has four Rolls Royce engines, totalling seventy-five thousand horsepower," Carter said looking up from his computer console. "Just looked her up on the web, sir. Not a lot of information about the boat itself, just the engines. Shallow water jet propulsion. Range ten thousand nautical miles, maximum speed forty-two knots with twenty-six knots as a cruising speed." He whistled. "Forty-two knots, that's impressive." He smiled at the Lieutenant Commanders face.

"So was the bridge, it was more like an aircraft cockpit. A very impressive machine I would have given my right arm to see the engine room. Back to normal duties," Withers said as he watched *Sundancer* move off into the distance, wishing he had that turn of speed.

James sat at his console beneath the sea. "Well, we have run diagnostics and one of our sensors was knocked offline. It is back up and running now and was in the right quadrant for us to miss the early warning alarm. What caused it to go offline we are, as of yet, unsure and we are still working through that. I have spoken with the *Sundancer* surveillance team and they were taking the opportunity to run a software upgrade on their systems while under the cover of ours," James explained via video link to Charles and Ralph. Charles had breakfasted on the deck with Anne and Ryan and discussed the near disaster that had occurred. He was still angry at the events that could have compromised the secrecy of their headquarters location. Anne had calmed him down and suggested that after breakfast he should talk things over with Ralph and James in the quietness of the library, over coffee. The cooked English breakfast, Earl Grey tea, fresh fruit and Anne's company were enough to cool Charles down.

"James, we must ensure that we never take any security measure offline for whatever reason without back up cover. Doesn't matter if it's *Launch One, Mercury, Jupiter, Sundancer* or headquarters. See to it. I will put a proposal to the New Zealand Minister in charge of the Environment for a permanently manned conservation station on Curtis Island to monitor the effect of climate change on the reef, grasses and wildlife. We will pay for and construct the station underground to minimize damage during construction. We will pay for the upkeep and manning of the station. I know they have looked at this in the past and side-lined it for cost reason. At least if we get caught in the area again, we will have an excuse, of sorts." Charles looked at Ralph next to him and James on the screen. "Your thoughts, gentlemen?"

"If we were still refuelling, it would have been a disaster, that's true. The fastest disconnect we have done in trials was eight minutes. If we could stay on station and disconnect without the need to move away at high speed, it would make life easier. I will make sure that all software updates have to be approved from here. I can only apologise for the mistake." James said. "We can link the station to our tunnel with another airlock."

"I concur with James. The software update was a bad coincidence, and in all the years we've been operating, it's the first failure. The conservation station is a genius idea, gives us a legitimate reason for being in the area." Ralph put his coffee down. "The sensor worries me though. It went offline and we don't know why. How can that happen?"

"We are running through the diagnostics and one of the software guys is checking the code." James rubbed his forehead with his thumbs. "At this time, as I have said, I do not have an answer."

"James, keep the guys on it until we know what happened and keep me advised. Now go and get yourself some breakfast, talk later." Charles disconnected the call and looked up as Max entered the library and went straight for the coffee.

"Right bloody cock-up for sure," Max said pouring himself a coffee and carrying the pot over to the table where Charles and Ralph were sitting. "Reckon the sensor was hit by something similar to the one off Hawaii," Max said, topping up the others coffee. "Marge told me she initially thought a submarine, whale or squid might have struck it due to its depths. When she recovered the unit it was obvious a migrating whale had hit the unit. They have improved the design since then to account for similar impact forces. The ones around Curtis Island are the old models and not scheduled to be changed for a few months." He sat down. "And," he paused for effect before saying, "I have some more information from our trawl of the data we downloaded from the Hawaiian offices of our friend Axmann."

"Let's hold that over till Duke is awake," Charles replied, supressing a yawn. "It's been a long day."

"Boss, it is very important. Duke, Ryan and I finished work on it at 2am this morning. We just had breakfast with the surveillance room team to do a quick review. Duke and Ryan went to freshen up and will meet us here shortly." Max looked red eyed.

"Seems we have all had a rough night's sleep except those scheduled for the night watch. Okay, Max let's have it. I can see your busting at the seams." Charles leaned back and rested his chin in his hands. "Tell me more," he sighed.

"Well, you recall what I said about Hitler and Himmler and their focus on finding ancestors and descendants of the Atlantean race." He waited until Charles and Ralph nodded. "Well, we can overlay more detail onto the map that we found. We have found more information from the research carried out by the Ahnenerbe Institut. If we add that to the searches done by Axmann and his cohorts, then we have a more defined centre of city of Atlantis. For some reason, they seemed to have halted their work on the Canary Islands, Cape Verde, the Bahamas and Bermuda quadrant. And this is the interesting part—they moved further to the West. The east coast is what they settled on including the Gulf of Mexico." He stopped as Duke and Ryan entered the library.

"I was going to lighten the atmosphere by saying the reason behind the Bermuda triangle disappearances, but the Gulf of Mexico rules that out!" Charles laughed.

"Don't laugh too soon," Duke said, joining them at the table and waited until Max poured him a coffee. "These people, no matter how distasteful we think their activities were, brought together the top people in their fields to do the research and the sheer amount of data is a testament to that. They were very close to discovering the centre of Atlantis, if it ever existed of course. They just lacked the deep sea submersible or equipment needed to map the sea floor in detail." Duke leant forward. "We believe, and, yes, we are taking two and two and coming up with four point one, that based on their detailed research and maps and the detail we now have of the sea floor, located the co-ordinates where we believe Gustav Axmann will aim for as the target of the power centre of Atlantis."

"Let me get this right. You believe that Gustav Axmann will place a nuclear weapon at the exact centre of where he thinks Atlantis is thought to be, or to be precise, his masters thought it to be, to harness the power of Atlantis so that he can increase the magnitude of the nuclear explosion?" Charles asked incredulously.

"Yes, boss" Max answered. "But do not dismiss the idea. In this area there are many black smokers and asphalt volcanoes and one that is particularly large. If he were to drop the bomb on top of or in or on one of these smokers or asphalt volcanoes, well, I hate to think of the consequences to the eastern seaboard, or the tsunami that would race across the Atlantic to our European and African neighbours."

Charles leaned forward and rested his elbows on his knees. "So, Max, the map, black smokers, asphalt volcanoes, Atlantis, Axmann," he said ticking each item off on his fingers. "What ties them altogether?"

"The exact locations of three asphalt volcanoes, well, within a few tens of metres, on a map we found in a folder marked *T4R*. When we clicked on the folder, we found other sub folders named *Atlantis, Himmler, Sumerians, and Ahnenerbe*. But the most interesting of them all was *The Rise of the Fourth Reich*. When we opened this folder, we hit the mother lode. Hundreds of scanned documents from Hitler and Himmler. But the pièce de résistance was a new overlay of the map that we found on our search which defined their latest conclusion of the location of Atlantis." Max rubbed his hands together before taking a sip of coffee and continuing. "We have found receipts for a survey ship dating back five years, the area to be surveyed was the same as detailed on the overlay map. The overlay map focuses off the Gulf of Mexico. We are still sifting through the rest of the receipts and documents. Just breaking through the password security and encryption was a big enough job, whatever else is in there someone wanted it kept under lock and key." Max refilled his coffee and sat back smiling. "And the location could not be more worrying."

"Why?" Charles looked inquisitively at Max.

"The rich oil and methane deposits will without any doubt truly magnify the effect of a nuclear blast beyond our comprehension."

"Well. We can advise the United States and they can monitor the area in question for any suspicious activity, but in the meantime we can wend our merry way to Borneo and Sumatra." Charles looked across at Duke and Ryan. "Do you concur?"

"I do. They can satellite survey the area and station parts of the fleet there. If they used a nuclear submarine, then no one would know. I'll get onto that now." Ryan got up and clinched Max's right shoulder. "You did well. Now we leave it to the big guns."

Max laughed. "Those big guns needed our little organisations help last time, don't forget. And Marge did mention the Gulf of Mexico sensors picking up anomalies."

"You're right, Max, and you have helped. Your focus now is on the tigers and Orangutans." Duke patted Max's shoulder and left.

"We keep on our course as planned," Charles stated flatly. "Ralph, ensure we are ready for safe passage through the Java Sea and check on the surveillance systems. Meanwhile, Max, your first job is the readiness of the helicopter, launches and vehicles. You can, of course, continue your work on the data. That is important, extremely important. Now, if you excuse me gentlemen, Anne wanted a game of Pétanque." Charles stood and walked over to the library door and decided to forgo his usual visit to the bridge that he was accustomed to do whenever he left the library on his own and turned around and took the lift down to deck five. He exited the lift and walked over to the balcony that looked down onto the lounge area below. It gave the lounge a light feel, with the double deck height. He ran his hand on the polished wooden rail as he walked round the balcony and took the curved carpeted staircase down to the lounge. Chris and Cathy were walking in to the lounge from the deck.

"Hi, Dad, how are you this morning?" Cathy asked, running over and giving him a big hug.

"I'm fine, just a rude awakening to start the day."

"Yes, we heard. They had no right to stop us," Chris remarked.

"In fact, they had every right," Charles said. "My worry was why we did not see them till they were right upon us, but that's sorted out now."

"Mum's setting the Pétanque up," Cathy said. "She asked us to join in but we want to be with the research team making sure all the equipment is on-board. If any is missing, now is the time to know. We can grab anything we need from the Tonga warehouse."

"Didn't you make sure everything was correct before loading?" Charles asked Chris.

"Yes, of course we did, Dad. But, as you know, things got a little speeded up at the last minute and something may have been left on the submersible when it had to close its hatch and get below," Chris replied, glancing at Cathy.

"That's true and could be the case. Okay join us when you've finished then."

"Oh no, not until we have had a look over the submersible in the moon pool," Cathy said. "Mum told us it has arrived and we haven't seen it yet."

"Okay, but keep it quiet, Duke does not know about either the moon pool or submersible and I would prefer to keep it that way for now," Charles said with a finger in front of his lips.

"Okay, Dad, you're the boss. Come on," Cathy said, grabbing Chris by the arm and dragging him towards the stairs. "Not the lift. We take the stairs, because the exercise is good for you."

Charles watched them go, before walking out into the sunshine and wandering down the length of the teak deck, past the swimming pool to the games area where Anne sat waiting for him.

Chapter Eleven

Tonga and the Java Sea

The run to Tonga was peaceful with a calm sea and balmy days. Charles relaxed on deck, occasionally popping onto the bridge to see the Captain and review their progress. He checked with Ralph that they were secure and that all *Sundancer's* security and surveillance systems were functioning. They were, so Anne took him in tow and ensured that he relaxed for the rest of the trip. Having their son and daughter, Chris and Cathy on board, helped a great deal. As a family they were apart quite often while they were on their different projects around the world, but thanks to video calling they managed to keep in touch, but there was nothing like actually spending quality time together even if some of that time was spent reviewing the state of an ongoing project or planning a new one. Amidst the work they played Pétanque and swam in the pool and put on a few pounds, thanks to the chef's amazing meals. Max, with the help of three crewman, polished and waxed the three cars that were stored on-board in the garage and *Sundancer's* four tenders before giving the helicopter a thorough clean. In truth Max supervised most of the time checking that everything was up to his high standard while he relaxed with the family.

The stopover at Tongatapu was regretfully short; just a day and a half to pick up replacement dive gear, an air compressor and two new generators that *Launch One* had offloaded for them and left in the organisations workshop. Cathy and Chris found two pieces of equipment they wanted plus some other items that they decided would be useful. Nuku'alofa was one of the Langham's favourite island destinations, with its azure blue seas, rolling surf, coral reefs and wonderfully friendly people. They had purchased a large parcel of land that was being unused, and using the organisations farming expertise, they developed the land in two ways. Firstly a large area was planted with native plant species whilst the other area was revitalised with natural fertilisers and planted with export crops of yams, taro, and cassava plus plenty of coconut trees. The area was then handed back to the islanders. Max had disappeared for the night to see an old flame, and the chef went ashore in his never ending quest for fresh ingredients.

Charles and Anne stayed on *Sundancer* for the duration, and welcomed Deborah Welch, the New Zealand High Commissioner, and Ataata Ha'apai, the Tonga Minister for Lands and Natural Resources, for an informal barbecue on the rear deck. They touched on the subject of their encounter with the New Zealand Navy off Curtis Island. Charles explained in detail how the encounter had unfolded and they all made light of the incident.

Charles discussed land development, and agreed with Ha'apai the purchase of further land to undergo similar treatment. Two new school buildings were discussed and Charles agreed to fund those as part of the deal. The Captain allowed the crew shore leave on rotation, and at ten thirty that night gave three blasts on the yacht horn to signal their call to return. Charles and Anne escorted their guests to the quay and their waiting cars and bade them farewell just as Max turned up and drove the Range Rover up the lowered ramp and into the brightly lit garage. *Sundancer* left Tonga late in the evening; Charles and Max were on the bridge as they left port. Just the glow from the display screens lit the vast bridge. Deeks sat at his console on the port side, the Captain in his chair in the middle and Franklin slightly in front and to the right of the Captain. Charles saw that everything was in order and decided to leave the team to do their work and walked over to the bridge door. "I'll leave you guys to it," he said and left the bridge.

"How is the research coming along, Max?" asked Captain Whitcome after Charles had left. Max stood beside the Captain who concentrated on piloting the superyacht with light touches on the small joystick, guiding *Sundancer* sideways from the quay using the thrusters before easing the joystick forward and to starboard gently propelling *Sundancer* further away from the quay so he could turn her northwest. Once clear of the quay, he checked the GPS navigation screen and looked at the safe passage through the maze of reefs and adjusted their course to put Monu reef off their port side and to steer round the top of Ualanga Uta Reef, staying south of Polo'a Island and Atata Island heading out into the South Pacific Ocean. Their journey would take them between Fiji and Wallis and Futuna before running between San Cristobal and Vanuatu into the Coral Sea towards Indonesia

"With the latest information that Grant, Ralph and myself have, I think we can now be pretty certain what Axmann is up to," Max said quietly, not wanting to ruin the quiet ambience of the bridge. "Everything we have points to the Gulf of Mexico area.

There is one file that we are having major issues trying to decode, which may be the key to the whole thing."

"Take over, Mr Franklin. Course is plotted in. Comfortable cruising speed, if you please."

"Aye, sir, First Officer has the bridge," Franklin confirmed. "Captain, do you want to run on two or four engines?"

"Two will be fine, Mr. Franklin. You can choose the inner or outer pair," Whitcome replied.

"Captain, I would like to run on all four engines at lower revolutions and charge all the battery banks," Deeks commented, spinning round in his chair.

"As you wish, Mr. Deeks. Everything is okay, I assume?"

"Everything else is fine. Just battery bank three needs topping up. I will get the team to clean the solar panels. They may be dirty or dusty."

"Mr. Franklin, all four engines then, if you please, and you have the bridge," the Captain said standing up, placing his Captain's cap on his head. "I will be with Max in the surveillance room, and then in my cabin or on the after deck, if needed." Whitcome made his way to the bridge door. "Come on, Max. Show me what you have found."

"Great," said Max. "I think you will be both impressed and intrigued."

In the surveillance room Max sat at the spare console and showed Whitcome what they had found. "Where are the maps and overlays?" Whitcome asked.

"I'll bring them up now," Max replied, tapping the keyboard till a map appeared on the screen.

"That is a very old map. I would hazard a guess that it must date back to the fourteen hundreds, if not before," Whitcome said, leaning towards the screen.

"We are not sure," Max said. "But you can see where Atlantis is outlined. Now if we overlay with this map"--he keyed a few commands—"it outlines the American, European and African continents." He held up a finger. "Now if we then allow for continental drift then we have this." After a few keystrokes the map morphed into the shape of the world today. "Which means Atlantis now lies here." He pointed to the Gulf of Mexico. "For my next trick, I will overlay that map with the latest one we found in the hidden Axmann folder and, hey presto—we have a match." Max sat back satisfied while Whitcome leaned closer to the large screen deep in thought.

"That they match is true, but only if, and it is still a big if, Atlantis was or is real depending on which way you think. You have certainly joined all the dots and come to the same conclusion as this man Axmann, of that there is no doubt. But the categorical evidence of the existence of Atlantis is still very weak and based ultimately on fables rather than scientific analysis," Whitcome said rubbing his chin.

"That's true enough but!" Max said, looking earnestly at Whitcome in the dimly lit room. "Put it this way. If this Axmann believes it to be true and has followed the same clues to identify its actual or mythical location, which we have validated, then whether or not Atlantis was or is real or not does not matter. The location matters in its own right. And from everything we have uncovered from the computer data, the location is where he may use one of his weapons."

"I assume that Duke will be relaying all this to the Unites States Government?"

"Yes, he has been on a video call with them for about forty five minutes now in the video conference room next door. It is not an easy thing to explain, I suppose, without a fair amount of trust."

"Well, trust is on Duke's side. He has known the President and most of his staff for many years," Whitcome said, but his eyes were all over the data on the screen. His hand motioned in front of the screen, his long slender middle finger tracing the longitude and latitude lines across and up and down. His forehead creased as he leaned closer to the screen. "Max, remove the last overlay please," he asked without breaking his concentration of the screen.

Max typed a few keys and the last overlay he placed was removed. "Why? What are you thinking?" He stopped typing and looked questioningly at the Captain.

"There is something not quite kosher about these maps. Yes, I agree on the surface that they look okay, and I can quite happily follow what you have said. But they have been altered somehow, I can see it but I cannot put my finger on it, if you know what I mean?" The Captain rubbed his chin and then rested it in his hands. "Put the overlay back on."

"What can you see?" Max asked, putting the overlay back on.

"That's the problem. I know for sure they are not right but I still cannot identify why. Look, print me copies of each map, plain and the overlaid variants, and let me concentrate on them." Whitcome stood as Duke came through the door. "Everything alright?"

"The President agrees the risks are too high to ignore anything at this stage," Duke said as he took his comb out of his top pocket and ran it through his hair. "The British Prime Minister has requested two aircraft carriers, which are on their way. Thomas and his team are on board one of them. *Jupiter* and *Mercury* have just linked up with their American counterparts and are heading for the Gulf. Marge has had to relent and agree to the American Submarine Commander of the *USS Alaska* as the number one of the task group. The president has sent three Ohio class submarines and one Virginia class submarine to the area, and two Los Angeles class submarines are being diverted there. In addition some surface ships are heading that way."

After leaving the bridge, Charles walked slowly down the starboard side, running his hand along the gunwale, stopping and leaning on the rail in the steamy heat of the early evening watching the maelstrom caused by the thrusters as they forced the superyacht away from the quay. The maelstrom eased as the distance between *Sundancer* and the quay increased. Abruptly the thrusters stopped and the wash of water eased. A faint ripple down the hull was the only indication of the change to forward movement. Charles tapped the rail and walked under the light of the half-moon that sat in the darkening blue sky, which flickered with stars further towards the stern. He made his way down the three flights of teak steps that were illuminated with soft blue led lights to the main deck and walked towards the stern some fifty metres away where he again leaned on the rail and watched as *Sundancer* slowly picked up speed leaving the lights of Nuku'alofa fading into the distance, only the curving trail of moon lit phosphorescent water from the stern of *Sundancer* to the quay betrayed her journey. He could see people lining Fakafanua road, who had gathered to watch *Sundancer* leave port. He turned and leant with his back to the rail raising his eyes to the moon and stars before lowering them to take in the vastness of *Sundancer's* sleek superstructure. The breeze was cooling and soothing and was just enough to flutter his fringe and the longer lengths of hair behind his ears. He could see the vast mast high up on Star Deck that housed the radar systems, searchlights and communication antennae arrays. He had been very careful with the designers to reduce the ugliness of the equipment that was to be housed on the mast and the brief to the designers was to simply hide them. He was pleased with the result and the way the Star Deck, his second favourite sanctuary on board, was blended into the highest most deck to render it invisible except from above. On the next deck down sat the sleek shape of the helicopter. He smiled at the thought of how Max reacted when he first sighted her. Like a child with a brand new toy, he just could not wait to open the door and take a seat even though he had been on many training flights in both the manufacturer's trainer and simulator. This was his machine, which was different; it was his baby.

The Bell 525 Relentless was an impressive machine by any standards, with an equally impressive specification. She shined under the subdued blue glow from the deck lights. He felt *Sundancer* heel gently as she turned to port picking up speed. He looked up at some movement that caught the corner of his left eye and saw a deck hand changing the signal flags. He moved to the port side so he could continue to watch the coastline before they entered the South Pacific and the endless expanse of ocean for the next week. His eye fell to the deck as he suddenly felt very tired and drained. He spun round and held the deck rail for support and with some effort stood upright, his arms rigid and took deep breaths of the sea air. That refreshing salty, ozone air that supposedly had rejuvenating powers, did little to help. His legs felt listless and he could feel the power draining from his arms as he fought to keep upright. His mind felt tight and tired. He could feel a headache starting and his thoughts became clouded, and he was unable to think clearly. He took his radio from his belt clip, checked the channel and pressed the call button. "Anne, come to the stern main deck, please, out." He released the call button.

A clipped female voice came over the radio. "I'm on my way now, out." Anne did not need to say anymore. She knew he was in trouble and needed help.

He clipped the radio back onto his belt clip and shook his head in an attempt to clear the fuzziness. He lifted his head and saw the lights of the coastline receding, a wonderful sight highlighted by the moonlight that reflected on the water. He felt rather than heard the increase in power as the four Rolls Royce engines powered up at the demand from the First Officer on the bridge. The breeze increased and the sound of the water being ejected by the water jets increased to a soothing rhythmic swooshing sound.

"Charles, what's wrong?" Anne asked as she came up to Charles and took his arm.

"Not sure, suddenly just felt very weak again. It's just the darn MS fatigue again. I've obviously overdone it again. Darned, if I know how."

"Okay, that doesn't matter at this moment. Well, let's get you inside and comfortable on the settee where the doc can take a look at you," Anne said helping him slowly along the vast deck, passing the games area, the swimming pool, galley, barbecue, dining area. They entered the lounge where Anne helped him sit down on the settee. She picked up the phone and called the doctor and asked him to come to the main deck lounge immediately. She then saw one of their smartly dressed stewards coming over to her, looking anxious.

"Is Mr. Langham okay, Miss Anne?" he asked with a worried look, clasping his hands together.

"Yes, just very tired thank you, Chen. He could do with a nice cup of coffee, and can you close the deck doors and set the air conditioning for eighteen degrees?"

"Sure Miss Anne. I'll get some on the go now for him. Would you like a cup?" he asked with a smile breaking on his face.

"That would be lovely," she replied as she sat beside her husband, still holding his hand. Charles sat there quietly with his eyes closed, breathing shallowly and slowly.

"Okay, let's take a look at him."

The doctor had arrived without Anne noticing and knelt beside Charles, his knees planted on the edge of the settee, his trade mark doctors black bag beside him. He took Charles by the right wrist, feeling for his pulse. "That's fine. What happened?"

"He called me on the radio, and when I got to him, he said he felt very tired," Anne said quietly.

The doctor took a blood pressure kit from his bag and put the blood pressure cuff on Charles. "I think it's just the fatigue that he gets with his MS. Tell me he has not been overdoing it again, please?" the doctor asked Anne while checking the blood pressure read out.

"Come on, doc, you know Charles. When does he not overdo it and drive himself to the limit! He had quite intense talks over dinner," Anne said, a smile brightening her face.

"Well, he needs to rest for at least the next twenty four hours, forty eight would be better and I will keep an eye on him every few hours. I will talk to the chef about the best diet for him over the next few days as well. Oily fish, vegetables and fruit."

"I'm okay, doc, just a little tired that's all," Charles said from behind closed eyes. "I don't need all this fuss." He sat up a little more upright and opened his weary eyes "A dose of Remy Martin and Columbian coffee is all I need."

"Charles, on board *Sundancer* I have the last word medically, and to be utterly honest, they are the last things you need." The doctor stated firmly "And you will do as I say." He turned to Anne. "Talk to Max, Duke and the Captain. Tell them that Charles needs absolute rest, mentally and physically, for the next twenty four hours and is off limits, doctor's orders. If they need to see Charles, then I suggest that they see you instead."

"I'll put the word out. Anyway, we are now at sea for the next seven days so there should be nothing to do but relax," Anne said, taking a cup of coffee from the steward who placed the cup for Charles on the marble table in front of the settee.

"True enough." The doctor smiled. "That's good and just what he needs." The doctor put his equipment back in his bag, closed it and stood up. "Well, I have crew medicals scheduled for the next day or so to keep me occupied. I will see Charles in a few hours. In the meantime, he can put his feet up in the cinema and watch a movie. The bursar tells me there's some new releases on board." He checked his watch. "I'll see the chef on my way as it's nearly dinner time already."

"That's a great idea. Thanks, doc," Anne said and watched him leave. She called Chen over. "Chen, we will have the fresh coffee in the cinema please and tell chef to send up two dinners in accordance with the doctor's wishes for Charles."

"Yes, Miss Anne." Chen bowed and went to the stairs.

Anne held Charles by the hand and helped him up. "Come on, lazy bones, let's go watch a movie."

Chapter Twelve

Thomas

The two American *Nimitz* class aircraft carriers dropped anchor in the Bristol Channel to the cheers and flag waving from the thousands of people watching from any vantage point they could find on the seafront. The two one hundred thousand ton mammoths of the sea with a complement of six thousand souls and ninety fixed and rotary wing aircraft were quite an imposing and reassuring sight for the local people, who were stunned by the attack on London and lived in fear of another attack. The sight of these two huge ships, towering twenty storeys above the waterline, with four and a half acres of flight deck, helped to some extent to allay their fears. Small tenders circled the vast ships like ants, keeping the fleet of sightseeing boats at bay whilst the vast decks were a hive of activity as helicopters and reconnaissance aircraft were raised from the lower decks and positioned for take-off, while air crew checked the aircraft and ratings moved around in a well-rehearsed routine.

Thomas had not wasted any time on the trip across the Atlantic, using the time to ensure that his team had everything packed and ready to depart for the shore as soon as the ship came to rest at anchor. He had visited the Commanding Officer and made certain arrangements that, on sight of the letter from the President, were agreed to, and kept secret. The weather had changed from bright sunshine to cloudy with a light drizzle as they reached the helicopter assigned to take them ashore, which stood in the three and a half acre hangar beneath the flight deck on one of the four lifts. Thomas kept an eye out for Wozniak, the FBI guy, who he desperately wanted to avoid. The team opened the rear doors and loaded their equipment. Thomas talked to the pilot, who was suiting up in a full radiation suit as the helicopter started to rise on the huge lift to the flight deck. Thomas gave his team the signal to board the helicopter, pulled on his radiation helmet and climbed into the seat beside the pilot. When the lift locked in place on the flight deck, the Flight Deck Handler came over straight away, having been briefed on their priority clearance and gave them the lift off signal. The pilot gently raised the large Sikorsky Seahawk off the deck and headed for the mainland. Thomas smiled to himself as everything went like clockwork and any confrontation with Wozniak had been neatly avoided.

Jerry Wozniak was looking for Thomas, and was furious to find the cabins assigned to Thomas and his team completely empty. He immediately made his way to where Thomas was storing all his equipment and slammed the door shut when he found that empty as well. He gruffly made his way to the bridge, barging his way through crew members without a second glance. "What the hell is going on?" he shouted to no one in particular as he entered the bridge, when out of the corner of his eye, he got a split second look at the face of Thomas in the co-pilot seat of a Seahawk that was lifting off the deck and turning towards the coastline. "Where the hell are they going?" he asked the Commanding Officer, his arm held straight out pointing towards the Seahawk.

"And who may I ask are you to come barging onto my bridge shouting?" asked the Commanding Officer, getting up from his chair and turning to see who was yelling at him. He had expected a visit at some time from the FBI Chief after the briefing he had from Thomas during a dinner conversation they had had on the voyage over, and he guessed that the man standing in front of him now was the FBI Chief.

"I, sir, am FBI Chief, Jerry Wozniak, and I want to know where that helicopter is heading." His face had reddened and his shirt collar and underarms were wet with perspiration.

"I have no idea. It is not under my direct control," the Commanding Officer replied.

"But it is one of your helicopters, is it not?" Wozniak said with a hint of sarcasm.

"You are correct in that assumption. I am, however, not in command of it at this time."

"You do know who is on board, though?"

"I am aware of who the passengers are," the Commanding Officer replied casually "The Presidential warrant stated that I was to provide any assistance required on a confidential basis. He asked for a helicopter and pilot and he got them." The Commanding Officer smiled. "Who am I to argue with my Commander in Chief, The President of the United States?"

"He must have filed a flight plan?" Wozniak asked angrily.

"No flight plans were filed, as requested by the holder of the Presidential warrant." The XO cut in. "You can follow them on radar if you wish in the flight control room. Though knowing the passenger, I do not think that will help. I know the pilot he chose, one of our very best and fully trained in low level flying and the art of flying below the radar."

"Damn," Wozniak slapped his hand on the back of the XO's chair. "I knew he would pull a fast one. Can you contact the pilot and tell him to return?"

"No, sir, I cannot not. The pilot is now under the command of someone who holds a Presidential warrant. We cannot interfere."

"He is supposed to be working for me, under my direction."

"That's exactly what he said when he asked for the chopper, and I said we had just one to spare," the XO said, unable to control a grin that was appearing on his usually stern face. "I suggest that you take it up with the President."

"Well then, I need a helicopter and a pilot immediately to follow that one." Wozniak said with his raised voice pointing through the bridge window to the receding Seahawk.

"Cannot do," said the XO. "We have all available craft loaded and lined up for take-off."

"How in damnation did Thomas get one, then?" Wozniak fumed.

"Presidential warrant." The XO picked up a long tabulated list and ran his finger down the list. "Scheduled the day before yesterday." He placed the list down and shrugged. "We can put you ashore by boat, if you like."

"Yes, now!" He turned to leave. "I will get my stuff and be back in a few minutes." He turned and stormed off bridge.

The Commanding Officer looked at the XO with a smirk on his face. "The sooner he's off my boat, the better. It's quite choppy so with any luck he'll get a soaking and cool down."

"I will assign him one of the rigid inflatable boats then." The XO picked up a microphone and called down to the boat crew and arranged for a rigid inflatable boat to be launched ready to take the FBI Chief to shore.

"And make sure the rigid inflatable boat returns as soon as he is ashore." The Commanding Officer picked up a telephone beside his chair. "Put me through to Thomas on the Seahawk." He waited a few seconds. "Thomas, heads up for you. Jerry Wozniak is aware that you have departed and we will shortly be putting him ashore by boat."

"Thank you, Commander. He will have trouble catching up with us. He has no idea where we are heading. But thanks, anyway, Thomas out."

"My pleasure, Thomas. You have the Seahawk and pilot for the duration of your stay. Good luck and may your God be with you. Out."

Thomas looked out at the devastation of London and glanced at the pilot who grimaced at the sight below them. They both shook their heads in their radiation suit helmets.

"Where do you want to put down?" asked the pilot.

"We need to get some of the radioactive earth but without getting a full dose ourselves. As close to the epicentre as we can and as far away as we can." He pulled his map out, which was marked with radiating red circles. "According to the boffins at the Pentagon, just here. I'll plug the co-ordinates into the flight computer." He read the figures from the map and typed them into the computer. "Hard with these thick gloves on," he muttered.

"Okay, that's two miles northwest of our current position,"

said the pilot and eased the helicopter into a gentle turn. "How long will you be on the ground?"

"As short a time as possible. I want Graham to be able to take some altitude shots while Bill takes some air samples, then we head for Chequers, where these samples will be collected." Thomas replied. "We stay at Chequers for the rest of the day and overnight, then it's off to Cardiff and Southampton. I'm in no hurry to get back to the ship. All I've got to look forward to is listening to Wozniak mouthing off at me for a while." He laughed. "Boy, that guy gives me the creeps."

"Here we are, your collection point." The pilot brought the chopper to a hover and then into a slow descent to the ground, picking a spot where he could get the wheels onto clear ground amongst the scattered rubble and keep the rotors clear of the surrounding heaps of broken concrete and bent steel bars. The air filled with dust caused by the down draft from the rotors.

"Geiger's off the scale, skipper," Bill said to Thomas through the radio built into his suit.

"Right. You got the gear ready?" asked Thomas.

"Yep, I'm ready skipper, got the collection trowel, collection bags and the radiation container all set up and ready to roll."

"Edwards, you've got the countdown. The rest of you stay here and do not remove your helmets. Let's go, Bill." Thomas opened the door, jumped down and quickly slammed the door shut.

Bill got out of the chopper both hands full of gear. Thomas came over and slid the rear door closed and led the way through the rubble looking for a good patch of earth, free of detritus. He carefully knelt down. Bill followed suit beside him and placed the container on the ground and unlatched it, but left the lid closed.

He took the miniature trowel from the plastic bag.

"Just here will do. Two separate scoops into two glass vials, then they go into the lead lined box," Thomas said, opening one of the bags and removing a glass vial. Bill carefully scraped away the top surface with the trowel before digging some earth and carefully empting the trowel into the glass vial, which Thomas then sealed shut with a clear lid. Thomas opened the other bag removing the second glass vial and they repeated the process taking a sample some 100mm deep. With both samples collected, Thomas opened the container, which had three separate internal sections. He placed the soil samples into two of the sections while Bill placed the trowel back into its own bag and carefully placed it into the third section. Thomas closed the lid, pulled down on two levers, closed the clasp latches and spun the combination. "Okay, back to the chopper." Thomas said picking up the container. "This goes in the rear most locker in the lead lined container."

"Skipper, times up," Edward shouted over his helmet microphone.

Bill wasted no time getting to the helicopter and opening the rear locker ready for Thomas to place the container within. Thomas and Bill jumped back in the helicopter, which lifted off before they had time to get seated properly and strapped in.

"Straight up, three thousand metres," said Thomas to the pilot.

"Okay, here we go." The pilot put the helicopter into a straight up ascent.

"Wow, hold on, my stomach is gone. Can we slow down a bit, please?" Bill shouted.

"Sorry," replied the pilot, "don't want to hang around. Nearly there now."

"Well, can we stop on the way down to collect my stomach?" laughed Bill.

"Sure we can," laughed the pilot. "Do you want to descend at the same rate we ascended?"

"You just try it!" Bill said so loud everyone on board laughed. He sighed as the helicopter came to a hover and he slid the door back and collected two small flasks of air samples and took a Geiger reading. He looked at the reading and slammed the door shut. "Better get out of here, boss, that reading was way off the scale!"

"He's right, boss, we are nearly at our limit of exposure. I suggest we keep at this altitude or higher till we are clear of the radiation zone," Edward advised.

"Graham, are you getting some good shots?" Thomas asked

"Sure am. High resolution shots all the way, and I think I've got the epicentre a few times," Graham replied, still looking through the viewfinder and clicking away.

"Decontamination, here we come, guys. "Thomas plotted some co-ordinates from his map into the GPS and pointed to the location. "Pilot, make you way there and you'd better put the hammer down. You will have to line up exactly with the grid on landing. It's going to be a tight fit. Everyone stays on board when we land till the helicopter is decontaminated. They will give us the signal to disembark when they have finished cleaning this machine. They will attach a skirt to the port side of the helicopter, which will be attached to a tunnel. We must leave through the skirt and proceed down the tunnel, to the decontamination tent, where we will be sprayed in our gear, then we have to strip for final decontamination. William, we will put our sample containers on a table in the tent, where they will be decontaminated, as well. We take them with us when we leave."

"Can we use the helicopter afterward?" the pilot asked.

"Once it's decontaminated and clean, it will then be thoroughly checked for radiation inside and out. If it's clear, then, yes, we can. If not, we'll borrow another one off the British. I'm sure the Prime Minister will help, if we need one," said Thomas as they flew south of the Thames. He looked at the ground below them. In every direction he looked there were the carcasses of what were once tower blocks, houses, shops and theatres, which now lay shattered and smouldering amongst the remains of what once were probably cars, busses and trucks. Empty foundations littered with rubble, smouldering stumps of trees. The destruction was everywhere and endless.

"Utter destruction as far as the eye can see. Hey guys, look, there are people down there wandering around. Hey, they are waving at us." Bill shouted. "We have to do something!"

"Not a lot we can do for them, mate. They are too close to the impact zone and would have received a lethal dose. They'll be dead before anyone can get to them," Thomas said, unlatching his visor and looking through his binoculars. "Poor souls, skins burnt, blistered and peeling, looks to me like an entire family, parents with a couple of kids. God almighty, there's more." He closed his visor and looked at the pilot. "Get us out of here please, can't this thing go any faster?" He could see Graham still using his camera.

The helicopters nose dipped slightly as the pilot increased speed, then lifted again as he regained altitude. Everyone remained silent as they flew over the wasteland that was once the thriving area of south London, until they finally reached the end of the destructive zone of the bomb and passed over green pastures, small woodlands and intact houses.

"Over there," said Thomas pointing. "That's our landing zone."

"This all took some forward planning, boss," Edward said, looking at the extensive range of military vehicles, trucks, four wheel drives, tanks and tents linked by tunnels in the landscaped ground next to an imposing country house.

"Yes, it has. That house is Chequers, the British Prime Ministers country residence and our base for the rest of the day and overnight." Thomas smiled. "We have some powerful friends and allies. An Osprey will be arriving shortly to take the sample to RAF Marham, where a Tornado GR with in-flight refuelling and canister drop capability will drop the samples for *Sundancer* to pick up and analysis. After which, Charles will get the samples to the United States for further analysis and storage."

"What do we do now, boss?"

"We find out as much as we can from the British, do our own reconnaissance, examine all the photographs for any evidence and try and track down the entry point of the weapon before we join either *Sundancer* or Marge on the submarine," Thomas replied as the pilot deftly and with intense concentration lined the helicopter up horizontally with the landing grid lines before letting her drift slowly to the ground. A buzzer sounded.

"Wow!" the pilot re-marked below his breath and flicked a switch, which extended the landing gear. "Never tried a belly landing in one of these, and don't really want to try one today."

Thomas gave him a sideways glance. "Forgotten anything else?" he asked with a grin on his face.

"Don't think so, but we'll certainly know in a few seconds," the pilot replied smiling as the helicopter touched down and settled on its landing gear. "No, we're down in one piece, so all's good."

Four men in white protective suits rolled a tunnel extension towards the helicopter and clipped it into place around the doors, then departed. Another group started to hose down the helicopter with a white coloured liquid.

"Okay everyone, you know the drill, off we go." Thomas unclipped his seat belt and opened his door, jumped down and then slid the rear door open. He saw the pilot climbing from his seat and across to the port door. He opened the rear locker and removed the sample container before he led the group through the long circular white tunnel and stepped up into a low tent that encompassed a tubular frame, a large yellow bin and a table. He placed the box on the table and motioned to Bill to do the same and Graham to place his camera on the table. Surrounding the floor was a narrow channel. On the floor of the tent were seven red circles.

"Each person stand in a red circle," Thomas directed. "On the command, lift your arms parallel with your shoulders and stand with legs thirty five centimetres apart. And keep within your circle." He watched as the tunnel was sealed at both ends of the tent. High pressure scalding hot liquid showered them from every direction from the roof, the floor and the sides. "Now!" Thomas shouted and everyone lifted their arms and spread their legs. He lost sight of everyone in the steam. After ten minutes or so the shower stopped and the liquid drained into the narrow channel and out through six outlets. "Okay, now strip off the radiation suits and all your clothing and place them in the yellow bin, then stand back on the circles. Don't be shy, your life is at stake."

After everyone stripped naked and stood back in their circles the showers started again, this time a liquid at body temperature. "Okay, arms up and legs apart!" Thomas shouted over the noise. After a few minutes a soap like liquid appeared. "Wash yourselves everywhere. Every crack, your ears, noses, hair!" he shouted. After some minutes the soap was replaced by a clear cool liquid. "Filtered water, rinse thoroughly." Thomas looked around and saw that everyone was taking things seriously. The water stopped and the temperature rose and hot air blasted in. The door opposite the tunnel opened and Thomas led the way, taking the sample container box with him. Inside the next tent were towels and clothes on pegs named with each operative's name. "Get dressed team. We have a delivery date to meet."

He could hear the roar of an aircraft getting closer and closer. "Ah, the Osprey has arrived."

He led the way through the tent, down another tunnel to the outside air where he breathed deeply. He watched as a team in white protection suits collapsed the tent and folded it into a cube while another team retracted the tunnels and gave the Seahawk a final rinse. A large enclosed army vehicle reversed up and the tent and tunnels were loaded and sealed in. Thomas walked over to the Osprey, which had landed and waited for the canopy to open. He passed the box and bag to the pilot, who stowed them. As Thomas walked away the aircraft lifted vertically into the sky and hovered before its rotors tilted, transitioning the Osprey into horizontal flight, quickly accelerating into the distance. Thomas led his team to the house, where he was greeted on the steps by

Malcolm Brooke, the Secretary of State for Defence. "You must be Thomas, Welcome to the United Kingdom." He shook hands with Thomas warmly. "The Prime Minister is waiting to see you and your team. We will talk over dinner, if that's alright?"

"That's great by us," replied Thomas. "And thank you, by the way, for the great organisation of the decontamination unit. Exactly as I requested."

"The least we could do. Please come this way," Brooke said and led them up the wide stone stairway into the house. "I assume that the aircraft is taking the samples to your carrier for identification."

"Eh, well, yes and no. It's going to RAF Marham actually, and from there to a location out in the Indonesian Ocean ,where it will be tested for formal identification of the isotope," Thomas replied choosing his words very carefully, knowing that the material would transfer to a F35 lighting and make its way to *Sundancer.*

Chapter Thirteen

Axmann Sets the Stage

The courier company contacted the police after repeated attempts to locate their driver had failed. With more deliveries in the same location they could not understand why he had turned off his location tracker and not finished his delivery round. They were visited by a police detective who very attentively reviewed the tracking log and delivery schedule and had taken copies when he left. The detective ordered a helicopter search initially in a thirty mile radius of the last known delivery. The truck was white with a black roof that sported a large bright iridescent yellow star designed to stand out in both daylight and the dark of night. It had, and within the hour the truck had been sighted, and the detective drove to the location of the courier vehicle, and while, on route, called in the local highway patrol. Two highway patrol cars were on scene when he arrived, blocking the road in both directions, lights flashing. As he exited from his unmarked car one of the highway patrol officers came over to greet him.

"Hi, I'm officer Martinez. The truck is over there, but no signs of a body from what we can see or a struggle for that matter. No foot prints in the surrounding area. We've called in the crime scene investigation forensics team, and they should be here soon. We have sighted the truck but haven't touched it. Just closed off the road."

"So no one has touched the truck?" asked Detective Taylor, leaning into his car to retrieve his hat, sunglasses and a pair of latex gloves.

"No, as I said, we have just cordoned off the area."

"Well, let's go take a look," Taylor said. "Show me the way."

He patted the young highway driver on the elbow. After a short walk the truck became visible. "Well hidden from the road and definitely not an accident. This was driven here on purpose." He scanned the ground. "No footprints either," he said pulling the latex gloves on and opening the door he looked inside. "No ignition keys, no dust or grime anywhere. This has been wiped clean."

He pulled the hood catch and stepped round to the front of the vehicle and lifted the hood. After a quick look he said, "GPS tracking unit is still there but the wires have been cut." He picked up the ends of the wires and examined them closely. "Cleanly cut as well." He looked around him slowly. "This is a professional job. I doubt the CSI team will find anything. Let's take a look in the back." He slid open the side door. "Just as I thought. Still packages neatly laid out, so that tells us a few things. It was not driven very fast or those packages would be scattered, and either they knew exactly what they were after or they took nothing." He slid the door shut. "Let's go back to my car. I have a manifest of what packages should still be on the truck. I want you to check through them. I am going to talk to the recipients of the last few deliveries and see what I can find," he said as they walked back to the unmarked car. He opened the door and took out a manila folder and leafed through the papers removing one sheet. "Take this list, and call me when you have checked it through. Oh, and let me know when the CSI team arrives."

"Okay," Martinez said and walked back to the truck.

Taylor sat in his car. Things did not make any sense. Nothing taken, everywhere wiped clean. A professional job. But why? He closed his car door, started the engine and headed for Palacios and Matagorda, where the last deliveries were made. On route he called the local mortuaries to see if they had any John Does, with no success. He then tried missing persons; again no success. He called the station and arranged for a copy of the driver's licence to be sent to his phone. He lit a cigarette, a habit he had given up around six times in the past six years but the career he had chosen was, in his mind, not conducive with not drinking or smoking.

He was still in contact with his wife and children, and although they lived apart neither could take the next step to divorce. They both still loved one another; it was just that Dianne could not come to terms with how he could live with some of the sights he had seen or the type of people he had to deal with. The drink was another factor but lower down her list, for he was always sober when he was with her or the kids. He never missed the children's birthdays and always remembered her birthday, invariably sending chocolates and flowers. Their wedding anniversary almost always heralded some jewellery and an invite to dinner, including the children. She always accepted and made sure the children were well dressed. One day they would be back together; when he did not know. He surmised it would occur only when he left the force and took up another career, but policing was in his blood like his father and grandfather.

He pulled over when he arrived at Palacios and picked up the list of last deliveries from the passenger seat, read an address, then put it back and picked up his map. Two of the last deliveries were close by, and the other three were on the other side of the bay, near the town of Matagorda. At the first two, both receptionists had confirmed the picture on his phone as the identity of their regular driver, who was always courteous and friendly. Back in his car he checked his map and drove to a small industrial estate on the outskirts of Matagorda. The two receptionists recognised the driver as their normal driver, but told Taylor that the last delivery they received was by a temporary driver whom they had never seen before. He was wearing the company uniform and knew the system so they thought nothing of it. Back in his car, he arranged for a police sketch artist to visit both companies. He checked his map and drove off to the other side of Matagorda, out into the countryside, and turned off up a long winding tree lined driveway.

Gustav Axmann was startled when he heard a knock on the front door. They now had all the parts they required and one weapon was on a trolley ready to go down to the boat on the Colorado River, covered with a tarpaulin waiting for the other weapon which, he had been advised by his son Albrecht, would be finished later that day. His detailed plan to vacate the cottage and workshop would then come into play. So a knock on the front door was an unwarranted shock. He got his stick, which lay against the settee, and with one hand on the arm of the settee eased himself up and slowly made his way to the front door. He undid the chain and unlocked the door and opened it to a blast of heat, which was a shock to Axmann after the comfort of sitting in the air conditioning. The next shock was seeing a well-dressed tall slender man of around fifty standing in front of him with a police badge in his left hand and a firearm on his right hip.

"Good afternoon, sir. I wonder if you can assist in an ongoing investigation," Taylor asked showing his badge.

"Of course officer, anything to assist," Axmann said. "How can I help?"

"We are investigating the disappearance of a courier driver. We know from the courier companies records that he delivered a parcel here a few days ago. Do you recognise him?" Taylor showed the photograph of the driver on his phone to Axmann.

"I did not see any courier driver, though my son may have signed for a parcel. Let me get him for you," Axmann left Taylor at the door and shuffled on his stick to the table in the lounge, picked up his mobile and pressed a speed dial number. "Albrecht, come to the front door, we have a police detective wishing to confirm the identity of a courier driver." He did not wait for a reply before disconnecting the call and dropping the phone on the table and returning to the front door. "Won't be long officer. May I ask what has happened?"

"The driver has disappeared and we have found his truck abandoned. We cannot rule out foul play at this moment in time. We are tracking his last known movements that is all."

"Ah, Albrecht, do you recognise the courier driver's face that this policeman has on his phone?" Axmann asked as Albrecht arrived at the front door behind his father.

Albrecht leant forward and looked at the face. He felt faint; he had hoped for more time. He took a breath and steeled himself. "Yes, he delivered a package here . . . let me think, two possibly three days ago. We have had a lot of deliveries lately, which makes it hard for me to be precise. But, yes, I do recognise him." He managed to keep his voice level, which surprised him as his heart rate had risen and he could feel the sweat forming on his hands, which he involuntarily rubbed on his jeans.

"Well, that's all I need to know, Thank you for your time." Taylor replaced his sun glasses and returned to his car. He needed to look at the times of the last five deliveries again. His gut told him Albrecht was hiding something; the hesitancy, then the eager confirmation was all wrong. His gut was never wrong and had served him well for the past thirty years. Back in his car, he turned around in the gravel driveway and made his way down the twisting drive to the main road and back into town. He turned the air conditioning up to cool down just as his cell phone rang. He took the call on hands free.

"It's Officer Martinez," the caller said. "The forensic boys say there's nothing to be found, wiped clean all the way through. They even found the bit of scrub that had been used to wipe the foot prints and cover the tire tracks from the road to the truck. Whomever it was, they were extremely thorough."

Taylor pulled over. "Have you got the time stamps for the last five deliveries?" he asked.

"Sure, you gave me the print out," Martinez replied.

"Give them to me, starting with the first one, at Palacios," Taylor said, getting a ballpoint pen and pad from the glove box.

"He did the first two in Palacios, and then three in Matagorda, two on an industrial park, and one to a private residence," Martinez replied.

"The two to the Matagorda industrial estate were delivered before the one to the private residence?" Taylor queried.

"No, they were the last two on the tracker before it was disconnected and the van headed out of town and dumped off the 616," Martinez advised.

"Okay, so the place I have just left, the private residence, were the last people to see the driver alive," Taylor remarked. "Are the forensic team still with the van?"

"No, the van is on its way to the precinct" Martinez answered.

"Right, I'm heading back there now. Where is the artist?" Taylor asked, starting his car and pulling back into the light traffic.

"He's at the Matagorda industrial estate. He has completed one sketch and is now doing the second."

Gustav looked at Albrecht through dead, evil eyes. "What are you not telling me Albrecht? I can see that you are hiding something from me." He led the way into the lounge and poured himself a schnapps, which he used to take his pain medication, poured another schnapps and lit a cigarette, his hands shaking slightly and lowered himself on the settee.

"The courier driver is dead," Albrecht said quietly, looking into his father's eyes. He knew better than to avoid them, which he would take as a sign of weakness to be used against his adversary. He had seen it happen to many people, who ended up dead.

"And how do you know of this?"

"He died at my hands, father." His father stiffened and glared at him, but he continued with his prepared explanation. "He came into the workshop before we could stop him and saw everything. We had no choice but to ensure his silence. He could have destroyed everything if he spoke to anybody about what he had seen. When we said it was a deep sea sensor, he replied that it looked more like a bomb."

"Where is the body?"

"Eaten by sharks, miles off the coast. Nothing remains. I saw to that myself."

"And how did you dispose of the truck?" Gustav asked quietly, finishing his schnapps.

"We did the two deliveries to the industrial estate on the edge of town, disconnected the tracker, then dumped the truck in scrub and wiped it clean."

"Which has now been found," shouted Gustav. "We move now. Get everything loaded up. We will split as planned the F150 and the boat. The bombs are complete, yes?"

"Yes father, the eight kiloton is on the trolley ready to go the boat and the ten kiloton is just having the last of the outer casing sealed and will then be ready to load onto the trolley."

"That's good, that is good, and just in time it would seem," Gustav said, lighting another cigarette. "Well, don't just stand there, get moving. We are out of here within the next hour."

"Yes, father," Albrecht said, and left the lounge and made his way to see Julian Beech and tell him the news. He found him next to the ten kiloton bomb on its cradle.

"Is it ready?" he asked.

"Yes, sealed and ready. So what's the buzz?" Beech asked, wiping his hands on a cloth.

"We evacuate the base." He looked around to make sure everyone was present and seeing they were he called out. "Everyone gather round please, I have some news." He gathered his thoughts as everyone moved closer. "We have finished our work here and believe that our security may have been compromised. We will be evacuating this base immediately. We will break into two teams as planned. Load both weapons onto the launch, break everything down in here. Spray all surfaces and the floor before we leave. I want no finger prints or DNA left here. The F150 team, you know your route to the airport and you know what you are allowed to take. Everything else remains here to be burned outside. Okay, you know the plan in detail. Let's get to it."

He moved to the trolley loaded with the eight kiloton bomb while everyone else went to get on with their allotted tasks. Beech joined him and they took the trolley down to the river to load the bomb on to the launch, where they placed it under a tarpaulin and returned to get the ten kiloton device. They passed Gustav on the path struggling with a satchel tucked under his arm; he was carrying a small suitcase with his walking stick in the other down to the boat.

"Hurry up, you two. We haven't got all day, you know," he mumbled

"The eight kiloton is on board. We will be back with the ten kiloton and our gear in a few minutes," Albrecht said between quick breaths. "Then we can set the bonfire and leave."

He doubted his father heard him as the distance between them increased. But that did not matter so long as they could get out of here before the law returned. They entered the workshop and lifted the ten kiloton bomb from the cradle and swung it on the trolley and disconnected the hooks.

"Right, let's get our stuff."

He led the way to the cottage and into their room. Most of their stuff they had not bothered to unpack, so it did not take long before they both had their suitcases closed and on the trolley either side of the bomb. He saw some technicians loading the F150 while others were carrying boxes out to the bonfire site. "Come on, let's get this to the boat," he said to Beech, and between them they swung the trolley round and headed for the door. The path was difficult with the extra weight of the 10k bomb and two suitcases, and it was not long before they rolled it onto the wooden jetty and transferred everything to the boat. Albrecht swung out the side davit and Beech connected the karabiners to the receptacles on the bomb casing.

"Okay, winch her aboard," Beech called. Albrecht started the winch, and once the bomb was clear of the gunwale, they swung the bomb on-board and lowered it to the deck.

"You get the boat started. I'll run this back to the workshop and check everything is clear and set the bonfire."

Albrecht jumped off the boat, grabbed the trolley and headed up the path. He checked the bungalow first and everything was clear; only a few tins were left in the kitchen, which he grabbed. He crossed into the workshop, where he smiled. Everything had been cleared and only the big F150 sat facing the double door. He went outside and looked at the bonfire pile, which stood over two metres tall and three metres wide. He threw the cans on top and removed the caps from two five litre tote tanks of fuel and poured them over the pile. He dumped the empty plastic tanks onto the pile, struck a match and threw it into the pile. The whoosh as the fuel ignited and the heat wave made him take a few steps back. He stayed for a few seconds to make sure the fire was really well alight before heading to the workshop and opening the two doors. He ushered the F150 out. When it was clear of the doors, he closed them then walked over to the driver side of the F150.

"Michael, you know the route. You've got the airline tickets. Stick to the plan. No deviations and we will see you back home in Brazil. Good luck, everyone."

He tapped the side of the huge vehicle and said, "Off you go."

He watched the F150 roll down the drive before making his way down to the boat. He untied the bow line, then the stern line and jumped on board. He handed the lines to Julian Beech. "Coil these up," he said as he sat in the helm seat and eased the eight and a half metre boat away from the jetty with a gentle purring from the twin four stroke outboards. As the river widened he increased power until they were out into the bay, where he turned on the GPS and radar and powered up till the boat was at full speed.

"Dad, we're on our way," he called down into the cabin. "Time to call the submarine."

Gustav came up into the cockpit. "Already done," he said. "Head straight for these co-ordinates. Should be a couple of hours at this speed. We will load the ten kiloton into the catches on the submarines side and take the eight kiloton down below."

"I hope we have got the side clip attachment dimensions correct," Beech said quietly.

"We're going to get only one chance to clip it in place with this boat rocking about, so I double checked all the measurements," Albrecht replied, reading the GPS. "The water is more than deep enough to sink this without a trace."

They saw the submarine surfacing and slowed to come alongside. Albrecht carefully lined up with the clip attachments. Hatches on the submarine opened and crewmen climbed out and caught the lines thrown by Beech and Albrecht, who tied the boat off. Using the davit and winch they lifted the bomb off the deck and swung the bomb over the boat's gunwale. With the help of a few submariners, they carefully lined the bomb up to the clip attachments until it clicked into place in the submarines side holder. Albrecht checked the attachments before unhooking the karabiners. They transferred the eight kiloton bomb, suitcase and lastly helped Gustav transfer carefully and gently from the rocking boat to the submarine and down the ladder. Albrecht opened the bilge cocks on the launch and watched as water slowly entered.

"Pass me a shotgun," he shouted across to a sailor on the submarine who bent down and shouted through a hatch and waited till a shotgun was passed up, which he threw to Albrecht who caught it. Standing at the entrance to the cabin, he aimed at the floor and fired the shotgun repeatedly, making a hole in the bottom of the boats hull ,which increased the flow of water into the boat, flooding the bilge and rising quickly out of the cabin into the cockpit. Satisfied he jumped onto the submarine and signalled the crew to untie the boat. He watched as the boat settled lower in the water before slowly disappearing from sight beneath the waves.

"Okay, let's dive," he ordered. The crew on deck disappeared down hatches, which they closed behind them. Albrecht climbed below sealing the hatch behind him. He looked at the Captain and said, "Clear to dive."

"Dive, dive, dive," ordered the Captain. The submarine started to move forward with its nose down as it dived into the Atlantic depths. Gustav came into the control room.

"Captain, here is the first location that I wish to go to."

He pulled a map out of this pocket, unfolded it and laid it on the chart table smoothing out the crease. The Captain came over and looked carefully at the map. He noted the co-ordinates then transferred them to his own chart and plotted the course. He gave an order to the helmsman, and then looked at Gustav.

"You know what this location is meant to be? Surely, you know it is mythical," the Captain spoke quietly with a slight grin on his face.

"We will see, Captain, we will see," Gustav said seriously before handing the Captain another sheet with numbers on. "The second location is here. A more difficult task for us all, but one for which we will need further assistance from our friends ashore. How close can you get us?"

The Captain looked at the map and transferred the location.

"Wow, that's eighteen hundred miles from the nearest point of the coast where I can safely land you. I can get you as far as here, just off the coast." He pointed to the map. "We can put you ashore at night in our inflatable dinghies. You will need a lot of help from our friends ashore if you are to achieve your goal of getting there." The Captain traced his finger along the map following a road from the coast to Gustav's location. "All ports of entry are under intense security."

"We still have friends, my friend. I will call them after we have positioned the first weapon and set the timer. Now, it may be faster if we go via the Saint Lawrence and travel through the Great Lakes to Minnesota, don't you think? But for now one thing at a time. Tell me when we are over the first target. I will be resting in my cabin," Gustav said, a weariness in his voice as he shuffled slowly down the gangway, leaving the Captain looking at the map and pulling more maps from his locker.

Chapter Fourteen

Sundancer Battles Through

Charles opened his eyes and saw that the cabin was dimly lit. He turned to his side and saw that Anne was sitting up reading a book. Charles sat up in bed and stretched his arms in front of him.

"Good morning darling," he said and kissed her on the cheek.

"Morning, would you like a cup of tea now?" Anne turned and clicked the Swan Teasmade on.

"Yes, that would be nice." Charles stifled a yawn. "Wonder where we are? Feels like we have picked up speed a bit."

"Not sure. Anyway, how do you feel today?" Anne put her book on the bedside table.

"I feel great, so far. The doctor was right, I needed to rest but after five days I am ready to rock and roll again."

"Oh no you don't. You will be taking it easy and you will not be overdoing it. Just remember the CNS therapist and all that good work that she did with you!" Anne said with the tone of voice that Charles knew meant arguing was futile. "You can still do what you used to do and just as well, but it just takes a little longer... remember that."

"Yeah, I know. It's just that there is so much to be done. So much that can be done." He pressed a key on the keypad inlaid into his bedside table and a television screen rose from its cherry wood unit at the base of the bed. He pressed a few buttons and the superyachts navigation display appeared on the screen. He picked up the keypad from its recess in the bedside table and typed some commands which over-laid the radar display on the GPS. He saw now what the Captain on the bridge was seeing. Anne passed him a mug of steaming hot tea. He felt *Sundancer* turn to starboard. He saw the two points picked out on the radar, one off each stern quarter seemingly closing in on *Sundancer's* position in the Banda Sea. He watched the display and saw the speedometer slowly increasing. The Captain was getting the radar points to show their hand; he was pulling them in.

Charles sipped his Earl Grey tea. He switched view to the security status screen and saw that *Sundancer* had been put in lock down overnight. He opened the electrically operated curtains to their windows and found the aluminium security screens were closed. He knew then that all the outer doors and all windows were sealed, making it impossible for anyone to gain easy entry into *Sundancer*. The only entry or exit was via the Star deck hatch, but he also knew that, at this time, it could be used only as an exit, the outer keypad would be in lockdown mode. He glanced at Anne, who was watching the screen.

"We are in lockdown. I think that the Captain is concerned about those two radar blips. He is increasing speed and changing course to get them to reveal their hand." He flipped through some more screens while he spoke. "The boys in surveillance have contacted the authorities. They have also sent some hi-res images of the two vessels."

"How far away are they?" Anne asked.

"Around one hour sailing time, if Whitcome carries on his present course of action. But these people will have high speed inflatable boats with them, and that is how they attack. Hard to pick them up on radar, but our motion and infrared systems will pick them up with ease. And I think we can almost guarantee they have not come across that technology before."

"So, what do we do, just sit around waiting for them to get closer?" Anne looked at Charles wondering what was going through his mind. He was too casual.

"The planned response Miles Channing and Ralph Cohen have developed for this scenario is to wait until the pirate boats are sighted then to use the bow and stern weapons to puncture their inflatable tubes so much that they have to return to their mother ships. In the meantime *Sundancer* will accelerate to her top speed and out of harm's way."

Charles sipped his tea and continued before Anne could ask a question.

"If, however, the mother vessels keep closing in, then a missile will hit the bow of the leading vessel as a warning."

"And if one of their speedboats reaches *Sundancer* and they get on-board?" Anne asked quickly, finishing her tea and placing the cup on the bedside table.

"One thing to remember. They cannot get into *Sundancer*. But if they boarded then in that scenario all the deck lights would be switched on and the guys in surveillance will use the deck guns. We will not risk anyone going on deck armed or otherwise or opening a bulkhead door."

"So, we are safe?"

"Yes, we are safe," Charles replied, swinging his legs out from under the quilt and onto the floor. He walked easily against the motion of the superyacht to the bathroom and had a quick wash, brushed his teeth and dressed. Anne got out of the bed, picked up the keypad, retracted the screen and placed the keypad into its recess on Charles bedside table. She came up beside him in the bathroom and put her arms around him.

"Where are you going?"

"To the bridge," he replied and waited while she dressed and combed her long hair. "Come on, let's go see what Whitcome is up to." He opened the door and led the way down the wide luxurious corridor to the lift. Just as they got to the lift *Sundancer* lurched, the bow digging deep as the Captain cut all forward propulsion. Charles put his arm out to steady Anne as they entered the lift. "A warning on the intercom would have been nice." Charles commented beneath his breath as the lift rose up six decks to take them to the bridge deck. Charles, as he always did, being the gentlemen he was, let Anne out first and followed her into the corridor that ran the width of the superyacht and through the door on to the vast bridge. The bridge was dark. The Sea View deck that housed the formal dining room, library, helideck and bridge was equipped with glass in the windows that could be darkened and lightened electronically. The Captain had used the electronics to darken the bridge windows to their fullest extent. The crew could see out, but no one could see in. He was running now with no navigation lights and, with the window shutters down, the ship was dark and impossible to see in the night sky except by radar. The eerie glow on the bridge was the result of the multiple display screens shedding their dim light across the room. Charles looked around the room and, besides the Captain, the First Officer and the Technical Officer, he saw Duke Warren, Max and Miles Channing seated at a display table reviewing the imagery. Charles walked over to the Captain, who sat in his bridge chair and put his hand on the chairs armrest.

"What is going on?" he asked the Captain.

"That's a fair question," Whitcome replied. "We have a situation whereby we have two vessels that we presume are pirate vessels mirroring our every move for the past three hours. They have their running lights and beacons turned off. Grant believes that he has sighted and is now tracking three inflatables that are heading towards us from each stern quarter with one of them staying back, which he thinks is co-ordinating everything. Again they are all in blackout mode."

"So why the sudden stop? Nearly threw us out of the lift."

"Yes, sorry about that, sir. Miles wants to take out that third inflatable, the command one, and Grant wants it slightly closer for a very clean shot," Whitcome explained.

"How can we shoot at them when we have no proof that they are pirates?" Charles questioned.

"This is a known pirate area and their actions are such that we are a hundred percent sure they are pirates," Whitcome replied, without taking his eyes from the display in front of him. He looked up, suddenly pointing to a bright burst of light in the distance. "That's a direct hit. Forward ten, Mr. Franklin. Might as well get moving again," he continued as the light grew in intensity before quickly dying away.

"I assume that was the shot then Miles?" Charles questioned

"Yes, Charles. We have reason to believe that that was the

pirate leader and he and some of his crew are now very wet indeed. If you look at this image, the shot took out one of his main tubes and his fuel tank. By stopping dead, we could get a clearer image and target more accurately. No one died, but we did see weapons on our infra-red camera, which confirmed out pirate assumption." Miles Channing explained. "Now I suggest we hit full speed and evacuate this area. It's bound to get hostile if we stay around here."

Just off *Sundancer's* port bow a fountain of water lifted high skywards and sent a spray of sparkling water onto her deck. "Full speed Mr Franklin, if you please," Captain Whitcome ordered casually.

"Miles, we need to take out their guns so they can't hurt anyone else," Charles commanded. "Grant is well within range and we can use the extreme long range camera to sight accurately with the laser guidance system."

"I can see from the display that he's already targeting and about to shoot," Miles said. Charles walked carefully over to Miles, balancing against the movement of *Sundancer* beneath his feet. He stood beside Miles and looked at the screen. He could see on the display exactly what Grant, who was in the surveillance room, could see through the camera. He watched as the sight moved slightly to the centre of the pirate ships gun just as it fired again at *Sundancer*. He felt *Sundancer* move heavily beneath his feet as she turned hard to starboard.

"Grant is co-ordinating with Franklin to avoid any of the incoming shells," Miles said. "He's using the tactical defence system, which interfaces with Franklin's main sixty five inch screen. Franklin can see instantly the computer calls for a course change based on the computers projection for the shells trajectory. We played with this during our Tonga stopover last year and tidied up the interface and interlocks when we integrated the new camera system. It's good to know our simulation runs were on track."

Charles focused on the display and saw the pirate ships gun disintegrate in front of his eyes. "Bloody Hell!" Charles exclaimed, looking up to see a fountain of water off their port quarter. He looked back at the display and watched as the camera moved and focused on the gun of the second pirate vessel.

"Grant is going after the gun on the other pirate vessel," Miles explained, "which has picked up speed now to get within range. See, he has fixed on the centre of the gun." At that moment the gun exploded and all that could be seen on the screen was smoke. "Job done. All we need to do now is get the hell out of here and keep an eye out for any other pirates on route. Mind you, I think these guys will be warning their brethren to steer clear of us."

"Of that I have no doubt. What about the inflatables?" Charles questioned. Miles switched the display screen to show the radar image and pointed to three blips.

"They are all returning to their mother ships. We are safe and clear."

"Thanks. Good job crew." Charles patted Miles on the back and walked back to Anne. *Sundancer* gently rose and fell beneath his feet as she turned back onto her original course and carried on gently accelerating to full speed. Anne was standing next to the Captain, holding on to his chair with both hands. He put his arm around her shoulder.

"Captain, how long before we revert to cruising speed?" he asked.

"When Grant or Miles advise me that we are out of harm's way. Until then we are running up to full power on all four engines," Whitcome replied. "Hopefully not too long now. We're burning fuel at a horrendous rate." He touched a keypad and the bridge windows brightened to a lighter tint. He picked up a handset and pressed two keys. "Grant, status report please," he said into the mouthpiece. He listened for a while before saying, "That's good news, thank you." He replaced the handset. "Mr. Franklin, you may reduce your speed to twenty six knots please. And do it progressively please, we don't want the chef throwing breakfast all over the floor do we? Run on the two outer engines only."

"No, sir, we don't. I'm starving. Twenty six knots with slow reduction in our speed. Outer engines only, aye sir," Franklin replied without turning round. He placed his right hand across four polished stainless steel levers topped by mirror polished red knobs and gently eased the two inner levers back, slowly decreasing the power output of the two inner engines till they were just ticking over. He then spread his fingers to cover the two outer levers and eased them back till he had *Sundancer* cruising at twenty six knots. He carefully adjusted the levers until the two engines were balanced on revolutions. "Twenty six knots, outer engines only, sir," he told the Captain. He looked over at the Technical Officer.

"Martin, inner engines are in neutral as requested."

"Thanks Franklin. I will shut them down for now," Martin Deeks replied, leaning forward in his chair and flicking two switch covers up, pressing the red buttons beneath.

"Speed twenty six knots, back on course and switching to autopilot, Captain," Franklin announced.

"Grant has lifted the security screens, Captain."

Martin continued seeing the status change on his security screen. "The three inflatables are in a huddle together not moving, and seem to be waiting for the two main vessels, which are heading their way. I can assume they are supporting the one we hit."

"Well, I think we can now leave the fun and games to the experts, while we go and have breakfast," Anne said, taking Charles gently by the arm. "You two coming?" she asked Duke and Max, who had been standing and quietly watching the action while the bridge and security crews did their business. "You too, Captain."

"Sounds like a plan. Come on, Duke," Max answered making his way across the bridge to where Charles and Anne were opening the bridge door.

Duke followed Max grinning from ear to ear. "Good to see that we are on a well secured vessel with a totally competent crew."

His remark directed at the Captain but just loud enough for everyone on the bridge to hear.

"Thank you, I will join you shortly," the Captain said to Anne. "Just as soon as I have done a handover following that little fracas." With the bridge empty of visitors, the Captain asked Franklin to join him with Martin at the navigation table. "We were burning fuel at a high rate. We are currently here and have this course plotted to our destination." He ran his finger along the line plotted on the screen. "At our current fuel load can we make our destination without refuelling if we have to run for the same sort of duration at full throttle again?"

Martin was tapping on a separate area of the screen, which

allowed him to monitor and calculate fuel use, amongst other functions, while Whitcome was talking. "Yes, we can with quite a safety margin if we run on two engines at cruising speed. We left with a full fuel load in all tanks. I have a fuel vessel meeting us when we anchor at Sumatra."

"Are all systems functioning properly?"

"Yes, and we have green across the board, and with the two inner engines off, the engine technicians will be giving them the once over. Not really required but while they are down we might as well take the opportunity," Martin replied.

"Thank you, Mr Deeks. Now, Franklin, protocol on board dictates that if a sudden dramatic turn or increase in speed is required, three short quick blasts on the horn are the appropriate warning. We failed to do this. It will not happen again. Nether the less a good handling of the yacht, thank you. Okay, back to your stations. First Officer, you have the bridge. I will be having breakfast. If I am required you know where to find me."

He stood, looked around at the bridge as Franklin returned to his command chair and Martin walked back to his console. He sighed quietly to himself at a job well done and at the experience and depth of knowledge his crew had. Franklin's skill at controlling the one hundred and eighty five metre, fourteen thousand five hundred tonne superyacht's seventy five thousand horsepower in tight fast course changes with speed alterations to complicate things was superb and confirmed his choice as First Officer was correct. It had been the first occasion when those skills had come fully into play and he had excelled. The security team's use of their equipment to quickly identify and track the probable pirates and then sight them with that new camera array was beyond belief but he would never forget the accuracy of Grant's targeting. Yes, he knew it was all computer controlled laser guidance systems, but still Grant was in control. He closed the bridge door behind him and made his way to the informal dining room on the main deck, where the breakfast, served buffet style, would be. He enjoyed dining with Charles and Anne whom he had known for many years, and at the request of Charles had had a great say in the design of *Sundancer*.

Chapter Fifteen

The Identification

Detective Taylor sat at his desk in the untidy open plan office lit with the dim flickering light from the fluorescent tubes that hung from the off white ceiling on old rusting chains. The office was never what one would call really busy but had that buzz of background activity that always made it feel edgy. He looked at the photograph of the courier driver and the renditions of the driver's face given to the police sketch artist by the last people to receive deliveries. The two renditions were remarkably similar, which meant to Taylor that they were of the same man, but they were totally different to the man in the photograph identified as the missing courier driver. The shape of the face was round not oval with a full head of close cropped hair. He rubbed the stubble on his chin and held one of the sketches in his hand.

"Put this sketch through the data base, get it to the CIA, FBI and Interpol and see if we can get a match." He handed one of the sketches to one of his team, a young officer called Robert Corby. "That house I went to were probably the last people to see this guy before he disappeared."

"What did they say when you questioned them?" asked Corby.

"They just said that they saw the courier driver when he dropped off a package." Taylor replied. "I have a gut feeling that they did not tell me everything. Between their house and the next drop off point, something happened to the real driver. Get moving with the search on the sketch and see if facial recognition comes up with anything. I have a feeling it will." He watched as Corby walked off to the scanner and picked up the other sketch and wondered who the guy was. He grabbed his car keys, opened the left hand drawer of his desk, withdrew his service revolver and placed it in the holster on his hip, put his sunglasses on and walked across the office, briefly stopping by Corby. "I'll be in my car. Call me as soon as you get something." He left through the front doors, took the six ornate carved stone steps down to the pavement two at a time and crossed the layby to his car.

He had spontaneously decided he was going to ask those people a few other questions. He racked his brains trying to recall the son's name. Albrecht, yes that was it. A very Germanic name. From that region of Europe anyway. He started his car, loaded the address into the cars GPS navigation system and set off. While driving he picked up his radio microphone and called Officer Martinez and asked him to meet him at the Axmann house. During the drive his mind pondered over the questions to ask. He decided on the psychological approach, the courier driver's attitude and manner, was he upset, cheerful, talkative? He would show them the sketch and see if they recognised the face. What would there reaction to the sketch be? Shock, nonchalance, violence, that sort of thing? He turned off the main road and headed down the long winding drive lined by trees. The trees were quite thick either side of the driveway, but he could see through the shadow an expanse of green lawn, then in the distance more trees.

He pulled up outside the house and switched off the car's engine. He opened the car door and lit a cigarette before getting out. He looked around him, waiting for Martinez to arrive. It was another warm, humid afternoon and he noticed the stains on his shirt at his arm pits, he sighed. So much for that new under arm deodorant. He paced back and forth in front of the house. Everything looked too quiet and the doors to the workshop were closed, unlike the last time he arrived, when they were slightly ajar. There were no sounds of air conditioners as there was last time, either. He walked to the workshop doors and noted they were not chained or padlocked; he listened but heard no sounds coming from the inside. He turned around at the sound of a car, its tires crunching on the gravel as it came up the drive. He saw it was Martinez in his black and white police car. He indicated to Martinez to park alongside his own car. Martinez got out, leaving the car door open and walked over to Taylor, his partner in the black and white speaking to dispatch and letting them know where they were.

"All seems quiet," Martinez commented.

"Yes, a little too quiet. Let's take a look around. Get your buddy to stay by the cars on alert."

"Henry, stay by the cars. We are going to scout the place," Martinez called over to his partner, who was still talking on the radio. When he saw his partner wave in acknowledgement, he turned and walked in the direction Taylor had taken to the left side of the workshop. He caught up with Taylor, who was looking through an old frosted and dirty window.

"Hadn't we try and knock on the front door first?" Martinez asked.

"I just wanted a quick look first. Don't think no one is home though," Taylor replied as Martinez followed him back around to the front and over the grass to the house. Taylor rang the bell by the front door and waited half a minute and rang it again. "As I thought, no one home. Let's take a look in the workshop. I don't think it's locked," Taylor said and walked over to the workshop with Martinez in tow, gun drawn and held in both hands ready. Taylor flicked the hitch open and carefully pulled the left hand door, which although large and old moved with ease. Someone had been oiling the hinges. The workshop was dim, so he quickly lifted his standard police issue torch from his belt and shone it around the workshop. He looked for the light switch, which he saw on the right hand wall. He flicked it on and saw that the workshop was empty. He clipped the torch onto his belt and entered the workshop. He could see where items had sat on the floor through the outlines in the dust. He saw tire tracks and pointed to them. "Big four wheel drive tire tracks. Cabinets have been here and we have an unusual arrangement of imprints by this back wall beneath the window, and plenty of foot prints."

"Taylor, look over here," Martinez called. Taylor came over and Martinez pointed to the wall, where someone had drawn an image.

"Sure don't think that is right."

"No, nor do I. Let's take a look in the house," Taylor said turning towards the side door, which he found unlocked. Across the small pathway he tried the side door to the house and was surprised to find that unlocked. He entered the house and held his nose against the musty odour that hit him. Martinez followed.

"Texas, PD," Taylor called loudly and drew his gun. "Texas PD, come out with your hands raised." He stood his ground carefully looking left and right; Martinez moved beside him. "Okay, let's do a sweep," he said quietly, and they moved off, clearing each room, guns at the ready and shouting to each other as they did until they arrived back at the door. Taylor dialled a number on his phone.

"This is Detective Taylor, send a CSI unit to my location now." He put the phone in his pocket. "Get your partner and let's give this place a good search starting outside while this place airs. It stinks." Taylor walked out and round the house and came to an area where a large bonfire was still smouldering. He picked up a stick and carefully starting easing items which looked interesting out of the smouldering pile, papers, booklets, small metal canisters and glass bottles. He knelt down and carefully looked at them, rubbing his jaw, deep in thought.

Martinez came up beside him. "I'm going to see where this path goes," he said. "Looks like somebody was trying to destroy a lot of stuff." he remarked at the sight of the bonfire. "Not that old either."

"No, it's very recent. Just a few hours old, I would say. It's still very hot in the centre. Come on, let's follow that path of yours." Taylor stood up stiffly. "I could do with the walk."

"It heads in the general direction towards the river," Martinez said as they walked down the track. "A trolley with something heavy has been down here, at least once. You can clearly see the track mark," he continued, kneeling down and running his fingers along the grooves. "The soil is still loose at the sides of the track marks, so they are relatively new." He stood and the continued to walk until they came to the jetty. "Very convenient. No way of knowing if it is has been used recently until the CSI guys get here."

"Nice spot for fishing," Taylor said, looking around. "Not overlooked, private from the road, own boat jetty on a quiet, wide stretch of the river." He spun on his heels." House hidden from the river." He looked at Martinez. "What do you reckon, drugs?"

"No, they would not have bothered taking all their empty chemical containers or waste by products, and there is no sign of drug paraphernalia in the house," Martinez replied. "Usually when we bust a drug house after the cooks and dealers have left we find all the empty chemical containers have been left full of the waste by products for us to clean up."

Taylor walked to one of the jetty support posts that stood about waist high and knelt down. "There's a clean area on this post which shows where a rope was recently tied." He walked to the support post at the other end of the jetty. "Same rope marks here, so we have four wheel drive tracks and signs that a boat was moored here. Did they split up? Did some of them leave by boat, some by big four wheel drive?" He stood up, his knees aching. I must be getting old, he thought to himself. He looked at the jetty floor and carefully knelt down. "Trolley wheel marks where it was spun around," he said, pointing to an area on two of the timbers. Martinez knelt beside him and ran two of his fingers across the marks and looked at the soil on his fingers before rubbing the soil between them.

"Same as the soil where the tracks are back there. Still dampness to it, so you are right, it's recent. They packed up and left not long ago. Soon after you left, I would say." Martinez stood up and said, "Might as well get back to the house. The CSI guys will be here soon."

They walked back up the track to the house, keeping an eye open for anything that may help. They found two CSI operatives clothed in white overalls sifting carefully through the bonfire, which they had spread further out with rakes to cool the embers. Specimen bottle, bags and jars already containing some items. They rounded the house and walked in the front door, where more operatives in white overalls were taking photographs and dusting for prints.

"Please do not come in until we have finished, Detective Taylor," said one of the operatives. "I know you want to know what we find, but we have had less than five minutes." he laughed.

Taylor laughed loudly. "Okay doc, I know. Call me as soon as you have something." He turned to Martinez. "Thanks for the back-up. I don't think there is much more we can do here."

"Anytime, just call," Martinez replied, saluted and went to his black and white, got in and drove down the tree lined driveway. Taylor watched them leave and returned to the workshop and looked carefully at what Martinez had shown him. He took out his pad and pen and copied the image and words that were below it. He put the pad away just as another CSI operative walked in who he recognised.

"Can you photograph this and see if you can match it with anything and check these tire marks. Also over there where there are some imprints of some sort," he said pointing to the back of the workshop. "There were some cabinets or something like a laboratory set up. See if you can work out what they were doing."

"Of course, for you anything. The air smells funny, a sort of metallic mustiness. You wouldn't realise that because you smoke too much. I'll take some samples and see if we can identify what gaseous particles are present," the CSI operative said before putting on her protective glasses. She paused before replacing her mouth mask to say. "Now, if you would leave, please. You're contaminating the scene."

Taylor looked at her. "Of course, Sarah." He turned to leave. "I have a bad vibe about this place," he said solemnly. "I need you and doc to work fast for me."

"We'll do our best as always," Sarah replied.

Before Taylor was out of the doors, the doc arrived looking hassled. "Sarah, we need to check this whole place for radiation contamination. I have the CBRN team on route. They will be here in a few minutes. I have every member of our team assembling at the end of the road. I will get the Geiger counters so we can start an initial sweep. Detective Taylor, I strongly suggest you join our team at the end of the road and await for us there. You may need to be decontaminated."

Taylor rubbed the back of his neck and looked questioningly at doc.

"Who or what is or are CBRN?"

"Chemical, biological, radiological, nuclear defence unit. They are flying in from Fort Leonard, Missouri, as we speak. They will take over until we are sure there is no radioactive agents or chemical agents on this site. Now, please do as I ask and go to the bottom of the road, Oh, and take your car with you. Now go, please," the doc said in exasperation.

"What about Martinez and his partner, what's his name, he

was in the house and workshop with me and by now they must be well on their way to back into town?"

"You'd better call them and let them know what's going on. They may need to be checked for decontamination," the doc said." Now go, get out."

The doc waved at Taylor with his arms hurrying him out through the doors. Taylor walked out of the door and jumped into his car and drove down the long winding tree lined drive, following the white overall wearing CSI people. He stopped half way and looked back at the house. What was happening here, he thought, just added to his gut instinct that they were the people who abducted the courier driver. He took his phone from his pocket and called Martinez and gave him the news and continued to the end of the drive, where he parked up next to the CSI van and got out of his car. He heard then saw two large helicopters appear overhead through the trees. He kept watching and walking until he reached the CSI team and joined them as the helicopters hovered above the trees. He watched as the first of the two huge helicopters landed close to them in the grounds of the house in an opening on the other side of the trees. As it touched down side doors were immediately slid open and people wearing hazmat suits jumped out and began to manhandle large bags through the doorways. The group dragged the large bags away from the helicopter towards the CSI team, keeping their heads low as the helicopter lifted off the ground slightly and moved further towards the house before landing again, this time its rotors slowing.

The second helicopter landed where the first machine had originally touched down, disgorging three people who headed towards the house and workshop while another four headed towards Taylor and the CSI team. Taylor watched as the last person got down from the second helicopter, slower and more deliberate than the others, with a clear sense of purpose and authority. The man looked around, taking in the scene before walking towards Taylor. Obviously this was the man in charge, thought Taylor. Two tent like structures were quickly being erected, one with some pipe work, both connecting to each other by large circular tubing. The man came up beside Taylor.

"You are Detective Taylor, are you not?" the man said slowly and distinctly.

"Sure, I am. Who are you?" Taylor asked, knowing full well he would not get a straight answer.

"That does not matter for now. I need you through decontamination first so we can talk about why you are investigating this house." He walked away to the centre of the CSI team. "Everybody, listen please," the man said through his hazmat suit. "You may have been contaminated, with what we are not sure. We are assuming it to be radiation. To be on the safe side you will need to go through the decontamination unit that is being constructed. After that you will be examined and tested then probably placed in quarantine until we get the all clear."

There was a lot of murmuring and shuffling amongst the CSI team until Taylor spoke up.

"Quarantine, for how long and where?" he asked.

"It may not be required," the man said loud enough for everyone to hear. "And we won't know how long until all the tests are completed. After decontamination you will be taken back to Fort Leonard in the helicopters and held there until we get the all clear or otherwise. But not you Detective Taylor, for I need you here."

"Brilliant. I am here on official police business conducting an investigation into a possible abduction or murder that the persons who lived here, may or may not, have been involved with," Taylor said exasperated.

"Well, just count this in as part of your investigation," the man replied.

"I have authority and jurisdiction here. Give me one of your hazmat suits," Taylor said in his most authoritarian voice.

"My department's authority overrides yours and, as for the hazmat suit, you are too late. I'm afraid that you may already be contaminated, my friend," the man replied.

"Not after I've been through decontamination, I won't be?" Taylor asked.

"Nice try, but no," was the man's clipped reply. "You will do as I say or you will be arrested."

Taylor gave him an exasperated look, lit a cigarette and stormed over to the first tent to start the decontamination procedure.

The man turned and saw two people walking towards him, a man and a woman both in white jump suits. "Ah, the two stragglers, doc and Sarah, over here, please" He motioned towards the CSI team. "Follow Detective Taylor, if you please, and do as the decontamination team tells you." He stood and watched them as they made their way over to the tents. He smiled to himself as they entered the first tent, turned on his heels and walked up the drive towards the house. Halfway he was met by one of his team, who removed his hazmat head gear as he got closer. The man followed suit and removed his.

"We have found no chemical traces, but we have detected trace radioactivity coming from the workshop floor and have high readings on the west and the rear walls. Otherwise, the house is clean. All the levels are low so there is no health risk unless you stayed in there for say a fortnight." the team member advised.

"Well, good news and bad news then. Okay, go tell the decontamination team, third level shrub and rub for the CSI team who entered the workshop and Detective Taylor. The rest are all clear. I'm going up to the workshop. Oh, and get Taylor to meet me up there after his decontamination." The man walked off towards the house, leaving the team members to carry on walking down to the decontamination area.

Having stripped and been washed clean and checked with a Geiger counter, Detective Taylor got dressed back into his clothes and thought to himself that this was all overkill and a huge waste of time and money, and went to find the doc. He found him getting dressed in his day clothes. "Thankfully my white coveralls protected my clothes. Otherwise I'd be just wearing one of their overalls and naked as the day I was born underneath," the doc said, buttoning the top two buttons of his shirt. "But not so. I see they have allowed you to get back into your original clothes."

"Bloody circus if you ask me. Look, doc, I am going back up to the workshop. I want you to get back to your lab and check this image that I found on the wall." He passed a sheet of folded paper to the doc. "It's important somehow. I've got to go back to the house. The spook wants to see me. When you see Sarah, tell her to join me." He placed a hand on the doc's shoulder. "Missing courier, now radioactivity. This is big."

"Sure thing. I will call you as soon as I have something," the doc said, walking off to find Sarah. Taylor watched him go. He pulled out his cigarettes and lit one. He took a long deep draw on the cigarette, exhaling the smoke slowly and commenced the walk back to the house. He entered the workshop and looked at the wall where Martinez had found the image. He frowned when he saw the wall had been scrubbed clean. He looked around at the floor and saw that the entire floor had also been swept clean as well. He looked around and saw patches on the wall where they had been wiped clean. He swore under his breath at the thought that all his evidence, at least all his evidence in the workshop had been wiped clean. He knew Sarah had photographs of the image on the wall, but the tire tracks and imprints left by the cabinets he was not sure. He walked from the workshop to the house and stopped as he saw Sarah walking up the driveway. He waited until she came up to him and noticed she still held her camera and implement bag. "Sarah, do you still have that image on your camera? Did you take shots of the tire marks and cabinet imprints?" he asked.

"I think so. Let me take a look." Sarah looked at the LCD display on the camera and toggled through the shots. "Yes, they are still there. Why?"

"The image has been wiped off the wall and the floor swept clean," Taylor told her, shrugging his shoulder. "I've never had that done before at a crime scene."

"This camera is wireless and I sent all the photographs to the lab as soon as the CBRN were called, so they will be on the server and the team will be working on them now," Sarah said reassuringly. "What about the house?"

"I was on my way there when I saw you walking up," Taylor answered, and they started walking slowly across the grass to the front door of the house, where people in hazmat suits were coming and going like bees in a hive.

"Okay, let's go see what they are doing and if there is anything left for me to see and test," Sarah said as she placed the camera in her bag. "Looking at that lot, I would say with some certainty that any evidence has either been removed or destroyed."

Taylor entered the house first and found large plastic bags and boxes loaded with household items. Sarah followed him into the kitchen, where an operative wearing a spray pack on his back was spraying all the surfaces while another followed behind, wiping the surfaces down. In the lounge the furniture had been removed and the carpet lifted. He looked at Sarah and shrugged his shoulders and walked outside to where the bonfire was. It now burned fiercely again with the added fuel of carpet, settee and wooden table, the thick smoke billowing across the bay. He angrily took a kick at the fire. "They have destroyed any evidence that may have been in there!" he shouted. "Why on earth would they do that?"

"Radioactivity," came a calm voice behind him as the man in the hazmat suit came over to them, his face calm and at ease as he removed his hazmat suit helmet. "Standard protocol, I'm afraid. Nothing I could do. Sorry if it interfered with your investigation, but we have all the evidence we need for ours. Yours, I'm afraid, is now at an end. Now I must ask you to tell me why and what you were investigating?"

"A missing courier drive. His last known delivery point was this house," Taylor said with some edge to his voice.

"Is that's all it was? Oh well, you will send copies of all your files to my office. Now I suggest that you get into your vehicles and leave immediately. Good day." He turned and walked away calmly, leaving Taylor and Sarah speechless.

"Well, all we have is what we got on camera. I will continue with what we got. Let's go," Taylor said, lighting another cigarette and patting Sarah on the shoulder before something at the edge of the fire caught his eye. "Hold on," he said. "That pile over there. I pulled those papers from the fire earlier. I need those." Taylor looked around and with no one else in sight, he gathered up the papers and looked around for something to put them in.

"Put them in here," Sarah said, opening her bag. Taylor carefully placed the papers in the bag. They walked to the front of the house and down the drive. "I'll see what I can recover from them when I get to my lab. I have a young lad who is pretty good at recovering and rebuilding fire damage papers." They walked in silence until they reach the cars at the end of the drive.

"Thanks, Sarah. Talk soon," Taylor said and got into his car as the doc came to his door.

"Your crime scene has been destroyed, Detective. I'm sorry about that but we will see what we have and do our best with what we've got. Good bye." He got into Sarah's car and they drove down the tree lined driveway to the main road.

Taylor stopped in a nearby layby, opened the car window and lit a cigarette and waited. When he saw the helicopters overhead after about a three hour wait, he started his car, closed the window and headed to the precinct. He needed a strong coffee and to talk this over with Corby and Martinez. He called both and told them to meet him at the precinct. He was not finished with this investigation; he knew, now, that there was more to this than just a missing person. This was big and he would not let it go.

Chapter Sixteen

Conservation

Charles walked across the teak deck, looking at the coastline as *Sundancer* lay at anchor in the bay. A warm breeze wafted across the deck beneath a clear blue sky dotted with a few high wispy clouds and a very bright sun. He stopped at the port side and leant against the gunwale. The railing felt gritty in his hand and he wiped away some encrusted salt from the polished wood. He was quietly annoyed knowing that, as soon as the superyacht anchored in the Celebes Sea, the crew should have washed *Sundancer* down. He took the radio from his belt hook and called the Captain.

"Captain, I have encrusted salt on the aft deck rails. It will, as you are aware, damaged the varnish and leave the wood exposed. Get the First Officer to check and make sure that *Sundancer* has been or is properly washed down." He clicked off without waiting for a reply; one was not needed. He knew what would happen. Captain Whitcome would be feeling totally let down that *his* superyacht had not been properly cleaned to the required standard and the quality of the cleaning process had not been checked. The First Officer would now be required to walk the length of the superyacht, deck by deck, checking with the relevant crewmen that she was indeed properly cleaned.

Charles had enjoyed the past week, following the encounter with the pirate vessels. They had calm seas all the way, warm sunny weather and maintained a steady twenty one knots. He had had plenty of time to relax and recuperate from his relapse. There had been many laughs, especially when Cathy and Chris had teamed up to play Pétanque and badminton against Anne and himself on a few occasions. When Chris and Cathy had coerced Duke and Max to play Pétanque and decide which team to join, there was much cajoling from each side and the whole game turned into a hysterical farce. The chef had dutifully followed Anne and the doctor's orders on the dietary requirements for Charles's health and was very inventive with each meal. Charles had played chess with Max in the quiet of the library on a few afternoons, during which they discussed world affairs and their future conservation plans, deciding on a few options that they may take over copious cups of coffee and cognac. Cathy had decided to take on running the cinema and diligently searched through the film and TV library, seeking out comedy films before deciding it would be great for her father and the crew to run all the *Pink Panther* movies over the course of the five days.

The doctor had supervised Charles in the gym for an hour each day and, as the ship's doctor, taken it upon himself to insist that the rest of the Langham family should exercise as well in preparation for their placements. Ryan, Duke and Max at the insistence of Cathy, had joined in the fun. Charles had kept up to date on the nuclear attack on London and had been in contact with both the United States President and the United Kingdom

Prime Minister on more than one occasion. Thomas had fed the *Sundancer* surveillance team as much insider information as he could, as and when it became available. Charles continued watching the tree lined coast until he heard the distinctive sound of the Bell 525 Relentless approaching.

He looked up and watched as Max brought the Bell 525 Relentless helicopter in fast and low over the trees of North Kalimantan before dipping to skim the azure blue water of the Celebes Sea towards *Sundancer* as she lay swinging leisurely at anchor. Max had decided to do a surveillance run to check that the clearing was clear of any obstruction and, therefore, safe to land in, before he had the extra weight of passengers and cargo. The gorgeous summer's morning with its deep blue sky made the flight most enjoyable. He liked to be cool and fresh when flying and had pumped up the air conditioning to give him an eighteen degree Celsius temperature. Charles smiled to himself as Max flared the huge executive helicopter and gained height to land on the helideck. He had now completed the first cargo run and on his next trip would deliver Cathy, Chris and Anne to the Orangutan sanctuary, and then do another cargo run and later return with Anne. They had plenty of time as they waited for the airdrop that was on route from the UK. The Captain would launch the eight metre rigid inflatable boat once they had confirmation from the pilot on the exact position at which the drop had been initiated. The airdrop would be a one metre long metal canister dropped from one thousand metres with its parachute opening automatically.

Inside the canister were two vials containing radioactive isotopes, which would be taken to the laboratory cell located at sea level on deck one and isolated from the rest of the superyacht by double negative air pressure seals and hydraulic ram assisted suspension mounts. The whole cell could be slid out of the superyachts side and floated free if required for a five day maximum operational duration. Originally designed to be used as either an on-board or floating laboratory for investigating parasites, pathogens and animal diseases that arose at their reclaimed sites or dive site, other uses had been found. The equipment expanded mainly at the request of Marge. They had carried out research on why corals were dying and investigating the deaths of other deep sea species.

Charles heard someone walking towards him along the deck and turned as Duke came up beside him.

"You've been standing here for well over an hour and a half, Charles. What's on your mind?" Duke asked, leisurely leaning on the polished wood gunwale, taking in the view of the coastline of Eastern Borneo as they lay at anchor south of Tarakan Island.

"You know, it is just darn hard to comprehend the devastation that has taken place in London. Just look around you, serenity," Charles replied in a quiet voice as he turned and leant his back on the gunwale. Looking up he could see Max jump down from the helicopter, closing the flight deck door, slide open the large cabin door, look around inside before sliding the door closed. The black and red colour scheme with the gold pin stripes accentuating her lines had been Max's choice and certainly stood out, sitting four decks above on what was called the Sea View deck. The interior of the Bell 525 Relentless consisted of eight white leather executive lounge seats that could swivel, arranged around a central circular table that had been Anne's choice. The flight deck utilised three of the same seats but without the ability to swivel due to the bulkhead in which sat a tinted retractable window to allow crew and passengers to talk.

"We are surrounded by things of beauty, natural and manmade in as peaceful location as you could get. Yet, for some unfathomable reason, someone many thousands of miles away has unleashed the power of nature in the most abominable way. Yet, here we are untouched, and if it was not for technology we would be none the wiser about the atrocity." Charles looked at up the helicopter, seeing that Max was getting ready for his next run and crew members were loading suitcases and parcels into the cargo hold. "Even that, in those colours is a thing of beauty."

"But you are here because of the wanton destruction of a natural habitat to fuel man's desire for more material things that is driving wild animals and plants to extinction," Duke said, bringing Charles back into the here and now.

"Yes, that's true," Charles said thoughtfully. "But at least we can and are doing something about that."

"Which to this very moment, you may not be aware, I am still totally in the dark about what it is you do exactly or what it is that you have done," Duke chided.

"Let's get a drink and I'll explain," Charles replied and led the way down the vast deck to the bar and got a cold beer from the steward. "Simply put, we purchase, usually at well over the odds prices, the rain forest lands that had been decimated by greedy companies and turned into palm oil plantations, or whatever. We also purchase a very large margin of land all around to give us a large buffer between the area in which the animals live and the nearest human habitation. We then ship in all the materials we need to enable us to build facilities to cultivate native plants and trees. We even set up breeding centres for the local wildlife and insect life. We then employ local people and, under expert supervision, train them to build all the buildings we need to run the wildlife rescue centres, vet clinics, training, primate housing, operations, school, hospital and accommodation buildings, the lot. We take the best of these people and train them as leaders and educators. Vegetable gardens, solar power generation and satellite communications round off the facilities. The locals replant the area with the cultivated native trees and plants to regenerate the rainforest. Wildlife and insect life is restored as much as we can."

He looked at his beer, and then continued. "We ship materials in to build schools and help the local inhabitants and workers with better housing. Everyone in the surrounding community wins by helping the Orangutans, who are saved and protected in the surrounding rainforest and we rebuild the biodiversity. A few years ago we purchased two mines and the surrounding rainforest, closed the mines and have a permanent team working exactly the same way with the local people regenerating the area. Cathy is visiting the older operation for a few days, which is now run exclusively by locals with her as their mentor, sponsor, so to speak. She keeps in daily contact and provides advice, assistance, monies or sends out our own people to help them as needed. But she will be heading to Sumatra after a few days. In fact, she should arrive while we are there. Chris is south in East Kalimantan at the mine reclamation site, which still has a full complement of our own staff in situ and is more challenging physically."

"They will have contact with each other though, won't they?"

Duke asked.

"Oh, yes. We have a helicopter and an Osprey based at both the main East Kalimantan site and the Sumatra site, and video conferencing facilities at all three. Chris can get to Kathy very quickly, but Ralph and Miles are arranging to leave two guards with each of them."

"Good call. This is still a tricky area," Duke said turning around and leaning with his lower back on the rail looking up at the helicopter as its rotors started to slowly turn.

"Even with the support of the local and federal governments! Ah, here comes Anne and the kids," Duke said.

Charles smiled at them. "I take it you guys are off now?" he asked, as Anne gave him a hug.

"Yes, I'm going out with them and will be back later when they are settled in. We have two guards on site for Chris already, and the two guards for Cathy are on this trip. We're dropping Chris off first, when I've settled him in, we will fly onto Cathy's site. I'll stay there for a while and most likely come back on the last flight. It has taken longer than planned to choose the guards for Cathy. Miles and Ralph have been inundated with volunteers to guard her," Anne advised lightly with a raise of an eyebrow. "Miles and Ralph wanted objectivity, not emotion, when action may be required."

"I see, well they had better have made the right choice," Duke butted in.

"Oh, they have. The two members of the security team who did not volunteer for the duty are the ones that are going," Anne replied. "Anyway, we had better get going, see you soon." She kissed Charles and gave Duke a kiss on the cheek.

"See you in Sumatra in four days, daddy," Cathy gave Charles a kiss and a long hug before letting Chris have his turn for a hug while she went over to Duke and gave him an unexpected hug. Abbey ran around knowing something was going on.

"Usual routine calls you two, and if you need anything at all tell us and if it's urgent do not wait for the scheduled call. I'll see you in six months, Chris. Stay safe," Charles said and watched as they made their way up the outside stairs to the helipad.

"Abbey, stay here," he called to the Border Collie, who had started to run after Cathy. Abbey stopped, turned and at a signal from Charles came and sat by his feet. He watched and waved back as they all waved before getting into the helicopter. The helicopter lifted off the deck before tracking sideways and down along the side of the superyacht so that Cathy could give one more wave before Max increased power and the Bell 525 Relentless lifted higher in the sky and increased speed towards the mainland.

"Abbey is well trained," Duke commented. "Ah, yes, the reason I came out here in the first place. Grant has received some news. There's been some action on the East Coast of the United States, at a place call Matagorda Bay. Never heard of it before but a house and workshop there have been found to have radioactive traces. Won't go into the full details but it was the last drop of a courier driver whose gone missing and when the local police returned later the same day, the place was deserted. Whoever was there left in a hurry. The CSI team who were called in found faint traces of radioactivity in the house so they called in the CBRN, who found higher traces in the workshop. I have the isotope signature being sent through. Oh, and the old man's son was named Albrecht."

Charles turned instantly at the mention of name. He took a breath. "Albrecht? That is the name of the eldest son of Gustav Axman."

"It could be a coincidence, but I don't think so. I have the police sketch of the person, who allegedly drove the courier truck before it was abandoned, being sent through," Duke commented. "There was a strange drawing on a wall, in the workshop I think, with some writing beneath it. I have a photo of that being sent as well."

"How did you manage to get all this information?" Charles asked, resting his hand on the polished gunwale rail.

"I have some very good contacts, people in the right places who owe me one," said Duke. "I am having it all sent through to Grant, so that he can process it along with everything else we have."

"Any clues as to how they got clear?" Charles asked.

"The local detective believes they exited by boat and car. He has traced the car to a local rental agency, an F150. I have copies of the rental agreement and identification papers also coming through."

"Well done, Duke. If it's by boat, then we have two submarines plus the Ocean sensors in the area, we might be able to pick up some anomalies," Charles said.

Duke straightened up and ran his hands down the small of his back, arching backwards. "Good idea. It's a long shot but I'll get Grant and Marge onto it," he started to walk off down the long deck towards the lounge still arching and stretching his back as he went.

"Duke, before you go. Have we got confirmed identities of the people that the detective met at the house?" he asked

"No, we haven't, but I see where your mind is going," Duke

said. "I'll arrange for the detective to see the latest photographs we have of Gustav and his son for identification."

"Thanks Duke. I am sure the old man will be Gustav and the young man his son Albrecht, which will mean that he has both weapons with him and that he has two objectives. And see the doctor about your back!"

"Yes, I know. After you've seen what I've set out with Grant in the conference suite next to the surveillance room."

Charles led the way to the lift, which arrived in seconds, pressed the button for deck two, and led the way to the conference suite. Charles could see papers neatly laid out on the large oval cherry wood conference table and images on the two large display screens built into one of the walls. He could clearly see the azure blue water and tree lined coastline through the large rectangular porthole and glimpse a sight of the helicopter skimming the water. The ceiling lights were dimmed. Grant was seated at the table typing into a keyboard whilst looking at one of the display screens. He looked up as Charles entered.

"Hi Boss, come to see the fruits of all our labours?"

Charles sat down at the end of the table closest to the door and Duke chose a chair on the left hand side next to Grant. "Take it from the top gentlemen," Charles said, "and let's have some fresh coffee in here."

Grant picked up his handset that sat by the keyboard. "Fresh coffee for three, deck two surveillance conference room." He waited while the steward confirmed the instructions. "That's correct, thanks." He then looked at Charles. "What we have is all the evidence that has been collated from an address in Matagorda Bay. The address has been found to contain radioactive traces that have the same isotope signature as the material stolen by Gustav Axmann. What's more is this symbol." He pointed to the left hand display. "It was the symbol used by the Nazi party to signify the Fourth Reich and beneath it are the words *Ahnenerbe Institut,* and I think we know all about that place and what they did, thanks to Max and his earlier investigation. On the right," he pointed to the right hand display screen, "we can see the radioactive trace that Marge has sent in. Amazingly or not so amazingly, depending on whether or not you believe in coincidences, is that is we extrapolate, that line then clearly leads back into the general direction of Matagorda Bay." He made a few keystrokes. "These red dots show sounds picked up over the past twenty four hours by our sensors. They have been highlighted by the system because they are not the kind of sounds that the computers normally associates with or picks up in that region." Grant stopped as a steward entered and placed a silver tray on the table and commenced pouring the fresh coffee into three mugs and handing them round.

"Thank you very much. We will help ourselves to milk and sugar," Charles said to the steward who nodded and left. "Okay, what else have we got?"

"Well, firstly, before I start on new stuff. Again if we join the red dots they lead from Matagorda Bay up the East Coast. The sound is similar to that of an old style submarine, although at this point of the track just here." He highlighted a dot with a circle. "There was a larger different sound, similar to the sound of a small underwater earthquake, or something large hitting the ocean floor," Grant said before looking at Duke.

"Now, we also have the photo-fit of the person who completed the last two deliveries as the courier driver. We have identified him as one of Axmann's team from the data we copied from the Hawaiian office computers, and the name Albrecht was used by the old man who answered the door to the detective," Duke said. "At this stage we are the only people who know their identity."

"So the assumption is that Axmann and his cohorts were at the Matagorda Bay house and have left using a submarine along this track. But that track does not follow the radiation track that Marge found," Charles said, rubbing the back of his neck.

"Correct, but there is also a time difference of a few days between the two tracks," Grant said. "Which could be entry and exit tracks. We are not sure at this stage. The fact that both tracks can be extrapolated back to Matagorda sort of indicated that probability is highly likely."

"How is Marge doing?" Charles said, putting his coffee down.

"She picked up some samples of the radioactive water and passed them over to the US authorities, who have confirmed on examination that it traces back to the material stolen by Axmann," Grant said, looking at his notes. "She is now, along with *Mercury* and one of the American subs, trying to track the submarine while the other American forces try to track the ship that left the radioactive trace."

"How much of this does President Johnson know?" asked Charles.

"Quite a bit, but certainly not all, and they have not got the same amount of background data that we have to pull it all together," said Duke.

"Well, let's give them the full briefing and contact the British Prime Minister and brief him as well. Has Thomas come up with the source of the London bombing?"

"No, he is trying to track down some footage of the epicentre just before the explosion. His hunch is that it was a motor vehicle but so far all the potential sources he has identified were destroyed in the explosion. He is on his way to Southampton," said Grant. "He is also looking into any American satellites that may have been overhead at the time and has his team going through all ports of entry records searching for any single vehicle entry within twenty four hours of the explosions."

"Let's meet back here," said Charles, "in about three hours, with Max and a link to Marge, Keith and James. If we can hook Thomas in, then all the better. Duke, you'd better get onto those briefing calls. See you guys later."

Charles left the conference room and walked slowly along subtly lit corridors lined with windows and pictures. He passed the medical centre and gymnasium and stopped at the lift, where he pressed the button to the Sea View deck.

He left the lift and walked through the formal dining room into his sanctuary, the library, where he went to the bar, poured himself an Islay malt and sat down at his desk. He leant back in the chair and looked at the amber coloured liquid as he swirled the glass. A little early for a drink, but what the hell, he needed it. He took a sip and felt the liquid's warmth. He typed on the keypad that was recessed into the desk and a large display screen recessed into the wall at one end of the room came to life. He flicked through the TV channels until he came to the BBC world news. He watched for a few minutes, then changed to the superyachts music library and chose an Herb Alpert CD. He sipped his Islay malt, placed the glass on the desk and rose, walked over to the settee and lay down and closed his eyes. He let the music fill his mind so that he could quieten all the thoughts that were running through his over active brain.

Max entered the library. "Mind if I join you, boss, it's been a busy time," he asked.

"Sure grab a drink," Charles said. "Everything going okay?"

"Yes, the kids are settled in. Anne has been testing the communications system and chatting to the locals, making sure they are happy," Max said sitting on the settee. "I've been to see what Grant and Duke have done and they took me through it. It's good work."

"We have some decisions to make when Anne returns," Charles replied.

"I'll be flying in to pick her up any minute," Max said.

"You'd better call her before you leave and make sure she's ready to return," Charles said. "Otherwise you'll be hanging around for a while and that beauty up there could be a sitting target for any of the locals who don't take too kindly to our interventions."

Max dialled a number on his satellite phone and put it on speaker and heard a female voice answer over the speaker.

"Hello, Max. What can I do for you?" the voice was light and cheerful.

"Just calling to see if you're ready to be picked up," Max said into the handset.

"Eh, hold on a minute," Anne said. Muffled voices could be heard over the speaker but the voices were too indistinct to make out what was being said.

Max looked at Charles and shrugged his shoulder. "Women," he said.

"Max?" Anne's voice came over the speaker clearly. "Point

one, I heard that. Point two, yes, I am all finished here so you may come and pick me up."

"I will be leaving now," Max said and disconnected the call. "I'll have a talk to the team about getting satellite calls routed through our ship radios. Carrying the two is becoming a pain. We should be able to select a call on these." He touched the radio on his belt. "And the switching unit should connect the call to the computer and out through the ships communication system."

"It can and does already, if you read your briefing notes from Grant. That's why I only have the one radio," said Charles with a smile.

"So, how does it work?" Max asked.

"Simple, select extcall on the display, then either key in the number or select the name from the display and press connect. It is that easy. Now, go get Anne. I'm staying here. I've got some thinking to do and decisions to make."

"Right, boss, Max replied and walked to the other end of the library and out onto the helipad. Charles sat back, put his feet up, closed his eyes and tried to relax.

Charles was brought out of his reverie by a distant noise that grew louder by the second. His mind recognised the noise as that of the helicopter returning. He pulled himself up till his back was resting on the arm of the settee and watched through the thick glass wall as the helicopter slowly came into view, its undercarriage descending from its nose and belly as it crabbed sideways and descended onto the helideck. The noise lessened as the rotor blades slowed. He continued watching as two deck hands ran crouching to the undercarriage and hooked the helicopter to the deck restraints. He could see Max tapping screens, shutting the engine and electronics down before removing his helmet and opening the door and alighting the helicopter. He closed the door and walked to the large passenger door, which he slid open and helped Anne down. Anne looked tired and dirty after her time in the rain forest. Max helped her towards the glass wall and pressed a button that slid a thick heavy glass section sideways and escorted her into the library. Max walked back onto the helideck and closed the door which hissed as it sealed. He went over to the deck crew.

"After you have secured her, I want her refuelled and then give her a thorough clean, inside and out. There's some mud and a lot of dust in the passenger compartment." He walked to the nose. "And polish the windscreens, I hate looking through grime."

"Okay Max, leave it to us. I'll get one of the engine room technicians to give the engine a once over when she's cooled," said one of the deck crew.

Max patted him on the back. "Great idea, thanks." Max left them to it and went down the side gangway to the bridge, not wanting to disturb Charles or Anne. He found the bridge quiet with just Franklin the First Officer and Martin Deeks, the Technical Officer standing by the large navigation table screen.

"Hi guys, any news on the airdrop?"

"Hi, Max," said Martin turning around. "The pilot has radioed, and we are following his position on the screen."

"He will be dropping the load in around fifteen minutes. The rigid inflatable boat will be launched in five, if you want to tag along," Martin said.

"No, I will sit this one out. I've been back and forth all morning and it's time I had a late, very late lunch. Have you seen Duke?"

"He's with Grant and the Captain going over some of the data again," Martin replied. "I have a feeling that, after Sumatra, we will be steaming full ahead to the Atlantic."

"Right. I'll get some late lunch. See you later guys." Max left the bridge and took the stairs down to the main deck, where he hopped in the lift to the galley on deck three. He sat in the galley while the junior chef cooked him bacon and eggs on toast with a nice pot of tea. The phone rang and one of the stewards answered. "Yes, Mrs. Langham, fresh coffee and some fruit loaf. I will bring it up to the library now," the steward said and replaced the handset.

"Get it ready, and I'll take it up," Max said between mouthfuls. "I want to have a chat with them. I've nearly finished." He was sitting at the galley table, which was on the far side of the galley preparation area.

"Thanks, Max. It'll save me a trip. I still have to get the provisions ready for the Sumatra stopover," the steward said, grinding some coffee beans before adding them to the glass Bodum coffee filter jug. He then boiled some fresh water and let it cool for a short time before pouring it into the filter jug and fitting the plunger. He sliced two pieces of fruit loaf onto a plate, which he placed on a silver tray along with a cup and saucer and a mug. He added a jug of soy cream, a bowl of brown sugar and two teaspoons. He then added the coffee jug.

"Don't forget plates for the fruit loaf," Max said standing beside the steward looking at the tray before placing his plate, knife, fork and mug into one of the dishwashers.

"Eh, oh, yes, thanks." the steward said getting two side plates from a cupboard and placing them on the tray, re-arranging it carefully to look correct and balanced.

"That's okay, you owe me one now. Nice layout, looks neat," Max said cheerfully, picking up the tray and heading towards the service lift. He exited the lift and entered the formal dining room on the Sea View deck and walked through to the library and knocked before entering. He found the Langhams deep in conversation on the settee with Abbey curled at their feet.

"Ah, Max, grab yourself a mug and join us please," Anne said. "We are discussing Sumatra and the London incident." She grimaced as she mentioned London.

"Thank you," Max said, placing the tray on the low coffee table. "Do we need Duke, Miles and Ralph to join us?"

"That's not a bad idea. Yes, why not? I think you'll find them with Grant," Charles agreed.

Anne played mother while Max called the others and took two mugs from the bar and sat in one of the armchairs opposite the settee.

"So, what's on you minds?" he asked leaning forward, clasping his hands.

"Well, after Sumatra, which should take us, what two days at most? You have four airlifts in the Bell?" Charles asked, recalling that he had not seen the final schedule. He knew that it was the result of much discussion in his absence during the trip while he was under doctor's orders to rest. Normally he would have been shown the schedule for his final agreement, more a custom out of common courtesy than a requirement.

"Yes," said Max, "the scheduled first load is the new security equipment, so Miles and Ralph are on that trip. Mrs. Langham is on the second supply run with the new computers and cameras and the last two runs are veterinary and medical supplies. The doc is on one of those runs. Miles is staying overnight to complete the installations of his new equipment, and everyone else is coming back here overnight. The Captain has a re-fueller meeting us to top up the tanks. The following morning, I head back in with Anne and Ralph so they can finish off. The plan as it stands has everyone back here by lunchtime, all going well.

"I'm on the flight out with Anne. I want to see for myself how the team are doing and see the new cubs. So, anyway. Ah guys, come and sit down." Charles digressed as Duke, Miles and Ralph entered the library. "You are just in time. Any news on the photographs of Axmann and his son?"

"Yes, positive identification from the detective. We did not identify the names just asked him if those were the faces he saw," Duke advised.

"After the air drop is collected," Charles said, checking his watch, "which should be in the next ten minutes, I've told the Captain that we depart all speed to Sumatra. We are anchoring off the East Coast, which means we have a fifty kilometre helicopter ride to our reserve south of the Taman Nasional Berbak. Except for the compound, the ground is extremely damp, or should I say more like bog. We have extended the boardwalks but it is still not all complete. Insect repellent is, according to the doctor, a must. So nobody goes across without the right gear on and insect repellent applied. The area around the helipad has been cleared to allow for the extra size of the Osprey, so the Bell's rotors will be fine. But, Max, I want you to fly in high, hover over the helipad so we can ensure a safe landing and descend vertically down so as to avoid disturbing the big cats. As soon as we have everything finished in Taman, without taking any short cuts, we are going after Axmann and his next targets." Max and Duke sat back in their armchairs, coffee mugs in hand and looked at each other.

"Charles, may I ask why the sudden change of opinion?" Duke asked.

"We have six months before we are scheduled to collect Cathy and Chris. Anne and I have decided that we may as well use the time to some advantage and how better than to try and avert another disaster. The Captain has advised that there is a storm building on our route to the Atlantic, some six to seven metre swells. In the meantime, we have our submarines and *Launch One* in the area doing what we need done locally so we can carry on acting as co-ordination and research analysis until we arrive on site."

Chapter Seventeen

Somewhere Beneath the Atlantic

Albrecht quietly pulled aside the curtain that gave a level of privacy to the cabin Gustav was sleeping in. Albrecht gently shook his father by the shoulder.

"Sir, it's time to get up." He saw Gustav open his eyes. "The Captain says that we are nearing the drop position for the first weapon, and he needs to talk through in detail the second drop off." Albrecht took a step back as his father pulled the sheet back and slowly swung his legs over the edge of the bunk, his arms shaking slightly as he lifted himself into a sitting position. He was fully dressed and looked a bit brighter after his sleep.

"How long have I been asleep?" he asked before having a coughing fit and reaching for the metal mug and jug of water on the small side table. He lifted them over the small rails that stop them, sliding off the top of the side table. He poured a full mug of water and drank it down in just two gulps. He grimaced at the warm dusty metallic taste.

Albrecht checked his watch. "Around nine hours, sir. The Captain is in the control room."

"Bloody water is warm and full of dust. Okay, let's go," Gustav said, putting the mug and jug down, wiping his arm across his mouth and standing up grabbing for the hand rail. Albrecht extended his hand to help Gustav, who swept the hand aside.

"I do not need help. I am not disabled," Gustav snapped as he used his walking stick to move Albrecht out of the way as he barged passed. Albrecht let the curtain fall back and followed his father down the dingy cramped corridor to the busy but quiet control room.

"Ah, Mr, Axmann. We will be over the co-ordinates in exactly nine minutes," the Captain said, looking up from his navigation charts, which he was bent over examining with his navigation officer, who briefly returned to his electronic navigation screens.

"Has anyone checked the radio connection with the weapon?" Gustav asked.

"No sir," the Captain answered. "We cannot, because you have the controller."

Gustav placed his tattered brown leather satchel on top of the navigation chart, much to the disgust of the Captain, who knew better than to complain. Gustav undid the case straps and removed a small silver plastic box that had a small display and keypad on one face and two connection ports on one side.

"Power please, twelve volts." He removed a lead and plugged it into the box and passed the other end to the Captain.

The Captain dutifully plugged the lead into a connection on the nearest panel.

"Done," he said and watched as Gustav typed some commands into the box.

"Ah, I have a connection. Well done, Albrecht. This will work when we are well away as well, yes?"

"Yes sir. The unit in the weapon is powerful enough to connect at depth and distance. I fitted a seven hundred and fifty metre reel of ultra-thin trailing antenna wire with a floatation device on one end which will release automatically at five hundred metres," Albrecht said, walking over to his father. "That boosts the range to two thousand miles at this depth."

"I will program it just before we release it, just in case we cannot, for whatever reason, make contact again. Now, Captain, you wish to speak to me about the next location?" Gustav asked.

"Yes, sir. The St Lawrence Seaway will be very dangerous and we will stand a great chance of being seen and possibly captured. Our best course of action will be to move at night. I have double checked the charts and believe that the furthest I can get you up the St Lawrence River is to the first navigation lock, which is here at Saint Lambert. Unfortunately, that puts you on the Canadian side of the border. We can go no further. I will have to calculate tides very carefully, and we will need to move at night most of the time."

"Why can we not get to Lake Ontario, the river is navigable?" Gustav frowned.

The Captain looked horrified and answered, picking his words carefully, aware that Axmann was not at all happy. "I have looked very carefully to see if we could pass through the locks but, due to depths, hiding beneath another vessel and the way the water flows through the locks when they fill and empty will be too dangerous for us to even try and traverse them. To get through them unseen we would have to hide beneath another vessel. Tricky, but not impossible. We would have to guess their drafts correctly, and also the maximum drop in the height of water and the chances are high that we would be crushed. The inflow and outflow of water would batter us around and we would not be able to hold vertical or horizontal station. As I say, very difficult but most likely impossible. If I can get you close to Parc De Pionniers, which is here," he pointed to the map, "then you could transfer to a small surface vessel to take you all the way to Duluth."

Gustav stared at the map in silence, the index finger of his right hand running over his lips as he concentrated his mind, calculating distances and time. The fingers on his left hand ran long the map, tracing out the path pencilled in by the Captain, following each curve and straight. When he reached Gross-Ile, his hand stopped and his eyes alone traced an invisible line to his destination. The Captain was not getting him close enough. He had to get to the south of Lake Superior on the United States side of the border. Then it would be an overnight drive to his destination. Only he knew where that was; he had brought no one else into his confidence at this stage. He might send his son and heir Albrecht to a different location, for he did not think that he would survive this final attack.

"Right. We will do that." He took a pad and pen from his satchel and started writing numbers and doing calculations. When he finished, he turned to a new page and started again. He then checked the two pages and smiled; the final numbers were the same. He underlined the number and picked up the silver box and slowly typed the number on the keyboard, checking each number carefully before proceeding to the next. He checked the final number on the screen to what he had underlined on his pad. Satisfied he pressed the green enter key and waited for the confirmation bleep.

"Captain, are we over the location and what depth are we at and how deep is it below us?"

The Captain looked at the gauges on the hull wall. "We are exactly over your location and holding position. We have four hundred feet above us and one thousand three hundred beneath us."

"Release the weapon, set controlled descent by the wire to one thousand two hundred and ninety eight feet," Gustav commanded.

"Aye, sir," the Captain went to a small wall console that looked out of place to the rest of the submarines control systems. He dialled in a length of wire, accounting in his head for the height of the submarine. He lifted a red hinged cover and flicked the switch beneath.

"Weapon released. Descent rate is sixty feet per minute, drop duration twenty one minutes." On the outside of the submarine two hinged latches lifted up and the cylinder then held just by one length of wire started to lower. The spool of wire unwinding at a set rate under the weight of the weapon and friction brake in the spool. To avoid any undue issues the spool and release mechanisms were totally designed and built by Albrecht.

"Captain, when depth is reached, release the holding latch. Albrecht, contact our people, let them know our arrival time near Ile D'Orleans. Let them know that it will be just myself and a package. Tell them the size and weight. They will need to come by boat, a fast boat, say a fifteen metre cabin cruiser. They are to hire or buy one, destination Duluth. Divulge nothing else, no matter what they ask."

He turned to leave the control room.

"Captain, that weapon must land exactly at the co-ordinates

I have given. Keep control over the submarines movements and ensure that it does so. Let me know when the weapon is successfully placed and you have the exact co-ordinates checked and confirmed. I am going to lie down."

"Yes, father," replied Albrecht and left to see the radio operator in the next cabin.

"I will do as you advise, sir," replied the Captain, keeping his eye on the line feed readout. He lifted the hand mic from the clip to his left.

"Sonar, anything?"

"All clear. Just normal shipping at the extreme range of our sonar scans," replied the sonar operator over the speaker.

"Okay, be very vigilant. Keep a close watch. We are holding this position for the next thirty five minutes."

"Aye, sir. Sonar out."

The Captain walked across to the navigator. "Keep an eye on the weapons drop co-ordinates and keep us exactly over Axmann's drop location co-ordinates."

"Not easy with the currents that are running," the navigator said. "We will need to keep adjusting and account for the drag on the wire. So far the wire is two metres off plum."

"Keep on top of that location and account for the drag," the Captain said, tapping the navigator on the shoulder. "You have all the equipment you need to do so." The Captain returned to his seat and pressed a button by the microphone clip. "This is the Captain. We are silent running for the next forty minutes. Turn off all systems not required. No noise, no talking. Captain, out." He pressed the button and replaced the microphone and wiped the sweat from his forehead with the back of his hand. He could feel the submarine moving gently and knew the navigator and helmsman were making finite adjustments.

This was going to seem like a very long time. He lit a cigarette and could picture in his mind the cylinder on the end of the line being dragged by the currents at depth. He turned and looked at the spool readout. What was really down there that Axmann was so adamant about? Could there really be a power source left behind by a peoples who died out millennia ago?

"Captain, we are coming up on one hundred feet from the end of the spool and bang on target," the navigator called across the control room.

The Captain stood up and walked to stand in front of the spool counter and watched as the spool counter neared the reading of all zeros. "Spool at zero. What is the position if we release?"

"On target, Captain," the navigator replied.

The Captain flicked a cover up and pressed the release button, walked to his command chair and picked up his microphone and pressed a call button. "Sonar, confirm the position of the package to target."

"Sonar, Aye. The package is confirmed on target, Captain."

"Thank you, Sonar," the Captain replaced his microphone. "Lieutenant, release the spool unit. Navigator, commence new heading to the Saint Lawrence River. Make full revolutions. Periscope depth." He walked over to the periscope and waited until he was told that they had reached the right depth and he raised the periscope, snapped the handles down and scanned the surrounding ocean. He snapped the handles up and lowered the periscope. "Surface and charge the batteries," he ordered. "Open the forward deck hatch and let the crew get some fresh air. Lookouts to the tower. First sign of any vessel, we dive immediately."

He went to the radio room to find Albrecht and was told he had returned to his bunk to read. He wandered down the dark passageway and stopped at the bunk assigned to Albrecht. He slowly pulled back the curtain and saw Albrecht reading a book.

"Yes, Captain?" he inquired.

"We have successful placement and have commenced our new course. I thought you would like to tell your father yourself. We are heading for the surface to recharge the batteries and get some fresh air."

"Thank you, Captain," Albrecht said, slowly swinging his legs over the bunk and dropping down to the deck. "I will tell my father and get some fresh air myself."

"If we see another vessel we will crash dive, so be prepared," the Captain smiled and walked off down the gangway.

Albrecht followed the Captain, stopping off at his father's cabin. When he entered he found his father sitting up in his bunk, his forehead creased deep in thought.

"Yes, Albrecht, you bring me good news?"

"Yes, father, placement was successful. We are now heading to the Saint Lawrence Seaway. You can soon come on deck and get some fresh air."

"No, I will stay here. The dampness is causing me a lot of pain. Best I rest ready for our next operation. Can you get me a hot drink? Coffee, maybe? With lots of sugar and a dash or two of rum?"

"Yes, father. I'll be back soon."

Albrecht left and made his way to the galley where the chef

conjured up a hot coffee with four teaspoons of sugar and two large slugs of rum. He returned to his father, who sipped the coffee.

"Just what I needed. We have a long journey ahead of us and one can assume that the Americans and that troublesome Langham are onto us. They will be searching for us, you know. They will have found that we left by sea and will, undoubtedly, put two and two together and be searching for a submarine off the east coast."

"You really think so?" questioned Albrecht.

"Yes, I do. This Langham person is well equipped and has a smart team around him, and so is the new President and they have a lot of movement of naval vessels and submarines occurring at this moment. Searching for us no less, I would say. The Saint Lawrence will be dangerous, which is why I am having you dropped off early to make your way to my third target location."

"Why, we have no other weapons?" Albrecht asked in astonishment at the suggestion he would leave the submarine before his father.

Gustav spoke haltingly. "I need you to meet up with the others and return home. In my safe beneath my desk there is a small glass vial. Be very careful. Your task is simple. Empty that vial into the New York fresh water supply. You will not be able to fly with that vial. It would be too dangerous. Contact the freighter and get the Captain to change course to the Saint Lawrence River, and you will meet him in the estuary." He raised his right hand. "There will be no discussion on this matter. Now, go, get on the radio." Gustav handed the empty coffee mug to Albrecht. "I need to sleep." He waved Albrecht off with a gesture of his right hand, laid his head back and closed his eyes.

Albrecht closed the curtain and returned to the radio room. He sat next to the radio operator and placed the empty coffee mug on the table.

"Contact the freighter for me," he asked putting on a headset, "and then the F150 team."

"Okay, putting you through," the operator placed his headset on and spun the dial and spoke into the microphone, then gestured to Albrecht.

"Captain, this is Albrecht. You are to change course and proceed to the Saint Lawrence River and rendezvous with us. I am to board you there. We will radio exact co-ordinates later. Destination will be advised when I am on-board."

"Changing course now. Await your exact pick up co-ordinates," replied a voice over his headphones.

"Talk soon, Albrecht out." He removed his headset, picked up the coffee mug and stood. "Thank you." He took a piece of paper from his pocket and gave it to the radio operator. "Contact the F150 team and tell them to be at this location two weeks from today. They are to change vehicle on an urgent basis and destroy the F150 beyond recognition."

"Will do, Albrecht," replied the radio operator, who started to dial up the team as Albrecht left the little cabin and headed back to the galley, stumbling against the roll of the submarine as she ran on the surface. He entered the galley and refilled the mug with coffee, keeping it black and adding two heaped spoons of sugar. He headed for the conning tower and gingerly balancing the coffee mug headed up the ladder and joined the Captain in the salty fresh air.

"Change of plan. I hear," the Captain remarked.

"Yes. Looks like I am leaving before you take your trip down the Saint Lawrence River," Albrecht replied through sips of his steaming coffee. He shivered against the cold wind and salty spray. "Father has a back-up plan in case his primary plans fail."

"So worst case is two hits against the United States. Just hope I get the chance to get clear long before anything happens," the Captain said. He wanted to get back to Hawaii and to his girlfriend. It had been a long time since he had taken his forty five sports fisher out for a run and caught some game fish. She would need batteries charged, oil changes and a good clean. He kept in touch with Pat and she was eager for him to come home and get married. The thought made him smile. But first he had to accomplish his mission.

"I would suggest that as soon as you drop my father off, you get submerged and stay submerged for as long as you can. Don't forget that I, not my father, am the Fuhrer of the Fourth Reich, so he does not care what happens as long as he is aware that the two initial attacks are complete. He is ready to die. You, my friend, he will see as just collateral damage," Albrecht said, quietly but firmly. "I, he will protect at all costs."

"Advice taken and understood," the Captain said with a sideway glance. "This whole crew including myself are looking forward to returning home. I doubt any of them has a death wish."

"I would keep that to yourself whilst my father is on-board, or he will have you shot." Albrecht turned and leant on the tower surround. "I'm serious. He has always been immersed in the Reich and has spent his whole life, his very existence, in fact, on seeing the rise of the Fourth Reich, which he sees as his legacy. But recently he has changed. He's become more evangelical, more fanatical if you like, about completing his revenge for the death of his Fuhrer Hitler on England and America, and he does not care how many die in his cause." He turned and faced forward into the breeze. "How long will we remain on the surface?"

"Another thirty minutes or so to charge the batteries and give the whole crew a rotation on deck for some fresh air," the Captain said. "Unless we see a surface target first."

"I'm going to see if I can get my father on deck. He could do with some fresh air." Albrecht made his way to the conning tower hatch and climbed down the ladder into the control room and carefully made his way down the corridor, holding the rails against the rocking motion of the submarine as it rolled against the motion of the waves. He pulled back the curtain to find his father lying on his side in the bunk, tucked up tightly under a blanket in a deep sleep. He decided to leave him. There would be other opportunities to get him on deck during the long slow run up the American east coast. He saw a notebook on the small side table in front of the water jug and picked it up, keeping an eye on his father. He silently leafed through the book. Inside he saw that his father had been keeping a daily record since they had left Brazil. Not what he had hoped for. He had hoped that he would find some evidence of where the third bomb was to be sited and what was in the glass vial. But there was nothing. He carefully placed the notebook back exactly where he found it and quietly left the cabin and returned to his own bunk to think. Just as he lay down he heard the klaxon sound loudly.

"Dive, Dive, Dive, Emergency Dive, Run RED!"

The Captain's voice came loud over the speakers. He heard

running feet and felt the submarine alter its attitude, his bunk tilting down slightly. He closed his eyes to rest but decided to get up and go to the control room, where the atmosphere was a buzz of activity. He went over to the Captain, who looked at him.

"Not now, I have an urgent situation to deal with." He walked past Albrecht. "Dive Officer, make depth six hundred and fifty feet, twenty five degrees down bubble."

"Aye, Captain, make depth six hundred and fifty feet, twenty five degrees down bubble," the dive officer confirmed

"Captain, we have active pinging from at least two vessels, range five thousand and closing," the sonar operator's voice came over the speaker.

The Captain unhooked his microphone. "Sonar, keep me informed every thousand change." He clipped the microphone back in position. "Dive Officer, depth please?"

"Six hundred and twenty, Captain," replied the Dive Officer. "Levelling out at six hundred and fifty."

The Captain unhooked the microphone again and flicked a switch to speaker.

"Cut engines, silent running," his voice boomed around the submarine. "Sonar, keep watch, report changes in person." He flicked the switch back, replaced the microphone and turned to Albrecht as the submarine levelled off. "We have two American vessels in our vicinity. They must have seen us on the surface and are now actively pinging, sorry, searching for us. I have no doubt they will have a submarine search aircraft overhead very soon that will drop a sonar torpedo to search for us as well. So for now we stay still, here at six hundred fifty feet, our maximum depth and as silent as a mouse. There will be no talking, no movement until the sonar gives us the all clear." He shrugged his shoulders. "You had better inform your father."

"He was asleep when I left him. I'd better wake him up and let him know," Albrecht said.

"Walk softly please and make sure he does not wake with a start and make any noise."

The Captain saw the sonar operator walking slowly towards him.

"Captain, both vessels are still heading straight for us, and actively pinging. I've looked at some of our monitoring information and I believe that there is a thermocline at eight hundred feet, which will make us much more difficult to detect if we can sit within it."

The Captain rubbed his jaw and thought for a moment.

"Okay, let's hope the old girl can take the increase in pressure. Dive Officer, make eight hundred, forward five knots. Ten degrees down bubble." Everyone in the control room looked at the Captain questioningly.

The Dive Officer replied, his voice quiet and hesitant. "Make eight hundred, forward five knots. Ten degrees down bubble. Aye, Captain."

The tension around the submarine increased as the submarine creaked and groaned as she exceeded her normal operational depth. All eyes were on the depth gauge as the needle slowly moved around the dial towards the red line at nine hundred but stopped at the eight hundred foot mark. As the needle hit eight hundred and stopped the sigh of relief was discernible throughout the submarine.

"Eight hundred feet, Captain," the Dive Officer confirmed.

"Thank you, engines to zero revolutions, all stop, silent

running," the Captain said. "Sonar, back to your station, check and report please."

Albrecht walked softly and carefully to his father's cabin, quietly pulling back the curtain and saw his father still asleep. He went over to the bunk and sat on the edge and gently shook his father's shoulder.

"Father, wake up, please." He noted Gustav's eyes open. "Father, don't speak, just listen." He put a finger to his lips as his father sat up slightly and rested on one elbow. "We are being searched for by some American naval vessels. We are hiding in a thermocline, whatever that is, and running silent to avoid their sonar. So we must stay very quiet and not move."

"Okay, I am tired. I'll stay here and rest. Wake me when all is clear."

"Okay, father. I think that's best." Albrecht got up and left his father's cabin and quietly returned to his own bunk and lay down, suddenly feeling extremely tired. He fell asleep almost instantly.

In the control room the atmosphere was tense and the Captain wiped away a bead of sweat from his brow. The red glow from the lamps gave the submarine an eerie feel. Without any machinery running, the air was getting staler.

"They are both just one thousand feet away and still actively pinging," the sonar operator appeared and whispered in the Captain's ear and quietly returned to his post without waiting for an answer. The Captain looked over at the depth gauge, which sat at eight hundred. He looked around the control room, where everyone either stood like a statue or sat dead still. No one dared move or speak. Seconds passed like minutes, minutes like hours.

"They are right overhead, still actively pinging," the sonar operator whispered. "I don't think they can find us. The thermocline is masking our position."

"Okay, go back and tell me when I can move and decrease our depth. I have no idea how long she can stand this pressure on her hull."

"Okay, Captain." The sonar operator smiled and returned to his headphone and screen.

Chapter Eighteen

Marge's News

Grant sat listening to Marge through his headset in the subdued atmosphere of the surveillance room on board *Sundancer*. Two of his colleagues were on the other side of the room in front of an array of large screens and typing away at their keyboards. Jake, tall, slim, with masses of long black hair was continuing his analysis of the data copied from the Hawaiian office search. The other, a small tubby and notoriously neat guy called Bruce was still trying to break the password of the last remaining file folder; it was becoming a personal challenge to him while listening to Led Zeppelin through his headphones and lip synching silently to the lyrics.

"Marge, on that basis I will call you back when I have rounded up the others. Talk soon." He removed his headset and placed it on the console and walked over to Jake, who was typing search algorithms into the computer. "Jake, I'm going to find Mr. Langham. I'll be about half an hour or so."

"Okay. We've got enough here to keep us busy for a while," Jake replied, spinning on his chair. "Take your radio in case I need to get hold of you."

"It's always on my belt," Grant said, and tapped his radio as he left the cabin.

He found Charles Langham in the library, curtains drawn, lighting dimmed and the aroma of fresh coffee filling the air. Charles was sitting at one of the desks and looking at some satellite images on the large screen with Anne, Duke, Max, Miles and Ralph all sitting on one of the two settee suites around a low coffee table. The images were of the Sumatra reserve which showed very clearly the before and after effects of their conservation efforts.

"Look over here, that's a new area of deforestation and it is very close to our operation." Charles highlighted the area using the mouse pad on the desk. He thought for a moment then looked over at Duke. "Duke, I want you to organise the purchase of that land. Make a note of the co-ordinates and find the owner. If needs be, contact the local authorities and find out who owns it and how we can contact them." He looked back at the images and using the mouse pad highlighted another area. "And buy this tract of land as well. From these images, I would hazard a guess that it is being illegally logged. If we can buy that land it will provide a nice kilometre and a half wide connecting corridor to our existing reservation. We'll need to extend the fencing around those areas and join them to the existing fencing. Where the new areas border the sea, here and here, we will need to extend the fencing into the sea. How far out we will need to confirm with our experts."

"Sure thing, Charles. I know just who to contact. He owes me a favour." Duke smiled.

"Looks like the reports are right and all the buildings are up, including the hangar and track for the chopper and Osprey storage travel rigs. The village school is up and I assume this here, is the new fencing around the compound," Charles said running the mouse along a line.

"I think so," Anne confirmed hesitantly, looking at a sheet of paper. "This report, which is the latest, talks about the tiger fence being completed around the compound and sanctuary headquarters." She looked up. "Ah Grant, come in and sit down. We're reviewing your latest satellite images with the ones from last year."

"I'm sorry to interrupt but I have some urgent information from Marge that I think you will all want to hear. If I may, I will connect back with Marge from here and she can tell you first-hand what they have found."

"Go ahead, Grant. We can get back to this Sumatra discussion later," Charles said.

Grant went over to the desk that was close to Max, who was seated in an armchair next to the settee where Duke, Ryan and Anne were seated. He typed in some commands on the inlaid keyboard and soon had Marge appear on the large screen on the library wall. Charles shifted his armchair back from his desk and turned it slightly so he could stretch his legs.

"Marge, I am here with the team now. Can you tell them what you told me earlier?"

"Sure thing. Hi, everyone." Marge waved both hands. "We have had a sighting of a submarine running on the surface. It was based on the design of a German World War Two model with an upgraded conning tower. Two US Navy vessels both captured some video and watched as it crash dived. They have been tracking it through sonar but lost it in a thermocline. They contacted us and we closed in on its last known position. Now, the interesting thing is that the location is not far from the location identified by Max as the possible target location." She smiled. "I know, I know, but before anyone else says it, I found it truly amazing. So, we intend to leave the search for the submarine and head for the co-ordinate that Max identified just to check and be on the safe side. We will leave the submarine hunt to the United States Navy, who have a dedicated submarine hunter steaming this way at flank speed."

"Both you and *Mercury*?" asked Charles leaning back in his armchair.

"Yes, *Mercury* is actually on the far side of the search circle and will move in from that direction and should bisect with us near enough in the centre of the search area identified by Max."

"And what are your intentions for *Launch One*?" he asked.

"She's staying with the American forces on the submarine hunt. Anyway, she's much further to the North than us and would take way too long to get here to be of any use."

"Sounds sensible. But I would still have *Launch One* get underway to your location. If you are right, you may need the submersible. Have you seen the footage of the submarine?"

"I'll bring it up." Grant said and typed on the keypad. They watched as the image of Marge became a smaller window on the screen and a new window opened showing clearly a submarine with no markings running on the surface before diving below the waves. "That's all we have. But we can identify it as a U-boat of the type VIIC/41."

"A U-Boat from World War Two! Are you sure?" Ryan queried.

"Yes, we have a positive ID. The only changes are to the conning tower and dive planes," Grant said moving the mouse pointer across the screen to highlight the changes. "Which, I believe, is to house up to date electronics packages. Bearing in mind the technological advances made since it was built."

"And we do know that Axmann has at least one submarine in his possession," Max commented. "Marge, do you have the remote camera with you on *Jupiter*?"

Grant removed the submarine window and Marge once more filled the screen.

"Yes, we do. If we get a sea bed contact we can capture still images and video," Marge confirmed.

"Marge, what direction was the submarine heading?" Charles asked, rubbing the back of his neck with both hands, a habit when he had an idea forming in his mind.

"North, north west, as far as we could tell. Difficult to be certain, I have to say, but that is the best that we could calculate," Marge said.

"So," Charles continued, "if Axmann is on-board that submarine and he maintains his current track, then he is heading towards the north east coast of the United States, Canada or Greenland. My guess would be the United States. Marge, Grant, I have an idea. I want you to plot the position where the submarine was originally sighted. Work out her rough speed from the video footage and extrapolate her course. You can then calculate an intercept course and location for *Launch One* to head to. If we can get *Launch One* to that intercept location at full speed, then she can sit quietly and keep her sonar searching passively for a contact. Let's see if we can head him off at the pass. Grant, tell me, if we fire an electromagnetic pulse at the submarine, will it disable or ignite a nuclear weapon if one was on-board?"

"Man, I don't know. I would have to check with Keith," Grant said.

"Okay, well find out. For the plan to work we have some issues to resolve. If we disable the submarine but the warhead is protected from the electromagnetic pulse, then they could fire it at any time. If we disable the submarine but the electromagnetic pulse ignites the weapon, then both ways we lose. So we need to ensure that, if we fire the electromagnetic pulse, it disables the weapon. Otherwise we will have to leave well alone. We need to know from the Americans the effect of an electromagnetic pulse blast on their weapon design."

"I'll get onto Clive Harris, the Defence Chief. He'll find out pretty darn quick under the circumstance," Ryan said, getting up and walking over to a desk where he sat down, picked up a handset and dialled a number.

"What about the current search?" Marge asked.

"Leave that to the Americans. *Launch One* can use her electromagnetic pulse device if they get a confirmed contact, and if it's safe to do so. The submarine will have to surface once its electronics are disabled or they will asphyxiate."

"Understood, Charles. We will get onto it now," Marge confirmed.

"Okay, keep Grant informed of progress. Take care, Marge. Bye for now," Charles said and indicated to Grant to end the call. "Okay, back to the Sumatra images, please, Grant." Grant typed on the keypad and the screen changed back to show the two satellite images of the Sumatra reserve.

"Now, as I was saying, Duke, arrange the purchase of those two areas as soon as we can so we can commence reforestation and link the new area to our existing reserve giving the animals a safe corridor." He looked at Duke, who was writing down the co-ordinates. "You can come with us if you like. But, as I've said, it is a very boggy, the humidity is murderous and you will need to use insect repellent."

"Love it," said Duke. "Never been in the real forest, just the outskirts near the city."

"Ralph will take care of you. He's been there before."

"That's good to know," Duke replied "Is it that dangerous?"

"Tigers can be pretty dangerous. Don't worry, we only use darts, not bullets on the wildlife, but there are people who do not like what we are doing, so we take precautions and use live ammo for them," Ralph said.

"Miles, are you still planning on staying overnight to install some of the new equipment?" Charles questioned.

"Yes, it's too much to do in two days if something goes wrong so I would prefer to err on the side of safety and work late on the first day and buy some time, just in case," Miles explained.

"Okay, Miles, you can stay overnight but have one of your team stay with you."

"I'll stay," Ralph volunteered. "I know the equipment as well as Miles and could be of some help."

"Good call. Now, Grant, where is that airdrop?" Charles asked, turning in his seat to look over at Grant, who typed on his keypad and looked at the screen on the desk.

"My status screen shows that the boat has been launched," Grant said.

"Are we ready in the laboratory to receive it?" Charles questioned.

"Lab status is green and the doctor has doubled check the

approval checklists," Grant said. "The technicians have tested the mass spectrometer and it is ready."

Ryan replaced the handset. "Harris is not sure. He will contact his people at the Nevada nuclear weapons facility and find out. So we wait, I'm afraid," Ryan said.

"That's fine," said Charles, "we still go ahead as planned. We have just over three days sailing before we reach Sumatra and plans to make before we arrive. The facility should be up and running and this is Anne's and my first look since we purchased the land and sent our crew in to get the boundary fences built and all the building work complete. Our man on the ground, Norman Stafford, has been overseeing it all and has had a lot on his plate conversing with the local people and local government officials. The crew under him plus all the experts in their field, geologists, naturalists, veterinary surgeons, architects, the build crew, electricians, communications and IT experts, so he has had his hands full balancing a lot of egos, as you can imagine. Now, I need him elsewhere to work on a new project that Keith and Anne have identified."

"Do you have the manpower do take on another project?" Duke asked.

Grant, Miles and Ralph sniggered at the question and Duke sat up and looked at them and then over to Charles.

"Yes, Norman takes his entire team with him. Cathy will take over and promote those locals who have been training during the build process and train others to fill other roles. We have a new veterinary surgeon, of course, to look after the wildlife and she is already on site taking over from our roving vet."

Duke laughed loudly. "I am so pleased I joined your team. It is so much more relaxing than being a Senator!"

"No pressure, Duke, but Norman will not leave until he has designed and commissioned the fencing around the new areas that you have yet to purchase and he does not like hold up,." Charles said with a grin on his face.

"Oh great," replied Duke. "So how long have I got?"

Charles thought for a moment. "I would say around seven days, starting now," Charles replied.

Duke looked around the library. "When does he have to leave?"

"He was scheduled to leave five days after Cathy arrives from Borneo. But it will take him two to three days to survey the new fence area. Say another four to five days to agree the architects design and the building crews plan. Then order the materials in from our supplier and agree who will stay to oversee the build crew and who will make up the build crew. In the meantime, Ralph will be planning the safety and security of the build crew. So, I would say that within five days of landing we need to have secured the land."

"Okay, I'll start in the morning," he answered checking his watch. "There will be nobody around at this time."

"We are on the move," Max said, feeling the small forward movement and increased background hum of the engines.

"It is such a wonderful night I think we will have dinner on the aft deck," Anne said, picking up a handset from the table and pressed a key and spoke to the chef. "Chef, barbecue dinner on the aft deck tonight. Oh, say in an hour." She replaced the handset. "I've organised dinner on the aft deck. A relaxing barbecue under the stars at seven tonight, casual dress as usual," she advised everyone and the curtains opened and the lights became brighter and Charles turned the screen off. Max stood up followed by the others. Duke and Ryan stood in conversation while Ralph and Miles went over to Charles.

"We're going to call Norman and get the latest security information on the new proposed areas," said Duke and then called over to Grant. "Grant, can you join in? We may need some surveillance work."

"Sure," Grant replied and followed then out of the library.

"Charles, I'm going to nip down and make sure the rigid inflatable boat has been cleaned and check of the isotope protocols," Max said.

"Make sure the Bell is fully fuelled while you at it please," Charles said and watched Max leave followed by Duke and Ryan. Only he and Anne were left in the library. "I think I will have a small drink," he said walking over to the bar. "What can I get you?"

"An Islay Malt would go down nicely," Anne replied. Charles poured two double measures and sat beside her on the settee. "Cheers," he said. "Here's to the quietness of the next three days."

Chapter Nineteen

Action to Marge's News

President Johnson was sitting in the Oval office talking with Clive Harris, the Defence Chief and his Presidential Military, Advisor Stephen Anderson, when he noted the incoming video call from Ryan.

"Hold it, I've got a call coming in from Ryan, who is with Charles Langham on his yacht *Sundancer.*" President Johnson pressed the accept button on his screen. "Hello, Ryan, good to hear from you. I've got Clive and Stephen with me."

"Hi, Mr. President, Hello, Clive, Stephen." He could see Clive and Stephen in the background. "Well, I have some news on the isotope," Ryan said looking at the face of President Johnson on the large video screen on the conference suite wall that was situated next to the surveillance room. Grant had set him up there for his calls so he would be easily and quickly accessible should Ryan need him. "The isotope sample supplied by Thomas from the London blast is, I regret a match to the isotope data supplied from Nevada. And to cap it, all the data supplied from the sample of radiated water from the Atlantic matches as well."

Ryan looked up at the screen into the eyes of a very concerned American President before he continued.

"We are waiting for the isotope data from Matagorda Bay, which I am ninety nine percent sure will also be a match. I feel deep down that all this links back to Gustav Axmann. You are aware that the radiated water in the Atlantic has been traced back to Matagorda Bay, where a house and workshop have been found to have radioactive traces?"

President Johnson looked drawn and spoke slowly and clearly. "I have heard about the radiation found in Matagorda Bay, the area around the house is now in lockdown." He paused. "It is essential that any news of a link, however firm or tenuous to the Nevada nuclear facility, is kept confidential until I have personally spoken to the United Kingdom Prime Minister and explained the manner in which this has all occurred."

President Johnson then spoke firmly and quietly. "A local detective who was involved in Matagorda Bay was spoken to by the CBRN team leader who believes the detective will ignore his directions and continue investigating the missing courier driver. What a mess." He, then, sighed. "This morning I sent Michael Ricchetti, my Executive for National Security Affairs, to personally talk to him." The President took a drink from his china coffee cup and placed the cup carefully back on its saucer. "If we need to, we will arrest him and anyone else who refuses to keep quiet. It is absolutely essential that information about the Nevada thefts and the likelihood that other weapons exist is kept to a minimum. I do not want a panicked nation on my hands. Who else knows?"

"We have kept it very tight to our chests. The only people who are aware of this are those on board *Sundancer,* who you know and trust. The technicians who carried out the test are full time crew members on *Sundancer,* so we can trust them."

"The boffins have advised against any electromagnetic pulse blast near the weapon, by the way. They calculate that there is a chance it could detonate. Where are you now?" the President asked.

"We are currently at sea, one day out of Sumatra," Ryan replied.

"Have you heard from Thomas?"

"Yes, I spoke to him yesterday. He took a helicopter ride to Cardiff and reviewed some information, camera data, I think it was, but then they took off in a hurry to Southampton, all care of the Royal Air Force. He and his team were tracking the movements of a Toyota Prius through London and motorway traffic cameras records held in Cardiff. Thomas took a hunch and started his team looking through records of car shipments through the Port of Southampton and happened on a white Toyota Prius imported from the United States. When they spoke to the freight forwarders representative he told them that he recalled the car easily as the whole collection process was very cloak and dagger, James Bond like with code words and numbers. He went through the file with Thomas and what Thomas saw was extremely revealing. Thomas left with copies of the entire file, which included a copy of the collector's passport and export agents name and address in the States." Ryan took a breath and a drink from his coffee mug. "The address of the man who collected the car was flattened in the blast, so Thomas has split his team into two with some of them researching for relatives while he is trying to arrange a fast plane to New York docks for the rest of the team out of the Mildenhall airbase."

"I see," the President said. "Do we have a name for the exporter?"

"Yes, sir, we do, but I believe you will concur that it is totally fictitious from the sounds of it. GAUK.S.A, based in Brazil. I personally think it blatantly stands for Gustav Axmann, United Kingdom" Ryan said. "Thomas wants to investigate the freight forwarder in New York, see what they know, and trace the origins of any payments made."

"Thomas knows what he's doing. You are aware of what is happening in the Atlantic, I assume?"

"We're concerned that the two submarines you had in the search area have left on some wild goose chase," Clive Harris said curtly.

"Looking for some mysterious Atlantis relic," Stephen Anderson added.

Ryan sighed deeply and spoke with a hint of exasperation to his voice.

"In fact, Mr President, gentlemen, they believe that Gustav Axmann has used his submarine to drop a nuclear weapon at what he believes to be the centre of Atlantis, beneath which lies a cave where he believes there is some great unique power. Now, whether or not that is true, a nuclear weapon blast in that location would cause massive damage to the eastern seaboard and Western Europe. The location is the important part of equation and comes from detailed maps and information gathered in Hawaii. I have personally been involved in examining the material with Max and Grant. In the area are three Asphalt volcanoes in close proximity to each other. A nuclear explosion near those three would be unthinkable! I am just about to contact Marge, and Charles's Operations Manager, Keith Pritchard, to find out the very latest information on the two searches. Thomas told me he would be in contact with you as soon as he arrives back in the States. I will keep you informed of any updates, Mr. President."

"Ryan, hold on. You're telling me that you believe a nuclear weapon has been planted on the Atlantic seafloor near three volcanoes and you have been searching for it for days without notifying me or my staff?" There was anger in the President's raised voice and he continued. "Hold on a minute, Ryan. Is this the same weapon that you asked the electromagnetic pulse information about?"

"Let's not get into a slanging match, Ok? The answer is no, this is another weapon. We believe he still has one with him on the submarine. Mr. President, until we locate the weapon, which will be some fifteen hundred feet deep, there is nothing you or your military can do. We, sorry, I mean Mr. Langham's operation has the two best submarines fitted with the latest technology available to locate the possible weapon. Once located they will film the weapon and we can take it from there," Ryan said in a calming voice. "Unless, of course, we need Langham's deep ocean submersible, which is already in the Atlantic and on its way to the probable location."

"Thank you, Ryan. But I would appreciate not being kept in the dark in future. Talk to you soon."

Ryan disconnected the call and stood up, stretched. "Bloody politics!' he said out loud and left the conference suite and entered the surveillance room next door and walked over to Grant.

"Grant, can you connect me with Marge and Keith now please?" Ryan asked.

"No worries," Grant said and followed Ryan back into the conference room. Grant sat at the conference table and pulled the wireless keyboard closer and touch typed while looking at the screen. "Won't take long. I get Keith first, then Marge. Save Marge hanging around too long." After a few seconds the face of James appeared on the screen. "Hi, James, is Keith around?"

"He's sleeping. It's been an excruciatingly long day for him. Anything I can help with? I'm up to date with everything Keith was working on," James replied.

Ryan nodded to Grant happy that James was available.

"Okay, hang on a second while I add Marge to the conference call with Ryan," Grant said typing away.

Ryan refreshed his coffee from the bar area. "Grant, can I get you a coffee?" Ryan asked.

"Yes, please, white two sugars," Grant said. "Marge, good to see you," he said when Marge appeared on the left side of the screen. "Can you see me and James?" he asked.

"Hi, Grant, hi, James. Yes, I can see everyone. Hey, Ryan, how are you?" she asked as Ryan sat down in one of the cherry wood conference table chairs beside Grant and handed him his coffee.

"I'm fine. I have some news to tell you and wanted to see if you guys had any further news," Ryan said.

"I'll leave you guys to it," Grant said diplomatically standing up and leaving the conference suite with his coffee. He closed the door as he left to give Ryan some privacy.

"James, Marge, the news that we have on *Sundancer* and that I have just told President Johnson is that the isotope readings from the London device and the Atlantic sample information you sent us Marge are a match to the Nevada material," Ryan explained quietly. He saw the change in facial expressions of Marge and James. "A shock, but I think it is what we were all expecting."

"I agree, but the confirmation still comes as a shock," Marge agreed. "What about Matagorda Bay?"

"We are still waiting for the data to see if there is a match, but I think we know the answer to that one already," Ryan replied. "The President is angry that we did not tell him what we knew about the weapon we believe Axmann dropped on the seafloor."

"We told his Admiral of the Fleet, so he should get his facts right before throwing any accusations about. How is Thomas coming along?" Marge asked.

"He's tracked the bomb vehicle back to the United States," Ryan said. "He is on his way to Mildenhall to fly to New York with some of his team. The others are staying in the UK to try and attempt to trace relatives of the bomber. Where are you currently, Marge?"

"Oh, I'm in my cabin on-board *Jupiter*, hundreds of metres below the Atlantic searching for that bomb that we believe Axmann has dropped at the location identified by him to be the centre of Atlantis," she said her face surrounded by the grey metal of her cabin.

"Max's old hobby horse," Ryan commented with a grin. "You really think he has dropped a bomb? Any evidence of that?"

"It really is conjecture on our part. The submarine we saw that was running on the surface was in the distinct area highlighted on those old maps," Marge said. "We are searching the area from the north and *Mercury* is coming in from the south. We intersect each other in approximately twenty six hours from now."

"Who is tracking the submarine?" Ryan asked

"The United States Navy and *Launch One*," James butted in. "Plus, our sonar array."

"Okay, but I had heard they that had lost contact," Ryan said.

"That was true. They lost contact when it took cover in a thermocline. We picked it up on our sonar array triangulating with sonar from an American submarine. *Launch One* was on its way to the position we calculated as suggested by Charles and picked it up. She is tracking the submarine from a distance at the extreme range of her sonar. Looks like the submarine is heading towards Greenland," James explained.

"Ryan, any news on the effects of an electromagnetic pulse on the weapon?" Marge asked.

"That's a no go, I'm afraid. The boffins have told the President that it could detonate the weapon."

"I just cannot see how it would," James said thoughtfully. "I think they are being very over cautious and covering their arses, just in case."

"That maybe so, but we now have our orders," Ryan said.

"I accept that," James advised sternly. "But I still think they are being weak minded and increasing the ultimate risk."

"Marge, James, if there is nothing else?" Ryan said questioningly.

"Not from me," said Marge. "I should really get back to the sonar room."

"I think we have a track on the freighter. *Launch One* has detected a vessel running without its transponder on, north east of their current position. Once they are in camera range they'll send me an image for verification," James said. "Other than that it's now a waiting game."

"Okay, you two, I'll let you go, Bye, for now." Ryan pressed the red button and the call ended. He leant back in the chair. "Oh, boy!" he said out loud. He picked up his coffee mug and took a long drink, wishing he was back in Washington in the thick of the action. Being on *Sundancer* had its advantages though: the flow of information, the intelligence gathering was staggering; but, as with everything, the advantages brought with them disadvantages: the lack of face to face contact, not being at the coal face, so to speak. Although on balance the advantages outweighed the disadvantages, and he was better off and more effective on *Sundancer*. He walked next door into the intense atmosphere of the surveillance room and found Grant again.

"I'm finished in there now. Thanks for the help in setting up the calls," he said, patting Grant on the shoulder, who removed his headset. "Do I need to call anyone to get the coffee pot taken away?"

"I'm sure Jake and Bruce will finish the coffee. They drink gallons of the stuff. Hey, guys, there is coffee up for grabs in the conference suite," he called over his shoulder.

"On to it," replied Jake pushing his chair back and heading for the coffee.

"Look, I will probably want to make a few calls tomorrow after we anchor off Sumatra," Ryan said.

"That's fine. If I'm not here there is always someone in the surveillance room twenty four hours a day who can connect you," Grant replied.

"Thanks again, Grant. Do you know the whereabouts of the Langhams?"

"Relaxing on the aft deck lounge area I should think," Grant answered.

"Thanks, catch you later," Ryan said walking from the surveillance room down the plush corridor to the main lift.

"Pour me a mug as well please," Grant said to Jake as he sat back at his console and surveyed the key word search analysis from his data feeds. He personally wrote the coding that the computer system at the Kermadec headquarters used to search computer systems worldwide, including satellite feeds and government systems. An activity that they kept very quiet about. A high speed communication feed protected by a secure encryption code that Jake had devised allowed constant satellite connections between the Kermadec headquarters and all aircraft, submarines and locations worldwide. The system effectively gave the power of the headquarters computer system to all locations. For Grant it meant he could seamlessly use the power of the Kermadec computer while he was sat in the surveillance room on *Sundancer* as though he were in the Kermadec base.

"Hey, guys, we had better pool our resources together, someone is searching the Langham name and this vessel's name!" Grant exclaimed spinning his chair round to face Bruce and Jake. "Wake the others and get Miles and Ralph down here. I'll tell Mr. Langham." Grant put his headset back on and called Charles on his radio. "Mr. Langham, we have a situation. Our key word search has picked up the words Langham and *Sundancer*. Someone is doing research on you and this superyacht."

Charles picked up his radio and listened to Grant with grave concern.

"Well, we know they won't find much. Continue your investigation. Link in with James and find out where they originate from and who it is that's doing the search and keep me advised," Charles answered and turned his radio off and placed it back on the table between the two loungers that Anne and he were lying on. He lay back down and relaxed in the knowledge that they were in safe hands.

Chapter Twenty

Sumatra

Charles was on the bridge sitting in the Captain's chair as they closed in on their anchorage point just off the east coast of Sumatra, in the lee of Bangka Belitung Islands to the south and Pulau Singkep to the north. To their east was a small cluster of coral islands. The sea was calm, with just the occasional white cap and a few fluffy white clouds skipped across the blue sky. It was not that unusual for Charles to take command of the bridge; it was something that he enjoyed and, although he owned the superyacht, he always asked the Captain for permission, It was after all, *his* bridge. The bridge stretched the width of the *Sundancer* with external wings on either for close quarter manoeuvring. Charles sat in the centre in the slightly raised Captains chair, which gave commanding views out of the two hundred and seventy degree windows. At his finger -tips was a large display screen from which, at a touch of the screen, he could call up all the navigation, radar and superyachts systems. On the port side of the bridge sat Martin Deeks, the Technical Officer, who controlled all the superyachts electrical, hydraulic and life support systems and was in overall charge of managing the four engines. Franklin sat front and centre on the bridge surrounded by all the helm controls, autopilot and navigation displays and controlled the ships movements. The co-ordination between Deeks and Franklin was seamless.

"Reduce speed to twelve knots please, Mr Franklin," Charles called.

"Aye, Captain. Current speed twenty six knots, reducing to twelve knots," Franklin said, placing his hands across the throttle levers and easing then back towards him.

Charles looked at the navigation screen. "Steer five degrees to port," he said.

"Five degrees to port, Captain."

Charles watched the navigation screen as they closed in on their chosen anchorage spot. "Reduce speed five knots. Advise when reached," Charles called.

"Current speed twelve knots, reducing to five knots, aye, Captain," Franklin confirmed and carefully watched their speed as it slowly reduced. After a short while he called out, "Five knots, Captain."

"Bring her to a stop please, Mr. Franklin," Charles ordered the First Officer as they reached the GPS point highlighted on the screen.

"Aye, Captain, bringing *Sundancer* to a complete stop."

Charles could feel the slight reverse thrust as he watched Franklin pull the four throttle leavers into neutral, and then smoothly back into reverse. After a few seconds he pushed them back into neutral, all the while concentrating on his GPS navigation screen that showed his speed, course and position. "All stop, Captain. *Sundancer* is stationery on plotted GPS location."

"Thank you, Franklin. Set the anchor Mr Deeks, if you please," Charles gave the order to the Technical Officer.

"Anchor away, tracking chain length as she goes, have camera watching for impact and hold," Martin said. "Franklin, reverse engines, take us back ten metres please, slow as you go."

"Reversing engines, slow as we go," Franklin confirmed, pulling the four levers gently backwards while watching Martin for his next order.

"Okay, hold there, brilliant. We have a good anchor set," Martin Deeks confirmed.

Franklin eased the four levers back into neutral. "Engines in neutral," he advised.

"Thank you, gentlemen. Good work. Secure the winch, shut down engines. I want a twenty four hour watch on the bridge. I take it that the Captain, and I am of course referring to the real Captain, has set up a roster?" asked Charles.

"Yes he has, sir," Franklin replied.

"This area is notorious as we all know for theft and kidnapping. Miles Channing, the Security Chief, is setting up twenty four hour patrols consisting of two armed guards circling the main deck and one armed guard will be in the rigid inflatable boat that is going out on hull cleaning duties. That's your job to organise Franklin. Martin, you make sure that the tender garage is closed after the rigid inflatable boat had been launched and not opened again until the launch is ready to be retrieved," said Charles as he stood up.

"Will do, Captain," Martin said checking his instruments and shutting down the engines.

"I will liaise with Miles on the guard," Franklin confirmed.

"Leaving radar on and sonar active. When the tender has been retrieved I will have the surveillance team turn on the hull perimeter motion sensor systems."

"Thank you, gentlemen. That was an effortless manoeuvre, which I thoroughly enjoyed. I'll be in command when we leave here. If anyone needs me, I'll be with Max flying to the reserve," Charles said and left the bridge.

Charles found Max in the cockpit of the Bell 525 Relentless. "Are we ready for the test landing?" asked Charles as he leant into the cockpit, where Max was seated checking instrument readings.

"Just about. A few more boxes are on their way up. As soon as they are secure, we can be on our way," Max said. "Flight plan is programmed in and we have a full load of fuel. You might as well get in and get yourself comfortable, I'm just about to start the engines." Max flicked up two switch covers and pressed the buttons beneath. The rotors started to slowly turn. Max saw two crewman exit the library and walk towards the Bell 525 carrying a couple of heavy boxes. He jumped down from the cockpit and climbed into the passenger cabin and took the boxes from the crew and carefully secured them with bungee netting. He climbed out and closed the large forward passenger cabin door and checked the deck restraining straps were undone, jumped back into the cockpit and secured his seatbelt and flight helmet. Charles was doing the same. He closed the cockpit door, flicked a few switches before lightly gripping the collective and cyclic fly by wire controls. He scanned the four LCD screens. "Here we go," Max said increasing engine power and gently the nine thousand five hundred kilo machine rose from the deck. Max let the Bell 525 climb gradually before crabbing her sideways across *Sundancer*. Once clear of *Sundancer* and over the open ocean, he increased power and turning quickly to starboard headed for the coastline in the distance.

"What cargo have we got in the back?" Charles asked through the headset.

"The vet asked for his supplies to be bought over first, and Norman wanted the new communication gear and tracking collars."

"Fair enough. Hopefully we will be releasing some of the tigers over the next few days and the tracking collars are essential," Charles said and looked around at *Sundancer* lying at anchor in the distance and watched for a few moments as the rigid inflatable boat was launched from the garage with three men aboard. He then turned around and looked forward at the coastline, which was coming up fast. The view below changed from the deep blue of the deep ocean to a lighter blue green as they crossed into the shallower waters of the coastline, which then slowly transitioned to the intertidal mudflats that were full of birds who took to their wings at the noise of the approaching helicopter.

"Milky Stalks, if my research is right," said Charles. "We may have to fly higher on the next runs to avoid disturbing them."

"Yes, I agree, can't do for us to continually disturb them," replied Max concentrating on the screens in front as they flew over the dense forest that offered no landmark to navigate by. "Fifteen kilometres to go," he said, slowing the Bell 525 from two hundred and sixty kilometre per hour to a more sedate one hundred and twenty five kilometres per hour.

"Over there," Charles said pointing to a large clearing in the trees.

"I would like to be higher so we don't scare the cats. Come in from the west. The cats are housed on the eastern side of the compound."

Without replying, Max increased altitude and turned the helicopter into a slow turn, curving around the clearing and coming over the helipad from the west. He slowed the Bell 525 to a hover around two hundred and fifty metres and started his straight down descent, slowing as they neared the helipad. He could see people gathering below, looking up at the Bell 525 but keeping well back from the landing pad.

"The clearing is more than wide enough for this bird," Max said.

"I forgot. It would be. They do have an Osprey VTOL/STOL based here, which is how Cathy flew here from Borneo," Charles said. "I forgot that I signed off Norman's requisition to purchase two of the things, one for here and one for Borneo."

Max continued the slow straight down descent.

"Well, I suppose with everything that's been going on that's not really surprising."

To his front he saw the tracks leading to a large hangar where a helicopter sat on a trolley next to an Osprey VTOL aircraft on its own trolley on the rails. He extended the landing gear at sixty metres and when the lights on the dash turned green, indicating the gear was locked, he gently lowered her until he felt the wheel lightly touch on the ground before settling on her suspension. He cut power to the engines and shut them down and waited until the rotors slowed before removing his helmet and unbuckling his harness.

"Okay, we're down. You can remove your helmet and harness," he said looking at Charles. They jumped down and opened the rear passenger doors and began unloading the boxes and placing them at the edge of the concrete helipad, which was the same diameter as the rotors and highlighted by a yellow and black painted band. Norman Stafford came forward and up the three steps to the surface of the helipad. Norman was not a tall man but stout and strong with rough untidy hair and his imitable two days growth of beard on his deeply tanned rugged face. He wore khaki pants and a thick checked shirt.

"Hi Charles, leave that. The team can unload the helicopter," he turned to the group watching the helicopter. "Well, don't just stand there. There are boxes for the veterinary center and our new communication equipment and the tracking collars. Get them unloaded and take them to their respective locations," he barked. At once people came forward and started unloading boxes. "This way, Charles, I'll show you around. What are you going to do Max?" he asked.

"Hi, Norman. As soon as your team has unloaded the cargo, then I'm heading back to *Sundancer* to collect Mrs. Langham, Ralph, Miles and more cargo," Max answered.

Norman and Charles starting walking along a raised covered wooded walkway that was festooned with creeping vines and hanging baskets full of colourful flowers. The walkway linked all the buildings in the precinct square together and ran around another raised large concrete pad marked with a large white painted "H." Numerous spurs of the walkway led between the various buildings.

Norman was pleased with what they had achieved in the year since they arrived. In the beginning a team of six had been lowered by ropes from a helicopter with chain saws, tents and food. They had worked long days clearing enough of an area for a helicopter to land. Tree stumps were dynamited and the area flattened. They could then land a light helicopter, which shuttled continually backwards and forwards with people and supplies. The next task on Norman's list was to widen the clearing and start building the platforms on which the building would be erected. The survey team commenced their work, marking the locations of each platform and the route of each raised walkway. While the survey team carried out their work, others felled trees, while another team cut the felled trees into the posts, which would be used to construct the platforms. Timbers were dropped in by helicopter and some of the felled trees taken out to be cut at a local Sawmill into the timbers needed for the buildings. Next came the construction crew and the building of the concrete helipad and the start of construction of the buildings began.

Norman remembered the days as long, sometimes non-stop, through the night under the glare of spotlights powered by petrol generators. When the concrete helipad was completed they could use larger machines and bring in the vehicles they needed not only to move the wire mesh and steel gates for the tiger enclosures but to go and dart the tigers that would be situated in the sanctuary. Every morning Norman brought the whole group together to review progress and adjust plans, in order to ensure each building was completed per the priority schedule that had been carefully planned over many months by him, Charles, Keith, Anne and Cathy. As the building progressed, they moved into the accommodation blocks and life became easier. They had comfortable beds, showers and food cooked in the canteen. When it rained they were kept dry and the addition of roofs over the covered walkway were a welcome relief by everyone.

The walkway roofs were not part of the plan, and no man hours were assigned to the task. When Norman broached the idea at one of the meetings after a week of heavy rain when everyone had got continually soaked, every member of the team agreed to get involved and do the work in their own time. Ten months later and they were ready to commence receiving tigers captured by the authorities and local villagers and start the capture of the many tigers destined to live in the safety of the sanctuary. As news got out that there was a team capturing tigers, they started to receive calls from officials and village elders asking for help to capture tigers that were a danger to their villages. So more tiger enclosures were built to accommodate the extra tigers.

Norman had called Charles to discuss the growing tiger population. After many discussions with their wildlife experts and veterinary surgeons, it was agreed that the sanctuary could cope easily with the number of male and female tigers that were destined to live in the sanctuary. The balance of males to female tigers had to be right. Now fourteen months later, the original project was completed and the tiger release programme could start. Norman looked around at what he had created. He now just had to work on the expansion plan that Charles and Anne wanted and that Duke was buying the land for. At least that job was just tiger proof fencing. A simple but crucial project compared to the others in his ten years working for Charles and Anne Langham.

When Charles originally contacted him, it was to project manage the building of a new secure electronics assembly facility. Just the one job, nothing more. They got on tremendously well, and after the project was finished Charles had changed direction and, at a meeting at their luxurious house in Cheshire, England,

Charles and Anne had advised him in confidence of their future plans and how they saw him fit with those plans. He project managed the secretive building of their Kermadec headquarters and the building and fitting out of their Boeing 747-400. Then he managed their first famine relief project and, after a year in Borneo, he travelled the world managing different projects, some small and some very large. All the time Charles and Anne left him to choose his team and have full budget control. Against their detailed briefs for each project, he was left to plan everything, human resource, buildings and infrastructure required to achieve their goals. The trust both ways was earned and complete.

Norman led Charles away from the helicopter across the square to the buildings on the other side, a sly smile on his face.

"We left that area clear in case we ever had the need to land another helicopter and in the end decided to make it a permanent raised concrete helipad. We removed all trees higher than the buildings and planted smaller ones to replace them. Native trees, of course. All the buildings have hanging baskets to bring colour to the compound, not part of the plan but a crucial decorative and soothing element. We built all the buildings on one metre high stilts and they, as you can see, are all linked together by the network of covered walkways. This building is the reserves headquarters and communications centre and is fully self-contained with bathroom and small kitchen."

He then pointed to a timber clad building with a painted corrugated roof. The windows were small with wood shutters. Wire fencing enclosed the area below the buildings between the stilts.

"All the buildings are built in the same external style as you can see, and heavily insulated against the heat, cold and the sound of heavy rain on the roof. All have air conditioning, plumbing, telephone systems and electricity," he said, walking past the headquarters building. "This is the kitchen and dining room and beside it is the hospital."

He walked slowly on towards three buildings, which sat at a right angle to the kitchen and dining room.

"These are the accommodation buildings. The first is male, the second female and the third is the married quarters. Each room is like a hotel suite with lounge, bedroom, ensuite and kitchenette. Over there through the trees is the maintenance building and the veterinary centre and behind that the cattery where all the cats are currently housed. We'll go there later. Now, power and communications are behind the headquarters and kitchen dining buildings. I'll show you, through here."

He led the way between the two buildings to four large caged areas.

"Even though the whole area is fully fenced we have still enclosed the equipment in these cages." In three of the cages were concrete buildings and the last six high towers. "The cage and building on the left is the petrol and diesel store with pumps. The tanks go well below ground. The next one is the generators, the last one is the battery power storage system. All are fitted with automatic fire suppressant systems. The two towers on the left, are the communications arrays, the two in the middle are the solar power systems and the last two the wind turbines."

"Where is the school?" Charles asked.

"In the next precinct, this way. We thought it best to keep the children away from the work area."

Norman walked back into the main square and passed the

headquarters building, heading away from the accommodation buildings. He walked down a short path alongside which were parked many Land Rovers, some with canvas tops and some hardtops and Mercedes Benz Unimog all-terrain trucks. The walkway opened into another large clearing. The buildings were of the same style and linked in the same way by raised covered walkways.

"How do you get the vehicles to the buildings?" Charles asked.

"It was decided to keep traffic away from the main walking areas so the only buildings accessible by vehicles are the hospital, veterinary clinic and the hangar. Each have double doors at the rear with wide steps and ramps," Norman said, looking up as the Bell 525 rose high in the sky before turning towards the coast. "The vehicles, the buildings, fuel and everyone are protected by the usual active security systems installed around the perimeter fence and monitored by the security team in the headquarters building." He looked up at the ascending helicopter. "Wow, he went high before turning!" Norman exclaimed.

"He is following orders. I don't want the cats spooked and stressed unnecessarily," said Charles. "I like what I see so far. So, this is the school and what else?"

"Yes, the school is there on the left, the conservation room is over there, and to the right is the ablutions block and another three accommodation blocks. To the far left connected to the school is the playground, which is within its own cage. All to the plan and pretty much within our usual design rules."

"Not quite within the design rules, but close enough to pass muster. Each reserve has to be designed around its unique circumstances," said Charles looking around at the buildings.

"I'm happy. You've done a grand job. The walkway roofing was a brilliant addition. Now, let's get back to the headquarters building. It's hot and muggy out here and we need to discuss your next projects, the expansion here and the Tongan project. Then I want to talk about the cat release programme with Cathy and the veterinary surgeon and his team."

"This way, then. As you can see at each junction we have a map of the compound and directions board," Norman said.

Cathy came to the door of the headquarters building.

"Daddy, hi there," she called and started walking towards him.

"Hello, Cathy. How was the flight in the Osprey?"

"A bit disconcerting when it changed from vertical to horizontal flight but smooth enough and quite comfortable. I take it mum designed the interior layout and colours?"

"Yes, she did."

He kissed her on the cheek and followed her into the crowded headquarters building. Along one wall were people sitting at a long table that ran the width of the building, which was filled with computer screens, laptops and beneath the table computer towers. On the rear wall was a large map of the area, a chart of the sanctuary and a conference table with a few open laptop computers. Cathy led them over to the table.

"I've laid out the plans for the current sanctuary and the proposed land purchases. The chief veterinary surgeon is on his way over and should be here in a few minutes." She sat in front of one of the laptops. Charles sat next to Cathy, and Norman sat opposite in front of his own laptop that he had been working on before Charles arrived.

"The survey team had completed their survey and we now have

a full list of the supplies we will need and the persons required to complete the task and a preliminary project plan," Cathy said as Norman handed Charles a Gant chart and printouts of the supplies and costs. "The veterinary team have given their all clear for the area, plenty of food that is sustainable."

"Norman, I assume that you have seen this already and had you input?" Charles asked, looking at the Gant chart.

"Yes, it has been adjusted to include my recommendations, which unfortunately added two weeks to the project timescale."

"What caused the extra two weeks?" Cathy asked, pre-empting her father as this reserve was her responsibility for the next six months.

"Based on our experience on building this project," he said quietly. "The weather conditions, the rain and the humidity. The impact of the staff. Some were affected by lack of sleep until we had the accommodation blocks built and air conditioning running. Hence, we were six weeks overdue. The teams building those fences will be living in tents and will suffer the same as we did here initially. Those who are doing the work, experienced the early days here so will not be looking forward to going through that again. It is best to have a plan that will work, knowing the environmental parameters we have to work within."

Charles examined the Gant chart and the costing and looked up at Cathy. "Have you been through these in detail with Norman?" he asked.

"Yes, dad. I have agreed the costing and staff requirements and who is on the team. I left the Gant chart till you were here so we could go through it together," she answered.

"Well, it looks well thought out and thorough and we can

start as soon as we hear from Duke that he has completed the purchase of the land. I know that the supplier has stock, some left over from the run he did for us on this project." He looked at Norman and Cathy. "Start the preliminary work, get the orders ready to be placed. I want to start as soon as we have secured the land. Increasing their range will be great for the cats and give us room for about a dozen or so more."

Cathy looked up as the door opened and the chief veterinary surgeon entered the headquarters building.

"Hi Edwin, come and sit down," she said. "Anyone for tea or coffee?"

"I'll take a tea," Charles said.

"Coffee for me, Cathy," said Norman.

Edwin sat opposite Charles with Cathy to his right at the end of the table. He carefully laid a folder on the table and opened it, leafing through the pages until he found the one he wanted. Edwin Murray was a careful man who worked slowly and diligently in a manner that suited his nature and looks. Most people found him infuriating at first but once they got to know him they understood and made allowance for his slowness. He was neat and tidy and of a large build being six foot two inches tall and around one hundred and ten kilos. His grey hair and moustache were the only indication of his years. After many years working with wild animals in zoological establishments in England and the United States, he was contacted by Charles and Anne on the recommendation of Max, who had heard that he was looking for a new adventure. At their first meeting Charles had outlined his plans for the Amazon rain forest project and their upcoming Borneo project. He had jumped at the chance. Now, here he was, five years later, working with Sumatran tigers in the wild. An amazing opportunity.

"Nice to see you again Mr. Langham. It's been a long time, or so it seems," he said in his deep resonating voice.

"Around a year or so, I think," Charles acknowledged. "How are the cats fairing in their temporary housing?"

"Exceedingly well. It has given us a great opportunity in getting to know each animal and their individual traits and needs. We have used the time to give each a thorough medical examination and work out which animals to allow in bordering territories and which male to match to which female based on diversifying their genetics. We sent their DNA to the zoological database and that has led to a request from two zoos for specific males to take part in their mating program. I have the two forms here which I need you to authorise and sign, if you agree." He passed the two forms across the table while Cathy served up the drinks.

"Will their leaving affect our work here?" Charles asked reading the forms.

"No, from the DNA I would say that we have their siblings here." Edwin replied.

"That's okay then, they can be released."

Charles signed the forms and passed them back across the table. "When you arrange transport use our aircraft and send one of your people with the cats to ensure they get the best treatment available and are settled in to their new surroundings."

Edwin smiled. "Of course, Mr. Langham. Do you want a written report on the journey and treatment on arrival at their respective zoos?"

"Yes, that's a good idea. I am aware that they are not pets, but they deserve the best treatment we can provide and it is up to us to oversee that. If there are any concerns they return here," Charles said with a grin. "Now, the release program. Can we go over the protocols, safety measures planned, collar placement and release dates?" Charles stopped as his radio sounded. "Hello," he said into the radio. He listened to the caller. "We are in the headquarters building, see you in a minute." He disconnected the call. "That was Anne. She has just landed. Cathy, get a coffee ready for your mother."

Edwin took three sheets of paper from his folder and passed them round.

"This is the release program." He passed another three sheets around. "And this one details the collar placement and release protocols that will need to be followed. I have set this out so that the tigers experience the absolute minimum of stress and tranquiliser drug," Edwin explained. "It is done in such a way that we start with those tigers that are the furthest away from here. Two vehicles have cages on their decks. A third is available if required. The doors on these cages line up precisely with the exit door on the sleeping quarters of the tigers cage. We drug two tigers each time. Line the trucks up to exit doors. The tigers will be drugged via their meat ration, the collar fitted and the tigers slid into the cage of each truck and the doors closed. The collar will then be retested and the number annotated to the record of each tiger. When we get to the GPS location for the release of each tiger, the cage door will be opened electrically from inside the vehicles. We then make sure the tiger is okay and that's it."

"What happens if a tiger wakes up? How can you be sure it has taken the required dose of tranquilizer?" asked Charles.

"The first cube of meat, an inch square, will carry the correct dose according to the weight of each animal. Once they have consumed that they will be given a further few pieces of non-drugged meat. A guard with a tranquiliser gun will be close by at all times as will another guard with a high velocity rifle. It only takes two minutes to fit the new style collars, which are a lighter weight than the last ones I used. They have a new design of locking mechanism which is much easier to use." Edwin explained. "James did a grand job with that."

"I didn't know that James designed the collar. Good to know that all parts of the organisation work well together." He stopped as Anne entered the building. He turned in his chair and smiled. "Hi, darling. We are just about to go through the release times of each tiger."

"Hello, Mum," Cathy said, walking over to her with a fresh hot cup of coffee.

"Thank you," Anne said, taking the coffee and sitting down at the table next to Charles. "Where is the new veterinary surgeon? I thought she would be here."

Edwin passed over some spare sheets from his folder.

"She is busy completing some blood work on the tigers in the second release. This is the release schedule. We've already been through the release protocols and were just about to start reviewing the release dates and times."

"Great, I'm just in time then." Anne smiled. "I've seen the tiger matching information and been through it with Cathy."

"We've been very careful and believe we have the best choices in mating pairs and then the best adjoining territories matched." Edwin looked up from his computer printouts. "As you can see the first release operation is scheduled for ten thirty tomorrow morning. It consists of a mating pair going to the first area in the north east just here." He stood up and pointed to the map on the wall behind him. "We have a trip of three hours by track in the vehicles. It is the furthest release in the program. The second release will be another mating pair and two hours by track to just here the following day." He pointed to another area on the map just to the right and slightly below the last area. "These are the farthest ranges, which is why we only have one release each day. After this we will be working to two releases a day, some of which are just one tiger and that is usually a male."

"Charles, can we stay for the first two releases? I would love to be part of that," Anne asked, looking at Charles with a tilt of her head and a hint of emotional blackmail to her voice.

Charles sat looking at Anne and quietly thinking. His mind going over the schedule that he had carefully calculated with his team.

"A twenty-eight hour delay to our plans. We may be able to make up some of that time by running later into the storm. So, okay, darling, we will stay and see the first two releases. Now, let's go and see the first lucky four cats," he said standing up and stretching.

They made their way along the covered walkway and passed the veterinary centre to the tiger precinct. Charles was interested in the arrangement of the tiger compound. Each cage was paired with another with each having its own very large enclosure with trees, bushes, water pool and grass. The walkway was masked from the enclosures by a long hedge.

"The first grouping of paired cages, those nearest to us, are male and female tigers that we believe will make good mated pairs. Those furthest are single males. We hope to increase the female stock." Irwin explained as they stood by the nearest tiger.

"Do they have names?" Anne asked.

"Oh, mummy, of course not. They each have a code number that will be crossed referenced by the serial number of their collar when fitted," Cathy said with a mocked laugh.

"I thought they would have names by now," Anne said disappointedly. "If I was here, they would each have names."

"These are wild tigers and to keep them that way, they have minimal human contact. Hence the hedge masking us from the tigers. We are fighting for the survival of the species and need to keep the tigers wary of human beings," Edwin explained. "To name them would go against that by humanizing them." They walked along the front of the enclosures and watched as the tigers roamed around. "As you can see, each tiger has an exceptionally large area to roam and only those enclosures of male and females we are releasing together do not have visual barriers between them. Where we have males side by side the visual barrier extends for eighty percent of the enclosure."

"Why is that?" Anne asked frowning and looking at the tigers as they slowly paced along the enclosure fencing. One climbed a tree to lie on its branch, legs hanging over the edges. A male roared in response to seeing another male who roared.

"Just an attempt to try and keep them calmer," Edwin explained as they neared the end of the enclosures.

"We have walked around half a kilometre," Charles commented. "And in this heat it's tiring." He wiped the sweat from his forehead. They turned and walked along the other end of the veterinary building. "It was good to see even the tiger enclosures were one metre off the ground as well." They turned into the headquarters building. Charles looked at his watch. "Nearly dinner time. We will return to *Sundancer* and be back in the morning. Cathy are you coming or staying?"

"I'm staying here, Daddy." She gave him a hug, "See you in the morning."

Chapter Twenty One

Axmann Plans an Attack

"Have you found them yet?" questioned Gustav in a low guttural voice when Albrecht entered his dimly lit cabin. He lay on his bunk, his knees slightly bent up to his chest. He was not feeling at all well. The damp confines of the submarine was not helping his arthritic joints.

"We believe so, father. One of our contacts has reported that the Langhams have been sighted at a tiger sanctuary in Sumatra. They flew back to their yacht last night." Albrecht sat at the end of the bunk. "Their information states that the yacht is being refuelled and they returned to the sanctuary early this morning. What do you want me to tell him?"

Gustav eased himself slowly to a more upright position against the bulkhead and a little smile broke on his unshaven face.

"This contact, what numbers does he have, what weapons do they have, are they actually capable of doing anything?" he asked his voice quiet and condescending.

Albrecht ignored the patronising tone of his father's voice, realising it was the pain talking.

"He has fifteen soldiers at his call and I understand that they are armed with high velocity rifles and grenade launchers. They are well practiced in guerrilla warfare in the Indonesian rainforests. Most served in the Acheh-Sumatra National Liberation Front. They are already deep in the forest ready and waiting. So, tell me what you want to do?"

"*Tote Die Langham's, Destro ihnen, destroy ihre organisation.* Do I really have to spell it out for you? *Destro Ihnen!*" Gustav replied, leaning forward, his voice rising to a crescendo.

Albrecht gripped his father gently on the shoulders and eased him backwards against the bulkhead making sure the pillow was high enough.

"Father, please, calm yourself down. Getting worked up will not help. I understand fully want you want me to do. I just wanted to make sure, that is all." He got up from the bunk. "I will organise it now. You rest, because we have a long way to go. The Captain is taking us further away from the east coast to avoid detection, so the journey will take longer and we are heading into a storm, which will slow our speed."

"What crap! We should just run deep and fast. Tell the Captain or I will!" Gustav raged.

"Father, please listen." Albrecht looked his father in the eyes and let his voice carry enough authority to make his father listen without threatening his father's leadership. "We cannot run deep for long, and the faster we go, the less time we can spend at depth. Every time we surface we leave ourselves open for detection. Our current course and actions are the best, believe me. Now rest. I will be back when I have more news. I will send some food and drink in." He spun on his heels and pulling the curtain back left his father's small cabin and walked down the gangway to the radio operator, detouring to the galley to organise some food and drink for his father. A few of the crew looked at him. They had obviously overheard the exchange, he thought, more than likely wondering what the hell the shouting was all about.

In the radio room, Albrecht had the operator connect to his contact. His father had built up a following in almost every country in the world. Though originally made up of ex Nazi party members and SS staff who, like Gustav, had fled Germany at the end of the war, the membership now mainly consisted of the next generation of the original founding members. The fanaticism still flourished, in part thanks to Gustav's propaganda machine, his activities, and the monies he sent to help their causes. Albrecht was happy he could report to his father that the operation to remove the thorn in his side was activated. The contact had told Albrecht that it would take three to four hours to complete the assassination, and that he would report back as soon as he could; their mobile radio equipment was only short range, so he could not report until he returned to his headquarters. That meant Albrecht would have to wait up to seven or more hours to hear news of success or failure. That would not please his father. He decided to tell his father only that the operation was underway. He thanked the radio operator and left the radio cabin and headed first for the control room to see the Captain.

On *Sundancer,* Grant walked through the lounge and over to the teak table on the aft deck, where Charles sat having breakfast with Anne, Max, Duke and Ryan. Stewards walked from the outside galley to the table with trays loaded with English breakfast, pots of tea and fresh toast. The air was warm and humid after the air conditioned comfort of *Sundancer's* interior, and Grant loosened his tie and undid the collar button on his shirt. The cloudless sky a brilliant blue with a bright globe of yellow high in the sky. The sea was a flat calm turquoise blue.

"Grant, why don't you join us?" Charles called cheerily on seeing Grant. "There's a free place."

"Thanks, but I have already had breakfast. I will have a cup of tea though." He pulled the chair back and made himself comfortable. "I have some rather more disturbing news, though. Ralph and Miles are reviewing what actions to take and will be up soon, but at the moment we do not want anyone leaving *Sundancer*," he said with authority.

"What's going on?" Charles asked, placing his knife and fork down, his forehead creasing into a deep frown.

"We have intercepted an order to assassinate you and anyone close to you in Sumatra and to destroy *Sundancer*," Grant stated succinctly. "The transmission was in German and, as far as my boffins downstairs can ascertain, originated somewhere in the Atlantic and was received and acknowledged by a receiver in the northern region of Sumatra. The reply mentioned a timeframe of three to four hours."

Charles picked up his napkin and slowly wiped his mouth while deep in thought.

"I see." He looked around the table. "Well, I have some tigers to see released today and I am not going to forfeit that experience. I know Anne has been hoping to see the tigers released from the first day we started the sanctuary project. We will carry on. We have security guards and can use the helicopters for aerial surveillance. We will be safe."

"I somehow knew that would be the answer," Grant shook his head in exasperation. "Ah, here's Ralph and Miles. Guys, we were right," he called to them. "They still want to go."

"Sir, I am your security chief and therefore responsible for the safety of not only yourself but also Mrs. Langham, *Sundancer* and everyone on her and everyone at the compound," Miles Channing the Security Chief stated clearly without any expectation of disagreement. "I have discussed this with Ralph and we will proceed as follows. *Sundancer* will be on total lock down with all surveillance systems in operation, sonar and hull protection activated. All external doors will be secured and shutters sealed. Deck armaments will be raised and primed. Max will deliver four armed security guards to the sanctuary before returning to collect yourselves. My team will back up the sanctuaries own security team. Two armed security guards will accompany yourselves. The helicopter based at the sanctuary will be used as an armed aerial surveillance platform and will follow your every move once you leave the headquarters with the tigers. The sanctuary will be on lock down and surveillance increased. One of the Unimogs will lead the way, the other, along with two Land Rovers will follow, both with armed personnel. Thirty minutes before you leave, two Land Rovers and the helicopter will scout the route." He rubbed his hands together. "Well, that's it. I hope that is acceptable?" He looked at Charles and Anne.

Charles looked at Anne and placed his hand on hers.

"You still want to see the release?" he asked.

"It's what we have worked so hard for," she said and nodded." Yes, we go ahead."

"Miles you have your answer. We proceed as planned but with

obvious caution under you security screen. We will, of course, do as you advise at all times."

"I think I will come along if that's okay? I've only seen tigers in captivity, it will be a hoot to see one, let alone two, in the wild," remarked Duke, looking at Ryan, who nodded.

"Sounds like a good idea," Ryan agreed. "I'll come too."

Miles sighed the sigh of someone about to give up on humanity. "Great, now I have an ex-Senator and a presidential aid to worry about." He let his arms drop to his sides. "Okay, Max, I want the first chopper off the deck in twenty minutes loaded with my team of four. Drop them off and head straight back here. The rest of you be ready to leave in one hour." The authority in his voice made everyone aware who was in charge. Miles knew Charles would take it the right way.

Max looked up at Miles with a big grin on his face. "Good, still time to finish my breakfast then." His light banter had the desired effect and lifted the spirits of everyone.

Miles and Ralph walked away; Grant followed. The group had a mountain of things to organise not only on *Sundancer* but ashore as well. They returned to the conference room where a map was laid out.

"Look," said Miles, "let's take one step at a time. The easiest first. Grant, lock down *Sundancer*. Only external door available to be opened will be the library door to the helideck. Turn on the underwater hull and intruder protection system. The surveillance team are to monitor radar and sonar. I suggest you put both systems on auto alert."

"I'll set things in motion now and come back," said Grant as he stood up.

"Wait a second, there is a bit more," Miles said before turning to Ralph, "Tell the bridge all four engines are to be kept running. Now, we have the re-fueller arriving in three hours. The re-fueller is to be closely examined by our long range camera as soon as it's in sight. Every detail is to be examined for potential threats, and every crew movement for anything suspicious. When we lower the hatch I want two armed guards on duty at the hatch and above on deck and all adjoining bulkhead doors sealed. Martin thinks we will be pumping for a good hour and forty minutes. Now he controls the entire operation from the bridge, except the camera scan, which is down to your team, Grant. Tell him what we need him to do." Miles looked at both men. "Okay, get going and come straight back here. I'm going to study this terrain map in more detail."

Grant left and headed next door while Ralph headed for the bridge.

On deck Charles was just finishing his breakfast with Anne, Max, Duke and Ryan when the public address system sounded.

"Ladies, gentlemen and crew. All outer doors will be automatically closed in ten minutes. Please proceed indoors immediately. I repeat, all outer doors will be automatically closed in ten minutes, please proceed indoors immediately."

Charles pushed his chair back and stood up.

"Miles is taking this threat seriously. Come on, everyone inside." He pulled Anne's chair back as the others stood and followed him into the lounge. Stewards quickly cleared the table, loaded the dumb waiter and cleaned and closed the outside galley and disappeared below decks.

"Well, I'm off on my first run, see you later," Max said and headed forwards to the lift.

Charles made his way into the aft lounge settee and the others followed suit.

"Well, I have to wonder whether this is all an over-reaction."

He watched as the large glass doors to the aft deck slid closed and the window shutters rose up shutting out all light. The interior lights came on automatically, casting a soft warm glow across the lounge.

"I doubt that Grant and Miles would react like this if they did not have a credible threat," Duke said relaxing back into the deep cushions. "Do you have the details of the actual threat?"

"No," said Charles, "I have no more information than what we all heard together. But all this about a threat from Axmann, who is known to be in the Atlantic. I cannot see him having the resources to make a credible attack on us here and that is if he could locate where we are in the first place."

"Well, look at it this way Charles," Ryan said, leaning forward and resting his elbows on his knees. "You employ Miles to run the security operation of your organisation. You employ Grant to run the security surveillance. You employed them both as they were the best in their field. So accept what they say and let them do their jobs."

Charles cocked his head to one side as he heard the sound of the Bell 525 Relentless take off, the sound muffled by the dense sound proofing material in *Sundancer's* superstructure.

"Well, there goes Max and the first security contingent. We are next. While we wait I'm going to see what Miles and Grant are planning," Charles said slowly standing up feeling his muscle cramp a little.

"I'm coming with you," said Anne, holding his arm and

helping him up. "Looks like you are very stiff, my dear."

She led the way to the lift, holding his arm in the crook of hers.

Chapter Twenty Two

Axmann Attacks

The convoy of vehicles left the compound and Miles made sure that the gates were locked behind them and the security patrols were running in accordance with his strict instructions. Miles sat in the first Mercedes Unimog, driven by Norman, speaking continuously into his radio to Ralph, who was driving one of the Land Rovers that was scouting the route ahead and Max in the helicopter that buzzed around above their heads. The second Unimog with Charles driving and Anne, Duke and Ryan as passengers was sandwiched in the middle of the convoy just ahead of the two Land Rovers that carried the tigers, one driven by Cathy, one by Edwin. The track was just wide enough for two vehicles to pass each other if they drove carefully enough. The surface was rutted with tire tracks, through the continuous use by the tiger project tea, while they planted new saplings in the deforested areas and built the fencing enclosing the sanctuary. Every so often they would come to a wide clearing that was a junction of tracks with directional signposts leading to different sections of the sanctuary. The rainforest closed in thickly on both sides of the track and the canopy kept the track in a deep mottled shade. From the air, the track could be seen by the helicopter if Max flew low enough; if he went too high the track disappeared, hidden by the dense canopy. Max chose to fly low and slow along the track, repeatedly soaring high to turn around and come sweeping back down the track. The drivers kept the speed down to ensure a reasonably comfortable ride, which Charles was amused to find out was specified by the veterinary surgeon for the tigers, not the human passengers. Duke sat in the front next to Charles and took charge of the radio and relayed information from Mile to Charles and vice versa. On the dash was mounted a large GPS display, which showed their departure and destination points.

After what seemed an eternity, but was a shade over three hours, they came to a large grass covered clearing. Ralph parked up next to two wooden buildings, one a long drop latrine, the other looking identical to those in the compound. The two Land Rovers carrying the tigers left the convoy and drove across to the middle of the grass clearing where, as though choreographed, they turned around so that the cage openings faced the rainforest in the distance. The rest of the convoy parked alongside Ryan's Land Rover next to the building. The drivers of the two Land Rovers in the clearing stayed in their vehicles, where they could remotely open the tiger cages. The guards alighted their vehicles and started to scout the area while everyone else followed Norman into the building.

"This building housed the team who tidied up this part of the rainforest and built the northern fencing and gates." He walked over to large window and tapped on it. "Double glazed, built identically to those in the compound. Sleeps eight in the four bedrooms down that hallway. Rain water harvesting of course with the water stored and filtered. Power is by solar panels on the roof and wind turbine with battery storage and back-up generator outside. It hasn't been used for a few months now, but will be used again when we do the fencing extensions." He pointed out of the window. "The area where the two Land Rovers are had been cut down but not cleared by the locals, so we removed all the lumber and old oil drums and all the other crap that they left behind. You know, we took seventy cubic metres of rubbish out of here! Over there on the right was an area that had been devastated. As you can see, the saplings we have planted are doing very well. The area is now patrolled by our local tribe people. They take soil samples and check on the undergrowth plants and where necessary plant more." Norman smiled. "A great recovery, I think."

Charles nodded. "How about communication? I did not see any aerials outside." Charles asked.

"Aerial is camouflaged to look like a tree. There is full internet access and staff bring their own laptops, but we do leave the two way radio's locked in the desk. Weapons are stored here on site and locked in that cupboard by the desk." Norman pointed to a desk that sat beneath a large scale map of the area. On the desk was wireless router. To the left of the desk was a kitchen with all mod cons and dining area. The lounge area was devoid of television and, besides the three piece suite, had just a coffee table.

Charles looked around. "Good set up and quite comfortable and safe. So, now we have two cats, very eager I should think to get out of those cages," he said returning his attention to the two vehicles sitting in the centre of the clearing.

Everyone took a place by the window. Norman took his radio from his belt, looked around to make sure everyone was ready and pressed the talk button.

"You can release the tigers," he said in a clear voice. In the clearing Cathy and Edwin took the cue and looked at each other. On a signal from Edwin, Cathy pressed the release button on her dashboard; Edwin did likewise. The front of the two cages rose up. Everyone in the building held their breaths in anticipation. Anne breathed in deeply as, from the two cages on the rear decks of the Land Rovers, leapt the two tigers, who after a quick look around, bounded off across the clearing to quickly disappear into the trees like wraiths. Edwin looked at the laptop on the passenger seat and after a few keystrokes he called Norman on his radio.

"I have their collars on track. They are heading off in the same direction, northwest, and the female is leading the way and the male is following," he said cheerfully.

"Max, how are you doing?" Norman said into his radio. After a few a seconds the voice of Max came over the radio.

"They didn't hang around did they? All clear, I cannot see any vehicles or people on any of the tracks," Max said. "But I cannot see below the canopy elsewhere."

"Okay, keep your eyes peeled," Norman said into the radio. "We are about to move out."

"Well, that's it I suppose," Anne said quietly. "They are back in the wild where they should be and I doubt if we will see them very often."

"We have placed cameras with movement sensors along animal trails that we came across during our exploration. We know from evidence we found that they were definitely used by tigers," Norman explained to Anne. "So, we may see them, although fleetingly from time to time. You can access those sighting on the system."

"Great. But how do we monitor their health?" Anne asked Norman.

"The collars monitor certain life functions and Edwin and his team will be tracking them down occasionally to video and photograph them so they can check their body condition and weight, all accessible from the system as well," Norman advised.

"We might as well head back. Nothing more to do here," Charles said to Anne, seeing the two Land Rovers on the clearing turning round and heading for the track.

"We can track their movements from the compound and talk about tomorrow's release."

"Ralph, you take up the rear guard," Miles said and followed the others out. Miles waited until everyone was back in the vehicles before heading off slowly back onto the track in convoy, checking his mirrors to make sure the others were falling in behind.

Everyone was happy and relaxed as they drove back down the track to the compound. Charles looked at his watch, mentally calculated that they were still over an hour to drive. The radio chatter mainly about the two released tigers until Max's voice sharply broke through the chatter.

"Watch it everyone, keep your eyes peeled, there are people along the side of the track just ahead around the next bend," he called over the radio. "They will be on your right hand side as you approach."

"Everyone move to the left side of the track. Security team at the double come down the right side, guns at the ready. Everyone else keep sharp," Miles said into his radio as he rounded the bend and his windscreen shattered to a round of bullets. Norman pulled the Unimog sharply to the left side of the track while Miles got some quick shots off. The Land Rover in front of Charles pulled out and drove down the right side of the track, machine guns firing into the tree line. Charles watched as it skidded to a halt and all four guards spilled out taking cover and firing into the tree line. Up above, the helicopter swung high and came sweeping down along the track, two guards with machine guns, leaning out firing at the tree line, restrained by their lap belts.

Charles struggled with the Unimog steering realising that a tire had been punctured as he tried to aim the large vehicle to pass to the left of the Land Rover. He saw in his mirror another Land Rover coming at speed and watched it come along side and nearly made contact as he fought to keep the Unimog in a straight line. He flinched as his windscreen shattered followed by a loud bang and flying glass to the right side of his face. He grimaced in pain as he tried to keep up with the other Unimog and get away from the gunfire. He tightened the grip of his left hand on the wheel as he quickly wiped his sweat drenched forehead with his right hand and felt the blood that was running down from his right ear. He gingerly touched his face and his fingers felt glass shards but quickly he got his right hand back on the juddering steering wheel. He put the pain to the back of his mind and concentrated on steering the bucking beast that wanted to dive to the right rather than travel in a straight line. He fought hard until the searing pain building in his right shoulder became too much.

Max spun the helicopter around and came back in a low pass following the track until he was directly overhead of the security Land Rovers. He bought the helicopter to a hover and the guards opened fired on the tree line. One took two grenades and pulled the pins and held them at arm's length out of the helicopter. He look down and called to Max on his headset. "Max, ease her to the right a bit. That's it, hold her there." He dropped the two grenades out of the helicopter. "Give me three flash bangs!" he said to one of his men and held out his hand and took the proffered flash bangs as two loud explosions echoed below. He pulled all three pins from the flash bangs and threw them in a spread into the tree line and watched as they exploded. Two figures staggered from the tree line into the track and were instantly cut down by machine gunfire from the advancing guards. "Another two grenades!" he called. He took them, removed the pins and threw them deeper into the trees. "Max, let's move, we are sitting ducks here."

Charles managed to steer the stricken Unimog over to the far left side of the track cutting down numerous branches before bringing it to a semi controlled stop. He initiated the park brake before passing out and slumping over the steering wheel. A startled Duke looked at Charles, trying to take in the scene before pulling him upright in his seat. Seeing he was unconscious and covered in blood he grabbed the radio microphone.

"Charles has been hit. I repeat, Charles has been hit." He dropped the microphone and with Ryan's help undid the seat belt and pulled Charles from the driver's seat into the passenger seat. Edwin's Land Rover slewed to a halt beside them. Two guards jumped out of another Land Rover, taking up covering fire positions. Edwin ran around to the passenger side of the Unimog, squeezing between the trees and the vehicle and jumped in. He ripped Charles's shirt and inspected the wound.

"Gunshot wound!" He eased Charles forward. "The bullet is still in, it hasn't gone through and needs to come out." He rested Charles back in the seat. "We need to get him back to the compound or *Sundancer* quickly so the wound can be properly cleaned," he said to Anne who was visibly shocked and on the verge of panicking. Ryan held her tightly and quietly reassured her.

"Can Max do an airlift?" Duke asked.

"Well, we cannot go back to the clearing, so unless he can put down in the next junction we will have to drive out, which I would prefer not to do!"

"Max, can you set that thing down in the next junction?" Duke said into the microphone. "Charles has been shot in the shoulder and needs airlifting to *Sundancer*."

"I'll get her down," Max replied his voice loud and clear over the speaker. "It's just half a click ahead. I'll follow you guys."

"Right, let's get him into my Land Rover. Anne you are coming with me. Duke, Ryan, sorry, but you'll have to follow in one of the other Land Rovers," Edwin said taking charge.

Miles and Norman came in running low, both carrying automatic weapons at the ready. Ralph came round the back of the Unimog at a run nearly crashing into Miles and Norman.

"It's under control now," he said to Miles and Norman. "Just a few stragglers who are running into the rainforest. I've got some of the guys going after them. Their making a hell of a racket and leaving an easy to follow trail so we should find them. If not they will come to the tiger fence."

"I want them alive so we can interrogate them!" Miles stated. "Set up a guard and get that tire changed." He unclipped his radio. "Max, I want the four guards on your chopper back here in the Land Rovers as soon as you drop them off. Cover the Land Rovers on the way to the meet point. Out." He went round the side of the Unimog and helped load Charles into the Land Rover. He whistled to a guard nearby. "You, come here. Go with this Land Rover and keep your eyes peeled. Come back here after Charles is transferred to the chopper."

Max followed the Land Rovers before slowing as they approached the junction. He hovered and looked down at the junction clearing trying to gauge room for the rotors.

"It's going to be tight," he called to the guard in the passenger seat beside him. "Keep an eye of how close the rotors are to the trees on your side." He concentrated hard, his forehead knitted with lines as he lowered the helicopter down into the center of the junction. He wiped the beads of sweat from his eyes and looked around as they got lower. He noted the trees at the edge of the clearing being blown around by the wash from the rotors, another worry. He breathed a deep sigh of relief as he felt the skids gently touch the ground. He powered down and removed his helmet and ran his hands through his short cropped black hair. He looked around and saw the look of relief on the face of the guards and smiled. "Close, wasn't it?" he said. "It's alright for you lot, but I've still got to get this bird up. Let's get Mr. Langham on board." He jumped down and walked to the Land Rovers that came to a halt next to the helicopter. The guards stood helpless while Ryan and Duke loaded Charles into the rear of the helicopter, and Anne jumped in beside him.

A third Land Rover came to a slithering halt and Cathy jumped out and ran to the Helicopter.

"Is dad alright?"

"Get in the front," said Edwin. "Come on, Max, let's go."

Duke and Ryan climbed in and made sure Anne and Charles

were strapped in while Edwin looked at the facial wounds. Max jumped back in and looked around.

"Okay, close the doors, and strap in." He put on his helmet, looked around and slowly took the helicopter upwards carefully looking around at the swaying trees. "Cathy, keep an eye on my rotor distance on your side." He looked at her. "We'll be fine. I got her in, so I can get her out. I'll radio *Sundancer* on route to the compound. We will need to change to the Bell. This one doesn't have enough fuel." When he was clear of the trees he increased speed, the nose of the helicopter dipping down as they accelerated. He called the compound and arranged for the Bell's engines to be started and have personnel available to help with the transfer. He then called *Sundancer* and spoke to the doc. Then checked with Martin Deeks that the re-fueller was gone and breathed a sigh of relief when he heard it had departed. The last thing he needed was the full emergency response crew on the helipad. He looked around and saw that Edwin was cleaning and dressing the wound with the on board first aid kit. Max arrived at the compound at speed and saw a number of people waiting just back from the central pad. He came in low and swiftly landed the helicopter wasting no time, quickly shutting the systems down. He removed his helmet and ran over to the Bell and readied her for take-off, leaving the transfer of Charles to the others. He was pleased to see the engines and all electronics running. He put his headgear on and checked all systems were okay and waited until everyone was seated before taking off and heading towards *Sundancer* at the Bell's full one hundred and fifty five knots. He clicked his microphone. "Max to *Sundancer*, we're coming in hot. Be on the helipad in fourteen minutes. Have the doc and a wheelchair ready. Edwin is with us. Charles has been shot in the shoulder. Out." He clicked his Mic off and concentrated on flying. A few minutes later Grant's voice came clear over Max's headphones.

"*Sundancer* to Max. Message understood, doc will get his surgery ready to remove the bullet. We will be ready with the wheelchair." Max recognised Grant's voice. "Library doors will be unlocked. Weapons systems are deactivated. You are now on radar, clear for straight in approach."

"Get the crew ready to refuel me as soon as I land. Out," Max replied and turned his attention to landing. He extended the landing gear and slowed as he came round the stern of *Sundancer* and came in straight over the aft deck and lowered the Bell on to the helipad on the Sea View deck. He saw Grant coming though the library doors onto the helipad and pushing the wheelchair. He stayed on board to shut down the systems. Leaving Edwin, Duke and Ryan with Grants help to manoeuvre Charles from the Bell to the wheelchair. Grant pushed the wheelchair through the library with Edwin at his side followed by Cathy and Anne. Ryan and Duke walked round and opened the cockpit door.

"I don't think we are going to stay here tonight. Do you?" Ryan posed the question to the others.

"No, I think we will be heading at pace to the Atlantic," Max said. "Ralph is on his way to the compound with Miles. Norman is heading up the search squads. I'll be off to get them in fifteen minutes as long as the doc doesn't need Edwin. And those guys get me refuelled." He pointed to two crew members setting up the refuel hose. "Time for a coffee and then check in with the doc." He jumped down and they went through the library to the lift. Duke and Ryan left the lift on the main deck while Max rode down to the medical center by way of the galley for some coffee. Max met Anne and Cathy coming out of the medical centre, looking dazed and drawn. Max passed them each a mug of coffee from the tray he held.

"Any news?" Max asked.

"Doc won't say anything. He is removing the bullet and has him on an intravenous drip and giving him a pint of blood. The nurse has taken a blood sample, which she is testing now and Edwin has started to remove the bits of glass from his face. Doc is keeping him sedated until he is stitched up," Cathy said speaking for her mum. "They seem concerned that bacteria or infectious materials may have entered the wounds."

"So, what do we do, stay here?" Max asked.

"No, as soon as the others are on board we are heading to the Atlantic. I want to find the bastard who organised this!" Anne said firmly.

"Right," said Max, "I agree with that. I will tell the Captain to get underway and, as soon as Edwin is okay to leave, I'll go and pick up the guys on shore."

"Is it safe to get underway with dad the way he is?" Cathy inquired quietly. "I mean if the Doc is working on him?"

"Yes, dear. The doc says it will not make any difference," Anne replied. "Max, off you go. Come on, Cathy. I could do with a stiff drink."

Max headed for the bridge, sharing the lift with Cathy and Anne, who alighted on the main deck, where Max saw Duke and Ryan sitting in the lounge area, drinks in hand. They walked across to Anne and Cathy and took them in tow to the bar. Max continued up to the Sea View deck and entered the bridge. The Captain, John Whitcome, turned around in his chair when he saw Max enter.

"Well, how is he?" he asked.

"Doc and Edwin are working on him now. Mrs. Langham wants to get underway immediately and head for the Atlantic. I'll be off to get our two stragglers, Miles and Ralph, as soon as Edwin is ready to leave. Get underway and I'll catch up with you. I'll radio for co-ordinates if I can't see you."

"Okay, be careful. We'll take it easy and make sure that we keep within your maximum range," Whitcome said as Max disappeared out of the door. "Martin, Franklin, you heard the man, weigh anchor, extend stabilizers, make course North Atlantic as plotted, speed twelve knots."

"Yes, sir, weighing anchor, extending stabilizers, position thrusters on. All engines are ready," Martin Deeks confirmed.

"Course computed, ready to make twelve knots," Franklin replied.

"Thank you, gentlemen. Mr. Franklin, make twelve knots, balance revolutions," Whitcome announced. *Sundancer* slowly made headway and started a long slow turn to bring her round to a southerly heading. Max could feel her picking up speed beneath his feet as he returned to the clinically white medical center.

"You want to know if Edwin can leave?" asked the doc stitching up the wound left by the bullet.

"You are correct as always, doc. No rush, I just want to be able to get there and back," Max said, noting he was still carrying his coffee mug, which was now empty.

"Yes, yes, yes, I have Michelle here. So Edwin you may leave. Thank you for your work. For a veterinarian, you make a great doctor."

"From you, doc, I take that as a compliment," Edwin replied, removing his gown and latex gloves. "Let me know how the patient progresses."

"I will. Sincerely, you stopped a lot of infection by your early intervention. Now go and get back to your cats." The doc replied, without looking up from his work.

Max waited until Edwin was ready and led him through the labyrinth of plush corridors to the main stairwell and lift.

"This is some yacht. I never realised how big it was. I would get hopelessly lost," Edwin commented. "Three lifts, countless stairs, too many cabins to count."

"You get used to her quite quickly. The layout is actually quite intuitive once you get the hang of it," Max said as they entered the lift and pressed the button for the Sea View deck. "So we now go up five floors to the helipad."

"I like the glass lift. It gives you a chance to see around. I have heard that there are three cars and four boats on board. Is that true?" Edwin asked.

"Two eight metres long rigid inflatables and two big fourteen metre luxury launches. The fourteen are new and took over from the original ten metre launches. In the garage are a Mercedes, Range Rover and an Aston Martin," Max said leading the way through the library to the Bell 525. "But this is the second most expensive piece of kit on-board and she's all mine." He looked around and saw the two crew retracting the fuel hose back into its cabinet. "Climb in." Max took his seat and strapped in. "Helmet and belts on," he said to Edwin as he switched all the systems on. He looked around to see the crew were clear of the pad. "Here we go." He lifted the Bell off the deck, crabbed to starboard and swung away from *Sundancer*.

"Max to compound. We are on our way. ETA twenty six minutes."

Anne and Cathy returned to the medical center to see. The doc had them sit down in the ante room at his desk. The room was clinically white with a built in desk with two visitor chairs and the usual medical equipment and drugs cabinets to see to the everyday ills of the crew. In the opposite wall were two doors; one led to the day surgery designed to cope with broken bones, cuts and general emergencies; the other was the ward set up with four beds complete with oxygen and monitoring equipment. Pictures on the wall attempted to tone down the clinical look.

"So, doc, how is Charles and what is the prognosis?" Anne asked leaning on the desk, her face ashen.

"He should be okay, I think. We found no bacteria or infectious material. We have cleaned out the wound and facial cuts. We got the bullet out and Grant has that for forensics. The bullet tore through some muscle. We made the hole bigger to clean it and did the very best repair that we could. He will be very sore, which we can manage with pain relief," the doc carefully explained. "The only complication could be the onset of a Multiple Sclerosis relapse, but we will have to take that as it comes." He smiled and placed his hand on Anne's clasped hands, "He will be fine. It will just take time. I will keep him here overnight and release him tomorrow. He will be on light duties for a while and his right arm will be in a sling."

"He won't like that!" Cathy said. "When can we see him?"

"In about an hour when the sedation wears off. I will let you know as soon as he comes round."

"Thank you. Doc," Anne said and stood up, Cathy holding her arm.

"The entire crew are worried, you know. Could I recommend that the Captain gives an update on Charles and where we are going?"

"Let me think on that. I may want to wait until I have spoken to Charles," Anne replied.

"Okay, I will leave that with you," doc replied.

Anne and Cathy left the medical center. "Let's go and join Ryan and Duke and see what they think," Anne said as they walked down the corridor to the main central stairwell and took the lift to the main deck, where they found Duke and Ryan still there but this time Ryan was on a conference call. As Anne got closer she saw that he was on a call to President Johnson. She sat down beside Duke and Ryan on the sofa. Cathy walked over to the bar and ordered some drinks.

"Anne, I am so sorry to hear what has happened. How is Charles?" the President asked.

"To use the cliché, as well as can be expected. He is still sedated and the doc has just told me that he will be up and about tomorrow," Anne spoke quietly, still in a slight state of shock. Cathy sat beside her and passed her a cognac.

"So, these guys tell me you are heading for the Atlantic?" the President queried.

"That is correct. They are going to pay for shooting Charles. Make no mistake." She tilted her head at the sound of the approaching helicopter. "Max, Miles and Ralph are just returning. It will take some time to get to the Atlantic, so we have plenty of time to plan things through. I need to get an update from Marge."

"Anne, you have Ryan with you. He has my authority and will

act as your liaison with the fleet operating in the Atlantic. Please keep me advised of Charles's progress."

"I will do, Mr President."

Ryan leant forward and pressed the end call button. "Do you want me to connect with Marge?" he asked.

"No, we will do that in the morning and plan things from there. For now I just want to rest," Anne replied. She picked up her radio and spoke: "Bridge, as soon as the helicopter is secure make twenty six knots."

"Will make twenty six knots as soon as the Bell is secure," said the Captain's voice over the radio's speaker.

Chapter Twenty Three

The Northern Atlantic Ocean

Thomas watched the ramp door open and walked towards it from the cavernous interior of the aircraft. The interior lights were turned off. He looked into the blackness and felt a shiver run down his spine. The other two members of his team followed him and stopped by the jump indicator light that currently glowed red. He checked the GPS on his wrist; they were close. He did a last minute check of his gear. He looked at the dark sky and could see nothing below. The jump light changed to orange.

"Get ready, lads," Thomas said. "Don't forget to release the harness before you hit the water."

"We have done this before you know!" retorted Connor with a wry grin.

Thomas looked at his watch, and then at the jump light. When it turned green, he looked at Graham and Connor and said. "Okay, guys, let's go!" He ran to the end of the ramp and jumped into the cold blackness. He saw Connor and Graham follow him into the darkness and quickly lost sight of them. When he looked below he could see nothing but blackness. He regained a sighting on Connor and Graham when he briefly saw their beacon lights. He checked his GPS and altered his posture to change direction.

"What a time to go swimming," he said and looked at the altimeter on his wrist and saw it read two thousand five hundred feet and pulled out the pilot chute. He felt the sudden jerk upwards and looked up as the chute opened above him. Looking around he saw the other two members on this dangerous exercise do the same. The dark night sky was suddenly lit up by the blazing white light of a signal flare that slowly drifted in the sky. He looked below and briefly saw the outline of the submarine glinting amongst the choppy waves to his left below. He gently pulled on the toggles connected to the steering lines of the ram-air winged parachute to change his direction and lower his forward speed. The submarines deck lights lit up and a spotlight scanned the sky highlighting each parachutist in turn. He watched below as a deck crew in foul weather gear fought against the wind and rain to keep a rubber boat they were inflating on the deck.

He checked his altimeter placed his aqualung demand valve in his mouth, dropped the package that was hard against his rump, which fell to the end of its long guide line instantly hitting the water. With trained precision he punched his parachute harness quick release button, dropped clear from the harness, gripped his face mask, bit on the demand valve of his aqualung and entered the water as straight as an arrow. He went down deep and stroked for the surface. He looked around and sighting the submarine searchlight started to swim in its general direction. The searchlight soon picked him up and an inflatable boat came alongside and the crew, struggling against the heaving water, managed with some difficulty to drag him over the side. The searchlight scanned the water and picked up the second parachutist, the inflatable swung round, bouncing heavily through the waves collected him and then collected the third. Thomas breathed a sigh of relief that the most dangerous stage of the operation so far was completed. All they now had to do was the tricky transfer from the rubber inflatable to the deck of the submarine.

The co-ordination of the drop was planned by Keith, who, after trying various fast modes of transport decided it could not be achieved by any other outcome except a night jump. Thomas had reluctantly agreed, knowing that night jumps over land are tricky, and over water even more so. All the members of his team were capable of the jump but he chose the two most experienced, leaving the others in New York to follow the freight forwarders lead. Keith had kept in constant contact with both the aircrew and submarine throughout the operation until the three parachutists were safely aboard the submarine.

"Welcome aboard, Thomas," Marge said when Thomas entered the control room still in his wet suit. "Good to see you again. That was a very risky jump to attempt."

"You wanted me here, so I came," Thomas said cheerfully. "Hi, Mike, long time no see." He clasped Mike Holdsworth on his left arm.

"Good to see you again," Mike Holdsworth, the Captain of *Jupiter,* reciprocated. "You have certainly gone up in the world since I met you last, working directly for the President." His smile was full of warmth. "But you'll have to excuse me, I have a submarine to run and we need to reposition over the anomaly." Holdsworth turned and called, "Dive Officer, take us down, two hundred and fifty feet, ten degrees down bubble, all ahead flank speed. Navigator, set course for the anomaly."

"Dive, Dive, Dive," came the call from the Dive Officer.

"Well Marge, where can we get out of our wet suits?" Thomas asked shaking his arms.

"This way," Marge said, leading the way from the control room down a gangway. "After you have changed, I'll go through what we have found. Meet me in here." She pointed to a cabin on her right. "We have *Launch One* on route with *Deep Sea,* our submersible. She's five hours out and *Sundancer* is a day and a half out."

"*Sundancer* is on her way here! I thought Charles had been shot in Sumatra and would be in hospital?" Thomas questioned. "That's a hell of a long way away." Thomas could not understand why Charles was heading into trouble when he already had vessels in the area; plus there were both the British and American vessels around. The area was getting crowded.

"Yes, when Charles was shot, Anne took the decision right away to head this way. The medical center on *Sundancer* has a small but well equipped operating theatre and the doc is experienced at handling most situations. Anyway, Anne is out to get Axmann for shooting Charles. The Captain sailed *Sundancer* at almost her full speed to get here. They started off well, slowed when they hit a big storm in the Indian Ocean and then had mostly calm conditions through the Arabian Sea, the Gulf of Aden, the Red Sea, where they put the hammer down and then through Suez, where they refuelled. Charles has recovered pretty well over the past eight days and has mostly taken back command. Mind you, he still has the doc on his back keeping him well under control, and from what Anne told me he is confined to working no more than four hours a day."

"He won't like that," Thomas said and then chuckled.

"No, he doesn't. Now, this is your cabin, and the rest of your team are just here, next door. I'll be in the inner conference room port side next to the control room."

"Before you go, what did Mike mean by need to reposition over the anomaly?"

"We had to shift our position to the west to get within the return range of your aircraft," Marge answered and left them, returning to the Control room. "How long till we get back to the anomaly, Mike?" she asked the Captain.

"Two hours at the most. We are setting up to get more high resolution photos and video from the drone to work out the best way for *Deep Sea* to lift it. The tech guys are working on it now, and fitting a Geiger counter. Sonar have been doing some tweaks and hope to get some better readings" Mike said. "That was a dangerous jump those guys did."

"I know Keith tried every option to avoid a night jump but nothing else worked as well time wise, so Thomas went with it."

"Do they honestly think they can diffuse this thing if the *Launch One* submersible can bring it to the surface?"

"Thomas thinks he can. He has studied the photographs and the assembly drawings from Nevada."

"You're assuming that they used the parts that were stolen and built them the same way?"

"Yes, we are. We don't believe that they have enough expertise to deviate from the design of the Nevada construction of the trigger assembly," Marge replied. "Especially in the limited time they had. To design and make new parts would have taken many, many months of work and specialist equipment."

"Well, let's hope you and your experts are right because we are going to be right in its blast radius," Mike said with a grimace.

"The American's have a submarine closing in on us and an aircraft carrier, the *USS Nimitz,* just a few hours away. The *Nimitz* has some nuclear weapon specialists on board and I haven't told Thomas yet, but I think his nemesis Wozniak is on her."

"Well, that guarantees at least one explosion." Mike laughed. "I think he knows now. He's just come through the control room door," he said looking over Marge's shoulder.

Thomas entered the control room and walked over to the navigation desk, where Marge and Mike were standing looking at the plots while they chatted. "Should be fun! Wozniak will blow his lid. We ducked out from underneath him and headed to London, leaving him on his own," Thomas said cheerily. "I'll just stand and watch as he goes ballistic. He can't do anything to me, which will frustrate the hell out of him." He turned serious. "Now, what do we know, how deep, how big and why here?"

"Depth is easy. One thousand seven hundred feet. How big? Our best guess is around the ten to twelve kiloton range. Why here? Well he could not have chosen a worse location regardless of whether or not you believe in the Atlantis mythology. We are right on top of a cluster of black smokers and a very large asphalt volcano. The experts say if that thing were to blow, then the eastern seaboard would be devastated and the resulting tsunami would hit the UK and the European coasts hard. The volcanic eruption that could follow is an unknown quantity. There are too many things we don't know about it."

Mike rubbed his right eye. "The other question we have is where in hell has Axmann gone? The Americans have lost all traces of his submarine, so Marge here with the help of Keith and James have plotted his past track and are now analysing the sensor data in a radius at the termination of that track."

"So far we have three possible traces that we have passed onto the US Navy," said Marge. "We are, of course, analysing them further back at HQ, and James has programmed the computer to refine the frequency ranges, removing known natural sounds to hone in on a definitive submarine trace. Once that has been accomplished, then the program has to remove the known frequencies given out by the US submarines that have been close enough for the sensor array to pick them up. What will then be left is Axmann's submarine, if it is there. My personal view, for what it's worth, is that he is heading to the St Lawrence Seaway. One of the last possible positions was south east of Sable Island, well to the north of any American coastal target, and it would make sense for him to keep to the deep waters of the Atlantic Basins. It's feasible that he could make use of the St Lawrence Seaway to dive deep into the heart of the United States. But the US Navy disagrees and are still searching off the Washington coast." Marge was frustrated and it showed. "Of the three traces, it's the best trace we have and they ignore it!"

"It's' okay. Look, why don't you and I conference call Charles, Ryan, Keith and James and go through what we know for certain. If we believe truly and have enough evidence to indicate that Axmann has gone north, then Charles can call President Johnson with the data and our findings," Thomas suggested seeing how frustrated Marge was at the navy's inactivity.

"Oh, how I could scream at them!" Marge said loudly.

"Marge, don't worry. Come on into the conference room.

We'll get things sorted." He took her gently by the arm. "Mike, get the communication guy to video connect us with *Sundancer* and HQ and put the call through to the conference room."

"No worries," Mike replied.

Sundancer powered her way across the Atlantic Ocean on a heading that would pass them north of Bermuda. Captain John Whitcome sat on the bridge of *Sundancer* in his deep upholstered Captain's chair, examining the large computer screen in front of him, from which he could call up all the functions and navigation data of the one hundred and eight five metre superyacht. He looked at the weather radar and could see they were nearing the edge of the storm, which had slowed them down for the past sixteen hours. He called up his fuel load and looked carefully at the consumption rate. In his mind he calculated that if they kept up their current speed of eighteen knots to the edge of the storm, and then resumed thirty eight knots, it would necessitate another unscheduled fuel stop. At cruising speed they had a normal range of ten thousand nautical miles, but until this storm hit they had been running at thirty eight knots and their fuel burn rose exponentially.

"Mr. Deeks, fuel burn computation, please."

"At current rate, and assuming we return to full noise, we could either make St. Georges or Silver Lake. But I would prefer not to navigate through Pamlico Sound. St. Georges would be much easier and is, by far and away, much closer, Captain."

The Captain acknowledged Deeks with a slight nod of the head. "Mr. Franklin, set course for St. Georges and call the authorities for clearance. Let them know we are only there to refuel. Then complete the clearance paperwork."

"Setting course for St. Georges, Aye, Captain. Course heading plotted, changing course, slow long turn, maintaining current speed," Franklin said, keeping his eyes on the navigation screen while he slowly turned the small helm wheel.

"Mr, Deeks, contact the fuel bunkering company and advise them of our arrival time and fuel requirements. You will need to arrange payment as well."

"Aye, Captain."

"Thank you, gentlemen. I will go and advise Mr. Langham of our course change and reason," Whitcome said. "I will have my radio with me." He stood up from his chair, picked up his radio and walked across the expansive bridge to the rear door that led to the corridor that ran the width of the superyacht. He took the lift down to the main deck, where he knew he would find Charles and Anne in the quietness of the forward lounge with its large picture windows looking out onto the bows. Double glass doors led to the bow relaxation zone with a small swimming pool, hot tub and loungers. He walked through the lounge and passed the dining room and down the corridor towards the forward lounge. He saw through the tinted glass door that Charles and Anne were in the lounge sitting on the large circular beige settee. He knocked on the door and waited. Anne looked up and motioned for him to enter. The lounge was bathed in a soft light with the darkened glass adding to its serene atmosphere while music played softly in the background. Anne and Charles were in the middle of a game of dominoes. The doors to the bow area were closed.

"Sorry to disturb you," he said as he entered.

"That's okay, it must be important," Charles said. "I assume it's to report our course change?"

"Yes, sir." He grinned at Charles noticing the subtle course change. "Our fuel consumption rate since we left Suez requires that we refuel in Bermuda."

"That's fine," Charles said. "We have a conference call with Marge in twenty minutes, and I would like you to join in. We may have a few course changes coming up."

"I assume that the call will be in the library?"

"Yes, it more relaxing than in the conference room."

'When do we get out of this weather?" Anne asked.

"We should be in calmer seas within the hour Mrs. Langham. I will do some course checking. I think I know some of the optional destination points," Whitcome said. "I will see you in twenty minutes." He turned and left, closing the door behind him and returned to the bridge.

"So, as you can see ,Charles, the US Navy is not being sensible," Marge said, her face filling half the screen as she leaned forward over the table, her arms crossed and her chin resting on the back of her hands. James and Keith filled the other half of the screen.

Around the library Duke, Ryan and Max sat in a settee angled to face the screen, Charles and Anne had a steward pull two armchairs together in front of the screen and the Captain sat at one of the desks with a view of the screen. The steward quietly served drinks and some snacks.

"Marge, I agree. From what we have heard from Keith and James, your assumption is pretty much spot on, but still there are a few issues to wrap up. The main issue as I see it is that you, *Jupiter* and *Launch One* need to take care of the weapon you've found and someone needs to chase down Axmann and his submarine, and only *Sundancer* and the US Navy have the speed to do that," Charles said, looking around the room for any reactions. "We are heading for Bermuda to refuel, after which we will head at full steam to the co-ordinates you've given us near Sable Island. In the meantime, Keith, James and you need to isolate Axmann's submarine from the rest of the sonar sounds. Meanwhile, Ryan and Duke will put a call through to President Johnson. How does that sound?"

"Very good," Marge agreed. "*Launch One* is now overhead. We have an American aircraft carrier up there as well. I think it's the *USS Nimitz* with some experts on board to help with the defusing, and a nuclear submarine close by which is redundant in this situation and should be doing more pro-active work!"

"Marge, if they want a submarine there, let them. It can do no harm," Charles said, sensing frustration in her voice. "They cannot get their deep sea submersible on site for many hours yet, so work with them please. I want you guys out of danger so as soon as *Deep Sea* has lifted the weapon and passed it over to the aircraft carrier. *Jupiter* is to dive to her depth limit and put as much distance between her and the weapon in the shortest possible time. *Launch One* is to recover *Deep Sea* and also to get the hell out of there as quickly as she can."

"You're the boss," Marge said sharply.

"Charles, hi," Thomas said, nudging Marge slightly to one side. "I want to go down with the submersible and see if I can find out how they intend to trigger the weapon. Would that be okay?"

"If you think it's worthwhile, then there's room on *Deep Sea*. You had better transfer to *Launch One* quickly. They will not be hanging around with the launch of *Deep Sea*. Marge, are you okay with this?"

"It's a good idea, actually. We will surface next to *Launch One* and Thomas can transfer to her."

"Thomas, how long will you take to get clear once your task is done?" Charles enquired.

"I'll either stay on *Launch One* or commandeer an aircraft from the carrier using my Presidential warrant."

"Nice one. Okay, then let's get this show on the road, as they say. Talk to you guys soon." Charles leant forward and pressed a button to end the call then looked around for the Captain. "Captain, after we refuel we head for Sable Island. You will need to arrange a re-fueller to meet us there. I think we are going to go on a bit of a chase and burn a lot of fuel and I would like to have full tanks. Plot a course and check clearances on the St Lawrence Seaway. Tell chef if he needs any provisions, then he'd better email his orders in advance and have them waiting for him when we arrive in St. Georges. Oh, and let the crew know what's going on."

"Yes, sir. I will get straight on to it," Captain Whitcome said, as he stood up and started for the door.

"Oh, one thing. When do we arrive in Bermuda?" Charles asked, a sudden thought running through his mind.

"In about four hours, sir," the Captain replied after quickly looking at his watch.

"And how far are we from *Jupiter* and *Launch One*?"

"When we arrive in Bermuda, we will be approximately four hundred nautical miles away, or around ten and a half hours at thirty eight knots."

"Okay, thank you," Charles said dismissing the Captain. "Time to call the President, gents?"

"Yes, I think we have enough information to call him and I

feel confident that with what we have been told and shown by the team, he'll see things our way," Duke said. "Ryan?"

"I agree with Duke, Charles. We have enough."

"Okay, I will get the call put through. Do you need me, Anne and Max?" Charles questioned.

"No, I think we can manage," Ryan said with a smile.

Charles picked up his radio and spoke to the surveillance room and arranged for the call to be put through. "It will be through in a minute or so. Anne, Max, come with me, please." Charles stood up and walked from the library with Anne and Max in tow. He crossed the wide corridor and entered the bridge, where he found the Captain, Martin Deeks and Franklin around the large display table at the rear of the bridge. He walked over to the bridge.

"Okay, show me," he said to the Captain, resting his palms flat on the screen. Deeks and Franklin made room for the others as they arrived around the table.

"This is us, over here. We have *Jupiter* and *Launch One*. This line is our current course to Bermuda and this red line is our plot from Bermuda to Sable Island. This line is an estimated plot from Sable Island to the St. Lawrence Seaway, and finally this point is where we believe Axmann's submarine was heard." The Captain explained his finger tracing the lines on the large screen. "This here is our fuel computation for each stage at twenty six knots." He pointed to a table in the top left hand corner of the screen.

"Recalculate that based on thirty eight knots. What's our fuel reserve like for the Bell?" Charles looked at Max.

"We are at about forty percent," Max replied.

Charles looked at Martin Deeks. "Arrange for the helicopter refill tanks to be topped up. Max, you make sure the team fill the Bell to the brim before we get to Bermuda."

"What's our current speed?" Anne asked.

"Thirty two knots, Mrs. Langham," Mr Franklin said.

"If we rise to thirty eight knots, do we have enough fuel?" Anne asked.

"Yes we do, Mr. Langham," Franklin replied.

"Well then, make thirty eight knots," Charles advised smiling at Anne.

Franklin left the display table and walked over to his chair, sat down and grasped the four throttle levers and, gently, slowly pushed them forward, carefully adjusting each one to balance the output of each of the four engines. The increase in speed was imperceptible to anyone on board. "*Sundancer* now at thirty eight knots, sir," he called.

Charles stood.

"Thank you, Mr. Franklin. Captain, keep me advised of progress. We will be in the conference room next to the surveillance room." Charles led Anne and Max out of the bridge.

"What's all this about darling?" Anne asked Charles as they waited for the lift.

"What's Axmann's next target? What could he possibly desire to hit next? We know through Max, which has been proved correct, is that his first target is based on Third Reich research. So, is that still true for the second?" The lift arrived and Max selected the deck button when they were all in.

In the conference room Charles had Grant pull up the documents they had analysed from the computer data taken from the Hawaiian office.

"What I want to do is to search all the, let's call them, 'Atlantis Files,' for any reference to cities, towns, landmarks in the United States," Charles said looking at Grant.

Grant breathed out heavily. "Well, that will not be an easy task. May I suggest that first we pull up each of the pictures and map files we found and see if there is one on the United States?"

"It's a start," Max said looking at Charles. "It's what I did."

Chapter Twenty Four

The Atlantic Depths

On the bridge, Captain Whitcome sat in his chair, resting his right elbow on the arm of the chair and looked through the rain drenched windscreens with their wipers tracking back and forth before returning his attention back to the weather radar. The run north from Bermuda had been mostly smooth sailing and he had noted the storm early on their weather radar and had seen that there was no way to avoid it altogether. To try and go around the storm and miss it entirely was impossible. He decided on a course change that would keep them as far away from the center of the storm as he could while maintaining a course as close as possible to what he had originally planned. *Sundancer* cut through another large wave, sending white water cascading over the bow. Whitcome rubbed his chin deep in thought.

"Mr. Franklin, I think the ride is getting a bit too rough for our guests. Reduce our speed down to eighteen knots and turn eight degrees to port please. That should allow us to cut the waves more cleanly and take us away from the worst of this."

"Aye Captain, eighteen knots eight degrees port rudder," Franklin replied.

The rear inner door opened and Max entered the bridge covered head to toe in wet weather gear. He unzipped the jacket, threw back the hood and cast off the jacket by the wall.

"How long will it be like this?" he asked the Captain.

"Around another six hours. I have changed course again to take us away from the worst of the storm. So, maybe a little less, depends really on how fast it moves," the Captain replied looking around and laughing when he saw how dishevelled Max was. "Get wet?"

"You could say that. Took four of us over an hour to apply the clamps, tether the rotor blades and get the covers on the helicopter. It's only when you do something like that, that you realise just how darn big she is," Max replied, helping himself to a coffee from the bar at the rear of the bridge. "I assume our course change will add to our journey time?"

"Only a small amount. In two hours I hope to alter course back closer to our original. We will still be battling the storm, but I hope it will be less ferocious. I should be able to increase our speed." A thoughtful look crossed his face. "A submarine will still be slower than us." *Sundancer* moved, a gentle wallow as she crested a wave at an angle. "Four metre swells, cresting five metres. She is built for far worse than this but you had better check on Duke and Ryan, not sure how good their sea legs are."

"Last time I saw them they were doing fine. I was going to see Grant to find out the latest on the weapon that Axmann left in the Atlantic depths," Max said draining his coffee. He removed the oilskin trousers. "Won't be needing these anymore. I'll come back and let you know the latest." Max left the bridge and took the glass lift down to deck two and walked along the main corridor to the surveillance room where he found Grant, Jake and Bruce in the darkened room seated in front of a large display screen having an animated discussion.

"How's the weapon lift coming along?" he asked, entering the room and taking a seat. Grant looked round and smiled.

"*Deep Sea* is two hundred metres from the surface, with the weapon held firmly in her arms. *Launch One* is ready to receive her into the moon pool, but the United States wants to remove the weapon before *Deep Sea* enters the moon pool." Grant said raising his hands in mock exasperation. "In that weather, they must be mad. They'll drop the bloody thing back in the Ocean if they try that!"

"It does sound precarious and as you say they could drop the darn thing," Max replied. "What do Duke and Ryan reckon?"

"They are next door, talking to the President. Their preference, like ours, is to moon pool *Deep Sea* and remove the weapon in the calm of the moon pool bay, and then transfer the weapon ship to ship by helicopter. Thomas is saying quite categorically that it must be removed from the submersible in the moon pool and is throwing around a Presidential warrant and refusing to surface anywhere else!" Grant said louder than he meant to.

"The President has given orders that the weapon is to be taken into the moon pool and transferred to the *USS Nimitz* by helicopter," Ryan said standing by the door, Duke at his shoulder.

"And what's this?" Max asked looking at the large display screen that was the center of attention.

"A hunch, that's all. Just seeing how far you can get a submarine up the St, Lawrence," Grant replied. "Without being seen, of course. We are assuming that you would have to run at periscope depth at night and lie on the bottom during the day." He pointed at the screen. "The points we have highlighted are about the only locations where you can sit a submarine off the bottom and not be visible at low tide."

"So, tell me, what has Charles decided to do?" Duke asked Grant moving his feet wider apart as the superyacht lurched through a wave.

"Our planned route is shown on this screen. We reckon from our sonar data that Axmann and his submarine are rounding Sable Island to the east, and we are going to pass to the west. We believe that he is heading for the St. Lawrence Seaway to try and strike deep into US territory."

"Did the so called 'Atlantis files' provide any more clues?" Duke asked Grant.

"No. Came up blank. We could be totally wrong with the St. Lawrence, but we are taking the punt that there is nothing else in that area where he could feasibly head for if he wanted to strike the United States."

"Well, it's a reasonable deduction," Max commented. "Where is *Mercury*?"

"Let's see . . . she should be off our stern to port," Jake said, turning to look at the sonar screen. "Yes, there she is. She's running at one fifty metres depth, one kilometre off our stern, port side."

"Comforting to know," Max said.

"*Deep Sea* is in the moon pool," Grant said, and motioned over to another monitor. "You can see here that the gantry hoist is positioned above her and will start to lift her when the clamps are in mating position." Everyone turned their attention to the monitor and watched as *Deep Sea* was gently lifted clear of the water and moved rearwards as the moon pool doors slid closed beneath. The cavernous area darkened as the underwater lights went off. When the moon pool doors sealed closed with a loud hissing sound, the cavernous interior bay burst into light as the exterior lights came on. In spite of the rough weather outside, the gyro stabilizing system installed on *Launch One* kept her as steady as a rock. To one end of the bay sat two acoustic generation devices, four single man ride on submersibles, a smaller two man deep sea submersible and racks of scuba gear. To the other side was a large decompression chamber and an empty cradle with its four clamps in the open position ready to receive *Deep Sea*. The hoist gently lowered the submersible into its purpose built cradle guided by a laser positioning system. As soon as the laser guides were lined up the four clamps swung up from the cradle and automatically locked onto the submersibles sides. The weapon was held firmly in the grip of its two mechanical arms, drawn in close to the submersibles circular forward viewing windows. The claws at the end of the arms hooking into large metal clips. Four crew purposefully entered the moon pool room, splitting up in a well-rehearsed routine. Two made their way instantly to the weapon and examined the clamps. Another made his way to the submersible hatch while the fourth sat at a console that operated one of the overhead gantry. With practiced ease he positioned the gantry directly overhead of the weapon. The two crew secured four thick webbing straps to the weapon and indicated to the operator to lift the weapon a fraction. As the gantry hoist took the weight he motioned to the submersible operator to open the clamps. The clamps slowly opened and the weapon swung free on the webbing straps. One of the crew put his arms up to halt the gentle swing.

The gantry operator moved the boom until it was on the opposite end of the moon pool to the submersible and lowered it slowly over a large flatbed trolley. The two crew members followed the weapon, steadying it and lined it up centrally on the trolley. They carefully tied it down onto the trolley and removed the webbing straps. They watched as Thomas climbed out of the submersible and walked across the bay over to the trolley and carefully examined the weapon.

"It looks as I thought. There is no way of seeing whether it is armed by timer or remote," Thomas said into his throat microphone. "This box attached to the side is not usual and is not on any of the designs I have seen and was the connection point for the long cable we cut away before lifting. I would hazard a guess that it's a radio antennae."

"Thomas, this is James in the Kermadec headquarters. I am following you by video. Can you open that box?"

"Sure, just six star head screws. What are you thinking?" Thomas asked turning to and looking at the many video cameras in the moon pool until he saw the one that gave the best direct view of the weapon.

"Well, if I was the bomber, then I would have included a GPS tracker to initiate the weapon if it was moved laterally. Plus I think we should disconnect the radio receiver but leave the actual weapon decommissioning to the navy guys," James said wearily, his tiredness from the long hours showing.

Thomas looked around and grabbed a tool box and knelt down next to the weapon. Opening the tool box he picked up the power driver and inserted a star head driver bit and proceeded to remove all the screws. He carefully checked around the cover for any booby traps before removing the cover and water seal, "Okay, James, can you see this?"

"Yes, I can see quite clearly. Follow the antennae cable through the gland on the side of the housing to where it connects to that circuit board, and cut the cable. When you've done that, cut the two leads at the battery terminals. Cut the positive one first. Lastly, you can see the GPS tracker and display on the left hand side. Remove the black cable entering the base of the unit on the right, but do not touch the red cable."

"Okay, here goes." Thomas took some wire cutters from the tool box and cut the antennae cable, then the cables at the battery terminals. The GPS tracker screen remained powered on. "The GPS tracker must have its own power supply?" he commented as he felt beneath the GPS unit and undid the plastic cable locking nut and pulled the cable free. The screen readout of the GPS unit went blank. "All done!" he said placing the tools back in the box.

"Well done. The bomb can no longer be remotely detonated and is safe to move to the *USS Nimitz*," James declared happily.

"Well done, you two!" came a chorus over the radio from Duke, Ryan and Grant.

Thomas called two crew over. "Help me take this to the deck lift," he said as they arrived and proceeded to push the trolley over to the open doors of the large deck lift. They pushed the trolley into the lift and Thomas pressed the surface button. Once on deck, with the help of some of the crew from the United States Navy Sikorsky Seahawk helicopter, they loaded the weapon for its transfer to the *USS Nimitz*. Thomas and the *Launch One* crew stood back as the Sikorsky lifted off the deck and slowly made its way through the heavy wind and rain towards the *USS Nimitz*.

Thomas, dripping wet, went to the bridge to see the Captain. He was surprised at how differently set up the bridge was compared to the one on *Sundancer*. With five crew plus the Captain, it had a cramped business like feel, compared to the roominess and warmth of *Sundancer's* bridge. He walked across to the Captain, running his hand through his wet hair.

"Captain, the weapon is aboard the Navy helicopter, so we can now get the hell out of here," he said.

"Thank you, Thomas. I must say that's a relief and I will be a lot happier when we have at least fifty miles between us and it! Okay gentleman, you heard the news," Captain Simpson, a bear of a man with a ruddy face and thinning grey hair and full grey beard barked his orders in a deep gravelly voice. A product of the British navy, he was old school and gave orders rather than conversed with his crew. "Station keeping thrusters off, reset gyro stabilizers, full ahead flank speed. Navigator, set intercept course for *Sundancer*. Communications, get me Captain Holdsworth on *Jupiter*."

"Aye, Sir, connecting you to Captain Holdsworth on *Jupiter*," the young close cropped hair rating confirmed. "You are through, sir."

Captain Simpson picked up his handset. "Mike, this is Albert. We are heading for Sable Island at full speed. The weapon has been transferred to the *USS Nimitz*."

"Right, we'll set course for Sable Island and dive to our maximum depth until we are out of blast range," Holdsworth replied.

Thomas felt the acceleration as *Launch One's* two huge stainless steel propellers bit into the water and pushed the huge ninety five metre vessel forward through the waves, quickly gathering speed. The wave piercing design of the hull split the waves, cutting through them cleanly with only an imperceptible lift of the bows. "What's our maximum speed, Captain?"

"In fine weather we can reach twenty seven knots, but in these conditions we will be running at twenty one knots. We are much slower than *Sundancer*. We have the same engines, but only two because of the space taken up by the moon pool and our gyro stabiliser system is not up to her standard. Charles is looking at a new submersible carrying vessel design that will have increased speed and range. We have not finalised the design but in the latest schematics it has the capacity for two submersibles like *Deep Sea* each in a separate moon pool." Captain Simpson smiled. "I have a meeting with him next month where we should finalise and commission the build."

"Sounds exciting and expensive. What will happen to this vessel?" Thomas queried.

"I think it will be donated to some marine research institute, along with the submersible, once we have stripped out our software and armaments." The Captain shrugged his shoulders. "We won't need it."

"An expensive gift, but I wouldn't expect anything else knowing what I do about the man." Thomas looked down at his shirt front and trousers. "Well, I think I will go and have a shower and get changed into some dry clothes before I catch a chill. Where's my cabin, by the way?"

"Deck three, cabin seven," he Captain said. "You did well, Thomas, and thank you."

Thomas left the bridge and quickly found his cabin, stripped and enjoyed a hot shower easing his aches and pains. He quickly dried himself and changed into dry clothes and turned on the

TV. The BBC world news was covering the ongoing situation in London following the bomb blast. The number injured was increasing every hour and counted in the hundreds of thousands; fatality numbers were thought to be even higher but rescue crews couldn't even get anywhere near close to ground zero. The British Prime Minister had recalled the entire Royal Navy fleet of aircraft carriers, destroyers, frigates and submarines back to British waters. Some were ordered back to their home ports to help with the rescue effort, and some to patrol the waters around the United Kingdom. Airports and sea ports remained closed. The Channel tunnel access was blocked and under twenty four hour guard. The situation remained dire. Fresh water and foods were becoming scarce, due to contamination, and supplies from the United States and Europe could not arrive fast enough. When supplies did finally arrive, distribution to those in need was slow as routes were extended to avoid contaminated areas. Tent camps, holding hundreds of thousands displaced people, sprouted up around north and west of London with rule of law overseen by the army. Hospital tent camps rose up, circling all around London. Main food and water distribution centres were set up close to the camps. Those whose homes were unaffected were asked to take in the displaced. Rioters and looters were shot on sight, no questions asked. The Prime Minister's latest address to the nation announced that prevailing winds, carrying radioactive fallout heading east of London, necessitating the total evacuation of an area twenty eight miles wide east of London to the English Channel. The French Premiere had, in talks with the Prime Minister, initiated the evacuation of the French population across the Channel from the fallout zone. Another American aircraft carrier, the USS *Carl Vinson* and an American hospital ship, the USNS *Comfort,* had arrived to provide more personnel, supplies and hospital aid.

Thomas was not surprised that no mention was made of the nuclear weapon in the Atlantic, or of the search for Gustav Axmann or even of Charles Langham's involvement. Those details were known by only a select group of people and would remain that way forever more. Any documents released in the future would be heavily redacted. He winced as the news item showed a satellite feed image of the devastation and turned the TV off, recalling vividly the image of the couple with young children walking amongst the debris in the blast zone. He closed his eyes and tried to shrug the image away. He had seen many things in his life that we would preferred not to have seen, but seeing those children, he shivered, grabbed the door knob and left his cabin to find Graham and Connor and decide what to do next.

Chapter Twenty Five

Somewhere Near Sable Island

The submarine broke surface half a mile from the freighter, which altered course in a slow tight turn to get close to the submarine. The freighter Captain, with infinite skill in the choppy waters, manoeuvred the freighter to come alongside the submarine. Two crewmen threw large tires secured to ropes over the side, to act as fenders, while another two threw mooring lines to the crew members on the deck of the submarine, who looped them around cleats on the deck. Albrecht climbed out of the forward hatch and, stumbling on the pitching deck, turned to help his father. A crew member passed out a large rucksack, which Albrecht picked up and slung over his shoulder.

Gustav, with difficulty, slowly climbed the ladder with Albrecht kneeling down to help him. At the top of the ladder Gustav rested one knee on the damp deck. A light shower had arrived, slowly increasing in intensity. Using his walking stick, he struggled to stand up but defiantly managed it on his own. He stood in front of Albrecht.

"Well, Albrecht, this is it." Gustav spoke slowly and wearily. "We part company and I do not think we shall see each other again. Now go. You know what you have to do. Michael will be waiting for you onshore." Gustav turned, his head down, keeping himself steady with his walking stick.

"Father," Albrecht said, placing a hand on his father shoulder, his voice controlled to hide emotion. "I do not like this and I do not know what you intend to do. All I know is that it must be for the good of the future of the Reich. So, I will accept it. We will meet again someday, maybe not in this world, but we will meet again along with Mother, God bless her soul. Goodbye, father," Albrecht said quietly, noting his father avoiding his eyes. He turned and climbed the boarding ladder that had been placed over the side of the freighter.

The submarine crew released the mooring lines and threw them to the freighter crew, who coiled them on the deck. The freighter slowly moved away from the submarine and turned towards shore. The huge tires were hauled back onto the deck. Albrecht looked back and saw two submariners helping his father to climb down through the hatch before they followed him, closing the hatch behind them. He stood and watched as the submarine increased forward speed, slowly disappearing beneath the surface until only the snorkel could be seen slicing through the water. Albrecht stayed rooted at the side of the freighter, gazing over the side as his hands gripped the gunwales, his knuckles turning white. He didn't bother to wipe the rain from his eyes or were they tears? His eyes followed the snorkel almost hypnotically until that, too, disappeared beneath the surface. He sighed heavily, wiped his face and entered the bridge.

"Captain, how long to shore?" he asked removing his sodden coat.

"Three and a half to four hours. We have to keep a close eye on the radar to avoid unwanted attention," the Captain said. "Contact Michael. I need to know the exact drop off co-ordinates and time."

"Very well," Albrecht said, unclipping the VHF radio microphone and turning the tuning dial. "Michel, this is Albrecht. Do you read me, over? Michael, this is Albrecht. Do you read me, over?"

"Albrecht, this is Michael. You are faint, but I read you, over." Michael's voice came crackling over the radio's speaker.

"Michael, we need your exact GPS co-ordinates," Albrecht said slowly and clearly into the microphone.

"That could not be easier. We are at Dyers Point, Cape Elizabeth, Maine. Come into the rocky beach tonight. We will be parked in the car park at the top of the beach with our headlights on. We will flash them when we see you through the night vision scope. Keep your lights off."

Albrecht looked over at the Captain and asked, "When can we be there?"

"Say, eleven PM tonight."

"Michael, we will be there tonight at eleven PM."

"We'll be there. See you tonight, out," Michael's voice replied.

Albrecht replaced the microphone in its clip and gazed out through the windshield, wondering what his father was going to do with the other weapon. Where was he taking it? From what his father had said, he did not expect to survive this attack. Albrecht was accustomed to death and knew that the survival and rise of the Fourth Reich was all that really concerned his father. It has been his life's work. As the Der Fuhrer, he knew his own survival was paramount and was all that mattered to those under his command and those who surrounded him. After meeting up with Michael and his team, they would return home to collect the vial that his father had mentioned. He opened his pack and removed a map and laid it down on the chart table, smoothing the folds. He looked carefully and worked out that they had a very long drive to Florida. They would have to be exceptionally careful where they stayed overnight to avoid unnecessary attention. In Florida, they would sell the car and buy a fast boat to get them to Cuba, then refuel and carry on to Haiti, where they would pick up their tickets and fly home to Brazil. It would be a long, tiring and dangerous journey.

"Where do you head for Captain, after you drop me off?"

"It was to be home to Hawaii and await further instruction from your group," the Captain replied. "But now your father wants us to steam up the St Lawrence River, where we will pick him up after the submarine can go no further. We then take him through to the Great Lakes." He shrugged his shoulders. "From there I have no idea. It was going to be a pleasure craft until the group had difficulty in obtaining one, so it falls to me. The submarine will head for Hawaii after they drop your father off. We will meet up with them somewhere on route or in Hawaii, I hope. I presume your father told you about the loss of the mining freighter? Depending on what you want my group to do, we may have to review resources."

"I will keep that in mind. I have yet to formulate our future plans and activities. Once this chapter in our long history is finalised, I will then know what we have achieved and how far we are from the goals and aspirations of our forefathers." Albrecht replied, his voice serious and words carefully spoken. "My father's legacy will be hard to follow and I must not let him or our ancestors down. I will take the time and put a lot of effort and thought into developing our future plans, once I know how far we are away from the end goal as set out by our ancestors." Albrecht left the bridge and went down to the galley, grabbed a coffee and made himself a few sandwiches. He took them with him and sat on the deck to grab some fresh air. After he had been cooped up in the confines of the submarine for so long, the cool sea air was refreshing and helped him clear his mind. The coffee was strong and the sandwiches filled a small hole. He looked forward to a proper hot cooked meal and a nice red wine. He wished his father had advised him of his plans, but it was obvious that the only person who knew what his father was planning was his father. Everyone else knew just enough to accomplish their bit. Whatever it was that he was going to do, he was going to do it alone. He suddenly felt the full weight of his responsibilities.

The freighter slowed and lowered the high speed center console boat over the side. The Captain had taken the precaution of running without any navigation lights and had a crew member constantly viewing the radar screen. Albrecht climbed down into the lowered boat and joined the crew member who started the large outboard and spun the wheel to take them around the headland. The boat crested each wave, slamming down hard onto the next. Albrecht licked the salt from his lips as he looked at the shore line. Seeing some lights, he screwed his eyes against the spray and concentrated on the image he saw. The lights flashed. He pointed to the shore towards the car headlights. The crewman spun the helm and turned the boat towards the light. The lights flashed. The crewman slowed the engine as they neared the rocky foreshore until he felt the boats bow nudge the ground.

"I'll jump out here," Albrecht said. He jumped out of the boat into water up to his knees, quickly turned to grab his rucksack and pushed the dinghy away from the shore. "Good luck!" he shouted to the crewman.

"Thanks, and good luck to yourself!" the crewman shouted and spun the boat around and accelerated away into the darkness.

Albrecht splashed through the water towards the rocky beach foreshore and headed towards the headlights, which again flashed twice. As he neared the vehicle, the driver's door opened and he saw Michael standing beside the open door.

"Albrecht, hi," Michael called quietly, placing the night scope on the dashboard. "You are soaked through to the skin. Let's get you to the motel where you can change."

"Good to see you, Michael," Albrecht replied and headed straight for the passenger door, throwing his rucksack into the foot well and removing his jacket. "Let's go. Where are the others?"

Michael climbed back in and started the engine. "The others are at the motel. It's not far from here. I have a room booked for you tonight, plus a complete change of clothes, care of Anelie." He moved the gear selector from park to drive, released the handbrake and swung the car round and headed for the main road.

"You were told to get rid of this car!" Albrecht said when he recognised the F150.

"We did. We returned the car to the rental agencies branch on our way here two days ago. I bought this one from a dealer. The other was black. This is a dark blue so you wouldn't have noticed the change." He looked across at Albrecht, who was removing his shoes and socks and wringing the socks out.

"What's your plan?" he asked Albrecht.

"We head for Florida, sell this and buy a fast boat with long range tanks and head for Cuba, then Haiti, where we will store the boat safely for future use and fly home. I want to contact all our groups and find out who is still operational. By that time I will know what my father has or has not accomplished."

He wrung out his socks one more time then put them and his shoes close to the heater outlet vent. They sat quietly for the rest of the drive until Michael pulled up into the motel carpark and parked the F150 directly outside their rooms.

"Everyone is in my room waiting for you. I took the liberty of ordering some food before I left, which should arrive soon, if it's not there already. Your room is there on the right," Michael said pointing to the door just off to his right.

"Well, if you don't mind I'm going to have a hot shower and get changed first. I feel caked in salt and wet through to the skin."

"That's okay. Pop in when you are ready." They climbed out of the car. "But don't be too long or the food may get cold. Here's your room key." Michael threw the key to Albrecht, who caught it deftly with his free hand. Michael took the handheld VHF from the driver door pocket and clipped it on his belt, picked up the night scope and locked the F150. He watched Albrecht enter his room before he made his way to his room, where the three others were waiting. He smelt the aroma of the Indian takeaway before he saw that the food packed in foil trays and lids had been delivered. The girl, tall, blonde and slim wearing a jumper and jeans, was laid out on one of the beds asleep. The two men, both of medium build, one fair haired, the other had short black close cropped hair, were sitting in the chairs watching the TV.

"Albrecht is next door having a shower, but he'll be here shortly," he said quietly, not wanting to wake Anelie up. She was, he knew, in a relationship with Albrecht. No one was supposed to know. He had found out by accident while they were at the cottage and had kept the news to himself. He was on his way to see Gustav and was just about to turn the door knob to open the door to the lounge when he had heard shouting from within. It was a loud and aggressive argument between Gustav and Albrecht, and Anelie was the subject. Albrecht had shouted that his father had no right to tell him to forget his feelings towards Anelie. He loved her and he had to accept it. A fierce argument had ensued. Michael had walked away from the door and around the corridor seconds before it was aggressively opened and slammed shut. Albrecht stormed around the corner and nearly crashed into Michael. His face was red and his hands clenched tight; he said nothing, just stormed on past. Michael never let Albrecht know that he was aware of the argument or that he knew about Anelie. It was, in his mind, none of his business; besides he had a girl back in Brazil waiting for him and no one knew about her. Michael took the handheld VHF from his belt and opened the door and stepped outside. He pressed the speak button.

"Michael to freighter, we are all safe, over. Michael to freighter, we are all safe, over." He released the button and waited.

"Will pass on the news, out," came the short crackling reply. Michael smiled and went back into the room. He saw that Anelie was waking up.

"We might as well start serving this lot up," he said.

"Where's Albrecht?" Anelie asked in a yawn, while stretching her arms above her head.

"Next door, freshening up. He should be here in a minute. I told him about the food." Michael replied.

The door opened and Albrecht entered, his hair still wet from his shower, the stubble gone from his face.

"Hi, everyone, good to see you all again. Let's eat, I'm starving," he said, amongst much hugging and handshaking. Albrecht sat on the edge of the bed with Anelie while Michael and the others sat around the small circular wooden table. Michael removed the lids from the foil trays and passed them around with a fork each.

"After dinner, we need to get some sleep. I want to start early in the morning. We have a long drive ahead of us," Albrecht said between mouthfuls of the hot Indian takeaway.

"That's a good idea, although I have to say I'm sick of sitting in that thing. It's all we've done for days," replied Michael, spooning some more rice into his meal.

"Try being cooped up in a stinking submarine," Albrecht said and laughed. "We'll stop plenty of times to stretch and rest. Now eat, then sleep." He smiled at Anelie, who coyly smiled back.

Two hundred and twenty feet below the dark forbidding sea, Axmann entered the control room and walked over to the Captain, who stood next to the Navigator.

"Captain, we should be near the mouth of the St. Lawrence Seaway, yes?" he enquired sharply.

"We will be changing our course in...." the Captain looked over at the Navigator.

"Fourteen minutes, sir," the navigator answered looking at his fob watch.

"At that point we will be eighty nine kilometres from Cape Breton Island. From there we will be five hundred and seventy kilometres from the mouth of the St. Lawrence Seaway."

"This is taking much longer than we planned, so speed things up. We are losing time too much!" Axmann shouted and walked out of the control room hitting his walking stick hard on the metal floor as he went. He suddenly turned and pointed his walking stick at the Captain. "I have people to meet and a deadline. You know that, now go faster!"

"Sir, we will increase our speed, but we will then have to surface very frequently, which puts us in more danger of being seen as we get nearer to the coast," the Captain said quietly in as much of an authoritative voice as he dared. He immediately regretted speaking.

Axmann stood still, his hand shaking on the top of his walking stick. His emotionless eyes glared. "You dare blame your slowness on this submarine," he snapped. "You do as I say or get off this submarine now!" He stared at the Captain, his eyes threatening death. "Well, dare you not answer?"

"Sir, I will speed up the submarine. I will ensure we go as fast as we can. I am, as always, your servant at your command," the Captain spoke, his head down, his eyes averting Axmann's gaze.

"Yah, We will see, we will see."

Axmann turned, leaning heavily on his stick and made his way back to his cabin, muttering under his breath. He sat on his bunk, and, using both hands, swung both his legs up. He laid the walking stick at his side and turned the small reading light on.

He opened his notebook and reviewed his notes. He noted where they were and looked at his watch and started some long hand calculations. He leant down and lifted his satchel onto the bunk and pulled out a map and started to transfer some figures. With a deep sigh he folded the map and put it in the satchel along with the notebook, removed a brown plastic bottle and a small bottle of schnapps. He removed two tablets from the bottle and took them with two deep gulps of the schnapps. He placed the satchel on his left between him and the bulkhead. He closed his eyes and slept, a restless, disturbed sleep.

Sundancer slowed as she neared Sable Island. The Captain stood on the port bridge wing protected from the cold wind by a heavy dark blue wool overcoat, complete with the word *Sundancer* embroidered on the left breast. He peered through his binoculars, scanning the sea to the west. He lowered the binoculars. "All stop," he called as he opened the door and entered the bridge. "Mr. Deeks, prepare for refuelling on our port side." He made his way across the bridge and seated himself in his Captain's chair. "Mr. Franklin, station keeping please and keep the gyro stabilizer systems on. We are in quite choppy seas with a reasonable swell and we must think of our guests." He lifted one of the handsets at his side and pressed a few buttons on the keypad. "Miles, can you come to the bridge please? We are stationary in waters that could contain Gustav Axmann's submarine." He listened for a few seconds before saying. "Thank you, see you soon." He looked at the keypad and pressed a few more keys. "Mr. Langham, I wonder if I could possibly see you on the bridge. We are heaved too and lying just west of Sable Island. Axmann could be around and I would like to plan our next track." He listened for a moment. "Yes, Mr. Channing is on his way up. Thank you." He replaced the handset and looked around the bridge. "Gentlemen, Mr. Langham and Mr. Channing will be with us shortly. Make sure we are shipshape, please." He picked up his binoculars and walked back onto the port wing and watched the approaching vessel. Martin Deeks joined him on the wing and pulled his overcoat closer around him.

"That's our fuel, Captain. I just spoke to them and confirmed the code. We need forty two thousand litres to fill the tanks, which means we will be here for around two hours. Grant has scanned the vessel thoroughly, checked her on side scan, infrared and listened in on their radio! He's paranoid, that guy," Martin said.

"Exactly what he is paid for," replied the Captain, keeping his binoculars on the approaching vessel. The vessel slowly approached from the stern, coming alongside *Sundancer*. "Lower the fenders and port fuel hatchway. Standby for refuelling. Put fire team on action stations," he fired off the orders automatically and returned to the bridge. "Ah, Mr. Langham, Mr. Channing," he said when he saw them enter the bridge through the internal gangway door. "Thank you for coming. If I may firstly cover the reason for Mr. Channing's presence." He led them over to the large navigation screen at the rear of the bridge. "We will be stationary for around two and a half hours and lying in waters, which could easily contain Mr Axmann's submarine. So we are quite vulnerable."

Channing looked at the map and, with a few touches to the screen, overlaid the map with radar. Then another few touches he overlaid the ocean sensor array. "Man, we are very vulnerable, indeed. The sensor array stops at the continental shelf. I've seen enough. If you'll excuse me, I will instigate a full surveillance and readiness operation." He walked swiftly away and out of the bridge.

"Well, Captain, looks like it's just you and me," Charles said with a smile and leant on the navigation table with the palms of his hands. "So, what have we here?"

"I believe we are, well, we are here. Our planned route takes us through here then around here to the St Lawrence Seaway, some nine hundred and forty kilometres. *Launch One* is here, just four hundred kilometres behind us, with *Jupiter* shadowing her. *Mercury* is beside us off our starboard bow at periscope depth."

"Okay, Axmann is in the area, of that there is no doubt. We desperately need to find him. The United States Navy never picked up any trace and are now looking for him off the North Carolina coast and the Nantucket shoals."

Charles saw the Captain raise his eyebrows.

"I know, no doubt, that they have their reasons. Anyway, we know he is around here, so *Mercury* needs to do a sweep and *Launch One* and *Jupiter* can join in when they arrive. As soon as we get a position on his submarine, then we will follow him and stay outside his sonar range. I'm betting on his sonar being an older model. *Launch One* will take lead, while *Sundancer*, flanked by the submarines, which will follow at a ten kilometre distance. If we do enter the St. Lawrence, then *Sundancer* will stay behind *Launch One* flanked by the submarines. We will dock in Quebec with *Jupiter* and *Mercury* submerged beside us facing alternate ways. Under no circumstances will *Sundancer* enter any locks."

Martin Deeks walked up beside them. "We are now pumping fuel, sir," he said directing his words at the Captain. "Very professional outfit. The fuel hose came across on a gantry, and within minutes we were pumping. At the rate we are receiving fuel, I reckon on an hour and forty minutes, a lot faster flow rate than planned."

"Thank you, Mr, Deeks. Please let me know as soon as refuelling is complete," Whitcombe replied. Martin Deeks returned to his post on the port side of the bridge.

The bridge door opened and Miles entered and joined them at the table. "We are safe for now. I have the sonar and radar screens on permanent watch and the weapons systems at ready stations," he explained. "So what have I missed?"

Charles explained briefly to Miles what he had discussed with Captain Whitcombe and added, "I would like Keith and James to see what they can do to help track him down." He put up his hand to fend off any interruptions. "I know the sensor array does not extend this far but what else have they got that they can use? Radio intercepts, propeller wash detection, infrared, heat signatures from satellites?"

"I'll talk to them, Charles. *Mercury* has started an acoustic and sonar search grid based on the last co-ordinates that we received from James," Miles said. "And the United States has a nuclear submarine and two frigates on route to this area. Duke and Ralph spoke to the President, who has in turn spoken to the Navy and made them see the errors of their ways. After we refuel, I would like us to move close in to Sable Island. At least that way one of our flanks is covered. We will then sit and wait for *Launch One* and *Jupiter* to arrive."

"Okay by me," Charles said. "Not a lot we can do until things start to click into place. I think I will join Anne in the lounge.

Keep me advised of any changes." Charles walked to the bridge door and stopped as Ralph and Duke entered the bridge.

"Charles, we have a request from The White House," Ralph said, walking over to the navigation table, Duke following behind.

"Really, and what would that be?" Charles asked letting go of the door handle and walking back to the navigation table.

"They want you to use your electromagnetic pulse system against Axmann's submarine," Ralph replied.

"That was our original plan but they declared it unsafe!" Charles commented with a hint of sarcasm. "So what's changed? If something goes wrong are we the sacrificial lambs? Or is it that we are in international waters and expendable?"

"Well, actually Axmann and his submarine are not. And their experts have now decided that it is safe to use the electromagnetic pulse," Ralph replied rubbing his chin. "They believe that the thickness of the casing on the submarine together with the thickness of the weapon casing should prevent the beam from entering the weapon. The firing mechanism, is in itself, further protected. Also, and I don't know how, and didn't waste the time finding out, but they have located his submarine in the St. Lawrence Seaway and in Canadian territory. The President does not want to start an international incident by firing on the submarine. If it were suddenly to become non-operational and surface, then it would be much easier for all concerned."

"I see," said Charles. He thought for a moment and walked around the bridge before stopping and leaning against the Captain's chair. "Both *Mercury* and *Jupiter* are equipped with the electromagnetic pulse system, but I would not send both of them in and neither would I send one in alone. They would need a protective shadow." He walked back to the navigation table. "When *Launch One* arrives she can follow *Mercury* into the St. Lawrence. If *Mercury* stays just ahead of *Launch One,* then she should, and I emphasis should, be in the sonar shadow of *Launch One.*" He looked at the Captain who stood on the opposite side of the table. "What do you think?"

"I agree. We cannot send a submarine on its own. It would be picked up and reported by other vessels and that would cause an international incident. *Launch One* should hide her, but not sure if she would be hidden from another submarine's sonar," replied the Captain.

"For what it's worth, I think it's worth a try, if the two Captains agree," Duke decided to add his view.

"I agree," Miles concurred. "We can fire a concentrated beam at Axmann's submarine, which will negate any side effects on other vessels that may be nearby. I would prefer to transfer to *Launch One* to oversee the operation. Besides Thomas and his two guys are on board." He looked across at Charles, who nodded.

"Okay, let's put it to them. We have a few hours before *Jupiter* and *Launch One* arrive. Axmann's submarine is slow. I have no doubt that ours can catch up to him. You three," he motioned to Ralph, Duke and Miles, "let's convene in the surveillance room in two hours. In the meantime, find out the exact co-ordinates of that submarine." Charles pushed himself off the table, held his right shoulder with his left hand and left the bridge, leaving the others talking.

Chapter Twenty Six

The Seaway

The submarine Captain stood in the conning tower looking through the dense mist that had made the last six hours a lot easier for him. He shivered at the cold and regretted not putting on his parka. The cold and damp chilled him to the bone. He picked up his binoculars, his hands damp like everything on the conning tower that was touched by the mist. He squinted as he peered through them; he still could not see far enough into the distance for his liking. His eyebrows dripped with water droplets when he moved them away from his eyes, he wiped his brow with his hand and shook the droplets of water away. The St. Lawrence was forty four kilometres wide at the point where the Captain had made the decision to surface. He had seen the mist through the periscope and with nothing on sonar had decided to surface and take a look. As morning approached the mist had started to lift but he could still not see the banks either side through his binoculars, so there were even odds that no one could see them. The longer he stayed on the surface increased the chances of being seen, but running on the surface was enabling him to recharge his near empty battery banks. Behind him in the coming tower was a young seaman who was on look-out duty, conscientiously scanning the horizon through his binoculars. The Captain called down to the sonar operator, who replied that it was still all clear. The mist started to drift in banks of dense then clear areas and the Captain became more wary of their growing visibility.

"Keep your eyes fresh. Every so often give your eyes a rest from the binoculars and look at something close by," he said to the look out. "The mist is lifting and we must see before we are seen."

The navigator climbed up the ladder and stood beside the Captain in the conning tower and shivered, breathing in the damp fresh cool air.

"Sir, sonar reports three contacts eight kilometres ahead," he said.

"Thank you," he replied and scanned around with his binoculars. In the dim light of morning, and through a gap in the drifting mist, he saw the outline of houses to the east, the occasional light coming from a window, and the occasional flash of car headlights passing between houses. Then the mist closed in and visibility dropped to a few hundred feet. To the west was a black nothingness that he knew was just a flat silt shoreline. He could see nothing straight ahead.

"How are the batteries?" the Captain asked of the navigator, continuing to look straight ahead with his binoculars. He tried to calculate how far he could see when the mist lifted in swathes. Three to four kilometres, maybe five, it was so hard to judge in the mist.

"I will check, sir," the navigator said and disappeared down the ladder.

Suddenly he saw something, or did he? In the distance at eleven o'clock. A large white vessel.

"Lookout, come here, look ahead, eleven o'clock, and tell me the moment you see something," the Captain commanded as he continued to stare ahead, not taking his eyes away from his binoculars that stayed glued to eleven o'clock.

"Yes, sir," the young seaman said taking up his new position on the left side of the Captain.

The submarine continued slowly at ten knots, the mist dulling all noise and playing with the minds of the two men in the conning tower.

"Battery banks are fully charged, Captain. Sonar counts three contacts, now at six kilometres," the navigator called from the ladder, not bothering to come all the way up.

"There, sir, two vessels, one at eleven o'clock and another at ten o'clock. The furthest is a bulk carrier which is moving away from us. The other, I don't know," the lookout called.

"I see them now. Prepare to dive the boat," the Captain commanded. The navigator cleared the ladder as the lookout descended above him. The Captain did one last scan with his binoculars before descending the ladder, closing the hatch above him and spinning the wheel and throwing the locking handle.

"Dive, Dive, Dive. Navigator, place us in the centre of the water column in the deepest part of the channel," the Captain ordered, wiping his hands dry on an old rag.

"Aye Captain, diving to centre of water column. Helm five degrees down bubble, steer eleven degrees to port," called the navigator, plotting the course on the map and calculating their course.

The Captain grabbed the periscope handles and snapped them down and looked through the eyepiece. In front and slightly to his left were the two vessels, one was definitely a bulk carrier, the other he could not be sure. The atmosphere in the submarine had improved with the venting of fresh air; the stifling oppressive dank air had gone.

"Down scope," he called and snapped the two handles up. He walked over to the chart, where the navigator was working with a parallel ruler and divider, constantly referring to a book of tables. "What depth are we in?"

"Thirty one feet, thirty two feet. We are moving into deeper waters. We are at high tide. At low tide we will not have a lot of manoeuvring room."

"I am aware of that. The only ships we will encounter are those coming towards us, which will be off our port side, so as long as you keep to the left side of the channel, we will be in the clear. Increase our speed to twelve knots but slow down if we catch up with any ships ahead of us," the Captain instructed.

"Sir, we have three hundred kilometres to cover, which will take eighteen hours at that rate," the navigator looked pained. "That's a long time to be vulnerable and we could be run down from behind."

"Not if the sonar operator does as I have instructed," the Captain said quietly. "We will increase speed to sixteen knots as we get to deeper water and the seaway widens. Keep us in the centre of the water column."

"Yes, sir. I understand. Twelve knots increasing to sixteen when channel widens, center of water column," the navigator confirmed. "Sonar, keep me advised of all contacts," he called. "Helm turn starboard five degrees." He drew on the chart, mapping their location.

The Captain went back to the periscope, snatching both

handles down. He looked through the eyepiece and scanned all around. "Clear aft, clear starboard, clear port side. Two vessels ahead. One steaming away and one coming towards us. The vessel moving away is a bulk grain hauler. The one coming towards us looks new. It's large. I'd say just under one hundred metres in length. Must be some sort of research vessel as she's very wide. I reckon around fourteen metres with crane derricks, a mass of antenna arrays and radar domes." He scanned around then went back to the white vessel, his interest piqued.

"Sonar to bridge, sonar to bridge. Three contacts ahead. One off to our port side, two directly ahead," the sonar operator's voice came clearly over the speaker to the left side of the Captain, who immediately grabbed the microphone.

"Sonar, are you sure? I can see only two contacts!" the Captain said into the microphone.

"Yes sir, I have three distinct contacts," the sonar operator's voice replied over the speaker.

The Captain, microphone in his left hand, peered through the periscopes eye piece. "Sonar, I am looking through the periscope right now and there are only two contacts. One to port moving away from us and one mid channel heading our way!" his voice snapped into the microphone.

"Captain, one contact to port, two contacts dead ahead. Range five and a half kilometres." The sonar operator's voice had a tinge of exasperation to it. "Dead ahead, sir, we have one vessel with two engines. From the sound I would hazard a guess that they are water jets and one vessel with a single propeller. The single propeller vessel is, I would say, right in front of the other vessel, sir."

"Sonar, there is no other vessel in front of the other, I see only one bow wave."

"It is there, sir, maybe below the surface?"

"A submarine below the other vessel?" the Captain asked incredulously.

"Yes, sir, I guess so."

"Action stations! All hands to action stations! Load tubes one through four," the Captain called, hitting the klaxon horn button on the rail around the periscope staging. He hung the microphone up. "I'll be in the sonar room," he called over to the navigator. "Keep our course and speed."

Miles and Thomas stood on the bridge of *Launch One* in front of a bank of display screens. Miles flicked his eyes from screen to screen taking in the various images from side scan sonar, forward scan sonar, radar and thermal image displays. He looked out of the windows into the mist and could see nothing. He returned his attention back to the electronic eyes in front of him. He scanned them again, when out of the corner of one eye he noticed a change in one of the images. He moved back to the thermal image and watched.

"Captain, all stop. Communications, put Lisa on the speaker now!" he yelled as he toggled back the thermal image with one hand and the forward scan sonar with the other.

"Lisa here, Miles." Lisa's voice came over the speaker.

Miles could feel the vast vessel come to a halt, and he picked up the radio microphone. "Lisa, directly ahead is a submarine. She is sitting bang in the center of the water column. It has to be Axmann, so bring *Mercury* to a halt. Your range is three kilometres. Fire up the electromagnetic pulse and have the guys lock on to it.

"Will do, hold on," Lisa replied.

Miles turned to look at the Captain. "Captain, contact the American Commander and let him know what's going on. He will want to move his frigate in to do the arrest."

"Good idea, Mr Channing," Captain Simpson replied and picked up his telephone.

"Miles, we have a contact and are locked on with a tight beam. Our sonar operator says he heard torpedo tube doors opening, four he believes," Lisa advised.

"Okay Lisa, you are in range and in danger. Fire the pulse now!" Miles said.

"Firing pulse in five, four, three, two, one, Fire!" Lisa's voice came clear over the speaker. "We have confirmed a direct hit!" she said. "Recharging pulse in case we need to go again."

"Good girl. Come up to periscope depth, close in but move *Mercury* to port. I want you out of torpedo range, just in case. Arm your torpedoes, one and two and open their outer doors," Miles said coolly into the microphone before then turning to the Captain. "Close in, move *Launch One* over towards the starboard bank."

Captain Simpson looked at his navigation screen, taking in the depth and radar images and called out commands to the helmsman. *Launch One* picked up speed slowly and turned to starboard. Miles moved to the port window and stared through the mist; seeing nothing but swirling mist, he picked up his hand help thermal camera and stared at the point where he figured the submarine would surface.

"There she is, fifteen degrees off our port bow. She's coming up very slowly," Miles said, pointing to the submarines position, which no one else could see without the benefit of a thermal camera. He looked over at Thomas, who took a radio off his belt and held it up to his mouth and spoke slowly and very clearly.

"Security, Team one, take up your security positions. Team two, get two boats ready to launch, have weapons at the ready. I'm on my way down." Thomas clicked the radio back on his belt and said to Miles. "I'll have the boats lowered and in the water. Just give me the go, if and when you want us to board her."

"Thomas, hold on a minute," Miles walked over to the Captain. "Captain, deploy your deck guns, please."

A seaman on the port side of the bridge turned in his seat and sat looking at the Captain, who looked back and simply nodded. The seaman turned back and concentrated his attention on the control console in front of him and started to tap on the touch screen. On either side of the bow, two deck hatches hinged open and two guns rose from beneath the decks. The seaman split his screen into two segments and used the thermal cameras mounted on each gun to aim them at the submarine.

"Weapons armed and aimed on the submarine," the seaman affirmed, turning towards the Captain. "Awaiting your orders, sir."

"Captain, may I suggest that you contact the submarine and advise them that, firstly, they are disabled, and secondly they have weapons sighted on them and, thirdly they have no means of escape," Miles said drily.

"It would be my pleasure," Captain Simpson agreed with a smile and lifted up his handset. "Communications, put me through to the submarine, all frequencies."

"Oh, and tell them the US Navy will be with them very soon!" Miles added as an afterthought.

"German U boat, this is Captain Simpson of the vessel *Launch One*. You have been hit with an electromagnetic pulse by the submarine *Mercury* and are disabled and going nowhere. All your electrical systems are out of action. The USS *Kauffman* will be with us shortly to undertake your surrender and arrest. Please advise your intentions. Over." The bridge was quiet as everyone waited for a reply to the Captains message. The Communications Officer listened through his headset, looking at the Captain, shaking his head as he scanned frequencies.

"No reply on any frequency."

"Of course, Miles, they can't hear us!" Thomas exclaimed. "They have no radio, we put it out of action!"

Ahead, they could now clearly see the submarine, a German World War Two U-boat type VIIC/41. It sat motionless on the surface, all hatches closed and no one visible in the conning tower. Three hundred yards away to her side and facing her, was *Mercury* now riding just below the surface, only the top metre and a half of the conning tower visible.

Miles wondered what Axmann would do. He went over to the communications console.

"How do I video call *Sundancer?*" he asked.

"That screen there, allow me." The Communications Officer tapped the screen a few times till Charles Langham appeared on screen with a coffee cup in his hand.

"Charles, we have the submarine dead in the water on the surface. We have radioed them but, of course, they can't hear us as the electromagnetic pulse disabled their radio. Thomas and his two guys and some of the *Launch One* security team are ready to board and the USS *Kauffman* is heading up the St. Lawrence. Her ETA is less than one hour."

"Miles, that's great work. We are behind the USS *Kauffman* with *Jupiter* on our flank. Don't make any move against the submarine. That's up to the Commanding Officer of the USS *Kauffman*," Charles said easily. "Our orders are just to make sure the submarine remains inactive. Thinking about it, though, we can talk and listen to them answer. Thomas knows Morse code, so he could tap out a message on the conning tower. *Launch One* carry's hull microphones that Thomas could mount to the submarine so we can hear what's going on inside and hear their reply."

"I'm on my way," said Thomas, who had moved in to look at the screen when he heard the mention of his name.

"Lisa has the electromagnetic pulse charged and ready to fire again if required and is ready to torpedo them if needs be."

"That's about it, then. Get Thomas to repeat the message every few minutes and standby," Charles said. "Pass my compliments to the crews of *Mercury* and *Launch One*."

"Miles," the Captain called, "sorry to interrupt but we have an old freighter coming upstream."

"Well, keep them well over to their starboard side of the river," Miles said quickly returning his attention to Charles. "What about the Canadian coastguard?"

"The Captain of the USS *Kauffman* and the American Ambassador have already taken care of that at the highest levels. President Johnson has spoken to the Canadian Premier."

Miles and Captain Simpson watched as two rigged inflatable boats skimmed across the water, the occupants in camouflage fatigues and carrying automatic rifles. They slowed as they neared the stricken submarine. They both moved in bow first against the hull using the engines to keep them in place. One occupant leant over the bow and fixed a circular disk to the hull and extended two thin metal rods from its surface. In the other boat Thomas leant over the bow and with a large heavy hammer, started tapping loudly on the hull. After tapping for some time, the boats moved away and Thomas clicked his throat microphone.

"Miles, tune into the pick- up, which is now in place. I have tapped out in Morse code the same message Captain Simpson said on the radio. You should be able to hear any conversations now."

"Thanks, Thomas," Miles said and walked across to the Communications Officer. "Tune in."

"Already done, sir," the Communications Officer said quickly. "I'll turn the volume up." He tapped on the touch screen console and a babble of German voices could be heard.

"Anyone speak German?" Miles said, looking at the five people on the bridge.

"Miles, Thomas here. One of the voices is saying that they have two choices, scuttle the boat and go down with her or surrender. It must be the Captain. He is saying eh, hold on, my German is a bit rusty. He is saying that they have completed their mission and to surrender will not be cowardly. However, to scuttle the submarine and die of asphyxiation is suicide and the option a coward would take. He is allowing the crew to vote and he himself is voting for surrender. There is a lot of talking. I cannot understand what they are saying, too many voices." Thomas gestured to his helmsmen to move further away. "There is a lot of shouting and cheering. I think they are surrendering."

Thomas turned and looked up at the bridge of *Launch One*. "Miles, we are pulling back to a safe distance."

"Okay, Thomas, You may as well return to *Launch One*. Not a lot more you can do. We will hand over to the United States Navy, as their frigate is nearly upon us."

"Right, returning to *Launch One*," Thomas replied to Miles. He turned to the helmsmen of both boats. "Okay, guys, we're bugging out. Back to *Launch One*," he called and sat down as the boats increased speed and made sharp turns, spraying water over the occupants as they headed down the port side of *Launch One*.

"Miles, what's the buzz?" Lisa's voice called over the speaker.

"Lisa, dive your boat, move further away but stay within pulse range, please," Miles answered over his radio microphone. He turned his attention to the video screen, where Charles was still connected. "Charles, I take it you heard all that?"

"Yes, I did, thanks. As soon as you have Thomas and his team on board, pull back to our position and let the USS *Kauffman* and, unbeknownst to them, a submerged *Jupiter* will take your place. *Mercury* can remain on standby as well. We are heaving to and are thirty three kilometres from you," Charles ordered. "Any movement on that submarine?"

"With the cheering we heard, the belief is that they will be surrendering. One assumes the Captain has his crew gathering their possessions before disembarking, but who knows." He could feel the throb of the engines as they increased revolutions and felt the sudden movement as the thrusters started to move the huge boat around on her axis. "Okay, we are spinning around like a top and the USS *Kauffman* is just coming down our starboard flank. I can see *Jupiter* on our sonar. Still no movement on the submarine."

Launch One gathered pace and moved downstream to join up with *Sundancer*. Miles stood on the starboard bridge wing and watched the USS *Kauffman* come to a dead stop and let go her anchor. Almost at the same time, three high speed rigid inflatable boats, fully laden with marines, were lowered into the water and sped towards the still motionless submarine. Thomas came up beside him. Suddenly the deck hatches on the submarine swung up and hinged back to the deck as the crew of the submarine started to empty out onto the deck. Two figures appeared in the conning tower and descended the ladder to the deck. Miles entered the bridge and returned to the wing holding a pair of binoculars. He looked at the face of each ragged submariner in turn, and watched as Navy Seals entered each hatch and descended into the submarine.

"No Gustav Axmann in sight," he said to Thomas. He returned to the bridge and over to the screen where he was still connected to Charles Langham.

"Charles, Gustav Axmann, nor his son, are on the submarine! Well, they are not on deck, anyhow!" Miles said, shrugging his shoulders. "Navy Seals are entering the submarine, so we will soon find out if anyone or the weapon is down below. Hold on." He went back onto the bridge wing and watched as a Navy Seal climbed out of the submarine and spoke into his radio. Miles grabbed the radio off his belt and tuned in, listening to the Navy Seal. "Charles, no one is inside the submarine and there is no weapon. We need to get the GPS download and find out where the submarine has been."

"I don't believe it. Send Grant a camera feed of the crew to check them out. I'll talk to the Commanding Officer of the USS

Kauffman about letting Lisa on board to get the data." Charles cut the feed and put his hands behind his neck, interlocked the fingers and stretched. He looked across at Anne, Max, Duke and Ryan. "Unbelievable. He's one step ahead all the time!"

Gustav waited patiently for the freighter to arrive. He sat watching the water slowly and inexorably rise. The submarine had dropped him off by rubber boat at night under the cover of the darkness and the swirling mist. He sat patiently on the ground near the river bank on the eastern end of the island surrounded by trees, the cold of night combined with the dampness of the mist had chilled him to the bone. The thick blanket he held tightly around him did nothing to help. He shivered uncontrollably. He unscrewed the top of the schnapps bottle and took a long drink, swallowing another couple of painkillers. He looked at the bottle; it was nearly empty.

He had spoken to the freighter's Captain and heard of the submarines plight with disgust. The Captain of the submarine should have scuttled her with all hands, not surrendered to the Americans. If he had thought that the Captain would surrender, then he would have installed a radio activated bomb on board. But the thought never occurred to him. The freighter Captain told him he had about an hour to wait before he would be picked up. Beneath a bush near the river bank sat the bomb covered in branches to camouflage it from any prying eyes, which was unlikely at his location on Gross-Ile, in the middle of the river, six kilometres from land on either side. He would have to wait till high tide and knew the freighter Captain was timing his arrival to coincide with that.

The freighter passed the unfolding scene, the Captain slowing down ever so slightly so he could see what was occurring. He watched intently as the crew were, under armed guard, transferred by rigid inflatable boats from the submarine to the USS *Kauffman*. Two tug boats arrived alongside and proceeded to attach tow lines to the submarine. He increased his speed and left the bridge to shout at two crewman on the rear deck to get the high speed center console boat ready. He didn't like the idea of doing the pick-up in daylight. He would have to take precautions of some sort.

"Put two fishing rods in the boat and a few blankets to cover the weapon," he shouted through the bridge door to the two raggedly dressed crewmen in woollen hats and bulky anoraks. He already had a stinking headache and did not look forward to the eight days of tension that lay ahead of him till they arrived at Duluth. He knew the old freighter, which had already been boarded and searched by Canadian Customs and Immigration, would be subjected to at least one more by the United States, and on a much more vigorous scale now. And by then he would have Axmann and the weapon on-board. He knew Axmann had credible documents, and that he had a secure place to hide the weapon. Still neither though appeased his nerves or headache.

He slowed the vessel down in preparedness to launch the boat. He did not intend to come to a stop. He watched from the bridge wing as the two crew members winched the boat over the side and into the water. One crewman climbed down the ladder and positioned himself at the center console and started the large outboard motor. The other crewman climbed down the ladder and unclipped the winch cables, the boat instantly spun away from the freighter's side and away towards the island, where Axmann waited.

Axmann heard the outboard before he saw the boat. He stood up, slowly and gingerly, leaning heavily on his walking stick as he made his way to the water's edge. The boat nudged onto the beach beside him.

"Where is the weapon?" asked the crewman, who jumped out of the boat onto the beach and ankle deep into cold water.

"Over there beneath those branches," Axmann mumbled, his arm wavering as he pointed in the general direction of the weapon.

The two crew moved the boat closer to the weapon and, using the cray pot hauler connected to the center console canopy frame, lifted the weapon into the boat. They helped Axmann in and while one pushed the boat off the rocky beach the other used the outboard engine to reverse away. Once free of the rocky shore, the crewman clambered on board and the other pushed the throttle forward and spun the helm to catch up with the freighter, which was still heading up river. The Captain watched as the boat came alongside. One of the crewman expertly maintained the boats speed to match that of the freighter; the other stood, legs apart, balancing against the movement of the boat, reached up and grabbed the dangling davit lines and connected them to the lifting eyes fitted to the boat. He then jumped and grabbed the ladder and climbed up the side of the freighter. Once on deck he switched on the davit winch motor and carefully lifted the boat from the water. The helmsman switched off the outboard motor and tilted it up to its storage position. The boat swung over the deck and was lowered into its cradle. Without a break the two crew, using the cray pot hauler, lifted the weapon over the side of the boat and onto a hastily obtained trolley from one of the deck storage cupboards.

Axmann, by this time, had quietly disappeared up the ladder to the bridge. The two crew strapped the weapon securely to the trolley, used one of the cargo lifts to descend one deck and pushed the trolley to the rear of the hold. One held the trolley while the other inserted a hook into the rear cargo hold metal wall and eased the whole wall forward. They positioned the trolley into the rear area of the confined space, just a metre deep that ran the entire width and height of the hold. Making sure the trolley was secure, they closed the wall, which had been carefully engineered to look like a true deck wall, with weld beads all around, completing the illusion.

One of the crew reported to the Captain that the operation had been completed.

"Make sure there is a chair, torches and a sleeping bag and blankets in there for our guest, and leave the way open so he can be secreted quickly. He will not be seen if we are intercepted and will remain in there when we traverse the locks and canal systems," the Captain ordered, his voice hardly betraying his grumpy mood now that Axmann was on board his ship. "And make sure a bottle of schnapps and some sandwiches or rolls are there, as well."

"Should I run some kerosene around the edges to put off any dogs?"

"That's a sound idea, do so." The Captain smiled and watched the crewman leave the bridge.

"So, I am to be cooped up again," snarled Axmann.

"Yes, sir, but just as we traverse the locks, canals and cross the border into the United State. It will be essential, and we cannot have you above deck if we are near land. If you want fresh air then Hold One will be open at all times," said the Captain. "For most of the eight days you can be on out in the open down in Hold One," he said in an attempt to placate Axmann, thinking of having to put up with the grumpy old man for eight days.

"I'm going to my cabin to warm up with a hot drink and food and then I'll get some sleep," Axmann said, leaning on his walking stick and hobbling towards the bridge stairs. "Get some coffee and hot food sent to my cabin."

Charles sat in the luxurious main lounge on *Sundancer*, which opened up on the expansive rear deck. The large tinted glass doors were shut. Anne and Max sat with him on one of the three sumptuous light cotton curved lounge suites that surrounded a large glass topped marble table. On one of the other settees were Duke, Ryan and Captain Whitcome waiting for Grant to arrive with the download Lisa had obtained from the GPS unit on Axmann's submarine. The atmosphere was calm and the air conditioning system kept the temperature at a nice snug twenty degrees. Grant entered with Ralph at his side and sat down on the other settee.

"Well, all I can tell you is that the submarine went upstream to Gross-Ile, where it turned slowly back downstream. From what I can determine it took twenty minutes to make the turn. More than enough time to get someone and something ashore and retrieve a rubber dinghy," Grant said solemnly. "I think Axmann and Albrecht are ashore with their weapon."

"But, why would he want to leave the submarine? He could have gone a lot further up river," Duke looked confused.

"Actually, I have been looking at that. In a submarine of the height and draft of the type VIIC/41 it would not be easy. Gross-Ile is about as far as he could have gone. He would never have made it into United States territory. My thinking is that he has transferred to another vessel, a surface vessel. From where he was dropped off, he would need a boat to get to the mainland and could have gone either way. But then by road he would never get across the border nor would his weapon, but on a vessel there are a numerous hiding places," Captain Whitcome suggested.

"So, it's the simple task of finding him on a vessel among the myriad of vessels that are traversing the seaway every day?" Max shrugged. "Easy then!"

"Actually, it's easier than that," Grant smiled. "We have a starting point and rough time." He sat quietly for a few seconds, his elbows on his knees, his face resting in his hands. "We know from the GPS where the submarine turned around and the time from the start of the turn to completion and therefore we know the time window of when Gustav was dropped off. We can assume that high tide would be essential for a pick up, especially given the weight and size of the weapon and the extent and make-up of the shoreline of Gross-Ile." He opened his laptop and starting typing. "We would be looking for vessels that passed the island between nine thirty and ten thirty in the morning, which cuts it down a bit."

"Okay, get onto Keith and James back at headquarters and see if they can get any satellite images, CCTV footage, radio intercepts and heat signature on the island. While they are at it, get them to run a computer check on all the shipping going upstream from Gross-Ile, from nine thirty in the morning.

Names, type, manifests, you know the rest." Charles requested sitting comfortably on the settee. "One more thing. Get one of the analysts, along with Julie our psychologist, to try and figure out, based on what we know about Axmann and what he has done so far, where his next target would most likely be on the basis of him making for and using the St Lawrence Seaway." Charles leant forward. "He came a long way to reach this seaway, so it must lead him closer to his next target than by road alone."

"Okay," Grant said, closing his laptop and standing up." I'll get onto it right away." He left the lounge and headed for the central staircase.

"Captain, there is no point in hanging around here anymore, so let's head to warmer climes." Charles looked at Anne. "How does St. Thomas sound?

"Wonderful," Anne replied with a wistful smile.

"Captain, make for St. Thomas. Call them and make sure a berth is available," Charles ordered. "Is that okay for you lot?" he asked looking at Duke, Ryan and Max, who all nodded enthusiastically. Captain Whitcome rose from the settee easing the creases from his uniform.

"Any orders for *Launch One*, sir?" he asked wiping his cap down.

Charles sat quiet in thought for a moment. "I think *Launch One* should head back to Indonesia and check on the kids and provide some security backup for them. Plus, I think they would both like to use the submersible in the area. *Mercury* is to follow us. I want a leisurely run down to St. Thomas," Charles said. "Oh, and get the Lear Jet transferred to Antigua and the 747 to Fort Lauderdale."

"Yes, sir. I will get the crew to give *Sundancer* a thorough spruce up on the way."

"Thank you, Captain. When we get to the Thomas, you can roster the crew some time off and add a thousand dollar bonus in their next pay packets."

"Thank you, sir. I will see to it," Captain Whitcome said, donning his cap and heading to the bridge.

"Well, I think I will give Cathy and Chris a video call." Anne stood and left the lounge. "I'll be in the Library," she said over her shoulder.

"You know, I have a feeling where he will strike next," said Max, a crease forming on his brow. "He won't hit a city. He's already done that with London. I think he will go for something much more drastic, much more dramatic."

"Please!" Duke exclaimed. "London was drastic. Have you seen the latest news reports? Millions dead or injured. The whole place will be an exclusion zone for years. The British economy is in ruins, the country in recession and it's taking the rest of Europe with it."

"France has been badly affected by the fallout cloud. A great swathe of western France has been contaminated and many people are suffering from radiation sickness," Ryan chipped in.

"I didn't mean it like that. I reckon he will want to make one last real big hit, bigger than anything mankind has ever seen before!" Max said showing his feelings had been hurt.

"Sorry, Max, didn't mean to imply anything," Duke said with a smile.

"Ryan and I saw the British Prime Minister's speech this morning and the news reports. Anyway, what are you thinking?"

"I'm not sure. I think I'll go to the surveillance room and work it through with Jake and Grant." Max stood up. "Feels like we are getting underway." He walked over to the large windows. "Yep, we are turning round."

"What are you going to do with *Jupiter,* Charles?" asked Ralph

Charles took the coffee mug from the steward. "What the hell, might as well send them home via a stop in Saint Thomas. I'm sure they would enjoy the break."

"I'll call Mike and let him know," Ralph said, taking a mug from the tray held by the steward and picking up a handset from the table.

"Get Axmann into the hide. We are coming up to the first lock system," the Captain of the freighter said to the crewman, who was on duty watch on the bridge. "He is to stay there until we pass through this system of seven locks. Make sure he takes a book and a flask of coffee and something to eat. He will be in there for quite a while. Oh, he will need a torch as well as a bucket!"

"Yes, Captain," the crewman replied and left the bridge to find Axmann.

Chapter Twenty Seven

Albrecht Arrives Home

Albrecht drove up the long tree lined gravel driveway of his father's two hundred hectare estate towards the mansion that sat at its center surrounded by manicured lawns with lush forest beyond. He swung the car round the fountain that formed the center piece of the circular driveway in front of the ornate steps that led to the arched porch entrance of the mansion. To the left side of the mansion was the garage that housed Axmann's collection of new and vintage cars, one being a Mercedes Benz W31 type G4 three axle ex Nazi staff car, one of only fifty seven ever produced. He had overseen its complete restoration and ever used it only on special occasions, though never venturing beyond the grounds of the estate. The mansion was the office headquarters of the Axmann Empire and the living quarters for his top staff. Albrecht and Anelie stepped out of the car into the searing heat and humidity.

"Been a hell of a long journey, Anelie, but we are finally back," Albrecht said walking round the car and taking her hand. He look up at the sound of another car coming up the driveway. "They must have missed the turn," he laughed as Michael pulled round beside them and the three men got out. Michael led the group up the stairs to the front door, which opened before them to reveal a tall man with slick, fair hair dressed in a black butler suit and a tall woman in a black skirt and white blouse who had curly, greying, fair hair. They entered into the coolness of the mansions atrium.

"Master Albrecht, welcome home. Greta has arranged some lunch for you all in the dining room. Your rooms have been aired and are ready for you. Clean towels have been laid out if you wish to freshen up. The pool has been cleaned by the gardener if you would like to swim. You've been travelling for ten days?"

They stood in the large marbled floor atrium with an enormous crystal chandelier hanging from the vaulted ceiling that set off the two circular mahogany staircases, beneath which was a corridor that led to the rear of the mansion. Mahogany arches to each side of the entrance hall led to long corridors and numerous rooms. The walls were lined with mahogany panelling and large paintings adorned most of the walls. A Swastika flag hung front and centre.

"Thank you, Heinz. Yes, it's been a long trip and I see that all is very professionally organized, as always." Albrecht smiled and shook hands with Heinz. He looked at the group. "I think we would all like to freshen up," he said, then thoughtfully. "I would also like some time in my father's office. You keep it locked, I believe?"

"Yes I do, Herr Albrecht, on your father's orders, of course. But he did leave me with instructions that I was to open it for you on your return, if he was not with you."

"Thank you, Heinz." He turned to the others. "You get freshened up. We will meet you in the dining room shortly. Come, Anelie." Albrecht led the way from the large hallway through the arch towards the rear of the mansion followed by Anelie and Heinz. He turned left down the corridor and stopped outside the second door, standing aside as Heinz inserted a key and turned it. Heinz stood aside.

"Your father gave you the combination," said Heinz, stepping back.

"Yes, he did." Albrecht pressed six numbers on the numeric keypad and turned the knob, opening the door. "You can relax, Heinz. I was aware of your orders if the code was incorrect."

"Thank you, sir. I will be in the kitchen, let me know when you are ready to eat. I will leave you now."

"Thank you." Albrecht held the door open, feeling the pressure of its self-closing spring and let Anelie enter the office. He followed her inside and let go of the door hearing it close shut with a dull thud and the metallic click of the locking mechanism.

"Wow!" Anelie exclaimed, opening the curtains and looking around the room as light bathed every corner. The walls were adorned with faded photographs of Adolf Hitler, Heinrich Himmler. Maps of the world and oceanographic maps covered in pins, some connected by coloured string. Grainy group photographs of Gustav Axmann with Hitler and various other men in SS uniforms and Nazi insignia. By the wall, beneath the only large tinted window, stood an old battered desk with an old wooden high backed chair upholstered in red leather and sitting on castors. Next to the desk sat another low back wooden office chair also upholstered in cracked red leather. Along one wall was a glass fronted bookcase filled with three tiers of old books of all shapes and sizes. Two grey metal three drawer filing cabinets finished off the room's furnishings.

Albrecht motioned for Anelie to sit as he sat in the high backed chair and looked at the desk. A photograph of himself in a silver frame sat in the left hand corner next to an onyx desk lamp. A phone sat in the right hand corner and a large leather bound blotter pad with three pens sitting on it was in the centre of the desk.

"Well, here goes," sighed Albrecht. He pushed the chair back from the desk on its castors. He bent down in the foot-well and pulled the carpet back to reveal a safe. He spun the dial to the left, then to the right, then back to the left, then fully to the right. He grasped the handle and pulled the safe door open and let if fall open to the left. He looked inside and there lay a glass canister with a white metal lid. He gently lifted it out and eased himself backward into the chair, rolling it forward and rested the glass canister on the blotter pad, folding his arms on the edge of the desk, staring at the object. Inside the glass canister was a small glass vial sealed by a cork which contained an oily glinting clear liquid almost to a third of its volume.

"It is true, then?" Anelie exclaimed. "They did do it all those years ago. They created the doomsday bug?"

"Designed to kill all those who do not match a certain genetic profile. Yes. It is hard to believe and although it would seem that my father could never use it, he has ordered me to. Can I really go against his last wish?" Albrecht replied letting his head rest in his arms. "What were the reasons he did not use it? Why leave me with that responsibility?"

"Albrecht, you're not thinking of defying your father and not carrying out his wishes? How can you refuse? You cannot and must not think that way. To betray all your people! You are their leader. You are The Fuhrer, the leader of the Fourth Reich and must remain strong and committed to the cause, no matter what the cost. You swore your allegiance, we all did."

Anelie stood tall and strong as she spoke.

"I know Anelie. Sit down, please. But this has only been tested on a small number of people of certain races and genetic type." He looked sullen. "You know, in those death camps. It may not work now as expected. I don't know enough about this kind of science. There are no papers with it. It may have mutated, it may kill all of us. I just don't know if it is safe to use after all these years."

"No matter what the cost! That's what we all swore. Who developed the doomsday bug? The Ahnenerbe Institut! They were all the top experts in their fields. They would not have made a mistake!" Anelie had sat down and placed a hand on his arm. "You know you have no choice my darling."

"But to kill, possibly, every living person and every living creature on earth, will not help create the Fourth Reich, will it! Totally defeats the purpose! I must know that all the purest of the Aryan race will survive to see the rise of the Fourth Reich and the conquest of the world. I must have the confidence that animals will not be affected, neither will those humans of the Aryan race as intended. I have to think this through. Maybe I have to test some, to see which races it destroys and which it leaves untouched. Did they test it on animals? If we kill all the animals what will we have for food!" He carefully replaced the vial in the glass canister and returned it to the safe, carefully replacing the carpet.

"I have to think this through thoroughly myself and decide what to do. Then we will need to discuss things," Albrecht said sharply before rubbing his eye and saying. "Sorry, didn't mean to snap like that. It's been a long journey, we are both tired, so let's freshen up and eat. We can come back to this later."

He held Anelie gently by her arms and looked into her eyes. "The others must not know about this. The only living people on earth who know about the doomsday bug are my father, myself and now you."

Chapter Twenty Eight

Gustav Commences Final Run

Gustav had spent seventeen long cold dark hours secreted in the special hideaway on the freighter as they slowly moved along the St. Lawrence Seaway and through the Great Lakes. Now after ten days of sailing they were closing in on Duluth. Using a torch he had managed to read and make notes of the thoughts that came to his mind. He had managed to add more details to his plans and pass notes to the Captain for the radio operator to pass onto his contact, who was to meet him near Duluth. When they were in the openness of the Great Lakes, the crew opened the hideaway so that he could spend many hours in the open, down in Hold One, where at least he could get fresh air and stretch his weary legs. Most of the time he sat in the chair and wrote in his notebook or poured over maps making numerous calculations. At breakfast, lunch and dinner he was asked to remain in the secret compartment. Now his excitement grew as they neared Duluth and the final hours of his plan drew near. His final hours drew nearer.

The Captain had advised him that he would be taken ashore at night in the small boat, and dropped off exactly nineteen point four miles north of Duluth, next to the MN61, where his contact should be at three am in the morning. The Captain had specified the GPS co-ordinates, which Gustav had included in his last communique. He sat, growing impatient. This part of the journey had given him too many opportunities to think and he had to fight not to become morbid. He worried that Albrecht may not have the guts to use the vial; mainly, he thought, because of Anelie. He had sent a coded message by relay to Albrecht with precise information on where to find the formula and test data on the liquid in the vial. There was nothing else he could do now. He knew the Captain had slowed down in order to arrive at the correct time. For Gustav that just meant more time down in Hold One. He looked up at the dark night sky with its myriad of stars and a bright moon. Not ideal conditions for a covert landing mission but it would have to do.

Gustav stood up and gathered the notebooks and maps that lay on the deck, picked up the chair and returned to the hideaway, leaving the access panel ajar. He sat in the chair and started to pick up all his possessions and placed them, carefully and neatly, in his satchel, taking his time to ensure that everything was in the correct place and in the correct order. It took him a long time but also helped to pass the time. A crewman came to the hideaway.

"Are you ready to go ashore, sir?" he asked politely.

Gustav smiled. The crew had all been very kind, especially this one. "Yes, I am, thank you."

"Come this way, please."

The crewman stepped aside, letting Gustav out and two crew to enter to retrieve the weapon. They manhandled the trolley on which the weapon sat, carefully through the tight entrance. Once they were clear, one of the crewman closed up the access panel so perfectly that on inspection it could not be seen. The crewman led Gustav to the bridge, leaving the other two crewmen to load the weapon into the boat.

The Captain took his eyes off the radar and looked briefly at Gustav, still holding the helm wheel. "Once you are ashore, we are refuelling in Duluth and then heading back to Hawaii, where we will await orders from Albrecht. How far away do I need to be, to be safe?" he asked hesitantly.

"If all goes according to my plan, nowhere will be safe, not even Hawaii nor Europe!" Gustav stated. "If my plan fails, then you will be safe enough here."

"I don't know what you intend, but I wish you all the best, Reichsleiter."

The Captain snapped his heels together and saluted in the straight arm style of the SS.

Gustav left the bridge and climbed into the small boat that hung from the davits. The boat, complete with the weapon, Gustav and one crew member, swung out over the side of the freighter and was slowly lowered into the water. The other crew member climbed down the ladder and jumped into the boat and unclipped the winch clips. The engine fired and the boat swung away from the side of the freighter. The helmsman looked at the GPS navigation screen and altered course to aim for the GPS point that he had entered onto the system. Gustav pulled his coat closer around him to ward of the cold wind. The other crew member checked the weapon was secure and sat down next to Gustav.

"I checked on the VHF and our colleagues are already waiting for you at the meeting point," he said, moving closer to Gustav to speak loudly into his ear against the noise of the wind and engine.

"How long before we arrive?" Gustav shouted hoarsely.

"Five minutes or so!" The crewman shouted in response.

Gustav sat back and held on as the boat leapt up the crest of a wave to crash down on the other side. The boat rocked and bucked across the waves. The helmsman pulled back on the throttle and changed course, causing the boat to pitch and roll nauseatingly between the waves. He turned the boat to port to crest another wave.

"Sorry about this. A couple of large boats must have passed this way and the wind is picking up. Nearly there," he said, turning his head to shout to the two passengers.

Gustav felt sick but that would be a sign of weakness, so he persevered and breathed a sigh of relief when the rolling stopped. He felt the boat slow down and the crewman next to Gustav stood up and, grabbing the handrails, made his way past the center console to the bow, where he grabbed one of the coiled lines and tied it to a cleat on the side of the boat. He felt the hull touch the bottom and jumped over the side into knee deep water and waded ashore, paying out the line behind him. He pulled hard on the line when he heard the engine note increase and the line go slack. He tied the line around a rock and coiled the tail of the line before returning back to the boat. He helped Gustav climb out. While Gustav walked up the beach, the two crew used the cray pot hauler to unload the trolley carrying the weapon. They sweated, despite the cold, as they hauled the weapon on the trolley up the beach. They breathed a sigh of relief when two other men appeared and spoke to them.

"Gustav said you could do with some help," the first man, burly with a pale face and long hair, said. With the four of them they soon had the weapon up the beach and at the rear of the vehicle, a big black four by four. They loaded the weapon into the rear and covered it with a cloth. Gustav sat quietly in the rear. The two freighter crewmen opened the rear door and looked at Gustav, who raised his head and looked back.

"Goodbye, Reichsleiter," they said, clicking their heels and saluting. Gustav raised his right hand in reply.

The two men said goodbye to the two freighter crewmen and climbed into the four by four. They watched the freighter crewmen walk away, pulling the trolley back down the beach. The driver started the engine and drove off, heading towards their destination.

After some time Gustav spoke.

"Arnulf, please turn up the heater. I am very cold."

The driver looked in the rear view mirror and nodded, turning up the heat.

"No problem, sir. Just let us know if you get too hot. Our plan is to drive through till six PM, when we will stop at a motel we've booked. There we will meet the others. We have booked dinner at a small restaurant nearby."

"How long from there to my target destination?" Gustav asked grumpily

"Only three to four hours. A good jumping off point if I may be so bold," the driver replied, his eyes watched Gustav in the rear view mirror. "It's a very small town that is used to tourists, so we will not stand out."

"I have a private room?" Gustav asked, his voice weary.

"Yes of course, Reichsleiter. We also have a bottle of your favourite schnapps. The room has a shower and a bath. We have the table booked for seven thirty PM so you can take your time while you freshen up."

"Thank you. I have been stuck in a stinking submarine and confined to a small filthy hole on the freighter. My arthritis is very painful."

"You will find some pain killers and anti-inflammatory tablets in the small brown paper bag in the seat back pocket with a small bottle of mineral water. The freighter Captain told us you might need something."

"Thank you, again," Gustav replied, investigating the contents of the brown bag. He took the bottle of water and downed some tablets before falling asleep.

"Here we are. Our Motel is at the end of Main Street," Arnulf said, turning off the highway and down Main Street into a small town. He looked in his rear view mirror and saw that Axmann was still asleep.

Chapter Twenty Nine

St Thomas

Max entered the main lounge on *Sundancer,* which lay moored in a berth at Yacht Haven Grande Marina, St. Thomas. After the long run down through some rough seas they had entered the calmer, warm waters of the Caribbean. As they had entered Long Bay the Captain had guided *Sundancer* to port and briefly moored at the cruise liner quay at Havensight. Max drove the Mercedes Benz onto the lowered garage door, which was then raised to the height of the quay. Max drove the Mercedes Benz off the door and onto the quay and around to the marina carpark. With the garage door lowered and sealed shut, Captain Whitcome had then swung the superyacht round and guided her aft first to the extra wide floating concrete quay, which would be *Sundancer's* berth for the coming weeks. By guiding *Sundancer* in aft first, the Captain was assured of the fastest departure if the need arose.

"Ah, there you are!" Max exclaimed, walking across the deep pile rose wool carpet through to the rear of the vast main lounge that opened up onto the immense rear deck of the superyacht, to where Anne and Charles were seated listening to some Herb Alpert music. Anne and Charles turned and looked at Max, who was dressed in black shorts and a white tee shirt with the *Sundancer* monogram embroidered into the left chest pocket.

"What gives?" said Charles, who was dressed for the heat in beige shorts and light brown polo shirt. His hair still wet from a swim in the pool, which had helped loosen his stiff shoulder muscle, still tight after the bullet wound.

"Before I get that that, I am happy to advise that the Lear Jet has landed at St. Thomas airport and the Boeing 747 is at Nassau airport."

"Good. The crews can have some downtime after they have re-fuelled, re-stocked and completed any necessary maintenance," Charles said cheerfully.

"They were so ordered and all requirements have been satisfactorily completed and logged," Max said smiling. "Oh, and the Bell is fully fuelled and re-stocked."

"What about security?" Charles questioned.

"Armed security are posted on both aircraft," Max replied.

"Good. Now everyone can relax for a while and enjoy the weather."

"They have been advised. They have booked into good hotels close to the airports. Now, what I came to see you about." Max sat down on the settee. "I think I have worked out where Axmann might target and it ties in with the results of Grant and Keith's work on tracking vessels through the Seaway and the Great Lakes." He smiled a beam of a smile. "Also it ties in with the results of the analysis carried out by Julie."

Charles picked up his coffee and thought as he breathed in the fumes. There was nothing better than the smell of fresh Columbian coffee.

"Okay, let's have it."

"Well, there were two freighters of interest, both near Grosse Ile at about the time the submarine was captured, and both would have been close to Grosse Ile at high tide, which they would have needed to do a pick up. Every vessel using the St. Lawrence Seaway or the Great Lakes have to, by law, have their transponders on. Well, Grant hacked into the ports system and put a marker trace on them so our computer could follow them both through the lakes. One stopped at a refinery in Lake Huron, taking on a load and headed back to the Atlantic Ocean. We checked her manifest and it was okay. The other carried on to Lake Superior." Max said smiling with delight.

"And?" Charles said, pausing from savouring his coffee to nudge Max on.

"Well, the second did a strange thing. It slowed and cruised around for a while just off the coast, about twenty kilometres from Duluth before carrying onto Duluth. We tracked it to a fuel depot where it refuelled before heading back towards Lake Huron. It did not drop off or pick up any cargo!"

"That's interesting. Why would a freighter make the long journey through the lakes for no pay?" questioned Charles, placing his coffee cup on its saucer on the marble table. "Okay, you have my attention. So what do you think his target might be?"

"I think he may have in his mind to set the weapon off in Yellowstone National Park right on top of the super volcano!"

"You've told Duke and Ryan?"

"No, I came straight to see you, boss"

"Get Ryan and Duke up here. I think they are playing table tennis in the games room," Charles said and looked at Anne.

"If he sets off the super volcano that's below Yellowstone, then millions could die as a result and a nuclear winter could occur right across the United States and parts of Europe."

Max tapped the keypad on the table and called the games room.

"Duke here, who is calling?" said the disembodied voice of Duke.

"It's Max. Duke, can you and Ryan come up to the main deck lounge now, please. We need to talk about Axmann," Max said.

"No problem. I was losing, anyway!" Duke answered.

"Are we okay here?" Anne said, looking shocked and ignoring Max's voice in the background. She picked up her coffee cup and saucer.

"For a while we would be, but it would be much better if we were in Auckland," Charles said, leaning back and getting comfortable into the corner of the settee on which he and Anne sat. "Yellowstone is a huge area, a little under nine thousand square kilometres with so many points of entry it would be almost impossible to track him." He turned back to Max. "Get Grant here and tell him to bring his laptop."

"Right away, boss," Max said and punched a number on the keypad.

"There are six of these super volcanoes in the world, if my memory serves me well. Yellowstone, California, New Mexico, Toba Indonesia, Taupo in New Zealand and one in Japan," Charles said, stretching his arms above his head and yawning before wincing as a stabbing pain hit his right shoulder. He looked over at the bar and called to the steward. "Another coffee all round please, and get three more ready."

"You need to get the Doc to look at that again," Anne said to Charles.

"I know, I'll go and see him after we've heard what Max has to say."

While the steward busied himself behind the bar getting a Bodum of coffee ready, Charles leant forward and tapped a few keys on the table keypad, shutting the music off and changing the temperature of the air-conditioning. He kept the glass doors to the vast aft deck closed.

"So, Max, what can you tell us about this volcano?" Anne asked.

"Well, from the research I did with Grant, it's huge, to say the very least. The upper magma chamber holds six thousand square kilometres of magma, the lower magma reservoir holds twenty nine thousand square kilometres of magma. Estimates are that ninety thousand people would die instantly. Ninety percent of the population within one thousand kilometres would die. The air would be thick with dust, which would kill more as it forms a cement in the lungs. Within three to four days a fine ash would cover Europe. Flights would be grounded, vegetation killed off and farmland destroyed. Two thousand million tons of sulphur would be ejected, which would result in a cloak of sulphuric acid aerosols around the earth with devastating results. Global temperatures would drop by ten degrees and take six to ten years to return to normal. Cheerful, isn't it?" Max said, like he was reciting.

Grant, Duke and Ryan had arrived and sat quietly while Max spoke of the effects of a Yellowstone eruption.

"I think we need to contact President Johnson," Ryan said. "If you guys are right, we have an emergency of global proportions on our hands."

"I agree. But first let's get some more information around us, the type that President Johnson would ask about." Charles picked up his refilled coffee cup and took a drink. "Grant, show me on the screen where the freighter cruised around near Duluth, then pinpoint the Yellowstone Caldera and routes linking the two."

Grant opened his laptop and started typing. A large flat screen television rose from its cabinet between the three curved settees and an image of the United States appeared. Grant continued typing and two red circles appeared joined by three coloured lines.

"There you are. The blue line is the fastest, the green line the most direct and the yellow line is the slowest route."

Charles looked at the screen. "But once he is in the locale he could detour on many different routes."

"That's true," agreed Grant. "Except to gain the most effect from his weapon he would want to get as close to the center of the super volcano as possible."

"Or a hot spot," cut in Ryan. "We did some work on this with a University and the Geological survey group and there are many hot spots where the public are not allowed to go due to the high temperature below the surface. Logic dictates he would head for either the Sour Creek resurgent dome or Mallard Lake resurgent dome. Although, to be honest, I don't see how he would be successful, because there are few roads and he has the weapon to transport."

"Grant, any way we can trace any vehicle from the freighters drop off point?"

"No, Charles. We have searched through all the CCTV and satellite feeds and came up with zilch," Grant replied. "The problem tracking the vehicle is that we have no idea of what make or model vehicle he is using. As far as any traceability is concerned, he is invisible until we get some clues."

"Okay, so how long would it take him to get from the drop off point to Yellowstone?" Charles asked Grant.

"Anywhere from eighteen to twenty four hours without an overnight stop," Grant advised. "That's if he goes by road. If he flew then a darn sight faster!"

Charles looked at Ryan and Duke, rubbing his chin, deep in thought. All they had to go on was a hunch, but previous hunches had proved right all the way down the line. He looked back at Grant. "Would that weapon leave any trace of radiation that could be tracked?"

"Nope, been there, tried that as well."

"Well, then, there doesn't seem to be a lot we can do except let the President know of our concerns and all the facts that we have at hand. Ryan, Duke, your thoughts?" Charles said.

"Not a lot to go on, and the conclusion is pure conjecture, but I agree. We cannot afford not to let him know. Ryan?" Duke looked at Ryan, who sat beside him very quiet as he took in all he had heard and tried to make sense of it. He looked up, his brow creased.

"We make the call. You guys have been right all the way down the line so far based on as little information as we have before us now," Ryan said. "I'll talk to him. Get him on the screen, please, Grant."

"No worries, but he may know already. We've been liaising with Homeland Security and the FBI since the submarine was captured," said Grant, typing on his laptop. "Connecting now. If you want I can have the maps and movement tracks displayed on his screen. Just give me the word."

"Now, how did I not know to expect that from you guys?"

The face of a solemn President Johnson appeared on the screen.

"Hello. Ryan. I see you have Duke and Max with you. I'm alone in the Oval Office, so you can speak freely."

"Good afternoon, Mr. President. I also have Anne, Charles and Grant here. Mr. President, we have reason to believe that the madman, Gustav Axmann, has landed ashore, near Duluth and may be heading to Yellowstone National Park with his weapon."

"Hi, Anne, Charles. My security chief briefed me on some of this an hour or so ago. If what they told me and what you say is true, then we have a very serious problem. What makes you think he has landed near Duluth?" President Johnson asked.

Ryan nodded at Grant, who typed on his laptop and displayed the tracking information on the screen.

"Firstly, the second track, which as you can see, Mr, President, shows the freighter circling around before heading to Duluth, taking on fuel and then it tracks right back to the Atlantic. The first track shows where the freighter slowed down near Grosse Ile, which is where we believe Axmann was dropped off by the submarine and picked up by the freighter." Grant explained as he displayed both tracks.

"Not a lot to go on," President Johnson said. "However, we know that Axmann has at least one nuclear weapon at his disposal and the movement of the freighter was very unusual."

"Mr. President, Max can describe what would happen if the weapon was set off in Yellowstone," said Duke.

"I am aware of those consequences, Duke, and it is unthinkable that someone would contemplate such an action. But we have seen with London that this man has no conscience, which I need to take into account in my judgement on what actions to take. Grant, please email me the tracks. Now I must get on. It's imperative that I have the National Guard and Homeland Security put a military cordon around Yellowstone National Park without delay. Thank you for the information, and please keep me updated. Good day."

"No worries, Mr, President, sending them through to you now," Grant said as the screen went blank.

"Okay all, there is nothing more we can do except keep up the surveillance and see if we can trace this guy and his son. So, Grant, keep behind your guys. Max, increase security around *Sundancer* and all our assets. Besides that, we can relax and hope the Americans find these guys," Charles said, curling one leg beneath him. "Max, tell the Captain to have *Sundancer* ready to go at a moment's notice. And the same with the Lear Jet and the 747. Grant, have your team monitor for any seismic activity and scan for possible radio messages from Axmann and his cohorts. In the meantime, I am going to take Anne, Ryan and Duke for lunch downtown. Max, you're driving and, therefore, invited."

"Where are we going?" Max asked, standing and brushing his shorts down.

"Cuzzins Caribbean Restaurant on Prindsesse Gade. You don't have to change, you can go as you are," Charles replied with a smile. "No suit or cap required."

"Right, I'll just go and talk to the Captain and then I'll fetch the Mercedes," Max said, heading for the lift.

Grant stood and closed his laptop. "I'll bring Ralph and Miles up to speed. Miles may want *Sundancer* anchored offshore."

"Yes, I think he might. But we can move just as quickly from here, which is why we are stern in and have two engines ticking over. If you guys get a sniff of anything, we will move offshore, until then I think we are safe here."

"I'll tell them."

Grant walked across the deep carpet through the lounge towards the central staircase.

"Right, let's go."

Charles uncurled his leg and stood up putting his hand out to help Anne. Duke and Ryan were already standing and deep in conversation. Charles looked across at them. "Everything all right?" he asked Ryan, who looked pale.

"Just concerned about my wife and children," Ryan said.

"Where are they?"

"Chantilly, west of Washington."

"Can you reach them?"

"Yes."

"Call them, and tell them to fly to Miami. I'll send the Lear Jet to pick them up from there. They can stay with us on *Sundancer* for a while."

"Are you sure?" Ryan asked.

"He's sure," said Duke. "Call them now."

Ryan took his cellular phone and made the calls while they walked downstairs and left *Sundancer* through the lower gangway door.

Chapter Thirty

Axmann's Final Hours

Axmann awoke from his restless sleep, yawned deeply and swung his legs off the bed. He had slept on top of the bed fully clothed to save time this morning. He felt exhausted, totally drained, but he knew very soon he would have a very long sleep. He looked at his watch and saw it was a little after four a.m. The previous night he had managed to obtain the keys to the big Chevy four by four when they returned from the restaurant by saying he had left something in the glovebox. He had kept the keys and called it a night, retiring to his private motel room. He stood up and started to gather up his maps and notes, placing them in his satchel and quietly and carefully opened his motel room door and looked around. It was cold and dark with heavy cloud cover. He closed the door very slowly until he heard the latch catch and crept over to the Chevy. He pressed the button on the key fob and as quietly as he could opened the door and climbed in. He carefully pulled on the heavy door and slowly let it close. Now for the hard bit, he thought. He put the key in the ignition and turned it. The engine started and was not as noisy as he thought. He put the selector in reverse and took off the park brake. With just a gentle pressure on the accelerator, he slowly backed away from the motel block, turning the steering wheel to swing the vehicle around. When he was far enough away, he put the big Chevy into drive and again gently touched the accelerator, trying to keep the engine noise down while he crossed the carpark to the main road.

He looked in the rear view mirror and smiled when he saw no movement or lights coming on. He turned onto the main highway and swiftly accelerated up to the posted speed. He was on his way. This was his time, his moment to savour. He eased off the accelerator to maintain the posted speed. He did not want to draw any undue attention to himself. He had four hours at most to get to his destination and wanted to reduce that time as much as possible without gaining the attention of any police patrol vehicles that may be around. He turned on to North Fork Highway and headed west towards the eastern entrance to Yellowstone National Park.

He drove carefully on the near empty road, ensuring he obeyed all the road rules as the road curved left, then right, winding its way to the park through tree lined mountains. From the east entrance he had calculated he had just one hour to get to the Fishing Bridge, where he would stop, arm the weapon and drive it off the bridge into the water, right above the Sour Creek resurgent dome. When the weapon was fired, he hoped that it would initiate the eruption of the super volcano. He felt tired; his eyes were dry, and the rising sun irritated them. He startled himself when he heard the deep rumbling and quickly corrected the steering, moving the Chevy off the shoulder back onto the road. He looked at his watch through tired eyes and yawned. He decided to pull over onto the grass verge between some trees.

He opened the driver's door and stretched and leant over the passenger seat and took the schnapps bottle, unscrewed the cap and took a deep gulp. He screwed the cap back on and swapped the bottle for a thermos flask. He unscrewed the top and poured the steaming liquid into the plastic cup. He sipped the bitter coffee and stretched his back. He was way too old for this sort of operation. The drive had been long and tiring. He had expected the road to be straight all the way, but it had turned out to be full of twists and turns as it wound its way through the mountains, forcing him to concentrate very hard and use the brake and accelerator almost continually. He removed a bottle of pills from his satchel and poured two in his mouth and downed them with the coffee. He replaced the cap and put the pill bottle carefully into the satchel. He put the screw cap back on the flask, drained the cup and screwed it on the top of the flask.

He stretched against the steering wheel, jumped down from the vehicle and opened the rear door and climbed up into the rear and pulled the thick blanket off the cylindrical weapon. He pressed two clips in and opened a metal panel. Beneath the panel was a control panel consisting of two digital timers and three buttons. He checked the top readout against his watch and adjusted the clock. He then turned his attention to the lower readout. He needed two hours to get to the eastern entrance and one hour from there to his target, the Fishing Bridge.

He checked his position on the map. He adjusted the lower digital readout adding three hours to the timer. He pressed the weapon status green button which lit a green bulb below it. The weapon status was good. He pressed the red arming button, which lit a red bulb below it. The weapon was armed. He was now on the clock. His own life was on the same clock, which was now second by second running down. Second by second he had less time to live and less time to carry out his final act. He covered the weapon with the blanket, climbed out of the rear and gently closed the door. He climbed up into the driver seat, started the engine, put the gear selector in drive, eased off the footbrake and pressed hard on the accelerator, spinning the rear wheels, throwing stones rearwards.

He drove on, following the black snaking road down through the valley. The landscape of tall trees and mountains rolling into the distance before him and behind him in the rear view mirror. The sky turning from night to day as the sun rose higher in the sky, the occasional white cloud floating across the blue sky. In the distance he saw the road widen into five lanes, one eastbound lane for those leaving the park and four westbound for those entering the park. The lanes entering the park were covered by a wooden structure made up of connected triangular shaped roofs, stretching to the right to what looked like a single storey office building. Beneath each of the four triangular shaped roofs were toll booths and barrier arms across the road. This was the eastern entrance to the park. On the far side he could see four highway patrol vehicles parked up and a military helicopter. He slowed down and pulled over amongst some trees and switched the engine off.

He looked carefully at the scene before him. The patrol vehicle and helicopter were empty, so he assumed the officers and pilot were in the small building on the right hand side. If they knew who he was, then there was no way around, unless he went the wrong way down the east bound lane at high speed or crashed through one of the barriers. He had to keep his head and remain calm and drive through the toll booth, pay the entry fee and not bring any attention to himself.

He looked at his watch. He sighed deeply. He had only one hour and ten minutes to get to the job done. He took out the map and laid it across the steering wheel. The only route was through the eastern entrance. He thought about the worst case scenario. If he was stopped he needed to buy enough time and cause enough distraction so he could get to the weapon and press the blue button, which would initiate the weapon instantly. He started the engine and pulled out onto the road and drove down the road towards the toll booths, choosing the left most booth. He slowed and pressed the button to lower the window. He pulled the Chevy level with the booth window.

"Just you, sir, then that's thirty dollars," the attendant said with a smile, his eyes looking at the composite picture on his desk. He instantly recognised the man he was serving as the man the picture. He kept cool and composed as instructed.

Axmann handed thirty dollars across. "Thirty dollars."

"Your receipt and guide to the park. Have a nice day, sir," the attendant smiled, his right hand reaching for the red button beneath his desk, which he pressed.

"Thank you, I will," Axmann said, taking the receipt and guide and placing them on the passenger seat. He closed the window and accelerated slowly away from the booth. In his rear view mirror, he saw police officers and military personnel running to their vehicles and helicopter. He pressed harder on the accelerator and looked at his watch, then again at his rear view mirror.

Suddenly, two helicopters buzzed overhead, one swooping low over the road in front of him before lifting just as he went underneath, the other peeling away into the distance. Axmann accelerated harder, the tires screaming as he hit a hard left turn forcing him to brake hard, the helicopter still overhead. He could see figures with weapons leaning out of the sides. He hit the accelerator again, too hard, the rear of the Chevy weaving from left to right. Axmann fought the steering wheel to straighten the rear of the Chevy, stamping on the brake, then the accelerator. The helicopter swooped low and flew alongside the Chevy.

"Stop, pull over and exit the vehicle," the voice of an officer barked from the helicopter over a speaker. A marksman half out of the helicopter waited for his cue.

"Over my dead body. Sieg Heil!" he shouted and stood on the accelerator. He looked at his watch again. Twenty minutes. Just twenty minutes was all he needed. He turned the next corner and slammed the brakes on hard, sliding the huge Chevy to a slithering sideways halt. One of the helicopters sat across the road; some distance behind were two police cruisers. Marksmen raised their weapons and aimed them at Gustav. Above him the other helicopter hovered. He saw a man in the front looking at him through high powered binoculars. He saw him turn to the man seated behind him. He heard the side window of the Chevy shatter.

The helicopter landed beside the Chevy and the man in the front opened the door and stepped down, covered by the marksman who had taken the shot. He straightened the jacket to his dark blue suit and adjusted his tie. He went over the Chevy and looked through the missing driver's window, put his hand in the air and waved for the others to come forward. Two men jumped out of the helicopter and ran to the Chevy, both wore casual clothes. The older man, with greying hair, in a knitted jumper over a checked shirt and black slacks, opened the rear door and uncovered the weapon. The younger man, with long fair hair, wearing a white shirt and beige chinos, joined him at the rear of the Chevy. The older man opened the panel and they both looked at the digital readouts. He reached in and reset the countdown clock and pressed the green button. The green light stayed on. He then pressed the red button and noted the red light went out. He looked across at his colleague, who nodded. He pressed the blue button and they both watched in anticipation as the clock and timer readouts went blank. The older man looked across at his colleague and breathed deeply.

"Thankfully, they were amateurs when it came to the timing mechanism." He sighed, stood up and shouted. "All clear. Take it away." He looked in the front and lifted the satchel and had a quick look inside and saw the maps and notebooks. "We'll take this with us."

"How did you know the right sequence?" The younger man asked as they strolled back to the helicopter.

"I didn't. A quick process of elimination," the older man said, climbing in to the rear of the helicopter. "Home, James," he said jokingly to the pilot. The man in the blue suit jumped into the front and made a circling motion with his right hand. The pilot powered up and lifted off making room for the second helicopter that was now hovering nearby.

Police patrol vehicle closed in around the Chevy while another drove to the eastern entrance and closed entry to the Park.

Axmann's body was removed from the Chevy and placed into

the rear of the second helicopter, which landed alongside the Chevy. His body was joined by his weapon both would be flown to a Homeland Security base. He would get no funeral, just an autopsy and cremation, with his ashes stored for prosperity in some deep vault.

The driver left the motel room to find the Chevy that should have been outside his door, was missing. He banged on the door of Axmann's room and got no answer. He went to the reception desk and convinced the manager to open Axmann's door because the occupant was very elderly and he was getting no response. When they got to the room and opened the door, they found it was empty. Although the bed was made, there was the indent made by someone lying down. Everything that should be in the room was there, though no possessions of the occupant remained. The manager shrugged, looked at Arnulf as though he had wasted his time, and went back to his post at the reception desk. Arnulf returned to his room. He decided that there was no point in waking the others and called Albrecht on his cell phone.

"Albrecht, this is Arnulf. Your father has gone and taken the truck and cargo." he said pacing his room.

"Where has he gone?" Albrecht asked, panic in his voice.

"I don't know. I have no idea when he left, either. All I know is that the Chevy has gone and his room is empty!"

"Okay, Okay, Keep calm," Albrecht said gathering himself together. "Return to your homes and gather all your personnel belongings. Leave nothing that could identify you and make your way here immediately. Get the others to do the same. There is nothing more you can do there."

"I will awaken the others and start our journey today," Arnulf replied and turned the phone off. He dropped the phone on his bed and went next door and banged on the door to wake the others. He found them awake and huddled around the television set. The news reporter was standing at the eastern entrance of Yellowstone National Park.

"I am standing at the eastern entrance to Yellowstone National Park, which has been closed since the early hours by the National Guard and Homeland Security."

The young female reporter stood at the side of the road with the entrance to the park in the distance. "Information is scarce, but what information has been released to us by Homeland Security suggested that a tip off was received by the FBI. The tip off suggested that an attack would be made somewhere within the borders of Yellowstone National Park. Security was increased overnight with the National Guard and marksmen taking up positions in and around the park. No other details have been released so far."

She stretched her left arm out towards the park entrance.

"The attacker was identified by a booth operator who alerted the local National Guard who, it would seem almost instantly, stopped the vehicle and shot dead the driver. Since we have arrived the whole park has been on lock down. Reports from locals tell us that there has been a lot of helicopters coming and going. We have no information on when Yellowstone National Park will reopen. I am Rebecca Hayter for NB3 News."

Arnulf snapped the TV off and looked at the other two men.

"We leave for Brazil now. Our Reichsleiter is dead and the authorities have the weapon. Pack up and be outside in five minutes."

He returned to his room and called Albrecht.

"Albrecht, I have just seen the morning news report. Sorry, Reichsleiter Gustav Axmann has been shot dead and the authorities have the weapon. The reporter said the FBI were tipped off." he said, opening his suitcase and throwing things in it.

"Arnulf, I knew one way or the other the Reichsleiter would not survive his last mission. We have work to do, to carry out his last wishes and our quest for the rise of the Fourth Reich. Come home now."

He placed the phone back on its receiver and sat quietly in his father's office, alone.

Albrecht looked at Anelie.

"My father is dead. He failed on his last mission. Langham is to blame. I will avenge his death."

Ryan sat in the lounge on *Sundancer* talking by video link to President Johnson. Charles, Anne and Duke sat and listened.

"Ryan, we put a lockdown on all the park entrances based on the data we received from you guys. The photo-fit picture of Gustav Axmann was circulated to all the booth attendants and one pressed the alarm. Gustav was shot dead by a marksman in one of the helicopters," President Johnson said.

"That's great news. Was his son with him?" Charles asked.

"No, Charles, he was on his own. The bomb is being examined and the scientists believe it was in the ten kiloton range, same isotope as the London weapon." President Johnson said from behind the Oval office desk, in shirt sleeves, collar open and tie pulled down.

"What damage could it have done?" asked Duke.

"We think it was large enough to initiate the Yellowstone super volcano, if that's what you mean. We do know that he had help. The vehicle he was driving was hired using false identification papers and three days before the submarine was apprehended. Who they were, was his son among them, where are they now, we have no idea. Homeland will not stop looking."

"Mr. President, I think Albrecht will be out of the country. His father would have ordered that to ensure that he could take over and carry on if something happened to him. Albrecht will now step up to the mantle and carry on trying to resurrect the Fourth Reich. The war continues." Charles said, sitting with his left arm around Anne.

"Well, one chapter closes another opens, I suppose. Duty calls. Speak to you all soon." The screen went blank.

Charles looked around and said, "Let's head home via Cathy and Chris. We are about due to pick them up."

"I wonder what Albrecht will do now?" Anne said thoughtfully.

"I have no doubt that he will try and complete what his father failed to do" Charles replied.

About the Author

Gary Paul Stephenson

Gary has always had a love of the environment learning how to grow plants and vegetables organically from a very young age under the tutelage of his father's gardener. Being bought up around family dogs and his own pet Dutch rabbit engendered an ongoing love of animals. The turbulent British political scene during the 1980's and his international career, saw his interest rise in politics. During these early years, he started to write his first novel and many poems. Pressures of work, a growing family and increased worldwide travel for international companies saw his writing put aside, time at home spent with family and long country walks with wife and Border collie.

A holiday to see the land of his father led the family to take up permanent residence in New Zealand. Following the life-changing diagnosis of Multiple Sclerosis, Gary once again took to writing as a way of keeping his mind active and undertook a creative writing course to hone his skills which he passed with distinction in July 2014. With his love of the environment and interest in the short term view of politics, The Charles Langham Series was born.

Gary is married with 3 children and a grandson. Favorite pastimes include travel, wine making, propagating shrubs, growing vegetables and looking after two mischievous Dutch house rabbits.

Other books in the Charles Langham Series:
The Pacific Affair